BATTLE
MAGE

B alfruss clapped his hands together and the charlatans were lifted into the air and thrown backwards. They slammed into the wall and hung off the ground as he stalked towards them. Their clothing was pressed flat against their bodies and they struggled to breathe as he leaned towards them.

"I can command storms, summon fire and unmake stone. Animals have nothing interesting to say and no one can see the future, because it has not been written," growled Balfruss. "It's dangerous to meddle with things you don't understand."

"Enough," said the King, moving to stand beside Balfruss. "Let them down."

BATTLE
MAGE

STEPHEN
ARYAN

www.orbitbooks.net

ORBIT

First published in Great Britain in 2015 by Orbit

1 3 5 7 9 10 8 6 4 2

A CIP catalogue record for this book
is available from the British Library.

ISBN 978-0-356-50480-3

Typeset in Garamond by M Rules
Printed and bound by CPI Group
(UK) Ltd, Croydon, CR0 4YY

Papers used by Orbit are from well-managed forests
and other responsible sources.

MIX
Paper from
responsible sources
FSC
www.fsc.org
FSC® C104740

Orbit
An imprint of
Little, Brown Book Group
100 Victoria Embankment
London EC4Y 0DY

An Hachette UK Company
www.hachette.co.uk

www.orbitbooks.net

For Liz, still

CHAPTER 1

Another light snow shower fell from the bleak grey sky. Winter should have been over, yet ice crunched underfoot and the mud was hard as stone. Frost clung to almost everything, and a thick, choking fog lay low on the ground. Only those desperate or greedy travelled in such conditions.

Two nights of sleeping outdoors had leached all the warmth from Vargus's bones. The tips of his fingers were numb and he couldn't feel his toes any more. He hoped they were still attached when he took off his boots; he'd seen it happen to others in the cold. Whole toes had come off and turned black without them noticing, rolling around like marbles in the bottom of their boots.

Vargus led his horse by the reins. It would be suicide for them both to ride in this fog.

Up ahead something orange flickered amid the grey and white. The promise of a fire gave Vargus a boost of energy and he stamped his feet harder than necessary. Although the fog muffled the sound, it would carry to the sentry up ahead on his left.

The bowman must have been sitting in the same position for hours as the grey blanket over his head was almost completely white.

As Vargus drew closer his horse snorted, picking up the scent of other animals, men and cooking meat. Vargus pretended he hadn't seen the man and tried very hard not to stare at his long-bow. After stringing the bow with one quick flex the sentry readied an arrow, but in order to loose it he would have to stand up.

"That's far enough."

That came from another sentry on Vargus's right who stepped out from between the skeletons of two shattered trees. He was a burly man dressed in dirty furs and mismatched leathers. Although chipped and worn the long sword he carried looked sharp.

"You a King's man?"

Vargus snorted. "No, not me."

"What do you want?"

He shrugged. "A spot by your fire is all I'm after."

Despite the fog the sound of their voices must have carried as two others came towards them from the camp. The newcomers were much like the others, desperate men with scarred faces and mean eyes.

"You got any coin?" asked one of the newcomers, a bald and bearded man in old-fashioned leather armour.

Vargus shook his head. "Not much, but I got this." Moving slowly he pulled two wine skins down from his saddle. "Shael rice wine."

The first sentry approached. Vargus could still feel the other pointing an arrow at his back. With almost military precision the man went through his saddlebags, but his eyes nervously flicked towards Vargus from time to time. A deserter then, afraid someone had been sent after him.

"What we got, Lin?" called Baldy.

"A bit of food. Some silver. Not much else," the sentry answered.

"Let him pass."

Lin didn't step back. "Are you sure, boss?"

The others were still on edge. They were right to be nervous if they were who Vargus suspected. The boss came forward and keenly looked Vargus up and down. He knew what the boss was seeing. A man past fifty summers, battle scarred and grizzled with liver spots on the back of his big hands. A man with plenty of grey mixed in with the black stubble on his face and head.

"You going to give us any trouble with that?" asked Baldy, pointing at the bastard sword jutting up from Vargus's right shoulder.

"I don't want no trouble. Just a spot by the fire and I'll share the wine."

"Good enough for me. I'm Korr. These are my boys."

"Vargus."

He gestured for Vargus to follow him and the others eased hands away from weapons. "Cold enough for you?"

"Reminds me of a winter, must be twenty years ago, up north. Can't remember where."

"Travelled much?"

Vargus grunted. "All over. Too much."

"So, where's home?" asked Korr. The questions were asked casually, but Vargus had no doubt about it being an interrogation.

"Right now, here."

They passed through a line of trees where seven horses were tethered. Vargus tied his horse up with the others and walked into camp. It was a good sheltered spot, surrounded by trees on three sides and a hill with a wide cave mouth on the other. A large roaring fire crackled in the middle of camp and two men were busy cooking beside it. One was cutting up a hare and dropping pieces into a bubbling pot, while the other prodded some blackened potatoes next to the blaze. All of the men were armed and they carried an assortment of weapons that looked well used.

As Vargus approached the fire a massive figure stood up and came around from the other side. It was over six and a half feet tall, dressed in a bear skin and wide as two normal men. The man's face was severely deformed with a protruding forehead, small brown eyes that were almost black, and a jutting bottom jaw with jagged teeth.

"Easy Rak," said Korr. The giant relaxed the grip on his sword and Vargus let out a sigh of relief. "He brought us something to drink."

Rak's mouth widened, revealing a whole row of crooked yellow teeth. It took Vargus a few seconds to realise the big man was smiling. Rak moved back to the far side of the fire and sat down again. Only then did Vargus move his hand away from the dagger on his belt.

He settled close to the fire next to Korr and for a time no one spoke, which suited him fine. He closed his eyes and soaked up some of the warmth, wiggling his toes inside his boots. The heat began to take the chill from his hands and his fingers started to tingle.

"Bit dangerous to be travelling alone," said Korr, trying to sound friendly.

"Suppose so. But I can take care of myself."

"Where you headed?"

Vargus took a moment before answering. "Somewhere I'll get paid and fed. Times are hard and I've only got what I'm carrying."

Since he'd mentioned his belongings he opened the first skin and took a short pull. The rice wine burned the back of his throat, leaving a pleasant aftertaste. After a few seconds the warmth in his stomach began to spread.

Korr took the offered wineskin but passed it to the next man, who snatched it from his hand.

"Rak. It's your turn on lookout," said Lin. The giant ignored him and watched as the wine moved around the fire. When it reached him he took a long gulp and then another before walking into the trees. The archer came back and another took his place as sentry. Two men standing watch for a group of seven in such extreme weather was unusual. They weren't just being careful, they were scared.

"You ever been in the King's army?" asked Lin.

Vargus met his gaze then looked elsewhere. "Maybe."

"I reckon that's why you travelled all over, dragged from place to place. One bloody battlefield after another. Home was just a tent and a fire. Different sky, different enemy."

"Sounds like you know the life. Are you a King's man?"

"Not any more," Lin said with a hint of bitterness.

It didn't take them long to drain the first wineskin so Vargus opened the second and passed it around the fire. Everyone took a drink again except Korr.

"Bad gut," he said when Vargus raised an eyebrow. "Even a drop would give me the shits."

"More for us," said one man with a gap-toothed grin.

When the stew was ready one of the men broke up the potatoes and added them to the pot. The first two portions went to the sentries and Vargus was served last. His bowl was smaller than the others, but he didn't complain. He saw a few chunks of potato and even one bit of meat. Apart from a couple of wild onions and garlic the stew was pretty bland, but it was hot and filling. The food, combined with the wine and the fire, helped warm him all the way through. An itchy tingling starting to creep back into his toes. It felt as if they were all still attached.

When they'd all finished mopping up the stew with some flat bread, and the second wineskin was empty, a comfortable silence settled on the camp. It seemed a shame to spoil it.

"So why're you out here?" asked Vargus.

"Just travelling. Looking for work, like you," said Korr.

"You heard any news from the villages around here?"

One of the men shifted as if getting comfortable, but Vargus saw his hand move to the hilt of his axe. Their fear was palpable.

Korr shook his head. "Not been in any villages. We keep to ourselves." The lie would have been obvious to a blind and deaf man.

"I heard about a group of bandits causing trouble in some of the villages around here. First it was just a bit of thieving and starting a couple of fights. Then it got worse when they saw a bit of gold." Vargus shook his head sadly. "Last week one of them lost control. Killed four men, including the innkeeper."

"I wouldn't know," said Korr. He was sweating now and it had nothing to do with the blaze. On the other side of the fire a snoozing man was elbowed awake and he sat up with a snort. The others were gripping their weapons with sweaty hands, waiting for the signal.

"One of them beat the innkeeper's wife half to death when she wouldn't give him the money."

"What's it matter to you?" someone asked.

Vargus shrugged. "Doesn't matter to me. But the woman has two children and they saw who done it. Told the village Elder all about it."

"We're far from the cities out here. Something like that isn't big enough to bring the King's men. They only come around these parts to collect taxes twice a year," said Lin with confidence.

"Then why do you all look like you're about to shit yourselves?" asked Vargus.

An uncomfortable silence settled around the camp, broken only by the sound of Vargus scratching his stubbly cheek.

"Is the King sending men after us?" asked Korr, forgoing any pretence of their involvement.

"It isn't the King you should worry about. I heard the village Elders banded together, decided to do something themselves. They hired the Gath."

"Oh shit."

"He ain't real! He's just a myth."

"Lord of Light shelter me," one of the men prayed. "Lady of Light protect me."

"Those are just stories," scoffed Lin. "My father told me about him when I was a boy, more than thirty years ago."

"Then you've got nothing to worry about," Vargus grinned.

But it was clear they were still scared, more than before now that he'd stirred things up. Their belief in the Gath was so strong he could almost taste it in the air. For a while he said nothing and each man was lost in his own thoughts. Fear of dying gripped them all, tight as iron shackles.

Silence covered the camp like a fresh layer of snow and he let it sit a while, soaking up the atmosphere, enjoying the calm before it was shattered.

One of the men reached for a wineskin then remembered they were empty.

"What do we do, Korr?" asked one of the men. The others were scanning the trees as if they expected someone to rush into camp.

"Shut up, I'm thinking."

Before Korr came up with a plan Vargus stabbed him in the ribs. It took everyone a few seconds to realise what had happened. It was only when he pulled the dagger free with a shower of gore that they reacted.

Vargus stood up and drew the bastard sword from over his shoulder. The others tried to stand, but none of them could manage it. One man fell backwards, another tripped over his feet, landing on his face. Lin managed to make it upright, but then stumbled around as if drunk.

Vargus kicked Lin out of the way, switched to a two-handed grip and stabbed the first man on the ground through the back of the neck. He didn't have time to scream. The archer was trying to draw his short sword, but couldn't manage it. He looked up as Vargus approached and a dark patch spread across the front of his breeches. The edge of Vargus's sword opened the archer's throat and a quick stab put two feet of steel into Lin's gut. He fell back, squealing like a pig being slaughtered. Vargus knew his cries would bring the others.

The second cook was on his feet, but Vargus sliced off the man's right arm before he could throw his axe. Warm arterial blood jetted across Vargus's face. He grinned and wiped it away as the man fell back, howling in agony. Vargus let him thrash about for a while before putting his sword through the man's face, pinning his head to the ground. The snow around the corpse turned red, then it began to steam and melt.

The greasy-haired sentry stumbled into camp with a dagger held low. He swayed a few steps one way and then the other; the tamweed Vargus had added to the wine was taking effect. Bypassing Vargus he tripped over his own feet and landed face first on the fire. The sentry was screaming and the muscles in his arms and legs lacked the strength to lift him up. His cries turned into a gurgle and then trailed off as the smoke turned greasy and black. Vargus heard fat bubbling in the blaze and the smell reminded him of roast pork.

As he anticipated, Rak wasn't as badly affected as the others. His bulk didn't make him immune to the tamweed in the wine, but the side effects would take longer to show. Vargus was just glad that Rak had drunk quite a lot before going on duty. The giant managed to walk into camp in a straight line, but his eyes were slightly unfocused. Down at one side he carried a six-foot pitted blade.

Instead of waiting for the big man to go on the offensive,

Vargus charged. Raising his sword above his head he screamed a challenge, but dropped to his knees at the last second and swept it in a downward arc. The Seveldrom steel cut through the flesh of Rak's left thigh, but the big man stumbled back before Vargus could follow up. With a bellow of rage Rak lashed out, his massive boot catching Vargus on the hip. It spun him around, his sword went flying and he landed on hands and knees in the snow.

Vargus scrambled around on all fours until his fingers found the hilt of his sword. He could hear Rak's blade whistling through the air towards him and barely managed to roll away before it came down where his head had been. Back on his feet he needed both hands to deflect a lethal cut which jarred his arms. Before he could riposte something crunched into his face. Vargus stumbled back, spitting blood and swinging his sword wildly to keep Rak at bay.

The big man came on. With the others already dead and his senses impaired, part of him must have known he was on borrowed time. Vargus ducked and dodged, turned the long blade aside and made use of the space around him. When Rak overreached he lashed out quickly, scoring a deep gash along the giant's ribs, but it didn't slow him down. Vargus inflicted a dozen wounds before Rak finally noticed that the red stuff splashed on the snow belonged to him.

With a grunt of pain he fell back and stumbled to one knee. His laboured breathing was very loud in the still air. It seemed to be the only sound for miles in every direction.

"Korr was right," he said in a voice that was surprisingly soft. "He said you'd come for us."

Vargus nodded. Taking no chances he rushed forward. Rak tried to raise his sword but even his prodigious strength was finally at an end. His arm twitched and that was all. No mercy was asked for and none was given. Using both hands Vargus thrust the point of his sword deep into Rak's throat. He pulled it clear and stepped back as blood spurted from the gaping wound. The giant fell onto his face and was dead.

By the fire Lin was still alive, gasping and coughing up blood. The wound in his stomach was bad and likely to make him suffer for days before it eventually killed him. Just as Vargus intended.

He ignored Lin's pleas as he retrieved the gold and stolen goods from the cave. Hardly a fortune, but it was a lot of money to the villagers.

He tied the horses' reins together and even collected up all the weapons, bundling them together in an old blanket. The bodies he left to the scavengers.

It seemed a shame to waste the stew. Nevertheless Vargus stuck two fingers down his throat and vomited into the snow until his stomach was empty. Using fresh snow he cleaned off the bezoar and stored it in his saddlebags. It had turned slightly brown from absorbing the poison in the wine Vargus had drunk, but he didn't want to take any chances so made himself sick again. He filled his waterskin with melting snow and sipped it to ease his raw throat.

Vargus's bottom lip had finally stopped bleeding, but when he spat a lump of tooth landed on the snow in a clot of blood. He took a moment to check his teeth and found one of his upper canines was broken in half.

"Shit."

With both hands he scooped more snow onto the fire until it was extinguished. He left the blackened corpse of the man where it had fallen amid wet logs and soggy ash. A partly cooked meal for the carrion eaters.

"Kill me. Just kill me!" screamed Lin. "Why am I still alive?" He gasped and coughed up a wadge of blood onto the snow.

With nothing left to do in camp Vargus finally addressed him. "Because you're not just a killer, Torlin Ke Tarro. You were a

King's man. You came home because you were sick of war. Nothing wrong with that, plenty of men turn a corner and go on in a different way. But you became what you used to hunt."

Vargus squatted down beside the dying man, holding him in place with his stare.

Lin's pain was momentarily forgotten. "How do you know me? Not even Korr knew my name is Tarro."

Vargus ignored the question. "You know the land around here, the villages and towns, and you know the law. You knew how to cause just enough trouble without it bringing the King's men. You killed and stole from your own people."

"They ain't my people."

Vargus smacked his hands together and stood. "Time for arguing is over, boy. Beg your ancestors for kindness on the Long Road to Nor."

"My ancestors? What road?"

Vargus spat into the snow with contempt. "Pray to your Lantern God and his fucking whore then, or whatever you say these days. The next person you speak to won't be on this side of the Veil."

Ignoring Lin's pleas he led the horses away from camp and didn't look back. Soon afterwards the chill crept back in his fingers but he wasn't too worried. The aches and pains from sleeping outdoors were already starting to recede. The fight had given him a small boost, although it wouldn't sustain him for very long. The legend of the Gath was dead, which meant time for a change. He'd been delaying the inevitable for too long.

Carla, the village Elder, was standing behind the bar when Vargus entered the Duck and Crown. She was a solid woman who'd seen at least fifty summers and took no nonsense from anyone, be they King or goat herder. With a face only her mother could love it was amazing she'd given birth to four healthy children who now had children of their own. Beyond raising a healthy family the village had prospered these last twenty years under her guidance.

Without being asked she set a mug of ale on the bar as he sat down. The tavern was deserted, which wasn't surprising with everything that had happened. On days like this people tended to spend more time with their loved ones.

"Done?"

Vargus drained the mug in several long gulps and then nodded. He set the bag of gold on the bar and watched as Carla counted it, but didn't take offence. The bandits could have spent some of it and he didn't know how much had been stolen. When she was finished Carla tucked it away and poured him another drink. After a moment's pause she tapped herself a mug. They drank in comfortable silence until both mugs were dry.

"How is everyone?" asked Vargus.

"Shook up. Murder's one thing we've seen before, in anger or out of greed, but this was something else. The boy might get over it, being so young, but not the girl. That one will be marked for life."

"And their mother?"

Carla grunted. "Alive. Not sure if that's a blessing or a curse. When she's back on her feet she'll run this place with her brother. She'll do all right."

"I brought in a stash of weapons and their horses too. You'll see she gets money for it?"

"I will. And I'll make sure Tibs gives her a fair price for the animals."

The silence in the room took on a peculiar edge, making the hairs stand up on the back of his neck.

"You hear the news coming in?" asked Carla. There was an unusual tone to her voice, but Vargus couldn't place it. All he knew was it made him nervous.

"Some," he said, treading carefully and looking for the trap door. He knew it was there, somewhere in the dark, and he was probably walking straight towards it.

"Like what?" asked Carla.

"A farmer on the road in told me the King's called on everyone that can fight. Said that war was coming here to Seveldrom, but he didn't know why."

"The west has been sewn together by King Raeza's son, Taikon."

Vargus raised an eyebrow. "How'd he manage that?"

"Religion, mostly. You know what it's like in Zecorria and Morrinow, people praying all the time. One story has our King pissing on an idol of the Lord of Light and wiping his arse with a painting of the Blessed Mother."

"That's a lie."

Carla grunted. "So are all the other stories about him killing priests and burning down temples. Sounds to me like someone was just itching for a war. A chance to get rid of all us heathens," she said, gesturing at the idol of the Maker on a shelf behind her. Most in Seveldrom prayed to the Maker, but those that didn't were left alone, not killed or shunned for being different. Religion and law stayed separate, but it was different for the Morrin and Zecorrans.

"What about the others in the west? They aren't mad on religion, and no one can make the Vorga do anything they don't want to."

Carla shrugged. "All people are saying is that something bad happened down in Shael. A massacre, bodies piled tall as trees, cities turned to rubble because they wouldn't fight. After that it sounds like the others fell in line."

"So what happened to King Raeza then? Is he dead?"

"Looks like. People are saying Taikon killed his father, took the Zecorran throne and now he's got himself a magician called the Warlock. There's a dozen stories about that one," said Carla, wiping the bar with a cloth even though it was already clean. "I heard he can summon things from beyond the Veil."

"I didn't think you were one to believe gossip," scoffed Vargus.

Carla gave him a look that made men piss themselves, but it just slid off him. She shook her head, smiling for a moment and then it was gone.

"I don't, but I know how to listen and separate the shit from the real gold. Whatever the truth about this Warlock, and the union in the west, I know it means trouble. And lots of it."

"War then."

Carla nodded. "Maybe they think our King really is a heretic or maybe it's because they enjoy killing, like the Vorga. Most reckon they'll be here come spring. Trade routes to the west have dried up in the last few days. Merchants trying to sneak through were caught and hung. Whole trees full of the greedy buggers line the north and southern pass. The crows and magpies are fat as summer solstice pheasants from all their feasting."

"What will you do?"

Carla puffed out her cheeks. "Look after the village, same as always. Fight, if the war comes this far east. Although if it comes here, we've already lost. What about you? I suppose you'll be going to fight?"

There was that odd tone to her voice again. He just nodded, not trusting himself to speak. One wrong word and he'd plummet into the dark.

"People like you around here. And not just for sorting out the bandits," said Carla scrubbing the same spot on the bar over and over. "You know I lost my Jintor five winters back from the damp lung. The house is quiet without him, especially now that the children are all grown up. Fourth grandchild will be along any day, but there's still a lot that needs doing. Looking after the village, working with the other Elders, easily enough work for two."

In all the years he'd known her it was the most Vargus had ever heard her say about her needs. The strain was starting to show on her face.

He settled her frantic hand by wrapping it in both of his. Her skin was rough from years of hard labour, but it was also warm and full of life. For the first time since he'd arrived she looked him in the eye. Her sharp blue eyes were uncertain.

"I can't," Vargus said gently. "It's not who I am."

Carla pulled her hand free and Vargus looked away first, not sure if he was sparing her or himself.

"What about the legend of the Gath?"

He dismissed it with a wave. "It was already fading, and me with it. There aren't many that believe, fewer still that are afraid. It's my own fault, I guess. I kept it too small for too long. It would only keep me for a few more years at best. This war is my best way."

Carla was the only one in the village who knew some of the truth about him. She didn't claim to understand, but she'd listened and accepted it because of who he was and what he could do. It seemed churlish to hide anything from her at this point. He waited, but to his surprise she didn't ask for the rest.

"So you'll fight?"

"I will," declared Vargus. "I'll travel to Charas to fight and bleed and kill. For the King, for the land and for those who can't defend themselves. I'll swear an oath, by the iron in my blood, to fight in the war until it's done. One way or the other."

Carla was quiet for a time. Eventually she shook her head and he thought he saw a tear in her eye, but maybe it was just his imagination.

"If anyone else said something like that, I'd tell them they were a bloody fool. But they're not just words with you, are they?"

"No. It's my vow. Once made it can't be broken. If I stay here, I'll be dead in a few years. At least this way, I have a chance."

Reaching under the counter Carla produced a dusty red bottle that was half empty. Taking down two small glasses she poured them each a generous measure of a syrupy blue spirit.

"Then I wish you luck," said Carla, raising her glass.

"I'll drink to that, and I hope if I ever come back, I'll still be welcome."

"Of course."

They tapped glasses and downed the spirit in one gulp. It burned all the way down Vargus's throat before lighting a pleasant fire in his belly. They talked a while longer, but the important words had been said and his course decided.

In the morning, Vargus would leave the village that had been his home for the last forty years, and go to war.

CHAPTER 2

It felt good to be home. The air was damp and it smelled clean and familiar. Beyond the thick city walls, Balfruss could see endless fields of green, yellow and brown, hemmed in on all sides by dry stone walls. There was so much colour here. It had taken him years of being abroad to realise.

In the far east the changing of the seasons made little difference to the weather. The wind blew a little colder, the sun was a little warmer, but the land didn't change colour as it did here in Seveldrom. After being away for so long Balfruss no longer kept track of time in days or weeks. There was little point when he wasn't racing home to the loving arms of a wife and family. Before his thoughts became even more melancholy he focused on the city.

From his position at the top of the palace, Charas, the capital of Seveldrom was spread out before him. The city was a fortress with crenelated walls more than a hundred feet high. At the heart of Charas were ancient buildings steeped in history that were centuries old. Towering over them all was the cathedral devoted to the Great Maker. Its vast spire was slightly askew and its metal roof turning green in places, but it was still a remarkable sight. Stained-glass windows depicting former kings, queens and warriors twinkled in the sunlight in a myriad of bright colours.

Despite the cathedral's prominence it was hard to ignore the domed temple of the Blessed Mother and the shining spire devoted to the church of the Holy Light. Both were clamouring for attention in the New City, a recent addition from five centuries previous. The New City spread out on all sides from the Old, more than tripling the population. The outer wall was as high as the inner, protecting its people from the worst of the weather and potential threats, although there'd not been a siege for centuries.

Peering down at the streets from such a great height, Balfruss could see a riot of colour, from painted shop signs and striped vendor awnings in the markets, to flowers in the Queen's memorial park. Coloured glass filled the windows on the top floor in most houses in the Old City, a leftover fashion from the days when everyone had sung hymns to the Maker. In the New City it had never caught on, although the newer temples copied the stained glass with varied success.

Compared to other cities he'd visited, the architecture in Charas was simple, but there was a certain beauty in the uniform two- and three-storey buildings of the Old City. All the straight lines, blue slate roofs and lack of ascetic decoration spoke to him of strength and reliability, attributes commonly associated with the Seve people. It galled Balfruss when he heard jokes about Seves being a race of cow-breeding dullards.

It was hard to believe he'd been away for five years. If Balfruss were to look in a mirror he knew his reflection would show a man who looked much older than his thirty-seven years. Already there were spots of white in his hair and beard, and the purple shadows under his eyes had become a permanent fixture, as if he'd been born with them. There was also the unfortunate fact that he felt the wind more keenly on the back of his head. At least his beard kept his neck warm when it was cold.

"Glad to be home, Lan?" said Vannok Lore, coming up the stairs.

It was good to see that some things hadn't changed in his time away. Vannok was exactly as before, a massive man dressed in moulded leather armour with a sword at his side.

Having grown up together they had no secrets between them. No one else called him Lan, the name he'd been given at birth before his eleventh naming day. It was a leftover custom from a time when six out of every ten children died from the red pox before their tenth birthday. There hadn't been a new case in four hundred years, but the tradition continued.

Despite their years apart, when Balfruss had been studying at the Red Tower, they could still read the other with ease.

"I never thought I'd say it, Vann, but I'm happy to be home." Balfruss took a deep breath and then another. "Do you smell it? The green."

Vannok sniffed the air. "Was it so different in the east?"

"The desert is dry, spicy and hot. You can feel the air inside when you breathe. There are plants and trees, but nothing like this," he said, gesturing at the land. "I missed the colour, and Maker forgive me, the cold. The rain and the wind too."

Vannok laughed. "You weren't tempted to stay?"

"No. It wasn't home."

"Are you going to stay home this time?"

Balfruss smiled up at his tall friend. "Ask me again when it's done."

"We should go. The King will be arriving shortly to greet you and the others."

Balfruss followed him down several flights of worn stairs and along wide corridors towards the throne room.

"Have the others been here long?"

"Three were local," said Vannok over his shoulder, "but a couple arrived in the last day. Some have travelled a long way to help us."

"How many are there?"

"Eight, including you."

Balfruss was so shocked he stumbled and Vannok caught him by the elbow before he fell. "Eight? Eight Battlemages?"

It was Vannok's turn to smile. "Just wait."

Nowadays Battlemages were rare, but at one time they had been reasonably common. Seekers had combed every town and village for children born with the ability, but that was before the Grey Council had abandoned their posts at the Red Tower fifteen years ago. The tower still took in those who turned up at its doors, but every year only a small number of students were trained by a shrinking group of ageing volunteers. Most of the staff had drifted away once they realised the Grey Council were not coming back. Those trained after the Council left were shown just enough to stop them from killing themselves, or anyone else, before they were sent home.

When he and Vannok entered the throne room the other Battlemages were already waiting for the King. Balfruss immediately recognised two of them and the ache in his chest returned. As soon as they saw him they approached with warm smiles and open arms. Both were dressed in loose yellow robes, but that was where the similarity between the two ended. Darius was dark skinned with a rangy build, black hair and dark eyes, while his wife Eloise was pale and blonde. The only commonality was the mark of Ayilah, a red glyph tattooed on their faces, running in a vertical line from hairline to jaw across the right eye. It signified their status as a wielder of magic in the desert kingdoms.

"What are you doing here? I only left you a few weeks ago," said Balfruss.

"My wife is not one to be argued with," said Darius, shaking both of Balfruss's hands with an iron grip. Balfruss wanted to embrace his friend, but knew Darius's customs frowned on public displays of affection. "She told me what was happening. After all that you did for my country, how could I not come?"

Balfruss offered his hand to Eloise, but instead she kissed him on both cheeks and hugged him tightly. "Stop scowling, Darius," she said without looking around. "We're in my country now. It's not unseemly to show affection in public."

Vannok cleared his throat and Balfruss took the hint.

"Sorry, Vann. Let me introduce you."

"It'll have to wait." The King was entering the throne room, followed closely by his advisors.

Balfruss had never met the King before, but he could see why some called him the Grey Bear. Every hair on his bare arms and head was the colour of old ashes. Although nearly in his sixty-fifth year he was still a solid man in good physical shape. Stood behind him on one side were his three adult children, two broad and bearded sons and their slender and elegant sister. On the other side were two grizzled warriors who he guessed were Generals. One of them had to be Graegor, the mad one-eyed bastard they called the Foul, although never to his face. Much to Balfruss's surprise Vannok took his place beside the other Generals and they greeted him as an equal. It seemed as if some things had changed in his time away.

The King sat down, but it was clear he wasn't comfortable staring down at people from on high. The throne itself was basic, made only of wood with a gold lacquered crown painted on the headrest. The throne, like the other plain furnishings in the room, reflected what Balfruss knew about King Matthias's approach to the trappings of his station. He understood their necessity, but preferred that the money be spent on his people rather than garish decoration for pomp and ceremony. The noticeable lack of colour also spoke of the Queen's prolonged absence. It had been more than twenty years since her death.

Balfruss approached the bench and the other Battlemages made room for him to sit down.

"Thank you all for coming," said the King. "I didn't expect such generosity from my friends in the east," he said, gesturing at Darius and Eloise who approached and bowed to the throne. As the King offered more lengthy thanks to King Usermeses IV, Balfruss glanced at those beside him.

The golden-skinned man must have come from the south-western kingdom of Shael, recently invaded and conquered by the Mad King. It looked as if the journey had almost killed the Battlemage from Shael. His face was haggard, his clothes dusty and torn, and even sitting down he leaned heavily on a tall staff. A pale headscarf sat about his neck, covering the bottom half of his face, and his shaven head was covered with fresh bruises, scars and scabs. As if he knew he was being watched, violet eyes turned to calmly regard Balfruss. He smiled and the man inclined his head.

The others were an odd group, two dressed in brightly coloured clothing like jesters, and a thick-shouldered man who looked more like a blacksmith. The smith was uneasy, constantly fidgeting and clenching his fists.

The last Battlemage was a small man with jet-black skin and a wide face who Balfruss recognised as one of the First People, the tribes who lived on the coast, north of Seveldrom.

King Matthias drew his welcome to a close, and from the broad smile on Darius's face, Balfruss knew it had been the right length to satisfy desert customs. After giving their names his friends resumed their seats and the King's expression turned grim.

"The King of Zecorria is dead," said the King, his voice echoing around the room. "His son, Taikon, now sits on the throne and he's declared war on Seveldrom under false pretences. He's accused me of committing heinous religious crimes and with this he was able to form a pact with Morrinow. The other nations in the west were coerced or crushed to form an alliance. An army unlike any we've seen before marches towards my border. Our intelligence suggests that with them comes a man known as the Warlock, a powerful Battlemage with several apprentices. I have asked you here today because of him. We'll speak again shortly, but for now, please introduce yourselves."

Taking the initiative two brightly dressed men stepped forward to greet the King. Balfruss noticed both were sweating despite the room being pleasantly cool. It was also unusual to approach the throne without being asked. A couple of royal guards drew their swords and stepped forward but the King waved them back.

"Greetings your Majesty," said one of the men with a florid bow. "I am the Great Samkin. Thank you for your seeing us. We hope to serve you well."

The King pursed his lips and one eyebrow quirked slightly. Balfruss started to laugh, but Vannok gave him a vicious glare and he turned it into a cough. Darius was frowning and seemed on the cusp of action, but his rigid traditions would not allow him to interfere.

There was a long pause before the King spoke again. "And how many years did you train at the Red Tower?"

"Seven," squeaked one of the men, nervously wiping sweat from his eyes.

"And what did you learn?"

"I can control storms, unmake stone, summon fire and see the future," said one of the men, his robe covered with sun and moon symbols that had been sewn on.

"I can talk to animals," blurted the other.

Balfruss laughed and this time he couldn't contain it. A few of the others were smiling, except Darius and the smith.

"Perhaps a demonstration?" enquired the King.

"I'm very tired from my journey," said Samkin, ignoring the

laughter echoing around the room. "But my strength will soon return."

As Samkin tried to step back all eyes fell on Balfruss, who was still laughing. Despite the frowns he struggled to regain his composure.

"My apologies, your Majesty," said Balfruss, standing up and bowing deeply to the throne, "but these two men are charlatans. I assume that if pressed, they planned to trick you with sleight of hand. They don't have the ability to touch the Source."

"You can tell just by looking at them?"

"Yes, your Majesty. I can feel a kinship with my brethren," he said, gesturing at those beside him. "There is a pulse. An echo between us."

"He's lying," said one of the jesters. His bravado was spoiled by the tremor in his voice.

"A demonstration then," said Balfruss. He waited until the King gave permission before walking forward. Balfruss positioned himself opposite the two men who suddenly looked very pale. "As I'm sure you know, one of the first lessons is the physical manifestation of your will. Combine your strength and push me across the room."

"We don't want to hurt you."

Balfruss showed his teeth. "Try."

Both men began by waving their arms and then one made strange whooping noises. The other chanted disjointed words, but nothing happened.

"Is that it?"

The two men looked at each other and then nodded.

Balfruss clapped his hands together and the charlatans were lifted into the air and thrown backwards. They slammed into the wall and hung off the ground as he stalked towards them. Their clothing was pressed flat against their bodies and they struggled to breathe as he leaned towards them.

"I can command storms, summon fire and unmake stone. Animals have nothing interesting to say and no one can see the future, because it has not been written," growled Balfruss. "It's dangerous to meddle with things you don't understand."

"Enough," said the King, moving to stand beside Balfruss. "Let them down."

Balfruss released the two men and they dropped to the floor in heaps. One was on the verge of tears and the other unable to look him or the King in the eye.

"What are your names?" asked the King.

"Sam."

"Paedr."

"Where are you from?"

"It's a tiny village, Sire, right on the border with the west. Hasn't got no name." The speech of both men had suddenly become less formal.

"We came here 'cos everyone left. Emptied out their homes and come east."

"We knew the war was coming," said Paedr, "and needed work. Didn't mean to upset no one. Pretending to be a Battlemage seemed like the best way to get fed. We went two weeks without, besides what we could forage."

"We didn't want to starve," said Sam, glancing briefly at the King. "We're sorry we lied, Sire."

"And what did you do before coming here?" asked the King.

"Worked the land for a local farmer. But Paedr's good with numbers. Kept the books straight for everyone when taxes was due. Not many in our village can write or do their numbers."

The King gestured at his daughter, who stepped forward.

"I think they will be able to help Jonkravish," said Talandra. This was the first time Balfruss had seen the Princess and it was obvious she took after her mother. She was tall with a willowy build, whereas her brothers were big men with broad shoulders like their father. Her hair was long and blonde, held back in a simple plait, whereas their dark hair was cut short. Unusually she was dressed in trousers and a long shirt that concealed much of her shape, but no one would mistake her for a man.

"Who's Jonkravish?" asked Sam.

"Our quartermaster," said Talandra, turning towards the two men. She gestured to someone at the back of the room, who stepped forward out of the shadows.

"This is Jonkravish," said Talandra, nodding towards the Morrin. Like all of his people the quartermaster had a slightly wedge-shaped face, pointed ears, horns and yellow eyes. The two charlatans were visibly unsettled by him and were unable to meet his unwavering stare.

"He will give you a bed, meals and a job."

"We're not getting the lash? Or killed?" said Sam.

Talandra's smile was warm and generous. "No, but your jobs will not be easy. He is not an easy man to please."

"We can do it," said Paedr, a second ahead of Sam.

Balfruss approached the two charlatans as they turned to leave.

"I'm sorry, Sir," said Sam. "We didn't mean no upset."

"I am sorry," said Balfruss, offering his hand. "I lost my temper and I shouldn't have."

They looked at his hand as if it were a poisonous snake, but eventually both shook it before following the quartermaster out of the room.

"Perhaps you could introduce the others," suggested the King as he resumed his seat on the throne. "And yourself."

"I am Balfruss, Majesty. I know you've already met Darius, and his wife Eloise, but he's also my Blood Brother." The King and his Generals looked nonplussed, but Talandra nodded, familiar with the title and honour bestowed on him. As a reward for his efforts in the desert kingdoms the King had allowed Darius to make Balfruss family, even though they were not related. It made Balfruss part of one of the most powerful families in the desert, and part of their line of inheritance.

"The others I don't know by name," apologised Balfruss, "but I recognise a Kálfe of the First People."

The little tribesman stepped forward with a nod towards Balfruss. His flat face was ritually scarred and his forearms were covered with faded red and blue tattoos that were almost black with age. Bone ornaments pierced his ears, and a necklace of reflective yellow stones was his only piece of jewellery. His feet were bare but after a lifetime without shoes the skin looked as tough as old leather. He wore a vest and a loose pair of breeches cut off at the knee to be polite, but normally his people went naked except for a scrap of cloth to cover their genitals.

"I am Ecko Snapping Turtle," he said, touching two fingers to his heart and then his forehead. "I came to help because you have always been good to my people. We still speak of your great king, Kiele, and we remember him in our prayers. He was the one who watched over us when we first came to your shores. I come from my people to honour him. I hope your Great Maker will watch over me while I am on his soil."

"Thank you, Ecko," said the King.

The big plain-faced man stepped forward as Ecko sat down. Balfruss was surprised to see how tall he was, managing to tower over Vann, the biggest in the room. "I'm Finn Smith," he rumbled and that seemed to be all of it. His face was boyish, but Balfruss saw a terrible sadness in his blue eyes. "I was trained after the Grey Council left. Do you want me to show you?"

The King glanced at Balfruss who shook his head very slightly. He could feel more than an echo of power coming from Finn, and he knew the others felt it too. Finn's ability was wild and untamed. An immense force barely held in check by a thread of control. His training would have been rushed and it was possible Finn could prove to be as dangerous as the enemy.

"There's no need. Welcome Master Smith," said the King.

The last Battlemage, the weary man from Shael, stepped forward and bowed deeply to the throne.

"I'm surprised and pleased to see you," said the King. "The news we've received from your country has been limited but very worrying. Can you tell us what's been happening?"

The golden-skinned man shook his head and then looked at Balfruss. His purple eyes bored into Balfruss's skull and for a moment he felt dizzy. A rushing sound filled his ears and somewhere in the distance he could hear the murmur of voices. Balfruss stumbled, but caught himself before he fell over.

"Are you all right?" someone asked, but Balfruss was listening to the other voice in his head, the one that wasn't his own. In his mind's eye he saw golden-skinned people, a distant land of tall trees, and cities dotted with elegant spires.

"His name is Sandan Thule," said Balfruss, as he came out of his reverie. "And the news from his homeland is grave."

The King raised an eyebrow, but said nothing. Before Balfruss could explain, the voice came again more quickly, and with it more horrific visions. A tide of blood flowed along streets and the screams of agony were so high pitched they barely seemed human. Balfruss cried out and fell to his knees as he was exposed to images worse than any nightmare. Somewhere in the distance someone was talking, asking him if he was all right, but they seemed so far away. Slowly the tide of memories receded and the intense emotions that came with them eased. After wiping his face Balfruss managed to stand up with help from Thule but his knees still felt weak.

"*I'm sorry. It was the only way,*" came the echo of Thule's voice in his mind.

"Are you all right?" asked the King.

"I will be," replied Balfruss, swallowing the lump in his throat. "I've seen what's happened to his people. The Mad King,

Taikon, had already united the other nations in the west when his army came to Shael," said Balfruss, relaying the words for Thule. "When diplomacy and bribery failed, he invaded Shael. They fought, but it only delayed the inevitable. There were too many. They tried to smuggle out the Queen and a few others, but all of them were caught, tortured and imprisoned. When the people heard about the Queen there was an uprising. A few escaped in the process, but not many."

"How did he escape?"

As Balfruss turned to face the throne Thule pulled down the scarf covering the bottom half of his face. "He didn't."

A fresh purple scar ran across Thule's throat from where it had been cut. The wound was jagged, which was the only thing that had saved his life. It had stopped bleeding, but was still swollen.

"He was beaten, tortured and then they slit his throat," Balfruss explained. "It was badly done, so he lost his voice, but not his life. He woke in a mass grave on top of the bodies of his countrymen. This was only a few days ago."

The King came towards Thule with Talandra on one side and Graegor, the grizzled one-eyed General on the other. If Thule was intimidated he didn't show it and stood his ground.

"There are no words," said the King, clasping Thule by the forearms.

"He asks that you do not give up on them," said Balfruss. "A resistance is forming, but it will not be enough to free Shael unless the alliance in the west is broken. He is here to help you win this war because it's the best way to free his people."

"I will do all that I can to help your people. On my life, on my honour, I swear it," said the King. "By the throne of Seveldrom and the iron in my blood, I swear it."

Such promises were not made lightly, and once given so publicly the King was bound by ritual and custom to see it through. Even if he died before fulfilling it, his successor was duty bound to uphold the promise. Thule bowed his head and gratefully returned to his seat.

"I'm sure you're all tired from your journey. I offer you my hospitality and suggest you all get some rest while you still can. The war is almost here and when it arrives, it could be a long time before any of us have a full night's sleep again."

They all stood as the King left the room, followed closely by his children and Generals. The one-eyed General paused on his way out and looked across at Balfruss. For a moment Balfruss thought the General was going to approach, but something made him change his mind as he hurried away after the other warriors.

The joy of being reunited with his friends faded quickly as the stark reality of what they were facing loomed in Balfruss's mind. A war against an army of unprecedented size, led by a Mad King, a rogue Battlemage and his apprentices. Balfruss had come home to Seveldrom because his King had asked for aid, but now there were many reasons to fight and they were all standing in the room with him. They were his only family and he would do anything to protect them.

Despite the threat, surrounded by more Battlemages than he'd seen in many years, Balfruss felt excitement mixed with his fear at the thought of what they could accomplish by working together. They could change the world.

CHAPTER 3

As Vargus walked through the Charas city barracks a few men nodded or waved in his direction. After three weeks among the Seveldrom army he was already well known. As a veteran the younger warriors often asked him for advice then keenly listened when it was grudgingly given. Those who wanted to live past the first day of the war paid attention. Novices and men new to the sword from other trades also took comfort from his presence. It gave them hope that it was possible for a common man to survive, even fighting on the front lines.

A mature warrior with no rank was rare, but it happened on occasion. Vargus wore no medals, spoke plainly, and swore when it was appropriate. He drank with farriers and farmhands, warriors and merchants, and sometimes turned up for training resembling a three-day corpse after too many ales. He was also known to inspect the front window of a brothel from time to time. As far as everyone knew he was an ordinary warrior, the same as them.

What some found most surprising was that after so much soldiering he wasn't angry or bitter towards those in charge. When an order was given he followed it. In turn, officers liked him for his discipline and the example he set for others. More than one had bought him a drink and asked for a story.

Three weeks of hard training had stripped the last of the fat from his waist and every muscle in his body ached in a way that made him feel alive. Blood pounded throughout his body, a rhythm of life that he embraced with all avenues of pleasure that were available. The noise of so many warriors preparing for war was as sweet as any music he'd ever heard. The clash of weapons and stink of so much leather being treated made his skin tingle. The tanneries were hard at work as craftsmen turned the famous Sorenson cows into the hardest leather armour known to man.

In the distance came the repetitive hammering of smiths at work, turning out the last of the weapons. No man was without a sword or axe, but weapons were always lost or broken in battle. The King knew his business and was doing his best to make sure that everything was ready in time.

"Vargus," shouted Carnow. He was one of many southerners that had marched north under the banner of Graegor, the grizzled General. Everyone knew that it was Graegor's tactics that had helped the King win several battles in the last thirty years.

Carnow was rangy and red faced from a life spent living outdoors. Like other southerners he was dressed in a mix of green and browns to blend in, and had been trained since childhood with a blade and bow. He was more at home in a forest than a city, where his view of the stars was blocked by towers of stone.

"Carnow."

"Drinks at the Fox and Glove tonight?"

"Sounds good."

"Where are you headed?"

Vargus scratched at his stubbly cheek before answering. "Bwillam's asked me to look over another couple of units in training."

"What did you do to get that job?"

Vargus shrugged. "Just pointed out to a few of the lads what they should be doing. Bwillam took notice and told me to have a talk with some of the others."

Carnow raised an eyebrow. "And?"

"And I get paid a bit extra."

"How much extra?" asked Carnow with a scowl. "'Cos I've three girls and a wife back home that need feeding. You're piss poor with a bow compared to me, so if there's more pay for teaching, I could do with it."

"I'll tell Bwillam you were asking. See if there's anything he can do."

"That's good of you. New tooth?"

"Fitted this morning. Steel," said Vargus showing it off with a big smile. It wasn't the first he'd been forced to replace over the years, and he doubted it would be the last. "Cost me enough, but it's better than having to eat gruel for the rest of my days."

"Shit on that. First drink's on me tonight if you tell me about Marrow Hill. I heard from one of the lads that you were there. Graegor won't speak about it," said Carnow looking puzzled. "It's like he's embarrassed or something."

"I'll tell you what I remember."

"See you tonight," said Carnow, heading towards the Old City.

A few minutes later, as Vargus passed a temple of the Blessed Mother, he felt as if he were being watched. Not far away he saw a girl, who was maybe fourteen, stood in an alleyway beside the temple. Her face was thin, and faint blue stains from venthe addiction marked the corners of her mouth. She wore a dress that was almost transparent, revealing slender curves that were still developing. She beckoned him over, but he shook his head and kept walking. Another warrior passing the other way took her up on the offer. They moved further into the shadows beside the temple, a place devoted to purity.

In Morrinow most people were devout and the punishment

for speaking out in public against the Blessed Mother was severe. Having sex next to a temple was punishable by flogging for the woman and something more permanent for the man involving a small cleaver. There, priests wore chainmail and carried maces to enforce doctrine. Here, a chubby matron in white silk ignored the grunting warrior while rattling a collection plate at him.

A short distance along the street was a dilapidated shrine devoted to Khai'yegha. The wooden doors were warped, the paint peeling and the carved eye was all but invisible. The roof gaped in several places, birds roosted in the rafters and a terrible air of regret hung over everything. A shadow flickered at the corner of his vision and then it was gone. The only living things inside the temple were vermin. With a sad shake of his head Vargus walked away.

Outside the southern gates the grasslands were covered with a sea of tents and campfires. The army surrounded the capital, a nation in its own right on the move. The vast camp was a hive of activity with people preparing in a hundred different ways for the coming war.

Some men were roaring drunk, even though it was early in the day. Warbling music from pipe and drum drifted by on the wind, and not far away a group of warriors danced with each other, howling and laughing, even when they fell over. A lot of the warriors had time to spare and they sought pleasure or oblivion, because all of them knew this could be their last opportunity to enjoy themselves.

All over the camp dozens of people working for the quartermaster were busy at work, cataloguing food, weapons, armour and medical supplies. Those enjoying themselves pretended not to notice the black-capped field surgeons walking through camp. The crows would be in demand when the fighting began, with men screaming and begging them for attention, but like their namesake they were an omen best ignored until necessary.

Further south on the plateau, units of cavalry practised against dummies and friendly units, running drills and mock battles over and over, until it became second nature.

Smiths, grooms and farriers worked tirelessly to make sure the horses were in the best health, while general army staff made sure everyone else was well fed and equipped.

The rhythmic clang of steel on steel drew Vargus's attention. Lines of men dressed in leather and chainmail practised under the watchful eye of a drill sergeant. After only a few seconds Vargus could tell they were not used to thinking as a unit. Their moves looked rehearsed, learned through repetition, not instinct.

Not far away he saw pairs of men fighting viciously and with far less style. Their movements were not for show, and their only purpose was to maim or murder. Sword against axe, mace against iron spear, lance against morningstar. A fight against someone armed the same as you was fine in practice, but on the battlefield there was no time to swap partners until you found someone you liked.

A little further out units of men came together with a loud crash of shields. These men wore no armour and only carried wooden swords daubed with red paint. A balding drill sergeant called Kefi, barely half Vargus's height, watched them with a critical eye. He pointed sharply at those men covered with a lot of red paint. They were declared dead and dropped to the ground for the remainder of the fight. After a few minutes of watching the mock battle it was clear why Bwillam had asked him to speak with this group. The fight was very one sided, but the winning unit only succeeded because they were generally larger and heavier.

When the final man fell the other unit cheered at their victory. Kefi moved to stand beside Vargus, limping slightly on his right side.

Vargus acknowledged his presence with a nod but kept his

eyes on the men, picking out those who seemed the most capable. "Your assessment?" asked Kefi.

"Sloppy. They have discipline, but aren't taking this seriously. They're not thinking as a squad. They don't realise the odds they're facing, or what's at stake."

"Then I will leave them in your capable hands," said Kefi with a curt nod. "Good luck," he added, offering a wry smile as he departed.

The men gathered around Vargus and more than a few were surprised to see him. He knew a few of them by sight, but the rest were total strangers. Honesty seemed like the best approach.

"Do you want to live through this war?" he asked and silence greeted him. "Do you actually want to see the end and go home?"

"That's a stupid question," said a big man with a silver ring in each ear and a shaven head.

"Prove it."

Vargus unsheathed his sword and put it down on the ground. Vargus beckoned and the big man stepped forward.

"Try and kill me."

The big man frowned. "What are you going to use?"

Vargus showed him an empty hand. "This is all I need."

Without a warning he rushed the big man, screaming at the top of his lungs. The big man's reflexes were good. He managed to draw his sword and make a wild swing, but Vargus easily avoided it by stepping to one side. He riposted by ramming a fist into the man's stomach. The air whooshed from his lungs and the big man fell back, gasping for breath. After helping him into a sitting position, Vargus waited until his breathing returned to normal.

By the time Vargus had retrieved his sword all of the men were paying attention.

"I won't lie and try to pass off grape-flavoured piss as wine.

Some of you are going to die screaming for your mother. Maybe all of you. I was watching your training and I can see why most of you will die." Vargus pointed at a short man with red hair and big ears. "What's your name?"

"Orran."

He pointed at Orran's neighbour, a blond ranger from the south. "That man is your brother. You couldn't look more different, except maybe if one of you was a Vorga." A few in the crowd chuckled, easing the tension a little. The threat of violence faded, but their attention didn't waver. "He's your brother. When the fighting starts and he's beside you on that field, stood in that line, you should know everything about him. Not just his name and how many children he's fathered, or whether he likes big tits or small. You should know every thought in his head."

"How am I supposed to do that?" asked Orran. Every face in the crowd was equally confused.

Vargus shrugged. "It's different for everyone. You've seen the others. Some drink until they pass out. Some talk for hours until the sun comes up. Some go somewhere quiet together, if that's your thing. I really don't care. Spend some time together and do whatever it takes to know each other. Because tomorrow, or the next day, the sun will come up and we'll march to war. And the day after that we'll be fighting for our lives and homes."

All around him other units had stopped fighting and a large group of men gathered to listen. This was for all of them. It was a thin reed of hope to hold on to, and given the odds they were facing, they desperately needed it. It wasn't much, but it was better than nothing. If they actually listened then the benefits would be huge. As much as they needed to hear it, he needed them to believe it if he was going to survive.

"When the enemy charges, the noise will rise up and hit you like a giant wave. It'll be hard to believe something could be so loud. Before you can count your fingers they'll be breathing on you, screaming and trying to cut you to pieces. With so many of them, and less of us, all you can do is stare at the man in front. Look at how he fights, work out how to beat him, and get it done, any way you can.

"The problem is, you don't get to face just one of them, like in practice. There'll be a clump, or pairs, and you'll be outnumbered and about ready to piss yourself. I've seen it happen. I ain't ashamed to say I done it myself when I thought I was gonna die. Times like that, it doesn't seem like winning is possible."

The words settled over the men, spreading throughout the crowd. Every pair of eyes was locked onto him, but Vargus wasn't seeing them any more. He was looking into the past, where grey-skinned men crashed into him and the others on the front line.

He came back to the present with a start and saw only young men, eager for any knowledge that might save their lives when events didn't go as planned and it all went wrong.

"Except, you're not out there on your own," he said, pointing at Orran and then the ranger. "He's there with you. And so is he, and him, and him," he said, pointing at a skinny man with blackened teeth, a chubby man with long sideburns and several other men in turn. "They're all your brothers. Every single one. They might not be kin by blood, and I'm not a priest so this isn't a fucking sermon, but you're all the same. He's relying on you to watch out for him, and you know he'll do the same for you, no matter what. That is what makes him your brother."

Orran and his neighbour looked closely at each other and he saw others doing the same. "If he sees a blade coming at your head, he'll get in the way and he'll stop it. He will risk his life to save yours, because he knows what you've got to lose. He knows why you're fighting, and he wants to make sure you get home. He won't even think about it; he'll just do it.

"Focus on the man in front and deal with him. But keep an eye out to the sides, and make sure you look after your family. Because without them, you're already dead."

Vargus approached the big man he'd knocked down and offered a hand. He thought he would refuse, but with so many watching, the big man couldn't ignore him. Vargus pulled him to his feet and shook the man's hand.

"I'm Vargus."

"Hargo Ke Waugh."

"We're family, Hargo," said Vargus with a smile. "And I'll be with you, stood on your left, when the war starts. On my oath, on my life, I swear I'll do everything I can to see that you survive the war."

Hargo looked as if he wanted to speak, to thank him or make a similar promise, but in the end he just nodded. He offered a smile, enough for Vargus to know he wasn't sore about being knocked down in front of the others.

"Training is done for today," said Vargus, addressing those nearest him. "Go and do whatever you need to. But tomorrow when I come back, I expect you to know your brothers, and fight as if you want to live. I don't need to scare you with stories about what will happen if they reach the villages. So you think about that, and what I've said."

As Vargus walked away he felt the eyes of many on him, but didn't look around. The hum of conversation rose as he strode towards the city, his skin tingling with promise.

The next few days would either see the men become brothers in arms who would die for one another, or there would be slaughter on a scale never seen before in history.

CHAPTER 4

Walking through the streets of Charas brought back so many memories. Even though he'd never lived in the city for more than a few months at a time, Balfruss had been visiting all his life. It was the closest thing he had to a home.

While living abroad he'd sometimes dream of walking through the city, staring up at the stained-glass windows, the cathedral spires and uniform buildings. Damp grass would crunch under his bare feet as he wandered through the Queen's park, his nose full of rich aromas from all the herbs and colourful flowers.

The dream was always the same. He'd pause to watch bees aimlessly drift among the flowers and only then would he notice the cottage. Curiosity drew Balfruss towards it until he was standing at the front door of his childhood home. Although modest, the cottage was in good repair, the thatch tidy, the walls freshly painted and the small flowerbeds at the front were well tended. Herbs hung from nails beside the door, drying in the heat, filling the air with the scent of basil and mint. Through the window he could see soft cushions, comfortable-looking furniture and a welcoming home.

The cottage, along with his mother, was gone. The dream

always left him with a terrible sense of longing. He'd not had the dream in months, but similar emotions came to the surface as he approached Vannok's home. The front door opened before Balfruss could knock, his friend filling the doorway.

"Come in, come in," said Vannok, gesturing. "Don't let the heat get out."

As he stepped inside Balfruss noticed Vann wasn't wearing his armour or carrying any weapons, and yet he still seemed too big for the room.

"Close the door!" someone yelled from another room as Vann shoved it shut behind him.

"I knew she'd say that," Vann muttered, before gesturing at one of the chairs beside the fire. Vann poked at the blaze then added another log. Despite it being early spring the nights were still chilly.

"Something to drink?"

"Whatever you're having is fine," said Balfruss, not wanting to impose.

"But you're our guest," said Theresa, coming into the room, with a baby in one arm and a bottle of wine in the other. It had been several years since he'd last seen her, and yet Theresa looked exactly the same, a slender, beautiful woman who turned heads wherever she went. Standing beside Vann made everyone look short, but Theresa came up to his shoulder, making her tall for a woman in Seveldrom.

A little boy charged into the room squealing with glee, ducked between his mother's skirts, then tried to wriggle his way under the table. Vann's face split into a huge grin as he scooped his son off the floor and held him up towards the ceiling. The boy screamed and started to laugh as Vann threw him into the air.

"Fly, daddy, fly!"

Balfruss took the offered bottle of wine from Theresa, kissed her proffered cheek and gently pinched the baby's chubby little leg.

"How are you, Terry?"

"I'm well, although this one has been keeping us up a bit," she said, nodding towards the baby dozing on her hip.

"Who's this?"

"This is Jordie," said Theresa, turning the baby around and giving Balfruss a brief glimpse of blue eyes and a shock of blond hair before Jordie shyly turned his face away.

"The last time I saw you, Tannos was the baby," said Balfruss, glancing over to see Vann holding his son upside down by one ankle. The boy was still laughing. "And now look at him."

Theresa rolled her eyes and shook her head. "Open the wine, I know I need a drink."

Balfruss tried to help Theresa prepare the meal, but she insisted he stay out of the kitchen. Once, many years ago, he'd been determined to return the favour for the countless meals they had made for him. Unfortunately it had not been a great success and the look Theresa gave him made it clear her memory was just as good as his.

For the next hour he found himself entertaining Tannos while Vann looked after the baby. The boy seemed to have an endless supply of energy, and after chasing him around the room and hoisting him into the air over and over, the muscles in his upper arms started to ache. Instead he suggested another game, and by channelling a small amount of power, he created a globe of light filled with a moving spiral of colours. It managed to hold Tannos's attention until Theresa called them to the table, by which time he was exhausted.

It had been a long time since Balfruss had tasted such a rich and tasty beef stew. In the far east beef was rare and expensive, making it a delicacy reserved for the wealthy. For the last five years he'd been eating a steady diet of goat and lamb. There were a number of benefits to coming home.

He wolfed down every scrap of meat and all of the vegetables, then mopped up the gravy with bread until his plate was spotless. Vann ate at a more sedate pace, with Jordie balanced on one hip, but he seemed happy to share his meal with his son and didn't begrudge Balfruss when he finished the last of the stew.

Once they'd been fed the boys started to get sleepy, but before Theresa put them to bed Balfruss saw her exchange a pointed look with Vann.

"Is everything all right?" asked Balfruss.

Theresa raised an eyebrow. "You haven't asked him?"

"I didn't have a chance, love." Vann passed Jordie to his wife and pulled the dozing Tannos onto his lap, addressing Balfruss. "He's been acting peculiar. Not all the time, just now and then. He tells me he hears people talking when there's no one around. He says he has these feelings, but he doesn't yet have the words. I wondered if it's just a child's imagination or if he's sensing . . ."

"The Source?" asked Balfruss and his friend nodded.

"Can you test him?"

"I can, but even if he does have the potential, he's too young for the Red Tower. Most children don't manifest their abilities until they're eight or nine."

"Oh Gods," said Theresa, cradling Jordie to her breast. "Who would send their child away at eight?" As soon as the words were out of her mouth she clearly regretted them. "I'm sorry."

"It's all right. I loved being at the Red Tower. I'm glad I went." All of which was true, but he'd cried every night for the first two weeks. During that time it felt as if he were being punished, and that it wasn't the special place he'd been promised. He'd been so heartsick for home his chest had ached for days. In time the feeling receded, especially when he realised what being a Battlemage meant. A life free from the drudgery and routine he saw every day in his village. A life that would allow him to travel the world, make a lot of money and meet lots of exotic women.

In time his priorities shifted as he outgrew pubescent fancies and it became a chance to quench his thirst for knowledge at the same time as protecting others.

"You'll need to wake him up for this," said Balfruss, kneeling on the floor until he was level with Tannos's face. Vann gently coaxed him awake but the boy was tired and just wanted to go back to sleep.

"Will it hurt?" asked Theresa.

"No. If he has the ability, he'll be able to sense an echo of what I'm doing."

While keeping his eyes on the boy's face for any reaction, Balfruss drew power from the Source, slowly at first, trickling it into his being. Tannos didn't seem to notice, so he increased the amount of power, drawing more and more heavily until it flooded into him. The boy yawned and tried to curl up on his dad's lap, totally unaware of how much power Balfruss was holding with his will.

"He doesn't have the ability," said Balfruss, and Theresa let out a long slow breath, obviously relieved. Vann's expression remained unreadable, so it wasn't clear if he felt relief or disappointment.

Balfruss said goodnight to both of the boys, and while Theresa put them to bed, he and Vann got comfortable in front of the fire with a bottle of port.

"How are your parents?" asked Balfruss.

"My father died two years ago, mother is still well. She dotes on both the boys."

"I'm sorry about your father. He was always kind to me when we were young."

Vann shrugged. "That's because he liked you. We never really had much in common. He thought joining the army was the stupidest decision I ever made, and he never hid his disdain. He wanted me to follow in his footsteps and become a stone mason."

Balfruss cast his mind back. "What was it he always used to say?"

"People need a roof over their heads every day. They don't always need a sword."

Balfruss laughed but it quickly faded as his thoughts turned to his mother and absent father. Annoying as he was, at least Vann's father had been there for him while growing up. He'd made sure his family never went hungry and had been more of a father to Balfruss than his own. The last time he remembered seeing his real father, Balfruss would have been about the same age as Tannos. All he knew was that he'd been a soldier for the King. His mother had told him little else and after a while he'd stopped asking as it obviously upset her.

"My father was a difficult man," said Vann, draining his glass and refilling it.

"The only time I ever disappointed your father was when he caught me with a girl in the barn."

"I remember that," said Vann with an evil grin. "He was livid. I thought he was going to march you both in front of a priest of the Maker and insist he marry you."

Even though it was over twenty years ago Balfruss could still see Beth's face, bright blue eyes and long blonde hair. As children they'd talked about getting married, having children and growing old together in the village. He would work in the quarry and she in the bakery like her mother. They were just childish fancies shared on warm, lazy summer days that seemed to stretch on forever. Balfruss had been happy to play along, but he'd never shared with Beth his dreams of becoming an explorer and finding places no one had ever visited before, digging up ancient treasures and statues encrusted with diamonds. Bringing home huge amounts of gold so that his mother didn't have to work so hard all of the time.

"Sometimes I wonder where Beth is, how her life turned out."

"She's here in Charas," said Theresa, coming back into the room.

"It's true," said Vann, moving to the floor so his wife could sit in the chair. She kissed Vann on the cheek and gently ran her fingers through his shaggy hair. "I saw her the first time about a year ago, and a few times since. Apparently I look exactly the same as when we were children."

"How is she?" asked Balfruss, swallowing the unexpected lump in his throat.

"Doing well. She runs a tailor shop with a partner and she married a cooper."

"They're expecting their first baby in the winter," said Theresa. Vann raised an eyebrow. "It was obvious."

Part of Balfruss wondered what his life would have been like if the priest had married them that day. It was an idle thought, and yet even as it occurred he could map the path of their lives. While a home and family sounded nice, in time he would have ended up resenting Beth and their children for shackling him to the village and a life of routine. A life without adventure and surprises. An ordinary life.

Even if he had not been born with magical ability, Balfruss knew he would have outgrown the village of his birth. Some of his childhood friends had no desire to leave and were happy with simple lives, following in the footsteps of their parents, and even grandparents for some. He'd always needed more to feel a sense of achievement, a sense of peace. At times he envied them and wished he could be satisfied with less. Perhaps in time he might come to that place, but he wasn't there yet.

Balfruss gave them both one final wave. Theresa closed the door and joined her husband beside the fire.

"Did you have a chance to talk to him about his father?"

Vann shook his head. "I couldn't find the right moment. I felt bad enough asking him to look at Tannos."

"He's going to find out, Vann."

"I know, but right now he has enough on his mind. It will wait a little while."

Theresa had her doubts but held her tongue. Secrets this big never stayed buried for long.

CHAPTER 5

Talandra rubbed at her forehead, trying to dislodge the ache behind her eyes. It was late, or perhaps it had become early, and there was still much to do before she could even think about sleep. Her borrowed desk was covered with a scattering of missives from her spies, reports, maps, lists of weapons and men, and a diagram for a new catapult that an insistent engineer had pressed into her hand. A sea of letters and numbers swam before her eyes.

Her father had moved her and the rest of his advisors to the Kilgannon estate, close to the western border of Seveldrom and the two passes that led through the mountains to Yerskania. That put her only a couple of hours' ride away from the army, but well out of harm's way. Lord Kilgannon had given her a comfortable suite, but her favourite piece of furniture wasn't the bed but a desk large enough to hold all of her papers.

"You'll be no good to me if you fall asleep during the first battle," said King Matthias coming into the room. "You should get some sleep."

"Soon, father, I promise."

"You said there was news?"

Talandra searched for the latest message from her spymaster in the western nation of Yerskania. The tiny messenger, a messúz bat, had died not long after arriving. They lived such short lives and yet it had flown so far to reach her. She wondered what it might have seen on its journey.

It wasn't much of a tragedy in the grand scale, but it was also the first death in the war she'd witnessed first-hand. She'd held its fragile body in one hand and watched it gasp its final breath. Her inability to save the poor creature, and the feeling of being utterly powerless, still troubled her. Soon enough Sisters of Mercy would be providing succour to dying men, and they would be equally helpless to save them.

Talandra unrolled the tiny scroll and scanned the coded message again. "I have news from my network about King Taikon. There was an attempt on his life."

"Unsuccessful I take it?"

Talandra shrugged. "It depends who was behind the attempt and its purpose."

"Tell me," said the King, sitting down and getting comfortable.

"Before you ask, it wasn't one of my agents. None of them can get anywhere near Taikon. The Warlock and his apprentice Battlemages scare everyone, but the message does mention some public dissent in Zecorria, which isn't surprising."

"If their fragile alliance is to hold together, the war must happen soon. Even with everyone focused on destroying such a foul enemy," said the King, tapping his chest, "other issues will only be laid aside for so long."

There were a hundred stories floating around about the horrific religious atrocities her father was supposed to have committed. Burning down churches of the Holy Light, beheading priests of the Blessed Mother and burning holy books. While that might be enough for Zecorria and Morrinow to go to war, reports from her network indicated the other nations in the west had not voluntarily joined the alliance. The messages coming out of Shael were worse than anything she could have imagined. It sounded unbelievable that the whole country had been destroyed so quickly, but her people knew better than to exaggerate. Certain facts could not be denied. The capital of Shael had fallen, the royal family were dead or in hiding, and thousands had been killed and enslaved. Shael was gone and Yerskania, previously their strongest ally in the west, had been earmarked as the next target if they refused to join the alliance.

Vorga society believed in strength above all, so they would relish a chance to test themselves, and as ever the motives of the Drassi people remained a mystery.

But the people across the west were not happy. There had been a lot of talk about great acts of evil being committed by her father in Seveldrom. So far the only atrocities people had seen had been carried out in the west against their allies in Shael.

"My agents are already working hard to try and fracture the western alliance from the inside," said Talandra. "There are many rumours, but some claim the assassination on Taikon was a test. A crucible laid down in the holy books. Some think Zecorran fanatics were behind it, others claim a Morrin splinter sect. Whoever was responsible, it's changed things. Made them worse for us."

"How?"

"Before the attempt on his life, Taikon was nervous; now he's paranoid. He convinced himself someone was trying to steal the artefact he wears on his crown and in his panic Taikon swallowed it. Not long after the first attempt, he invited a second, in public."

King Matthias rubbed his chin before answering. "The artefact protected him."

Talandra nodded. "He was stabbed in the side, and as the spear left his body the wound closed, leaving no mark. His hold over the northerners is even stronger now. Now, many believe they fight in a holy war against an enemy of unparalleled evil."

Her father inclined his head with a wry smile, but it didn't stay on his face for long. "What's so special about the artefact?"

"In both holy books dedicated to the Blessed Mother and the Lord of Light, there are references to immortal prophets. It sounds thin to me, and my agents are trying to undermine it, but it's making both the Morrin and Zecorran priests squeal in delight. The alliance is tenuous, but if this religious fever spreads ... " Talandra trailed off and shrugged her shoulders. The other nations in the west were not as focused on religion, but even they couldn't ignore a leader who could recover from any wound.

Then there was also the issue of land. Seveldrom had huge grazing plains and rich farmland in the south which many envied. Talk of religious prophets might be the excuse that some used, but she knew others marched to war for their own reasons.

"It will happen soon," said the King. "They must be nearly here."

"That was my thought too. To maintain their momentum, blood must be spilled very soon."

"When do you think they'll arrive?" he asked.

"Tomorrow, maybe the day after at the latest."

"We're ready." He sounded confident and Talandra took strength from him. "I'll tell Wolfe to double the number of scouts in both passes."

"How is the new General performing?" said Talandra, changing the subject slightly.

"Vannok?" asked the King, raising an eyebrow. "Two years in post is not that new. Why do you ask?"

"Just idle curiosity."

"You're never idly curious about anything, Tala," the King shrewdly pointed out. "What do you make of him?"

"He knows his business. He isn't quick to anger and the men are loyal to him. He's a reliable man."

"And?" said the King, gesturing for her to get on with it.

"Did you know he and Balfruss grew up together?" asked Talandra.

"I didn't know that," mused the King. "And what do you make of the Battlemage?"

"I haven't decided. I'm going to do some more digging into his past, but he named Darius his Blood Brother. So he's well travelled and respected to have earned such an honour."

The King yawned and stood up. "You need to get some sleep."

"I will. I just have one more meeting."

"You look pale. Have you eaten?"

"Yes and I'm fine," she said, smiling up at him. He sighed, touched her cheek and turned to leave.

As her father's footsteps receded Talandra pondered orders for her network in Yerskania. It was the most central country in the west and despite the impending war its capital city, Perizzi, remained the main hub for all trade. And with trade came a constant river of information from all over the world that her people listened to. But they could also add to the river and watch as the stories spread throughout the west.

Perizzi was the key to the west, both strategically and geographically. Both the northern and southern passes through the mountains from east to west arrived at its gates. And with the largest trading port on the western coast it made the city critical. An army on the move needed to carry a huge amount of food, weapons and armour, which meant the docks would be busy for months shipping goods in before sending them back out through the passes. Accidents could happen, shipments could be delayed or sunk, food spoiled or poisoned and weapons damaged in transit. The number of opportunities to cause havoc from behind enemy lines was enormous, but only as long as Perizzi remained free from Taikon's influence. If it should fall under his direct control then her job would be almost impossible.

The war on the battlefield was not guaranteed and already preparations had been made for a strategic withdrawal. The Battlemages might change that, but for now she and her father had to rely on the facts. The west simply had more soldiers. Eventually the numbers would begin to tell, so in order to win this war the alliance had to crumble from the inside.

If the worst should happen and the western army should defeat them, then Perizzi would become even more important. It would be from there that a resistance would start, led by her people. Hopefully it wouldn't come to that, but she'd considered it and made plans for her father to be evacuated.

In the meantime she thought it was time for new stories to emerge about Taikon. While some might believe him to be a prophet of the Lord of Light, others would see his healing abilities as perverse and inhuman. Scripture was often open to interpretation, but no one would support Taikon if they thought his powers were fuelled by cannibalism and ritual sacrifice.

She left the details up to her agent, Gunder, to decide, but the people in the west needed to look a little more closely at who they were following. She also made it clear in her note that Gunder's first priority was to the city and the people of Perizzi. She gave him leave to do whatever was necessary to keep it free from outside influence. She sealed the note in a small tube and had a servant take it to the rookery.

A short while later Jonkravish, the army quartermaster, stumped into the room, his boots echoing loudly on the stone floor. Despite the hour he didn't look tired, but then Morrin were known for being a hardy race. His keen yellow eyes, set in his slightly wedge-shaped face, gave nothing away about his thoughts. Talandra had known him all her life and, unlike some, she wasn't intimidated by his unwavering stare.

Jonkravish wore no badge of office or stripes on his uniform to show his rank, despite being one of the most important people in the army. He wore no jewellery or visible displays of wealth, and his tall frame was still lean despite his age. As ever he was smartly dressed and his horns were buffed to a glossy black sheen. Talandra knew he spent little money on himself, and that it mostly went on his family. He had no vices, was incorruptible and utterly loyal. Spies from the west hated Jonkravish with a passion.

"You look awful," said Jonkravish as he sat down.

"Thank you."

Jonkravish's smile was mostly hidden behind his shaggy beard, but she knew it was there. "You're too skinny as well. You should eat something and then sleep."

"So I keep hearing. I will. Very soon."

"You wanted to discuss supplies, yes?"

"Yes. How are the staging points progressing?"

Jonkravish regarded her silently for a long time before answering. "Heavily armed warriors guard them at all hours. The caches hold spare weapons, food and a few surprises," he said with a vague wave of a hand. "The army must retreat, yes? We are ready when it happens."

"Good."

"But that's not why you asked me here," said Jonkravish. "You've never taken an interest in me before."

"That's not true. I've known you all my life. As has my father."

"And your grandfather before that. I meant an interest in my work, not my personal life, but you knew this also. Do not play your word games with me, child," rebuked Jonkravish with a shake of his head. "Do you doubt my abilities?"

"Of course not."

"Then you think your father, and his Generals, are incompetent. Bumbling fools, not worth the salt in their blood, yes?"

"No."

"Then speak plainly, girl. Time is short and my patience is not what it was."

Talandra sighed. "Before the war began, I received regular reports from Morrinow. In the last three weeks a large number of Morrin left their homes and businesses here in Seveldrom, to return home to Morrinow. My sources tell me that few of them arrived. I have no proof, but I believe they were murdered on the road. My agents tell me that Seveldrom, and my father, are being blamed for their deaths to fuel the propaganda about him."

Jonkravish sat back and folded his arms. In the glow from the candles his white and purple marbled skin looked almost translucent. His neatly trimmed hair and beard were completely grey, but as a young girl she remembering seeing patches of black. Jonkravish stared at nothing for a short time before focusing on her again. "You have a question?"

"What can you tell me about the Morrin extremists?"

"It would be them," agreed the Morrin, nodding his shaggy head. "They are one of the reasons I left my country. At the time, many thought they were nothing more than a group of disgruntled youths, making trouble in the streets. But I saw many people offering them support, and every day their numbers grew. Now I hear they have a seat on the Council and their voice can always be heard somewhere in public, spewing poison on the wind."

"That was a long time ago. Now they have the majority on the Council. I suspect the Warlock is partly responsible for that."

"Perhaps. Or perhaps it was already moving that way, yes?"

"Do you have any contacts or friends back home?" asked Talandra.

"Yes. But do you not have spies in Morrinow?"

Talandra shrugged. "A few foreigners, but they've fallen silent. I'm worried they've been imprisoned or murdered."

A brief silence filled the room as Jonkravish considered what she was angling him towards. She didn't need to mention the risk to those involved.

"You want me to ask my friends to spy for you?" said Jonkravish in a whisper.

"No. I know how your people feel about such things. I'm merely interested in . . . talk."

It was said two Morrin could not pass each other on the street without stopping to talk for at least an hour. Although it was a callous stereotype, Jonkravish had sometimes joked that most of his people only went to temple to gossip, and prayer was the second-most popular pastime in church.

"I hear a lot of rumours, but I'd like to know which of them are true and which are propaganda," said Talandra.

"I will see that it is done."

Talandra let out a long sigh of relief. She hadn't been sure he would agree. "Thank you."

The old Morrin was about to leave when he saw something in her expression. "Something else worries you?"

"There are four thousand Morrin in the army, and perhaps four times that number in Charas. You know it's only a matter of time. Once the fighting starts, and the first bodies are carried through the gates, people will look for scapegoats."

Talandra glanced at his horns and winced at her poor choice of words. The racial slur was so old it went past Jonkravish without him noticing. She'd been spending too much time with Graegor and his foul mouth.

Jonkravish bristled. "I will not leave my post, or go home and hide in my house. This country has been my home since before your father was born. In Morrinow I was an outsider because I did not bow and pray to the Blessed Mother twice a day. Here I am a Morrin, yes, but also just another man on the street."

"I know, I know," said Talandra, trying to placate him. "I'm not asking you to hide. I already knew you'd say that."

Jonkravish hesitated. "Then who?"

"The Morrin Ambassador. Most of the western nations have embassies here, and they've accepted our protection. Ambassador Kortairlen seems to think there's no danger, or he's invincible."

"It's common in those who've not yet lived a century. I will send him a convincing letter."

"Thank you."

"You will get some rest, yes?"

Jonkravish waited until she nodded before getting to his feet. Looking down he affectionately ruffled Talandra's hair as he'd done when she was a girl. Although impolite, Talandra was tempted to ask his age. Morrin could live up to four times as long as men, and in his eyes it would seem only moments since her birth.

As the sound of Jonkravish's boots receded down the hallway, she made a mental note to ask him about her mother. Her oldest memories were fading and it would be nice to be reminded of what her mother was like from someone who remembered everything so clearly.

Talandra considered going to bed but there was still work to be done. She laid her head on the desk, telling herself she was just going to have a short rest. She was asleep in seconds.

CHAPTER 6

The morning was cool and the dull blue sky suggested little chance of rain. A poor day for growing crops, but well suited for the first day of the war.

Vargus watched as rangers withdrew from the southern pass, running past him and other warriors on the front line. The southerners were used to travelling long distances on foot. A short sprint to outdistance the enemy wasn't difficult for them, especially in light armour. Not for the first time Vargus envied the quality of their moulded leather armour. By comparison, his army issue armour was serviceable, but the blood he'd cleaned off it was a little disconcerting. Too late to do anything about it now.

The last of the rangers slipped behind the front rank and a few seconds later the order was given. The air throbbed with a loud humming, and a weak sun passed behind a black cloud. Hundreds of tiny distractions flickered at his eye corners, but Vargus stubbornly ignored them and kept facing forward. Up ahead a vicious rain of arrows fell onto the approaching enemy. Most of the soldiers didn't have time to raise their shields. Screams and cries of pain echoed off the stone walls. Vargus watched dozens of men die in a few seconds from the lethal rain. Another volley quickly followed the first and then another as the enemy came on, stubbornly pressing forward despite the slaughter. On raised platforms and tiny ledges cut into both sides of the pass, individual archers started picking targets and firing at will.

A faint westerly wind blew through the pass, driving dust into the face of the enemy, adding insult to the carnage. Vargus was glad the wind wasn't blowing the other way or else he and the rest of the army would be left smelling dead men for days.

Without looking around he knew that Hargo was stood on his right. He could feel him, a solid and reassuring presence. Orran was on his left and the blond ranger Benlor beside him. Not far away he could hear Black Tom, his stained teeth black from endlessly chewing tarr, day and night. Next to him was Curly, who'd fallen out of a tree as a boy and been bald as an egg ever since. Beside him was Rudd, the skinniest man in the squad who ate more than three men, and Tan, a rat-faced lad who'd grown up with Orran.

Nearby, a dozen others were known to him, each with their own stories of sorrow, triumph and loss, big and small. Dead wives and children lost to random acts of violence, tragic accidents and drawn-out illness. Farms burned down and families butchered in wanton slaughter by raiders. Finding ancient gold buried in a field, hearing their firstborn say his first word, and provocative stories of wild nights with foreign, mysterious women. Mundane and miraculous, all of their stories were a part of him now.

They'd bonded over beer and pit fights, rye spirits and shared miseries, war stories and old songs around the embers of a dying campfire. A brotherhood two weeks old and already it was stronger than many he'd seen in the past. They were his family now and the only thing standing between him and oblivion.

Despite their losses from the rain of arrows the enemy came on, stepping over the dead and leaving the injured where they fell. The western soldiers were close enough for Vargus to see they were Yerskani warriors, stout, pale-skinned men dressed in steel caps and leather jerkins. For the most they carried spears and slightly curved cleavers, the ancient weapon of their tribal heritage. The weapons and armour would have been mined, smelted and forged in the Yerskani smithies. Theirs was a nation of merchants, craftsmen, traders and sailors. They were not renowned for their prowess on the battlefield. It seemed a bizarre choice for them to lead the first attack when other nations in the alliance had warriors with more ferocious reputations. Vargus wondered who they'd angered to have drawn the short straw.

The Yerskani warriors approached with greater caution, triangular shields at the ready, but the archers were already pulling back. As soon as they were close enough for him to see their eyes, Vargus felt a wave of pity. Their spirit was already broken and the worst had not even started yet.

"They'd better do it now, or else we'll be in the bloody way," muttered Orran. Even as he finished speaking there was a loud thump from somewhere behind them.

"Down!" shouted Vargus and a dozen others along the line gave the order as well.

The front three ranks dropped to their knees, pulling their shields over their heads, overlapping with their neighbours.

For a moment the sky turned completely black. Vargus risked a glance around the edge of his shield and saw the shadow break up into thousands of smaller pieces as it flew overhead.

Horrible screams and shrieks rattled his eardrums as the caltrops slammed into the enemy, digging into flesh and driving men to their knees. The iron spikes were not heavy, but falling from a great height the momentum drove them through their armour and flesh with ease. Some tried to huddle behind their shields, but most still died as the caltrops shattered wood or rebounded, burying themselves in exposed limbs. Injured men stumbled and fell onto more spikes, and soon the floor of the pass was carpeted with the dead and wounded men screaming in agony. A few disciplined officers were attempting to rally those still able to fight, but it was hopeless.

A crisp note from a horn blotted out the pleas of the dying Yerskani warriors. Vargus rose to his feet with the others in readiness. Orders were being given, but it wasn't necessary. They all knew what they had to do. Drawing his short sword Vargus looked first to his right and then left. Hargo nodded grimly and Orran gave him a nervous grin, trying to mask his fear. He was on the verge of telling one of his dirty jokes but it would have to wait.

Taking a deep breath Vargus screamed a wordless battle cry that was taken up by hundreds of others all around him. Setting the pace he jogged forward towards the shattered front line of the enemy. The Yerskani warriors saw them coming, twenty men abreast, but there was nowhere for them to go. The sides of the pass were too steep to climb, and more men were filtering in from behind. All around them were corpses, blood, shit, gore, fallen weapons and more caltrops threatening to maim them.

A small number found the courage to ignore what was happening and face them on their feet. Here and there spears were lowered, one directly in front of Vargus, but he didn't think today would be his last.

Vargus's heart was pounding in his ears, a faint tingle running along his arms and legs. Without realising, he increased his pace, pulling slightly ahead of the others in line. Part of him wanted to be the first to reach the enemy.

To his credit the terrified man in front raised his spear, but Vargus parried it with ease and drove his sword into the man's guts. A second later the two armies came together with an ear-splitting crash as shields slammed into the broken front rank of the Yerskani. Their leather armour could not stand up to brutal punishment at close range, and many swords went straight through. Gouts of blood and chunks of flesh rained down on Vargus as limbs and pieces of men were sliced away.

Screaming at the enemy Vargus smashed his shield into the face of one man, stabbed another in the neck, kicked a third in the stomach and head-butted a fourth. He almost decapitated one man with the edge of his shield, and smashed the pommel of his sword into the face of another, shattering his jaw. Blood sprayed across his cheek from somewhere on his right as Hargo sliced open a man's neck. With his next blow Hargo cut deeply into an enemy soldier, splitting the man's collar bone and wedging his blade deep in the man's torso. From the corner of his eye Vargus saw someone try to take advantage before the big man could find another weapon.

Using his shield Vargus pushed back two soldiers and then slashed at the face of the man in front of Hargo. The soldier recoiled, more in surprise than pain, but it was enough. Hargo took up a fallen Yerskani cleaver and split the man's skull with one vicious blow. Like a mad butcher he started hacking the enemy soldiers into meaty red chunks. A laugh bubbled up from Hargo's throat. A slip of madness, a moment of joy amid the mindless slaughter. It faded when someone cut him across the ribs, but the weapon stayed in his hand as if it belonged.

Gone was the sky and the earth. Even the walls of the pass were no longer a part of Vargus's world. The only thing he saw was the enemy in front. First it was a tall warrior spitting curses through yellow teeth. With a growl he disembowelled the man and kicked him in the face on the way down for good measure. A broad man, bare-chested and rippling with muscles took his place, but he was quickly dispatched with a quick thrust to the groin that left him squealing like a slaughtered pig. After that the faces started to blur together. Vargus kept pushing forward, hacking and slicing, grunting and kicking. Suddenly there was no one in front and his momentum made him stumble and almost fall. A bloody hand touched his shoulder and he spun about ready to hack off the arm that came with it.

It took him a few seconds to recognise the man was Hargo. He lowered his sword and looked around for any pockets of fighting, but there was nothing to see. It was over.

All around him lay the dead and the dying. Vargus had no idea how long they'd been fighting, but gradually he became aware of his loud breathing and the painful burning in his lungs. His shoulders ached and his arms were covered with blood and gore up to his armpits. Orran, and some of the others, came to where he stood catching his breath, their expressions a mix of horror, relief and fear. Black Tom huffed, spat a wad of tarr on the ground but said nothing.

"What's wrong?" asked Vargus, spinning around and looking for the source of their alarm. Maybe this had only been the first wave and reserves were on their way. But there was no one in sight except warriors from Seveldrom. Any Yerskani survivors had broken ranks and were running for their lives. A trail of weapons and armour had been dropped in their wake as they fled.

Vargus looked at the others. "What is it?"

"It's not them," said Orran, wiping his mouth and spitting a wad of bloody phlegm. "It's you."

"I could barely keep up," panted Hargo. He was bent double, gasping for air. "You cut straight through them. It was you that broke them."

"No," said Vargus, emphatically shaking his head. "It was all of us. On my own I was a dead man. We broke them together. Hargo saved me three times over, and I know I did the same for him."

"Where's Tan?" asked Orran, looking around for his friend. No one had seen him in a while. Fearing the worst they started to search the battlefield.

They found his body buried under two others, a permanent expression of fear stamped on his narrow features. His eyes stared on and on at nothing, and yet none of them could look away. Nearby somebody groaned and they saw it was an injured Yerskani, bleeding from several wounds, but not quite dead. With a feral scream Orran launched himself at the man, stabbing him over and over again, until he was just a bloody sack of meat that didn't look like a man any more. Orran was crying by the end, sobbing with snot running down his bruised and battered face, but no one was laughing. He and Tan came from the same village and had known each other since they were boys. More than twenty-five years of shared memories, boys to men.

Eventually the tide of anger passed and Orran just slumped down on top of the dead, forgetting everything in the world but his sorrow.

Hargo picked up his weapons while Vargus and the others helped Orran to his feet. Black Tom and Curly wrapped Tan's body in a blanket and they carried it with them out of the charnel house towards the sprawling camp.

Vargus cast a final glance around the pass at the bodies, which were already attracting a swarm of flies and carrion. A bloody first day to be sure, but not what he'd expected. To say it had been easy would be a lie. Plenty of men had died on both sides, but for every one of theirs that had fallen, a dozen or more had died from the west. The sun was still not at its highest point and already the fighting was done. After such a crushing and brutal defeat he didn't think they would return today. Despite the victory, it felt like an ill start to the war.

That night, around a blazing bonfire, they all said their goodbyes to Tan. Greasy black smoke drifted into the air from his funeral pyre, and an old priest of the Maker said a few kind words about his life. There were no prayers, just quiet weeping from Orran, silent tears and grim faces from some of the others who knew him best. Theirs wasn't the only funeral that night, or the only pyre burning high, but it was the noisiest.

Before the fire had started to burn down a few of the men were drunk, but out of respect they pretended they were sober until Orran was well into his cups. By then it didn't matter, he wouldn't remember much of the night, let alone who'd been respectful and not.

Then came the stories and raucous laughter as Orran remembered the good times. He told them tales from their joint childhood of stealing apples, and how Tan had been caught fingering a farmer's daughter in a hayloft because she'd squealed so loud.

Later, men were dancing and singing old songs from the book of the Maker, often led by the tipsy priest. Their good mood was briefly spoiled when a priest from the church of the Holy Light offered to hear Orran's confession.

"Take your lantern, and shove it up your fucking arse!"

Orran would have gutted the priest if Vargus hadn't held him back and Hargo taken away his sword. The scrawny priest retreated and was soon forgotten when they tapped another keg.

War stories came next, and the crowd of men around the fire swelled until Vargus couldn't see any other campfires for the press of bodies. There was a giant sea of red faces, from which waves of laughter and snatches of song rolled in and out like the tide.

When talk inevitably turned to the day's fighting, Hargo and a few others spoke about Vargus's savagery and how many Yerskani he'd killed. Vargus was quick to share the credit, stressing that they were drunk and exaggerating. Orran, much the worse for drink, took offence when Vargus tried to deny they'd won because of him.

"I was there. I saw you cutting them bastards down like you

were scything corn," he said, swaying wildly. "It was like nothing I've ever seen."

Vargus put down his mug and sat perfectly still, waiting until the others noticed. Even Rudd stopped shoving food in his mouth and Black Tom paused in his endless chewing. It was only when a hush fell over the crowd that Orran looked over.

"The only reason I'm still alive is because we fought together. Remember when we met during your training? It wasn't that you couldn't fight. It was just you didn't really care. I said you were brothers, and you probably thought I was drunk, or preaching like them lantern boys." Orran sneered and Black Tom spat into the fire, making it sizzle. "Believe me now?"

Those closest nodded or grunted their assent. Vargus held Orran's gaze, and after a long moment the smaller man inclined his head. Vargus knew his unit had earned the respect of many others. They'd led the charge, and it was they who had broken through first, shattering the fragile will of the enemy.

A man moved into the firelight and took a knee in front of Vargus. "I saw how you all fought today and I want to join," he declared earnestly. "What do I have to do?"

Vargus pretended to consider it, while others looked on with a mix of surprise and amusement. "Well, I'll bend over and you can kiss my ring. How's that sound?"

The warrior looked suitably horrified and others laughed at his expression. Pulling the man to his feet Vargus clapped him on the shoulder. "This isn't a cult, and I'm not its leader. Sit and we'll talk."

That night more than a hundred men took the idea of the brotherhood back to their units, and from there it spread throughout the army like a forest fire.

Just before he fell unconscious from drinking too much, Vargus looked at the back of his hands. The liver spots were almost gone and the skin looked firm and much tighter.

CHAPTER 7

Nirrok crouched in the furthest corner from the throne, pressing his back against the wall and doing his best to go unnoticed. So far Emperor Taikon had not called on him, but that could change at any second. He needed to be ready to fulfil any of the Emperor's requests, as fast as possible, or risk his wrath for taking too long. At the moment he seemed obsessed with a colourful exotic bird that had a sweet, if somewhat loud, song. Apparently the bird was extremely rare and had been brought in from the vast emerald jungle to the north across the Dead Sea. No one had seen its like before in the west, making it utterly unique and therefore worthy of the Emperor's attention.

Nirrok wasn't a betting man, but would happily put money against anyone who thought the bird had a future. It would end up with a broken neck like the other toys and curiosities he lost interest in.

There was a loud booming at the main door before a herald stepped into the room to announce guests. He bowed so low his forehead almost brushed the floor before he straightened up.

"Most Holy, as you requested, your War Council is here. They await your pleasure."

Taikon put the songbird back into its cage and carefully made sure the door was locked before focusing his attention on the herald. The muscles in the sides of the sovereign's face jumped up and down as he clenched his jaw and Nirrok braced himself for another burst of violence.

"Send them in," said Taikon in a calm voice, much to everyone's surprise. The herald let out a long slow breath, bowed low and slowly backed out of the room.

Six burly men marched into the room, bowing low in unison to the throne. Four were local Zecorrans, dressed in heavy plate and chainmail, and the last two were horned Morrin warriors. All of them wore numerous badges or notches indicating their rank, and the servant guessed they were Generals. The Morrin were here as a courtesy, but they looked equally nervous and on edge as the others. Despite the room being fairly cool everyone was coated in a sheen of sweat.

Perhaps it was because he didn't know very much about war, but Nirrok thought it odd that the Generals were here in the capital and not with the army.

"What news of the war?" asked the Emperor, breaking the silence gripping the room.

"As you requested, Most Holy, the Queen of Yerskania has been punished for disobeying your orders," said one of the Generals. "She will fall in line now."

The bored expression slipped off Taikon's face and he became focused. "Tell me everything," he said with a friendly smile. The muscles around Nirrok's sphincter immediately tightened at the Emperor's expression.

One of the Generals stepped forward, a broad man with an oiled black beard. "We launched our first attack through the southern pass, relying heavily on Yerskani troops, with only minimal support. As expected, their armour and weapons were no match for the Seves. It was a bloodbath, Most Holy. They're still counting the bodies, but we estimate several thousand Yerskani are dead."

Perhaps feeling that he'd said too much and been speaking too long, the General bowed again and quickly stepped back.

"Have we heard from the Queen of Yerskania yet?" asked the Emperor.

The warriors conferred briefly before the same General spoke again. "No, Most Holy."

"So, we have no way of knowing if she understood the message."

The General swallowed. "Not yet, Most Holy. But I expect a response any—" Taikon held up a hand and the General immediately stopped talking, as surely as if his throat had been cut.

"Herald!" screamed the Emperor, his voice echoing around the bare stone walls.

Nirrok heard a frantic flapping of feet before the doors were thrown open and the sweaty herald appeared.

"Yes, Most Holy?" he gasped.

"Have we received any messages from Yerskania?"

The herald took a brief moment, no doubt to consider his options, before speaking. "No, Most Holy."

"Are you certain?"

A brief pause. "Yes, Most Holy."

Taikon stood up from his throne. "Go away," he said with a shooing gesture and the herald quickly withdrew, backing out of the room before closing the doors.

"Tell me, General . . . ?"

"Lorcha, Most Holy."

"Tell me, Lorcha, did my army win on the first day of the war?"

Lorcha looked at his colleagues for support, but they were equally lost for words. "I don't, that is—"

The Emperor moved closer, almost gliding across the floor, his hands behind his back.

"It's very simple, Lorcha. Did we win?"

Sweat poured down Lorcha's face and his eyes looked everywhere around the room for something to help. "More of our soldiers died than theirs. We . . . withdrew."

Taikon moved within arm's reach of the Generals. A lump formed in Nirrok's throat and he suddenly found it difficult to swallow. The air seemed too dry and hot. "We lost."

Lorcha wiped sweat from his brow, tried to speak and in the end just nodded.

The Emperor shook his head sadly, clicked his tongue and walked back towards the throne. As quietly as possible the Generals all let out a sigh of relief while his back was turned.

"And you estimate a few thousand of my soldiers are dead?"

"Yes, Most Holy," croaked Lorcha.

Reaching behind the throne the Emperor produced a small dagger. Nirrok covered his face with both hands, unable to watch, before peeking out between his fingers.

"Every death wounds me. Every single one. I feel it."

No one knew what to say to that. As Taikon approached the Generals with the dagger held low they all stiffened, bracing themselves for the worst.

"As they suffer, I suffer also," said the Emperor, holding up his empty hand before slicing his palm. "I think it's only right." The wound was shallow and a small trickle of blood fell to the floor but suddenly stopped. The red line across his palm knitted together, then vanished completely until no mark remained.

"We should all suffer," said the Emperor, grabbing one of Lorcha's hands and slicing it with the dagger. The wound looked much deeper as blood flowed freely to the floor.

"Gah!"

"That's one," said Taikon.

Taking the dagger in both hands he turned the point towards himself before burying it in his stomach up to the hilt. He didn't cry out in pain, but stumbled to one side and bent forward before pulling out the blade. Dark, rich blood ran down the front of his silk robe before it too slowed to a trickle and then stopped. It took a while, but eventually Taikon regained his breath and could stand upright again.

"That's two."

"Wait!" was all Lorcha managed to say before the Emperor stabbed him in the stomach. He screamed and tried to shove Taikon away, which sent him into a rage. With a feral screech Taikon launched himself at Lorcha, bearing him to the ground where he continued to stab the General over and over again. The other Generals quickly backed away and one tried to run for the main doors but found they were locked.

"Seven, eight, nine," said the Emperor as he stabbed Lorcha over and over. Gouts of blood flew into the air and a pool began to form around his body. A fetid stench of piss crept into the air and Nirrok guessed at least one of the Generals had pissed himself.

"Seventeen, eighteen, nineteen." By twenty Lorcha had stopped screaming. By thirty-two he was jabbing a cooling carcass.

When he finally stood up, his robe was soaked through with blood and more covered his arms and face. The Emperor seemed oblivious until the squelching of his sandals drew his attention and he noticed the bloody footprints he was leaving across the floor.

"Oh dear," he giggled. "My steward isn't going to be happy. I've made such a mess."

He sat down on the throne, spattering its finery with more blood before looking across at his songbird. It continued to chirp away happily, oblivious to the violence in the room. The sound of its song brought a smile to the Emperor's face and he seemed lost in thought. He wiped at his face, smearing blood across it like paint before spitting onto the floor. Picking up the jug of wine cooling beside the throne, Taikon emptied it over his head, washing off the blood from his face and neck. Unsatisfied he stripped off his robe, then kicked off his sandals until he was naked on the throne.

The other Generals were spread out around the walls, desperately looking for another way out of the room. They were unarmed and royal guards were stationed just outside the doors. A few glanced at the tall windows behind the throne. It was a long way down to the gardens. Even so, one of them seemed to be contemplating it as he started to edge towards the throne.

"What was the count?" the Emperor asked the room. "Anyone?" When no one answered he glanced directly at the far corner and Nirrok felt his heart skip a beat. "You! What was the count?"

"Thirty-two, Most Holy."

"Ahhhh," said the Emperor, as if the number itself held secrets that only he could determine. "Yes. I'd hate to start from one again."

With a malicious grin Taikon charged at the General edging towards the windows. The man's scream was extremely high pitched and he made it all the way to the window before the Emperor landed on his back.

"Thirty-three!" he said with glee, stabbing the General in his hand reaching for the window. Howling in pain the General lashed out, his elbow catching Taikon in the face with a crunch. As the General fumbled with the window latch the Emperor's shattered jaw knitted itself back together. In a panic the General shattered the glass with his elbow and then tried to force his way out.

"Thirty-four, thirty-five, thirty-six," said the Emperor, stabbing the General in both of his legs. Grabbing him by the waist the Emperor hauled the General back into the room before stabbing him in the eye with a wet squelching sound.

"Thirty-seven. Oooh, juicy!"

Nirrok couldn't watch any more. He covered his face with both hands and pulled himself into a tight ball. But he couldn't blot out the screams, the wet slapping noise of meat hitting the floor, or the growing stench of open bowels and death that flooded the room. Trying to think of better times Nirrok hummed a tune from his childhood, a rhyme his mother had sung to him before she put him to bed. He couldn't quite remember the words, but it had something to do with sleeping well and tomorrow being a better day.

Some time later, how long he didn't know, but eventually Nirrok became aware of the silence. Moving very slowly, so as not to drawn any attention to himself, he unfurled from his ball and peered out between his fingers.

The floor was awash with blood, bits of men, staring eyeballs and lots of pink, blue, white and red things he couldn't name. A boot, with a foot still inside it and no leg attached, had been placed on the ground not far away from where he crouched. Splashes of blood coloured the walls in stripes and a vast array of patterns that spoke of pain and suffering. Somehow there was even blood on the high ceiling, as if someone had thrown something against it over and over, creating a trail of blood marks.

The Emperor was back on the throne, whistling softly to his little bird. Without looking around he spoke. "Have this cleaned up," he waved vaguely at the scattered body parts. "And find me another set of Generals."

Nirrok moved to the doors, held his breath and gently pulled. To his surprise they were unlocked. Crying and laughing at the same time he stumbled out, running as fast as he could to find the palace steward before the Emperor blamed him for the mess.

CHAPTER 8

The northern and southern passes between Seveldrom and the west were choked with dead bodies. For two days the combined might of the west attempted to bully their way through and failed. In such a tight space their superior numbers counted for nothing and hundreds of lives were wasted, perhaps on purpose. The majority of those killed were from Yerskania and were poorly prepared for such intense fighting. It almost seemed as if they were being punished for something. Today was expected to be different, unless Taikon was truly mad and intended to waste his entire army.

Their days of rest in the city had come to an abrupt halt with the commencement of the war. The journey to the front had taken days, but it had offered Balfruss a chance to ride through the countryside of his youth and relive old memories. Much to his surprise it had left him more homesick than he'd been expecting.

So far he and the other Battlemages had not been needed, but they were ready, just in case the Warlock and his apprentices made an appearance.

The Battlemage Thule was out of sight, but Balfruss could feel him approaching before he came into view. A few days' rest had been a boon to them all, but Thule had needed it the most. The King's surgeon had attended to his grave injuries, using a combination of sleep, poultices and foul-smelling draughts to heal and build up Thule's malnourished body.

If the art of healing with magic had not been lost, Balfruss could have repaired Thule's wounds in seconds. Unfortunately only the First People knew a little of the Talent of Healing, and it would be gone in a few generations. Losing such knowledge was something Balfruss deeply regretted, piled on top of the other regrets in his life. Balfruss had spoken to Ecko about it, asking if the tribesman would teach him. His knowledge was limited but others in his tribe were very skilled. Perhaps Balfruss would visit them once this was over, if he survived.

"You look better," said Balfruss.

The wound on Thule's neck was covered with a white bandage and the shadows under his eyes were fading. The hollows of his cheeks were not as pronounced, and he barely leaned on his staff when walking. Sleep had been prescribed and Thule had slept for the first three days. On the fourth morning the surgeon had found an empty bed. Thule had risen before dawn and walked into the city to stretch his legs. Since then he'd been eating meals regularly and his portions rivalled those of Finn.

"*Finn certainly is an interesting man,*" said Thule's voice in his mind.

Balfruss frowned. He was still getting used to the idea that his mind was connected to Thule. It felt strange to hear Thule's words in his head. The idea that Thule could hear his thoughts was disturbing.

"*Only those on the surface. And only those with strong emotions attached. I did not mean to pry.*"

"It's all right. I am worried. Finn is incredibly powerful, and would've been without equal if he'd been properly trained. As it is, I don't know if he's a blessing or a curse."

"*We will soon find out. Do you feel it?*" asked Thule.

Closing his eyes Balfruss blotted out the noise of the bustling warriors and focused, reaching out with his senses in all directions. Somewhere to the west he could feel a presence moving closer. An echo of magical Talent. It was barely there at first, like a feather brushing against his skin, but with each passing second the impression in his mind grew stronger.

"Shit," he muttered as his eyes flew open. "Get the others."

But there was no need. They could feel it too and had rushed from their tents. They approached with eyes wide with a mix of fear and excitement.

"It is them?" asked Eloise.

"It has to be. No Battlemage is that powerful by themselves," said Balfruss, hoping he was right, because if it was the Warlock then the war would be over very soon.

The warriors couldn't sense the presence of magic, but they started to look nervous as the Battlemages spread out across the front rank. Conversations drained away to a trickle, then stopped all together. An unnatural silence gripped everyone as they watched the mouth of the southern pass for any signs of movement.

The pressure against Balfruss's mind increased exponentially, as if the thing coming towards them was too immense to comprehend. It felt as if a tidal wave was about to come rushing through the pass and crash down on them all.

His fingers began to tingle and the hairs on the back of his hands stood up from the accumulation of energy in the air. Finn was on his immediate left and Ecko on his right. They'd chosen their positions very carefully. Eloise was on the far side of Finn, as she was the most subtle Battlemage, and would be able to guide the smith if necessary. Even with the weight of the approaching force, Balfruss could feel a heavy pulse coming from Finn, a constant reminder of his strength.

"Remember," he said to Finn. "They might try to scare us with nightmares, or enter your mind to crumble your resolve."

Finn nodded. "I remember my training."

"Then relax," hissed Balfruss. "I can feel you gathering power already."

The big man stared at him for a few seconds and then began to take long slow breaths. There was an easing of pressure and the echo of summoned power faded from the smith.

Just past Finn's shoulder Eloise was looking in his direction. Without saying it she knew what he was thinking and shook her head. They were out of time. If they survived today, he would need to have a long talk with Finn about his power and additional training.

The minutes trickled by, but none of the warriors started talking again. They could see the tension in the body language of the Battlemages.

As he took a deep breath, Balfruss noticed an unusual smell that quickly saturated the air. It was spicy with a hint of rot. A mix of mouldy leaves and herb-baked bread. Those around him started looking for the source. Next came a slithering sound, and then a tap-tapping of metal striking stone, like a gang of miners hacking into rock.

What emerged from the mouth of the pass was an enormous slug-like behemoth with a pink segmented body that was so dark it was almost purple. Its body barely squeezed through the channel, even though it was wide enough for twenty men abreast. Metal-tipped tentacles, bony spurs and nodules along the length of its body helped propel its gargantuan mass at an incredible speed. When it reared up, its maw was lined with rows of sharp needle-like teeth as long as spears. A fetid orange cloud emerged from its mouth and an ear-splitting screech tore at their ears.

The warriors alongside him stared in horror at the monstrosity. It was unlike anything they'd ever seen before. Archers started to ready themselves while squad leaders made warriors form up in tight units. He could feel the fear coming off the warriors beside him in waves, but they all held on to their nerve and no one tried to run.

Balfruss had to admit that at first glance it was a well-constructed illusion, but he soon noticed several flaws. The ground didn't shake or tremble, and not even one pebble was disturbed by the behemoth's passage. If the monster had been real they would have felt its approach long before they saw it.

With a shake of his head Balfruss focused his will then drew power from the Source into his being. He reached out with his mind towards the beast as it howled and thrashed about. Balfruss stretched out one hand and made a sharp twisting gesture towards the creature. It gave one final scream and then vanished, leaving a ghostly after-image on the inside of his eyelids for a few seconds.

Channelling a bit of power, Balfruss amplified his voice. "It was just an illusion. Nothing like that really exists." Or so he hoped. There were rumours of giant worms that lived under the sand in the far east. But none of those stories mentioned tentacles.

He expected another attack, something more subtle to confuse or muddle their senses, but nothing happened. Instead he was slightly disappointed to see six cloaked figures walk towards him and the other Battlemages. Each was dressed in an identical purple robe with a deep hood which concealed their identities. From their varying heights and gait, he could tell that some were men and others women. Even without seeing their faces he knew none of them was the Warlock. These were the Splinters, his apprentices.

The intense pressure he'd felt earlier on his mind came from all six. Their combined will had been forged into a single weapon. A massive crushing force that could flatten mountains, butcher armies and turn the tide of a war, if unopposed.

Balfruss and the other Battlemages had planned for this. The only way to oppose the Splinters if they combined their power was to form a Link of their own with one Battlemage directing the powers of the others. Although Balfruss thought Eloise was better qualified as she had more control, they had nominated him to direct the Link.

"I will lend you my strength, brother," said Ecko. The little man wasn't physically robust, with spindly limbs and a body which was all sinew and bone, but when he joined with Balfruss, there was an enormous surge of power. It took Balfruss a few seconds before his pulse settled and he could breathe normally. One by one the other Battlemages added their strength to his, and with each it took him a little longer to adjust.

As each joined the Link it gave him some insight into them, allowing him to gauge their strength. Finn was the least well trained, but also the strongest by far and when he joined the Link it drove Balfruss to his knees. It felt like hours before the black spots stopped dancing in front of his eyes, but when he looked up the Splinters were only a few steps closer.

The air around him crackled with static. Blue motes of energy danced along his limbs, worms of blue fire chasing others across his clothing. The warriors nearest to him started to back away, giving him plenty of space, just in case they were accidentally hit by some magical attack.

"Balfruss?" Someone was talking, but he wasn't sure who it was. The edge of the grassy plain leading up to the mountain pass looked barren and desolate of life, but as his eyes adjusted he saw this wasn't true. The air teemed with pollen and a hundred types of insect crawled through the earth beneath his feet. Above his head a murder of crows circled and, even higher, birds of prey coasted on thermals scanning the ground for food. All around he could hear blood pounding in the hearts of a thousand mammals and birds. As Balfruss stared ahead he could see the slow beating of a fly's wings as it sailed towards him. Everything seemed to be moving so slowly.

In his reverie, Balfruss's expanded consciousness started to sense a broad connection and a thread of energy flowing through all living things. A vast lattice was forming, and his thoughts started to reach out towards an idea that was normally beyond his understanding.

"*Focus. You must focus*," said Thule.

The intruding thought brought him back to the present and the immediate danger. Turning his gaze towards the enemy he saw they were readying their first attack. It seemed crude and poorly constructed. A moving wall of energy laced with a thousand spears that would rip the soul from the flesh, leaving no visible marks on the skin. As soon as it was ready the Splinters released it towards him and the other Battlemages. His reaction was instinctive.

Balfruss knew that without the strength of the Link he would never have been able to repel such an attack. It would have instantly killed him and all those around him, but now it was so easy to tear their wall into shreds. Another attack came, faster than the first, but only slightly more complex. He dispelled that and then a third, which again was only a little more intricate.

"*It feels like this is just a test*," said Thule, and Balfruss could only agree.

The cloaked figures never moved, spoke or gave any outward signs that they were alive. Narrowing his eyes Balfruss channelled some power and a spectrum of colours normally invisible to his eyes were revealed. All of the Splinters were bonded together in a Link, but there was something else as well. A narrow black thread of energy floated in the air behind each, which disappeared into the distance. The black threads made him think of the strings of a marionette.

The Splinters' attacks never wavered and eventually the complexity and speed reached a plateau. There was no real thought or invention behind them, and the Splinters started to rotate between different types, as if following a pre-agreed pattern to keep him and the others off balance and distracted. They couldn't ignore the attacks as they were still lethal, and yet he felt as if the Splinters were there just to be a nuisance.

"Balfruss," said Eloise, also sensing that something was very wrong.

"I know," he said, gesturing for Ecko to come closer.

"Yes, brother?"

"This is a distraction. I'm going to release you from the Link. Warn the others. I think the real attack will come through the northern pass. You may be needed there."

While keeping one eye on the enemy, Balfruss focused on the essence of Ecko in the Link. It felt as if he were trying to cut off one of his arms, but gradually he found the contours of Ecko's power and released it from the collective.

When the next attack came it was more difficult to repel. The pressure against his shield was harder, and the toll on him and the others would be greater, but it was still possible to stop them.

Ecko spoke to a Captain and a few seconds later a scout galloped away on a fast horse. It was possible they would reach the others in time, but Balfruss had his doubts. Ecko took a few minutes to rest, sitting on his haunches and wiping the sweat from his brow. It was only then Balfruss noticed the sweat running down his sides. How long had they been like this, linked together, fighting the enemy?

There was a shift in the Splinters and one of their number separated from their Link, perhaps in response to Ecko. The tribesman was immediately on his feet and Balfruss could feel him drawing power from the Source.

The lone Splinter made no move to attack, but he reached out with a faint thread of energy which touched Balfruss, making him shiver. Looking down the line he saw each of his brethren have the same response one after another. When he sensed it moving towards Ecko the little man lashed out. The Splinter recoiled, and for the first time since they'd appeared, Balfruss saw independent movement. The Splinter cast back its hood, and even at a distance, it was obvious there was something very wrong.

The skin on the man's face was pale and a sickly yellow in places, and tufts of black hair clung to a scabrous skull. His eyes were two black holes in sunken pits, and pieces of flesh were missing from his face. Holes gaped here and there, showing the inside of the Splinter's mouth and white skull. With a hiss that showed rotting teeth and bleeding gums, the Splinter started to gather his power.

With a sad shake of his head, Ecko lashed out again, pulling one hand towards his chest in a tight fist. Something purple and pulsing plopped onto the ground in front of him. It throbbed a few times and then stopped. The rotting Splinter gasped then collapsed face forward on the ground.

Balfruss was poised on the balls of his feet, ready for the next attack. Much to his surprise the enemy withdrew. Their Link dissolved and the Splinters simply walked away as if signalled. Slowly he relaxed and then released the others one by one. When the last one separated, Balfruss felt smaller and the world seemed less distinct around him, as if his eyes were suddenly blinkered.

As his own senses returned he realised his clothing was drenched with sweat. He stumbled and would have fallen, if someone hadn't caught him with a strong hand. The same person gently eased him to the ground where he sat trying to catch his breath, his whole body aching as if he'd been fighting all day. Looking up at the sky he saw the sun had barely moved. An hour at most had passed while he'd been in the Link.

A warrior offered Balfruss a skin of water and he drank deeply. It was slightly stale and lukewarm, but tasted glorious. His mind was awash with emotions and thoughts he was only just starting to process. He was having difficulty forming ideas that would have been effortless only moments ago. Full comprehension of what he'd seen while in the Link was eluding him. Thoughts and notions were starting to slip away.

"Are you all right?" a woman asked, and it took him a little while to recognise the voice.

"I need a moment."

"Take as much time as you need. They'll not come back today," said Eloise. "Not after losing one of the Splinters."

"What did Ecko do? I didn't see."

"Tore out his heart."

"Did we warn the others in time?"

Eloise knelt down beside him and her expression told him everything. "Heavily armoured Zecorran soldiers punched a hole through the front line. Morrin berserkers poured in after. We're pulling back to the first staging point."

Despair crept into his voice. "What was this for? What was the point?"

"Without us, it would have been a slaughter," said Eloise, pulling Balfruss to his feet. Her tone was sharp, but she sighed and gently touched his cheek. "They would have got through eventually. Everything we do until the siege is only a delay tactic."

Balfruss sighed. "You're right. I just don't like being manipulated and tested."

Eloise grunted. "Me neither."

He cast one final look at the pass and wondered if they would ever see it again.

CHAPTER 9

Gunder sat down with a loud huff. His assistant, Sabu, locked the front door, lit two oil lamps, then pulled down the paper blind over the door. As the boy swept the floor Gunder went over the day's ledger.

He shifted his considerable bulk around on the stool, the wood creaking ominously at his weight. When everything was tidy and the money secure, he locked up and waddled down the road to his local tavern, The Lord's Blessing.

The wooden sign above the door had recently been repainted. The Lord of Light's flowing white robes were now edged with gold paint and the sign seemed to glow in the dark. The innkeeper's pious wife had requested the special paint from Shael in the south. This must have been before the war started, of course. No one spoke in public about Shael or the atrocities being visited on the population. Torture camps. Pits filled with hundreds of rotting bodies. Bonfires for the dead so large they turned the sky black for days.

With savage Vorga lurking to the south, and angry Zecorrans and Morrin to the north, few could blame the Queen of Yerskania for agreeing to join the alliance. Threats had not been necessary. Gunder noticed there were no rumours about threats being made against the mercenaries of Drassia. Apparently they were part of Taikon's alliance, but no one knew anything more and he'd been asking all the right people. Perhaps Taikon feared their reputation.

The inside of the tavern was well lit, with lanterns hung on the walls and a thick white candle on each table. A group of sailors and dock workers crowded around the fire, trying to get warm after a hard day working outdoors. A line of muddy boots sat by the front door.

About half of the tables were occupied by a mixture of traders, general workers and merchants. Most were stocky pale-skinned local Yerskani, but there were also a couple of masked Drassi mercenaries and the odd swarthy black-eyed Zecorran from the north.

Tantalising fishy smells wafted from the kitchen, making Gunder's stomach growl. As Perizzi was a coastal city it meant that seafood always dominated the menu. Primly dressed barmaids served drinks under the close scrutiny of the innkeeper's wife. All wore headscarves, but they were a stark white compared to the bright colours Gunder usually saw on the streets. Yerskani people were not known for being demure, but the innkeeper's wife didn't like customers getting too friendly with her girls. Masson, the tavern's enforcer, sat with a cosh resting across his knees as an added deterrent.

It was a fairly stuffy tavern but thankfully it was a safe place to have a private conversation.

"Over here!" said Ramalyas. The lean-faced carpet seller was a Morrin, but he didn't stand out as there were others scattered about the crowd. Most Morrin were amenable people, but Ramalyas had told him the voices of religious extremists had been growing louder back home. It was one of the reasons he now lived in Yerskania.

As Gunder eased into his chair he gave a nod to Zoll, the black-eyed Zecorran jeweller, and clasped hands with Iyele, a local vintner. A barmaid brought them mugs of the local black ale and took their meal orders.

"Just a small fish platter, if you please," said Gunder apologetically, patting his bulging stomach. "I'm trying to lose weight."

He dabbed at his sweaty face with a sleeve and adjusted his velvet cap. If anyone saw that his hair was briefly askew they pretended not to notice until he'd straightened it.

Conversation started light until inevitably it turned to business.

"It's the will of the Lord of Light that heretics be severely punished," said Zoll, "but I cannot believe all Seves have succumbed. I've traded with many good people in Seveldrom. A purge seems a little . . . extreme."

Gunder raised an eyebrow but said nothing. The jeweller was the most devout of their group, and yet even he found the war excessive. It gave him hope that others in Zecorria might also feel the same. The alliance was only a few months old and already it showed signs of starting to fray at the seams.

"I do not believe the stories about the King of Seveldrom," said Ramalyas. "I also want the war to be over."

"Really? Why?" said Gunder.

"Because it's killing my business. Silk from the far east is the best, yes? Customers will pay twice as much for such carpets. The silk from Shael is not so good and is unpopular right now. But with trade routes to Seveldrom and the desert beyond closed, I must dip heavily into my stock. Unless it's replenished soon, I will have a bare shop and an empty stomach."

"We're all being affected," said Gunder. "It's a difficult time."

"None of your family has been slaughtered," said Iyele, staring glumly into his ale. "When that happens, then you can say, 'It's been a difficult time.'"

The others leaned in closer, speaking in whispers. "You've heard something?" asked Ramalyas.

"A nephew of mine works at the palace. He overheard some people talking. There have also been several messengers coming and going in the last few days."

"The rumours?" said Zoll, nervously touching his oiled moustache.

"All true," said Iyele, shaking his head. "Her Majesty refused a suggestion from King Taikon," he said with a sneer. There were no suggestions from the Mad King, only orders. The propaganda from Zecorria claimed every nation in the alliance retained their sovereign power, but everyone knew the truth. Taikon ruled the west. So far his influence on Yerskania had been minimal and Gunder intended for that to continue. "The day after her refusal our warriors were given the glory of leading the charge against the Seve army. They engaged with the infidels, but soon realised they were doing so with little support. This continued for two days and many of my countrymen were needlessly slaughtered."

Yerskania was not a nation known for its warriors. They were merchants, craftsmen and sailors. They made armour and weapons for other countries. They didn't wield them on the battlefield. Their small army was normally used to chase down raiders in the countryside and bolster the Watch during emergencies. With the bulk of the army on the front line in Seveldrom it left the city vulnerable to outside forces.

"I lost two nephews and three nieces," said Iyele. "They are still counting the dead in the passes. I heard four thousand, maybe as many as five."

A heavy silence settled on their table. Gunder took off his cap, straightened his wig, then bowed his head in respect. They sat in silence for a minute before conversation resumed.

"Do you know what orders the Queen was given?" asked Gunder.

Iyele shook his head. "After a second day of slaughter, urgent missives from the palace were sent to Taikon. Heavily armed warriors from Morrinow and Zecorria took to the battlefield in place of my countrymen."

"Blessed Mother guide their hand," said Ramalyas, more out of rote than real belief.

The food arrived and they ate in silence, digesting the news and possible repercussions alongside their meal. Before coming to Yerskania, Gunder rarely ate fish or seafood. Here it was a staple of the local diet, and at least one meal every day contained something fishy. Because he didn't want to attract undue attention, and he was supposed to be a native, he ate like a local. There were a few dishes he enjoyed, but at times he tired of fish and chicken, and would have killed for a juicy steak. A little beef was imported from Morrinow, but the best came from the southern grasslands of Seveldrom. The current shortage meant the price of red meat was doubling by the day. Perhaps investing in spices had been a bad idea.

Gunder's smoked-fish platter was a modest portion compared to the others, and he devoured every mouthful with vigour. The other merchants were still eating by the time he'd finished and was greedily eyeing up a plum cake at the next table. When it was time for dessert he ordered crystallised slices of fruit, while the others ate pastries and honey-soaked cakes. Another round of ale was delivered and half was consumed before conversation resumed.

"I've heard some worrying rumours from the north," said Gunder. Zoll gestured for him to continue and the others leaned in closer.

"A friend in Zecorria told me there's been looting and burning of holy temples."

The others looked shocked, but Zoll continued to sip his ale quietly. Gunder noticed the Zecorran's nonchalance, but he waited for the others to spot it.

"What do you know of this?" asked Iyele.

"It's nothing," Zoll said dismissively, but when he saw their worried expressions he continued. "It's only a few pagan shrines, and no one was hurt. It's just a filthy little cult."

"Do you know who gave the order?" demanded Ramalyas.

"Who do you think?" said Gunder rhetorically. "And how long will it be until he decides churches of the Maker, or temples of the Blessed Mother are not to his liking?"

"He wouldn't dare," said Ramalyas aghast.

"It won't come to that," promised Zoll, but even he didn't sound convinced. Stories were already leaking out of Taikon's palace about him killing people because they stared at him in a manner that was displeasing.

"It's been a long day, my friends," said Gunder, getting to his feet and pulling on his cap. "Until tomorrow."

Taking his time and enjoying the cool night air, Gunder took a circuitous route back to his house. As a centre of commerce the capital city of Yerskania was a welcoming place to all travellers. It was often called the crossroads of the west and until the war it had seen visitors from all over the world. Traders used to come from as far away as the desert nations in the far east, along the silk road beyond Seveldrom. Now dark-skinned eastern faces were absent from the crowd and there were no tall Seves, strutting along proudly in their moulded leather armour. There were also no golden-skinned faces from Shael in the south.

Since the war began, visitors to Perizzi comprised tanned Zecorrans, lean-faced Morrin and masked Drassi warriors, following merchants and the nobility as bodyguards. There was the occasional blue-skinned Vorga, but everyone gave them a wide berth and didn't make eye contact. As if thinking about them had summoned one, Gunder rounded a corner and nearly walked into a Vorga.

Small for a Vorga at six feet tall, it glared down at him, its hand hovering above a dagger the size of a short sword. Dressed only in a kilt and vest, he couldn't tell if it was male or female. Both were equally brutal warriors. Its slightly damp pale blue skin glistened in the light from nearby lanterns.

"Are you blind, fat man?" it grated.

Gunder stared at the bony ridges around its wide jaw, doing his best not to look into its slightly bulging eyes. One of the Vorga's sail-like ears flipped away from the side of its head as it bent down towards him.

"Did you say something, coward?" it hissed, showing him a row of spiky teeth. He'd rarely been this close to a Vorga but now understood why some people called them frog-faced. In truth they were more reptilian, but they would take that as an insult as well. They came from the sea and were children of Nethun, Lord of the Oceans.

With a hiss and irritated click of its teeth the Vorga stormed off and Gunder heaved a sigh of relief. A minute later two members of the Watch walked past, trailing the Vorga at a discreet distance, just in case it caused some trouble.

Gunder zigzagged his way home across the city in case someone decided to follow him. Perizzi was bisected by the River Kalmei and was criss-crossed with bridges. Seven huge stone edifices and more than two dozen footbridges wide enough for three people walking abreast. Gunder trotted across one of the smaller bridges at a brisk walk before doubling back several times.

As soon as he stepped inside the house he knew something was wrong. There was a peculiar stillness to the air, a distinct pressure against his ears. Taking a dagger from a concealed sheath in his sleeve, he slipped off his shoes and crept through the house, moving silently from room to room. In the kitchen a woman with luscious red hair was sat at his table, casually eating an apple.

"You're late."

Gunder heaved a sigh and sat down opposite. "I wish you wouldn't sneak in, Roza."

"Any news?" she said, carving another slice of apple.

"Some," he said, then filled her in on the news about the Queen of Yerskania and King Taikon. "I suspect there will be a royal decree in the next few days."

"Do we know what he's ordered her to do?"

"No, but if it threatens the city, we must intervene. Send word to our contacts in the palace. We need to know what she is planning ahead of time. So, what do you have for me?"

"Rumours mostly, but I've heard one story from several sources about Taikon's health."

Gunder looked towards the heavens and pretended to pray. "We're not that lucky. He can't be dying."

"Sadly not. Not only can he heal any wound, but apparently he's now stopped eating. Servants have also seen people coming and going at all hours, so it looks as if he doesn't need sleep either."

"Shit," said Gunder.

"If he never stops working, night and day, the cracks in the alliance will disappear faster than we can create new ones."

"He's moving more quickly than we anticipated," said Gunder, rubbing a hand across his beard. It itched a lot, but combined with his make-up it helped make him look like a fat man.

"What do you want me to do?"

"The Warlock has been spreading stories about Taikon's childhood to fit the holy books," said Gunder. "Princess Talandra wants us to make sure a few different stories emerge. You know the sort. He casts no shadow. No reflection in polished surfaces. Red eyes. Take your pick. But keep them short, and let others turn them into something more. Trickle them in and send them to everyone we have. The whole network."

Roza frowned but didn't disagree. It would take a few days to get a message to all of his contacts in the west, and a few more before the first rumours could be trickled into the general population. But once the rumours had passed through a hundred mouths, they would mutate into something else. Soon people would be swearing they knew someone who had seen Taikon drinking blood and consorting with dark powers from beyond the Veil. Such rumours would spread quickly to all nations in the west, and become impossible to repress.

"It's going to take a while," pondered Roza.

"I trust your judgement. Move as fast as you can."

"What are you going to do?"

"Send an update to the boss."

"And then?"

"I've been ordered to make a new friend," said Gunder with a chilling grin.

CHAPTER 10

The others went ahead of him into the hospital tent, but Vargus lingered on the threshold. The massive space inside was full of beds and each bore a bloody man, injured from the day's savage fighting.

The enemy had hit them hard, and this time they'd come fully prepared, covered in heavy armour and armed to the teeth. Casualties had been high as they'd not expected the western enemy to be so brutal. They seemed driven by insatiable rage; many had screamed and cursed, declaring them evil, abomination and blasphemers. The manipulations and lies of King Taikon and his cronies had worked them into a religious frenzy. Some of the Morrin had even been foaming at the mouth, driven insane by narcotics or religious fervour. They believed their cause was righteous, and that they were fighting on the side of light. They were heroes, cleansing a putrid stain from the land which would usher in a new age of peace. Trying to convince them of something else would be pointless. Vargus knew if he were in their position it would sound like propaganda. This war would not be over quickly or solved with words.

Surgeons with black caps moved around the long hospital tent, tending to the worst injured, while nurses looked after the rest. Sisters of Mercy sat with the dying, cradling them, singing lullabies, cuddling and kissing them until their eyes glazed over and their hearts stopped. Incense burners sat in all four corners, and at regular spaces along the tent, but the whole place still smelled of blood and shit.

To Vargus's right a man started gasping his last breath, crying out for his mother as blood seeped through the bandages on his chest. A Sister of Mercy held him tight, paying no attention to the blood he spat on her clothes and face. A few more breaths and then he was gone. The Sister laid him out flat, crossing his arms over his heart and gently closed his staring eyes. Only then did she wipe the dead man's blood and spit from her face.

She glanced briefly at Vargus and he thought she looked familiar. She was tall, with wavy red hair and green eyes. Looking more closely at her face he realised it bore a passing resemblance to someone from a long time ago.

"I bet you need a drink more than me."

The woman offered a tired smile before turning away to wrap the dead body in a sheet with calm efficiency. Two stretcher bearers came in and took the body away. It wouldn't be long before the bed was filled with another dying man, pissing himself and bleeding to death.

"Are you just going to stand there?" asked Hargo from further down the tent.

Vargus took a deep breath then wished he hadn't as the smell of the blood and death stuck in his throat. Halfway down the tent a group of warriors had gathered around the bedside of Benlor the ranger. His right leg ended just below the knee where it was covered with a thick swathe of white bandages. Benlor's face was pale, yet he looked calm and at peace. He wasn't being tended by a Sister of Mercy or a priest, which was encouraging. Knelt at his side was his twin, Rennor, who looked distraught in comparison, as if he'd absorbed all the pain of his brother's injury.

The other lads wore sombre expressions, but were also grateful it wasn't them lying on the bed with one and a half legs. A few kept staring at the ground, not knowing where to look, or maybe they were counting their toes and glad to be coming up with the right number.

"If any of you start crying I will get up off this bed and strangle you," Benlor warned them. "I'm not going to die, am I Vargus?"

"No, you're not," he said, squatting down beside the bed. He offered Benlor the bottle of southern whisky he'd brought with him. "I thought you might fancy a drop. It'll make you feel better."

"Ah, my favourite," said Benlor, cradling the bottle to his chest.

"That's good whisky," muttered Black Tom. "Expensive stuff."

"How would you know, Tom?" asked Orran, but Tom just shrugged.

Benlor hid the bottle behind his arms. "Don't think I'm going to share it with any of you beer-swilling dogs."

"Don't be greedy now," said Rudd, licking his lips. As ever he was hungry, and thirsty. "We've got refined taste."

"Rudd, you couldn't tell the difference between wine and beer if you were blindfolded."

"Both get you drunk in the end, so what's it matter?" he asked the others. Curly shrugged, clearly confused as well.

"You see what I have to put up with?" said Benlor, and his brother forced a smile. "This whisky is exactly what the doctor ordered."

"It's not going to make his leg grow back though, is it?" snapped Rennor, gulping back a sob. An awkward silence settled on the group and the tension increased. Black Tom pursed his lips as if he were about to spit, changed his mind and swallowed with a grimace. The uncomfortable silence stretched on for a while.

"I'll tell you one good thing about this," said Vargus to the twins. "From now on, it'll be a lot easier to tell you two apart."

Rennor was horrified and on the verge of violence, until Benlor began to laugh. His whole body shook until tears ran down his pale cheeks.

"You sick bastard," muttered Rennor, but he too was smiling.

"Ben, we did all we could. I'm sorry it wasn't enough," said Vargus. The ranger gripped his hand tightly.

"Don't," he said, shaking his head. "Before I met you and we started the . . . " He trailed off, trying to find the right word.

"If you say cult, I will cut off your other leg," warned Vargus.

"I was going to say brotherhood. Fair enough?"

"I suppose."

"Before that, I was just another warrior for the King. I had my unit and we were friends, but nothing like this. I've lost a leg, but I'm still a richer man." His gaze swept over the gathered group. He wanted to say more, but didn't have the words. Hargo and the others understood. There was no need to say it.

A nurse came to check on Benlor and frowned at the group. "Do they all have to be here?"

"They're family," said Benlor.

The nurse stared at the men, none of whom looked even vaguely alike, and raised an eyebrow.

Vargus took the hint. "Get some rest. Safe journey home."

The others said their goodbyes and began to file out, leaving Benlor alone with his brother.

As he was about to leave the tent Vargus felt a prickle run up the back of his neck, as if he were being watched. He turned around, expecting one pair of eyes, but instead saw dozens. Along both sides of the tent, all of the wounded men were staring in his direction. Every warrior still able to move raised an arm in salute. A final farewell between brothers.

*

It was dark when Balfruss woke up in his tent. He must have slept for eight hours and yet still he felt exhausted and wrung out. The fight from earlier in the day had proven more draining than he had realised. Emerging from his tent, he saw Eloise reading by the fire and Darius adding spices to a pot of bubbling stew. His stomach growled at the smell, reminding him it had been a long time since his last meal.

"Just in time," said Darius, handing him a bowl, which he filled with rice and then a generous helping of stew.

"Where are the others?" asked Balfruss, blowing on his food to stop it burning his mouth.

"Asleep or resting. I'm sure the smell of food will bring them around."

"He won't come," said Eloise, fixing Balfruss with a pointed stare. He didn't have to ask who she meant.

"At least let the man eat first," Darius chided her.

"I'll speak to him," said Balfruss. "I promise."

They ate the rest of their meal without mentioning him. Ecko came to the fire to eat with them, but had little to offer in the way of conversation. Their shared stories and adventures in the far east meant little to him, although he listened with polite interest. Until recently Ecko had never left his tribe, or homeland, in the north. Unable to share stories and experiences of travelling abroad, Balfruss tried a different approach.

"Tell me something about your people. About their history."

"I could tell you many stories," said Ecko, mopping up the last of his stew with some flat bread. "Tales of the Weaver, the Sky God and the Underking, but they would only be reflections of what is true. Perhaps you should visit with us to learn about my people."

"Perhaps I will, one day," said Balfruss. "If we survive," he added with a smile.

Ecko tilted his head to one side, looking at him with one eye closed. "I think you will visit. Soon."

"You sound very sure."

"I can see more than you," he said with a wide grin, as if he'd told them a joke. "Thank you. Delicious stew," he said to Darius. With another smile he walked away from the fire and disappeared into the surrounding dark.

With no more excuses Balfruss rolled his shoulders and stood. He felt much better for the food and sleep, but wasn't sure he was up to this.

It wasn't hard to find Finn. He followed the sound of ringing metal and eventually came to one of the temporary smithies. Weapons needed repairing, armour needed fixing and there were never enough hands to do the work in an army of this size. New weapons were being brought in from the city by cart, but with a journey that took over a day's ride, there wasn't time to shuttle items back and forth for repair.

Finn was hammering at a sword, his face glowing from the heat and reflected light from the forge. Sweat dripped off his face and his shirt was stuck to his body. Strangely he didn't look tired, quite the opposite in fact. His rhythmic pounding echoed across the camp and Balfruss could see thick muscles jumping in his arms and shoulders as he worked. Although Finn's eyes were focused on the metal, Balfruss thought his mind was elsewhere. Finn didn't seem aware of his surroundings and paid no attention to anything except shaping the metal.

At first glance the other smiths were going about their work as normal. But every now and then one of them would risk a glance in Finn's direction, when they thought no one was watching. He might be able to do the work, but Finn made them nervous.

Eventually Finn seemed happy with the repair. He put

down the hammer and tilted the sword this way and that, inspecting his work. A bald man approached them, whose arms were as wide as most people's legs. The only indication of his status was a small pair of silver hammers worked into the backs of leather gloves hanging from his belt. He took the offered sword and gave it the once-over with an expert eye.

"Nice work."

"Any more?" asked Finn.

The master smith shook his head sadly. "Not tonight. You can come back tomorrow, if you want," he added. From his tone he clearly hoped Finn didn't. On the one hand he was probably thankful for the extra help, but on the other, Finn scared the other smiths because he was a Battlemage.

"Mind if I work on something of my own?" asked Finn.

"Suit yourself," said the master smith, before waddling away. Finn took a lump of something from his pocket and stuck it in the heat with a pair of tongs.

"Have you time for a short rest?" asked Balfruss.

Finn looked up at his voice, shading his eyes to see Balfruss beyond the glow from the forge.

"I've already eaten," said Finn. "She didn't have to send you."

"I'm not here about that."

"Then what do you want?" he said, stoking up the fire.

"To talk about your power."

"I'm busy," snapped Finn.

"Doesn't seem that way to me," said Balfruss.

"Well, I am."

"It won't take long."

Finn stared at him for a long time. "You're not going to go away, are you?" he asked, and Balfruss shook his head.

They moved a short distance away from the forge and took turns sipping from a water skin. Maybe he should have brought something a little stronger. It would have made this conversation easier for both of them.

He was trying to find the right way to start when Finn interrupted. "So what do you want?"

"Are you always this direct?"

The big man shrugged. "Don't know how else to be. You want to know about my curse?"

"What curse?"

"This power. It's a curse."

Balfruss started to laugh until he saw Finn's expression. "Tell me."

"It started about three years ago with pains in my head. Back then, life was good. All I'd ever wanted was coming true. I should've known to worry. The Maker doesn't like people being happy," Finn said bitterly. "The local priest wasn't a bad sort, but the Maker's book is full of people suffering, and the priest seemed to think it was a good thing."

"What happened?"

"Me and my cousin had taken over the local smithy. Business was good. Mostly it was repairs, but sometimes we made new stuff: scythes, axes, shoes for farriers and the like. Then I met a girl." Finn stopped talking and stared off into the dark. It was a long time before he spoke again and his voice was hoarse.

"The first time it happened I knocked over a drunk who was acting stupid. I did it without touching him, but no one noticed. They thought he'd tripped, but I knew. The next time was when I was angry and a couple of people were hurt when a roof collapsed. I tried so hard to keep it inside, but that made it worse. Eventually I couldn't hide it and everyone found out. I begged the Elder not to, but he sent a letter to the Red Tower for a Seeker. Two months later an old man turned up to test me, and that was it. I had to go away for training."

"How long were you away from home?"

"Six months."

Balfruss shook his head in disgust. "Is that all?"

"It was too long," said Finn. "By the time I got back everything was different. Someone else was living in my house. My cousin had taken on a new partner. And she ..." He trailed off again. Balfruss didn't need to hear the rest. "It's a curse," Finn said finally.

"It doesn't have to be."

"I didn't want this. I didn't ask for it. Can you burn this thing out of me?" Finn asked desperately. His temper flared and blue motes of energy danced between his fingers before pooling in the palm of his hands as a living flame. With an angry shake of his head Finn released the energy and the magic fire vanished.

"You can control it."

"I don't want to," snarled Finn. "It's dangerous and I almost killed people I care about. I want to get rid of it. Can you help me?"

"Not in that way."

"Then what good are you?"

Finn drained the last of the water and returned to his anvil where he began to take out his frustration on a misshapen piece of metal. Balfruss watched him for a while before walking back to his tent.

As he approached, Eloise looked up hopefully, but he just shook his head. Darius was snoring in his tent and Thule was finishing the last of the stew on the other side of the fire. He stared at Balfruss and offered a sympathetic smile.

"*Give it time*," said Thule.

Balfruss nodded because there wasn't anything else he could do. At the moment there was no way to reach Finn, but he had to keep trying. Some of what Finn said was true. He was dangerous, and unless he learned how to control his power, he could kill all of them and many more people by accident.

The events of the day finally caught up with him and Balfruss felt exhausted. It didn't take him long to fall asleep and when his dreams came, they were full of images from his own childhood and the ruined village he'd not seen in over twenty years.

CHAPTER 11

The army had pulled back and Talandra and the others had moved further east to another borrowed estate. Despite having only been in her borrowed rooms for one night Talandra had already filled them with books and papers. Every night dozens of messages were collected at the aviaries in the capital city and ferried out here to her by messenger. Now her new office was covered with numerous tiny scraps of paper written in code.

Talandra unrolled the latest message from her spymaster in Yerskania. As instructed, her network would begin planting the seeds of new stories about Taikon and his miracles. His mythology was shaky, built upon a mountain of lies, but so far people in the west were blind to the terrible truth. Perhaps they were so desperate to believe that a prophet walked among them they could overlook his insanity and the twisting of their faith.

Along the table, the Generals and her father were discussing the results of their latest strategy and its impact on the day's fighting. Her brothers were on their way back from the front line but would arrive too late to take part in the meeting. Besides, Hyram was happier mixing with the men than planning strategy, and Thias kept him out of trouble.

Her father had also requested that Balfruss join them this evening to give them his view on how the war was progressing from a magical standpoint. Like everyone else Talandra thought he already looked exhausted and the war was only a few days old.

"It's going very well," Graegor was saying. "The gullies and traps are doing their job. It was a bastard to dig all those channels, but it's working. They have more men than us, but that means nothing if we can keep splitting them up."

"They won't last much longer," said Wolfe, "and we don't have time to dig any more."

"Still, they've done their job and slowed the enemy," said the King, conceding the point and calming Graegor before there was another angry retort.

Talandra hadn't known it was possible to be angry all the time until, as a girl, she'd met Graegor. Even so, the old General had been particularly irate these last few days, and she didn't think it was the war that was bothering him. This wasn't his first war, so it had to be something else, something personal. The only problem was Graegor didn't have a family, or anything resembling a normal life outside his service to the King.

She made a mental note to ask her father a few discreet questions the next time they were alone.

The foul-mouthed General scratched at his eye patch and took a swill of ale. Surprisingly it was his first and they'd been at this for a while. As ever he was dressed in his black armour. Talandra realised she had no memories of seeing the grizzled warrior without it, or that hideous axe on his hip.

"What did our Morrin citizens say?" asked the King, turning towards her.

"It took a bit of convincing, but in the end they agreed. Seveldrom is their home, so they'll fight to protect it. They're on their way here already and should arrive in the morning. There's no moon tomorrow night, so they'll attack the enemy camp two hours past midnight."

Morrin had perfect night vision, making them ideal candidates to become assassins or spies. Unfortunately, most of them regarded such professions with disdain and contempt. Deception and even role-playing games among children were seen as grave sins. Acting troupes never travelled that far north as it was a waste of time. Morrin culture included strong religious doctrines that were gradually superseding the laws of the land. In a few years Morrinow would be a true theocracy, with religious leaders deciding the fate of the nation. That made it very difficult to find even one Morrin willing to break centuries of tradition and risk everything for the promise of greater freedom. However, asking Morrin who had emigrated to Seveldrom to attack enemy supply lines was something they could get behind.

"Who's leading them?" asked the King. His tankard held ale, but he'd done little more than wet his lips since sitting down.

"Kuldarran. He's a good man," said Vannok. "He doesn't panic."

"Good. So," said the King, before taking a deep breath. "Tell me about our casualties."

"Not as bad as we were expecting," said Graegor. "With all the traps and quick strikes, they rarely had time to engage our warriors. We'd pull back and the rangers provided good cover," he said with a nod towards Wolfe. High praise indeed. Something was definitely upsetting the old General.

"For every casualty we're still killing three to five of their men," said Talandra. "The worst we've suffered was when they broke through the northern pass."

Everyone in the room knew that the current tactics were designed only to slow the pursuit of the western army. Once both armies were clear of the Fosse hills and its uneven terrain, they would have to engage on the field. Even then it would be a gradual retreat to the city, and then came the part Talandra was dreading the most. A siege.

"How are the Battlemages?" asked the King, turning towards Balfruss.

"Tired, and despite killing one of the Splinters, our job hasn't been made any easier."

"Why not?" asked Graegor. "Don't you outnumber them now?"

"Yes, but it's not that simple."

"Why not?"

"Some Battlemages are stronger than others," explained Balfruss. "It's the same with the Splinters."

"Then can't you just push harder when you work together?" asked Graegor, getting irate.

"Graegor," said the King, with a warning note in his voice. Talandra could see Balfruss was starting to get annoyed.

"Do I tell you how to dig your traps or direct your warriors?" asked Balfruss. Graegor opened his mouth to answer but the Battlemage cut him off. "You know nothing about magic or how it works."

"It has been a long day," said the King to Balfruss. "And I know you have to travel back in the morning. Thank you for coming for this meeting."

Balfruss shook the King's hand and went out the door while Graegor glared at his back.

"How is morale among the men?" asked the King, moving them on. The other Generals looked at Vannok, since he spent the most time in the field. Graegor never left the King's side, and Wolfe never stayed in one place long enough to get a feel for the men.

"It was low after we lost the northern pass, but it's improved since then. Units are fighting better than I've ever seen before. It's uncanny," said Vannok, sounding genuinely surprised.

"It's not unusual," said Graegor. "I've seen it many times. Warriors pull together when they realise the only thing between them and the Maker is the men in their unit."

"It's not that," said Vannok, chewing his lip. "It's something else."

"Well, whatever it is," said Graegor, quickly losing patience again, "it's working, so don't pick at it like a scab."

"Do you have any news from the west, Tala?" asked the King.

Talandra filled them in on the latest from her spies about the change in King Taikon's health.

"More worrying is that a handful of Zecorran fanatics have put their religious prophecies together with a Morrin splinter sect. It was just a cult at first, but now it's something more."

"Meaning what?" asked Graegor.

"Taikon has the beginnings of his own religion."

"Maker's balls," spat Graegor in disgust.

"Why's he doing it?" asked Vannok. "The Morrin and Zecorrans would never give up centuries of faith for a new religion centred on him."

"He's trying to consolidate his hold. The more he ties his mythology into the Lord of Light's scripture, the easier it will be to convince them he's the long-awaited prophet. The fanatics are outsiders and they're desperate for power. They've banded together behind Taikon's banner because, at the moment, he's the most powerful man in the west."

"He's mad," said Graegor.

"I agree," said Talandra, "he's becoming more unpredictable every day."

"It doesn't stop him being dangerous," warned the King. "Don't lose sight of that. His father was an incredibly devious and sadistic man, yet he ruled Zecorria for thirty years."

"My network is doing all it can to disrupt the alliance from the inside," said Talandra. "This religious slant might actually work in our favour for once. The Zecorrans and Morrin have become idolaters. Right now the truth is our best weapon against Taikon. My people are working hard to try and help the northerners see that. There have been some protests in the north, and we're supporting all of the rebellions in secret."

The King stood up and the others followed suit. "I need to get some sleep and I suggest you all do the same." He gave Talandra a knowing look.

"Soon," she promised.

The others filed out to seek their beds, but Talandra stayed where she was.

A short time later Shanimel, her most trusted agent, sauntered into the room. Morrin spies were incredibly rare and despite having lived in Seveldrom for most of her life, it had taken Shani years to shake off centuries of tradition.

Dressed in deep purple trousers and a matching coat cut in the latest fashion, it made her pale skin look even creamier. Shani's black hair was tied back in a ponytail which showed off the curve of her neck and the slight points of her ears. Her modest horns, little more than studs, were hidden beneath the folds of her hair.

"You wanted to see me?"

"Yes, please sit down," said Talandra.

Shani glanced at the open door through which Talandra could see the shoulders of two royal guards. They would watch over her until she entered the royal apartments, at which time she could finally be alone.

Talandra explained the latest about Taikon and the start of his own religion in Morrinow and Zecorria. Despite Shani not being deeply religious Talandra could see how disturbed she was by the news. Seveldrom was her home but she still cared about her people.

"I assume you want to take steps to disrupt this cult?" asked Shani.

"Yes, and I think it will have to be something extreme. Burning down old temples to a forgotten God is one thing. The historians may weep, and a few dedicated followers, but the people won't be moved to interfere."

Shani raised an eyebrow. "How extreme?"

"Send word to Gunder. Tell him to burn down a church of the Maker in Perizzi."

Shani stared at her in shocked silence. Other faiths might rise and fall over the centuries, but people had been following the Maker forever as far as the history books could tell. She'd considered one of the other religions but they would not be as shocking and Talandra needed Perizzi to remain independent of Taikon's control. Eventually Shani found her voice again.

"That will not be easy."

Talandra grunted. "Gunder and his people will find a way, they always do. There's one more thing. High Priest Filbin is on his way to Perizzi."

The First Minister of the Church of the Holy Light was a disgusting creature, but also one of the most powerful players in Zecorria. He sat at the top of a huge network of priests that he ran like his own army. People who disagreed with him had a habit of disappearing or being the victim of unfortunate accidents. Talandra had carefully monitored his rise to power and had been collecting information on him for years.

"He decides to take a pilgrimage now? In the middle of a war? It can't be good news for Yerskania, or us."

"I thought the same," said Talandra. "But we might be able to turn it to our advantage. In Zecorria he's surrounded by legions of dedicated people and is untouchable."

"Surely you're not thinking—"

"No, although it did cross my mind," admitted Talandra, penning a coded note back to Gunder with her instructions.

"Filbin isn't someone who can be bribed, blackmailed or coerced," said Shani. "How do you intend to persuade him?"

"With the truth," said Talandra with a grin. "It's our best

weapon to remind him of who he is and how far his people have drifted off course."

From her expression Shani wasn't convinced but, underneath, Talandra knew she trusted her judgement. The Morrin woman took the note and looked over her shoulder again.

"Will that be everything for tonight?" she asked, raising an eyebrow.

Talandra cleared her throat. There was only so much she could say with others in earshot. "Yes. I have one more meeting and it's already late."

"Then I'll see you tomorrow," said Shani, heading for the door. Talandra watched her go, nodding to the guards on her way out.

Talandra tried to suppress a yawn, but her jaw cracked and her eyes filled with tears.

"Maybe we should talk tomorrow morning, Highness, before I leave," suggested Balfruss, striding into the room. "You look exhausted."

"No, it's fine. Come in."

Talandra rose to meet the Battlemage and they shook hands. Balfruss's grip was firm, but not crushing, and the skin on his hands was calloused from hard labour. She'd never seen him with steel in his hands, but if she hadn't known he was a Battlemage, it wouldn't have surprised her to see him wielding a sword.

Just like her brothers he was built like a warrior, with broad shoulders and thick arms. Whenever she stood beside her father and brothers, Talandra knew she looked out of place. They were dark of hair and eye, tall and broad like all Seves. She had the height, but was slender and not as curvaceous as she'd like. Her hair was blonde, her eyes a deep blue and her skin paler than most, three gifts from her late mother. The only visible kinship she shared with her family was a slightly hooked nose and the same smile, although none of them had laughed in weeks.

"I'm sorry about Graegor. He's a difficult man," said Talandra.

"That's putting it mildly," commented Balfruss.

"Drink?" offered Talandra, gesturing at the jug of ale.

"No, thank you, Highness."

"There's no need to be so formal in private. Talandra is fine," she said, waving at a seat.

"Thank you," said Balfruss, getting comfortable. "You have some questions for me?"

Talandra nodded and took a drink to buy herself time to study the Battlemage. Vannok had told her a little about their shared history, but most of it was tales of their childhood. At eight years old Balfruss left the village to start his training at the Red Tower. After that, Vannok only saw him two or three times a year. After Balfruss completed his training they only saw each once every few years in the capital city. Battlemages were in short supply and high demand, especially in those nations with few or no native practitioners of their own, like Morrinow. Balfruss was educated, respected, and a natural leader who others instinctively followed. The story of how he'd destroyed the giant worm was already becoming an urban legend and his fame was growing.

Despite knowing all that, Talandra still felt as if she were missing something important. She also had the feeling that Vannok knew more but had been unwilling to tell her. Perhaps it wasn't his secret to tell.

"I wanted to ask you about the Opsum Prophecy."

Balfruss snorted and then laughed. "I wouldn't wipe my arse with it," he said and then realised who he was talking to. "My apologies, Highness. It's a very sore point that's been responsible for countless years of grief. I can't even imagine how many lives have been wasted because of it."

"What do you know of the prophecy itself?"

"I can recite parts of it from memory. In short it talks about a child of magic who will reshape the world for centuries. But, with respect, what do you know about the Oracles who make the prophecies?"

Talandra rubbed her chin as she thought about it. "I've read they're Battlemages, or they were."

"Have you ever seen an Oracle?" asked Balfruss. Talandra shook her head. "They're mindless idiots who dribble, shit and piss themselves all day. They live in squalor and their own filth, worse than any animal. They endlessly talk gibberish and their minds are nothing but empty shells."

"Really?"

"They are not seers," scoffed Balfruss. "They're idiots who pushed themselves too hard before they knew what they were doing. They burned out their own minds. Some believe this makes them open to receiving divine messages."

"But not you."

Balfruss's expression darkened. "Do you know why it's called the Opsum Prophecy?" He barely waited for Talandra to shake her head. "Because it's the only thing he said for the first month. No one knows if it was his name, or just a random noise."

"And yet the Grey Council believed it so much, they abandoned their posts at the Red Tower to search for the one mentioned in the prophecy."

Talandra expected Balfruss to respond angrily. Instead he just looked disappointed and terribly sad.

"And just look at the results of their wise decision," he said bitterly. "When I was a boy, a Seeker passed through our village every six months. Remote places used to see them once a year, but it was enough. Children with any Talents, or the ability to touch the Source, were identified, accidents were avoided, and the Red Tower was busy with students. Now it's all but deserted. These days there are only a handful of Seekers, and each must cover entire nations by themselves. It's an impossible task." Balfruss shook his head. "In the last fifteen years, most children with any ability have died before, or during, puberty. Sometimes it's obvious how they died, other times they just die in their sleep. Whole families have been killed in terrible accidents, because children with no training couldn't control the power. Entire villages have even been destroyed. Those that find their way to the Red Tower are always ill-trained when they leave and you end up with—"

"Finn Smith," said Talandra.

Balfruss nodded. "He's incredibly powerful and no one died in his village, but he can never go home. People are afraid of him and what he might do."

"And what of the Grey Council? Where are they now?"

Balfruss scratched at his beard and sighed. "Gone to find their chosen one. No one has seen or heard from them in fifteen years. After what they did, it's good riddance to a bunch of arrogant bastards."

Talandra took another drink before asking the one question to which she really wanted an answer. "Do you think the Warlock is the one mentioned in the Opsum Prophecy?"

Balfruss took a moment before answering, running a hand through his beard which she noticed was dotted with patches of grey. There were also touches of white in his hair. Those, and the deeply etched worry lines in his forehead, made him look older than his years. He was probably the same age as her eldest brother, Thias, who hadn't seen forty summers yet.

"No," Balfruss said finally. "I don't believe the Warlock is the one. The prophecy is vague and it could refer to anyone. There have even been a few prophecies some claim were written about me. None of those have come true either. The Opsum is imprecise and the Grey Council interpreted it to suit their needs. I doubt they'll suddenly reappear and name him their messiah." Talandra heaved a sigh of relief. "Besides, they're most likely dead by now."

"I don't know whether I should be relieved about that or not."

"We are a dying breed," said Balfruss. "In two decades, three at most, the few remaining teachers at the Red Tower will retire, or die from old age, and then it will close its doors. After that, we will enter another Dark Age, where any child showing even the slightest Talent will be burned at the stake or drowned, like the bad old days."

"Could someone else not take on the responsibility? Form a new Grey Council?"

"A few have tried and failed. Most Battlemages don't see the point, or the profit, in such an investment of their time. It might generate a lot of goodwill, but that won't feed them. Besides, the money they can earn right now is considerable."

"You keeping say 'they'. Aren't you one of them?"

"Do you think I'm here for the money?"

Even if she'd just met him, a quick look at his clothes told her the answer. "I'm sorry. No, I don't. You were telling me about the Red Tower?"

"Someone might be able to form a new Council, but it will take a better man than me to make it work. I don't have the wisdom, or the patience, to be a teacher and a leader."

"I have just one more question about the Warlock. How powerful is he?"

Balfruss hesitated before speaking. "So far, he's only sent his apprentices against us, and there's much about them that worries me. From his actions so far I believe he's brutal and merciless, but I'll know more about him when he takes to the battlefield. We all will."

"Thank you for coming. I know it's late," said Talandra. "I appreciate your honesty and your candour. I may need to call on you again."

Balfruss stood and gave her a short bow. "I am at your service. Goodnight, Talandra."

She sat a while longer pondering what Balfruss had told her about Battlemages and the inevitable fall of the Red Tower. After a while she decided there was enough to worry about without adding to her list.

She hoped Balfruss was right and that all prophecies were just the ravings of lunatics. Otherwise their situation could become even more desperate.

CHAPTER 12

Vargus snarled at the Zecorran soldier, easily blocking a poor thrust with the edge of his shield. Screaming like a petulant child the man attacked again. His wild swing nearly severed the throat of the soldier to his right. Vargus swayed backwards and then came forward in a rush. His forehead crunched in the man's face, breaking his nose and spraying them both with blood. The Zecorran started to mewl like a child, so Vargus finished him quickly before he started to feel pity.

To his right Hargo was busy hacking apart his latest victim. He'd become very attached to the Yerskani cleaver, and used it with brutal efficiency. Unlike most, he fought silently and with savage grace, making each attack look as if it were a step in an elaborate dance. With precision Hargo lopped off one man's hand, then split another's face with the sharpened edge of his shield. Before either could recover, Orran moved in, stabbing each man through the chest with a short spear he'd picked up somewhere. All of the Seves were fighting in teams or pairs, watching out for each other and getting in the way of weapons that were meant for someone else. Vargus had witnessed one man step in front of a spear that would have killed the man beside him. With only his bare hands, and a spear through his ribs, the Seve strangled the Zecorran to death before he succumbed to his injury.

Vargus witnessed countless acts of selfless bravery that did little to change the overall course of the war, but they meant everything to the men on the front line. All doubts about the men who fought beside them, and how far they would go for one another, disappeared. They would do stupid and ridiculous things for each other, and sometimes they would pay off. The shakes, and the nightmares of what could have happened for being so reckless, would come later for those who survived.

The close-combat fighting skills of every man were being pushed to the limit, and then beyond. Rehearsing moves a thousand times was less instructive than half a day's fighting in a shield wall, when it often turned into a shoving match. The slightest thing could turn the tide, and yesterday it had been loose gravel under the feet of the enemy. One man fell over and then two more. A bloodbath followed as the Seves piled on, stabbing and chopping until it was just so much red meat.

Vargus and the others cut deeply into the enemy's ranks who broke off their attack and ran for their lives. Those not paying attention to the rout were cut down without mercy.

Vargus watched dispassionately as an archer picked off an enemy soldier who thought he was beyond the range of their bows. With a squawk of pain and indignation, the Zecorran soldier turned to face them, then keeled over with one arrow in his arse and another through his chest.

The other retreating soldiers saw their comrade fall and kept running, well into the foothills. Today's attack had been poorly organised because of the Seve night raid on the western camp. The Morrin citizens involved had proven their loyalty beyond reproach to King Matthias and their adopted home.

Tents had been set on fire, picket lines cut, meat spoiled, food wagons burned to the ground, and several senior officers killed in their beds. King Matthias and his Generals had thought there would not be any engagement today, and perhaps a reprieve for two days. Someone in the western army stubbornly ignored the problems caused by the raid and ordered an attack at first light. The result had been disjointed and doomed to failure from the start.

Whole units of men were wiped out with simple ambushes, while others fell into traps lined with sharpened stakes. Giving the western army no time to recover, the Seves shredded the enemy with archers, then slammed into their ranks with infantry. It was another demoralising defeat for the righteous army of the west.

So far no enemy soldiers had tried to surrender, and no mercy had been given. Vargus knew that would have to change when they fought on the plains, which would be soon, if not tomorrow. They were at the very edge of the Fosse hills. Behind him stretched fertile farmland, a few villages and copses of trees all the way to the capital. Today was the last day their tricks and traps would work. Tomorrow, the real war would begin on a scale not seen before. It was going to be bloody work.

"Back!" someone shouted. The buglers began to repeat two sharp notes over and over.

Vargus turned and ran as fast as his legs would allow. The Battlemages were coming.

Balfruss and the others watched as the last of their warriors ran past, trying to get as far away as possible from what they knew was coming. This was the third time Balfruss and the Battlemages had faced the Warlock's apprentices, and the last two occasions had been a stalemate. Despite the loss of one of their number, the Splinters' attacks were almost as powerful as the first time, but they were still without any subtlety or creativity.

If their situations were reversed, and a blunt-force attack didn't work, Balfruss would have tried assaulting the senses, commanding the elements, or finding a way into the minds of his opponents to unlock phobias and nightmares. The Splinters attempted nothing new and just kept battering away relentlessly, trying to wear them down. It was always the same, as if they had no original thoughts of their own. Someone had trained them, as their control was impeccable and it never wavered, but there was something very wrong with the faceless apprentices. They seemed hollow.

"*You already know why,*" said Thule's voice in his mind.

"I only have suspicions," said Balfruss. "No proof, and the dead body told me nothing. I need to speak to one of them, face to face, to know the truth. But I think that's unlikely to happen, don't you?"

"*Yes, unless we can lure one of them away.*"

"No," said Balfruss, casting around for Thule. As he became more comfortable with the mind link between them it was working over increasingly longer distances. It was also starting to work both ways and some of Thule's thoughts were bleeding into his mind. "No. I will not use one of our brethren as bait. The risk is too great."

"*Then we may have to do something rash. This stalemate cannot continue.*"

A few minutes later Thule came into sight, galloping to the front line on a Seve warhorse. He slid off the beast's back with athletic grace and gave the others a nod as he took his place in the line.

The Warlock's apprentices slowly came into view, walking in unison towards them, just like the last time. Five robed and hooded figures, faceless and nameless. And with them came that growing pressure against his ears. A crushing force of combined power and channelled will.

The others looked at Balfruss expectantly. He had suggested someone else take control of the Link, but it seemed as if they had decided he should take the lead again. One by one they added their strength to his. This time he was ready for all that came with it, and even managed to stay on his feet. It also seemed a little easier, although that was probably his imagination.

Sweat began to bead in his hairline as the Splinters launched their first attack and he focused to unravel it.

It was supposed to be spring, and although the last of the snow had melted, Vargus was pleased to be sitting close to a fire. In the middle of the battle, with the blood pounding and survival his only concern, he barely noticed the weather, hot or cold. But tonight there was a chill in the air, a last desperate attempt by winter to thwart the turning of the seasons. He edged slightly closer, trying not to set his boots on fire.

He took only a small sip from the wine skin before passing it around the fire to Hargo. The big man sent it on to the next man without taking a drink. He was too busy listening to the newcomer's story about a second assassination attempt on King Matthias.

"Do you know why they tried it?" asked the beefy Seve named Khasse, a battered veteran. His arms were criss-crossed with faded scars and one of his ears was gone. A ragged notch of flesh was all that remained. His nose had been broken so many times it listed to one side, and his joints creaked when he moved. His hair was grey and his beard bore only a faint memory of being black. Like Vargus he was older than most, but there was a reason he was still alive and others were desperate to catch his every word. In part to hear the story, but also to find out how he'd managed to live for so long.

"Because they've only had one good day in this war," said Orran.

Khasse smiled, showing a mouthful of battered and broken teeth. "Exactly. The Grey Bear's a canny fighter, I saw it myself years ago, but he's a better strategist. Him and the others turned what could've been routs into victory."

"Stop teasing. You're worse than my wife," grumbled one of the men. "Who'd they send to kill him this time? Some masked Drassi mercenary?"

"Nah, that was the first one. Not even Taikon's mad enough to try the same thing twice."

The wine skin kept moving around the circle and Khasse took a long drink, stretching out the suspense. Everyone around the fire was hanging on his every word, but from the slight glaze in his eyes this wasn't his first retelling.

"The assassin wasn't anything to look at," he said finally. "Anyone would walk past him and not remember his face. Like he was just some lad that wandered into the wrong place by mistake. Way I heard it, he tried that first, babbled and tried to back away, but old One Eye spotted something was wrong."

"Graegor? Saw it with his magic eye, did he?" scoffed Orran.

"Magic eye or not, I wouldn't bad mouth that black bastard," said Hargo, looking deep into the fire. There was something in his voice that made Orran and the others look at him in surprise. There wasn't much that scared the big man.

"He's right," said Khasse, reluctantly letting go of the wine skin and passing it on. "All of a sudden, Graegor starts shouting. Shoving the King back and calling for help. The assassin saw his game was up and went straight for the King. Dagger came out of nowhere. Graegor must have thirty years on the assassin, but he still cut that sneaky bastard in two. Left handed as well, 'cos of his missing fingers."

"In two?" someone asked. "Down the middle, like?"

"Not the way I heard it," said another man who'd wandered up at some point during the story. "It was the other General, Vannok. Took the killer's head clean off his shoulders and Graegor took a shit in it."

"I saw the body before they took it away," said Khasse, swallowing hard. "It was split from collar down to stomach, ribs spread open like petals of a bloody flower." He dared the other man to tell him different, but no one said anything. Everything they knew had come second- or third-hand, but Khasse had seen the body. There was no arguing with that.

The fire crackled loudly and when it snapped, more than a couple of men shifted uncomfortably. None of them actually jumped in fright of course.

"I heard Graegor tends to that axe every night, like it was his lover. Five hundred strokes on a whetstone," someone whispered. "Only way it's that sharp."

"I heard he's done it ever since he lost his wife and son. Someone butchered his whole family, so now he takes the axe to bed instead."

"Either way, I wouldn't want to be on his bad side. So keep stories like that to yourself, in case they find their way back to him," suggested Hargo and others made noises of agreement.

There would be seeds of truth in the stories. Even though Vargus doubted some parts, he saw no reason to stir things up. Their leaders were tough men. Each one had risen up the ranks through hard work and sacrifice. Not one of them was noble born. Now they were becoming something else in the eyes of the men, and he wasn't about to do anything to change that. The warriors around him needed to believe that the Generals knew better and could see them through this, because without saying it aloud, every man knew it was going to get worse before it got better, and that the war had only just begun.

CHAPTER 13

Gunder emptied a bucket of cold water over the High Priest. He came awake spluttering and gasping for air as the water ran down his face. He tried to move, and when that failed he looked at his surroundings, taking in the dirty warehouse, the stacks of old barrels and then the tray of steel implements beside his chair. In the background Gunder could hear the sound of the waves and the cry of seagulls, but they were never far from the ear in Perizzi. The High Priest would never know exactly where they were in the city.

High Priest Filbin, First Minister of the Church of the Holy Light of Zecorria and one of the most influential men in that country, tried to stand up, but the cloth restraints around his arms and legs kept him firmly in place. Gunder had taken great care when tying the knots so that they wouldn't mark the priest's flesh. The chair was nailed to the floor, and a gag sat around the priest's throat in case he screamed. At the moment that seemed to be the last thing on his mind.

"You will burn for this," Filbin spat and Gunder couldn't help laughing. Even in the face of torture and death, dripping with water like a drowned cat, the man was defiant. "The Church and King Taikon will see you flayed to death!"

"You're a funny man, Filbin."

"You will address me as, Your Holiness," he said, sounding deadly serious.

Gunder smiled and slapped him across the face. Filbin was so horrendously shocked Gunder had to slap him again on the other cheek. Even as the red marks began to rise, shock was replaced with outrage.

"You will be tied out in the sun," he promised. "Burned at the stake. Gutted and fed to my dogs!"

Gunder let Filbin ramble on for a while and make threats while he checked his torture implements. Some he'd bought from a retiring butcher: the cleaver, the skinning knife, the knocking spike and heavy mallet to drive it home. Others had been specially crafted, but this was the first time in years they'd all been laid out together. It was easy to stab someone and pull out their innards. It took real skill to kill a man and leave no mark, so the authorities never knew how it was done. Those were the murders that took real talent.

But all of that was a long time ago. The tools were a reminder of another time in his life, another man with a different name, before he began his work in Yerskania.

"What are you going to do with those?" Filbin asked eventually. It always surprised him when they asked. Gunder simply raised an eyebrow. The priest's anger drained away and was replaced with fear and dread.

"Please, please, I'll pay you whatever you want, just don't hurt me. I'm a good man. A pious man!"

Gunder turned away and took a deep breath to calm himself. His hands shook with rage as he struggled to control his temper. The urge to slash the priest's throat was overwhelming. He'd found His Holiness at a brothel that specialised in young girls, and from the manner of the proprietor's greeting, it was obvious Filbin was a regular customer. Officially he was visiting Yerskania, and the capital city, to pray at the local temple and offer spiritual guidance to the Queen, but no one actually believed it.

The number of rumours about the Queen and the Royal Family had increased dramatically over the last few days, and although no official declaration had been made, Gunder expected one any day. It would be something significant if Taikon had sent His Holiness to speak on his behalf to persuade the Queen it was in her best interests, and that of the people, to comply. Gunder suspected another slaughter of soldiers would follow if she refused.

More worrying for Gunder was that his agents in the palace had failed to send any information for five days. He suspected they had been compromised and were being tortured, or were already dead.

"What are you doing?" said Filbin, intruding on his thoughts.

"Deciding if I should cut off your hands or your feet first."

"Lord of Light protect me," chanted the priest. "Lady of Light save me!"

"They're not here," said Gunder, turning back and picking up the bone saw. "But this is," he said, tapping the blade. "Specially crafted, toughened Seve steel. Cuts through bones like warm butter. A lot of people used to die from shock when they sawed off limbs, because it took so long."

"Why are you doing this?"

"Then someone came up with blades like this one," said Gunder, tipping the blade this way and that so it caught the light. "A very special alloy. Now it only takes seconds."

"If you want money, that can be arranged," promised Filbin. "The Church will pay a substantial ransom for my return. More money than you can imagine."

"I'm sure," mused Gunder, pretending to consider it. "But I'm more interested in what's going on inside there," he said, poking the side of Filbin's oversized head with a finger.

The High Priest had seen at least fifty summers and was shaped like a barrel. His exquisite gold and maroon silk robe was stretched tight over his fat belly. His black hair was balding on top, and to compensate he'd grown a beard. Normally it looked impressive, but at the moment it was a soggy mess dripping with water. Despite his indulgences and unsavoury appetites, Filbin's mind was as sharp as his jet-black eyes.

"How much do you want?" he asked, sounding more like a Yerskani merchant bartering over the price of grain than someone begging for his life. Making deals with people in difficult situations was something he understood.

"It's not about money," said Gunder, moving to stand directly in front of Filbin. He bent down until they were at eye level. There was a subtle shift behind the priest's eyes.

"Who do you work for? Is it that bitch, Robella?" he asked, and Gunder shook his head. "Who then?"

Gunder maintained eye contact, but he lowered his voice slightly so that the priest was forced to lean closer. "I'm not going to tell you, Filbin."

"Stop saying my name!"

"What I want," said Gunder, ignoring the outburst, "is to know about your childhood."

His words gave Filbin pause, as again he had to reassess why he was tied to a chair. This wasn't what he expected from this kind of situation. His looked calm, but Gunder could read the slight twitches around the corners of his mouth, the brief tilt of his eyebrows, the shifting muscles of his jaw.

"It was an unhappy time."

"You have an old Talent," said Filbin. It was a logical assumption, but wrong. "Some weak magic that's letting you know what I'm thinking on the surface."

Gunder wrongfooted himself on purpose. "Your mother was a drunk."

"You're just guessing," scoffed Filbin, but there was a slight tightening around his eyes. A glance into the past for a moment.

"Your father was a miner. He often spent weeks away from home in the pit. Working hard to provide for you and your mother."

"That is a matter of public record. So far you've said nothing that's impressed me. What do you want?"

"Your mother would go out at night, and sometimes she'd come home with other men."

"How dare you!" Filbin strained against his restraints and the chair creaked.

"You spent long hours alone in the house with nothing to do. But then you found the Book," said Gunder, offering a friendly smile as he softened his voice. "The glorious Book and the Way."

"You're not a believer," spat Filbin.

"I find it ironic that you're devoted to a religion steeped in the ideals of purity, when your own mother was a cheap whore."

"I'll fucking kill you!" screamed Filbin, writhing and thrashing about in his chair. It creaked again, but thankfully didn't break. Given Filbin's weight, maybe he should have used more nails. "You will be tortured for days! Weeks! You will beg for death!"

"You knew what was happening in your parents' bed, and yet you never told your father. He knew something was wrong, didn't he?"

"No, no," sobbed Filbin, shaking his head. Gunder never moved a muscle and yet his blows kept hitting the priest, affecting him far worse than if he'd used the steel on Filbin's flesh.

"Your mother pretended that everything was normal when he came home, but it wasn't. Sometimes you'd wake up in the night and see your father stood at your bedroom door. You both knew he'd been crying, but he'd never admit it. A big man like him? Crying?"

Filbin's eyes were wide with horror and his mouth gaped like a fish. "How? How are you doing this?"

"He wondered, and when you were older, so did you. Was he really your father?" Filbin had run out of words. The wound was old, but still very raw. The priest was staring at something, but it wasn't anything in the warehouse. Perhaps it was a shade of his father, standing in the shadows. "He asked you once about your mother, didn't he?"

"Stop," choked Filbin, moments away from tears or another threat. "Just, stop."

"And you lied," whispered Gunder.

Filbin stopped begging and just stared into the past.

Gunder let him stew for a while. All of his information on Filbin had come from Talandra and her little black book of secrets. It wasn't one book any more, although that was how it had started years ago with a few secrets dug up by her network. Somewhere in the palace was a secret room, the walls lined with bookshelves from floor to ceiling, and inside each black notebook were secrets about all of the most important and powerful people in the world. Together with the facts, she had added notes on each person, their strengths and weaknesses, vices and family, all leading to how they could be manipulated. The Black Library, as it was known by some, was Talandra's most powerful weapon.

"One day you will meet the Lord of Light, and all of your sins will be laid bare before him," said Gunder, bringing Filbin back to the present. "You will confess all your sins or be turned away. Is that not what the Book promises?"

"Do not quote scripture to me," said Filbin. His voice was thin and hoarse.

"You will be judged. But do you really believe? In your deepest heart, in the darkest corners of your mind, where no one can ever see, do you really believe?" Gunder asked gently, as if they were two old friends. "I keep using your name because here, in this place, you are not the High Priest. You are not a spiritual leader, or head of the church. You are not even a priest. You are just a man and if I kill you, He is who you will see next. He will judge you. You cannot hide anything from Him. So, I'll ask you one last time, Filbin. Do you believe?"

Talandra's information had revealed that in Filbin's mind, lying to his father was the worst sin he'd ever committed. It was the one that could never be forgiven as both of his parents were now dead. The wound was buried deep inside and every action, every word, every thought since that moment rested on top of it. Decades of memory tried to press it down, flatten it out and smother it with triumphs and sins, big and small. But no matter what Filbin did, the sharp edges had not softened over time, and as Gunder forced him to turn it over in his mind, it cut him anew.

"I believe." The words were spoken so softly that Gunder thought he'd imagined it at first. "I believe," said Filbin, as tears ran down his cheeks from the memory of what he'd done.

Gunder smiled and with careful and precise gestures he swirled his fingers in front of the priest's face and then snapped his fingers. Filbin's eyes glazed over and he sat perfectly still.

Gunder spoke quietly and calmly, laying out the truth. Stripped of all pretence and pride, rank and status, Filbin responded without hesitation, speaking from his subconscious. There was no need to plant a suggestion. Filbin already knew what needed to be done when he got home, and how he should respond. All he needed was a little nudge to remind him of how far he and his people had drifted from their true faith. Filbin would become their ally in Zecorria against Taikon and his new cult, and best of all, he wouldn't even know he was working for Talandra.

Gunder watched as the hooded figure of the High Priest left the seedy establishment, flanked by two bodyguards. A short time later a girl came out of the building, padded across the street and casually leaned against the corner with her back towards him. She was small for her age and looked much younger.

"Well?"

"It happened just like you said. He woke up and was confused, then he just sat there, staring at nothing."

"Did he say anything?"

"No, he just looked really sad," said the girl. She was dressed in an ankle-length dress, but he knew inside the brothel all the girls wore next to nothing.

"And then?"

"Nothing. He got dressed and left. Never said a word, didn't touch me, barely even looked at me."

Gunder produced a heavy pouch, which he held out towards the girl. She quickly pocketed the money and risked a look over her shoulder at him.

"Is that it?"

"You're done. Never go back there. If they ask, tell them you couldn't stand it, not even for one night. They won't argue, or try to stop you."

The girl was young, but not stupid. "All this money, for nothing?"

"No. It's to make sure you forget everything you saw today," said Gunder, moving out of the shadows until she could see his eyes and murderous expression. With a flourish he produced a dagger in both hands from the sleeves of his expansive robe. "Because if you don't, I'll cut your fucking heart out."

The girl's eyes widened in terror and her throat tightened with fear. She tried to speak, to make a promise, but couldn't manage it. Instead she turned and ran, never once looking back.

CHAPTER 14

Balfruss felt exhausted after another long day on the battle-field. He and the other Battlemages were kept on constant alert, unable to properly rest in case they were needed. He managed a few naps, but afterwards felt just as tired and sandy-eyed.

Today had been the first day of the war on which King Matthias had been unable to use the mountain passes against the enemy. Today had been devoted to tactics and quickly responding to an ever-changing situation. Not being privy to the same level of news as the Generals, Balfruss only knew what he heard from others. By all accounts, today had been another victory.

The infirmary was still full of screaming and bleeding warriors but, according to Vann, it could have been a lot worse.

Despite barely moving, while warriors around him hacked at each other with bloody weapons, fighting with magic all day was equally tiring for Battlemages. Darius and Eloise were already asleep in their tent, Finn had returned to the forge, but despite his prodigious stamina, even he had dark shadows under his eyes. Ecko had gone off into the dark, away from the noise and fires of the camp, to reconnect with the spirits of the land. Thule rested on the other side of the fire, but his face was pinched and his eyes troubled.

Today the Warlock's apprentices had split into pairs and

Balfruss had been tethered to his Blood Brother, Darius, for the duration. Since she possessed a deft touch, as well as greater control over her power, Eloise had been tethered to Finn in an attempt to stop him endangering them all.

Thule and Ecko had rested while the other four defended, and when anyone began to tire they would swap partners as in a Drassi folk dance. Even so, it had been a long day of blocking a wider range of strikes and concussive forces than previously. He still thought the Splinters lacked imagination, as they rotated through a series of six different attacks. It was almost as if they didn't know how to do anything else, or they were simply following instructions and not allowed to try anything new. There was a third option, and his earlier suspicions had blossomed.

"*The others have noticed too,*" said Thule, his purple eyes glittering in the firelight.

"Then I don't need to tell them," Balfruss snapped and immediately regretted it. "I'm sorry. I have something else on my mind."

"*He nearly killed her today, although she would deny it if you asked.*"

Balfruss ground his teeth and forced himself to take deep breaths. "He won't listen to reason. He thinks his power is useless."

"*You're thinking like a Battlemage. You were taught for years how to use your power. He had six months. He saw his training as nothing more than a necessary chore to be endured. It took him away from his home, his life.*"

Thule's golden skin reflected in the firelight, rainbow colours dancing across his face and arms.

Balfruss could feel the other man's fatigue through their mind link, but he was starting to sense much more. The most prominent thought, which Thule made no attempt to hide, was a desire to free his people in Shael. If winning the war and killing every last soldier in the west was the only way, then he would do it. Nothing short of death would stop him. Thoughts of his country and his people burned in his mind like embers in the dark. It was for them that he had climbed out of the grave and travelled so far, while in so much pain.

Thule steered their conversation back to the immediate problem.

"You could try to appeal to his sense of patriotism, but I suspect he will ask what more you want from him."

"Then I will have to think of something else," said Balfruss, getting to his feet. "Another way to reach him."

As before, he found Finn by following the rhythmic sounds of pounding metal which led him to the smithy. The big man was hard at work, beating on the same black piece of metal Balfruss had seen him with last time. He seemed frustrated, as the ore looked exactly the same shape and colour as before. Finn looked as if he were working out some of his aggression, hammering the metal harder than was strictly necessary. With a curse he relented and stuck the metal back in the fire. It was only then that he looked up and saw Balfruss.

"Time for another lecture about my power?" Finn sneered. Balfruss swallowed an angry retort and shook his head. "Then unless you're good at mending shields, I'd go back to your tent and get some rest."

"What are you working on now?" he asked, pointing at the fire. "I saw you with it last time."

"Nothing. A joke," said Finn. He turned the piece of metal over and stoked the fire around it.

"I've not seen ore like that before."

Finn stared at him. "Do you really want to know? Because I've no time for games."

"By the Maker, I swear," said Balfruss, touching his heart. "No games, just simple talk. What is it?"

Finn pulled the lump out of the fire, twisting it this way and that. The black lump seemed to sparkle, as if studded with pieces of broken glass.

"It's a piece of star metal." There was a note of awe in his voice. "One night a few years ago, I saw a shower of fire falling from the sky. The local priest said it was an omen from the Blessed Mother. A warning that dark times were coming. I asked the village Elder the next day and he told me they were rocks made of pure evil, which didn't make sense either."

"What did you do?" asked Balfruss.

"I needed to find the truth for myself, so I tracked down where one had fallen. It took months, but eventually I found a farmer who complained of losing a portion of his crops to fire from the sky. He was happy to let me dig it out of his field and take it away. Saved him a job for another day. Inside the rock was this piece of metal. I showed it to every smith I could find, but none had seen anything like it, or knew what to do with it."

Finn fell silent and was lost in thought. His eyes became distant and he was probably thinking of better times. Balfruss didn't disturb him and inevitably his mind turned to fond childhood memories of long summer days with Vann. After months of reading and studying indoors, he was always happy to return home and spend it outside. The familiar sights, sounds and smells of the village refreshed him in a way he couldn't describe.

It was all gone now. His entire village, wiped off the map by a band of raiders. The only real home Balfruss now had was the capital city, although he owned no house within its walls. The money was there for a house and more, sat in the bank along with other possessions he'd picked up on his travels, but so far there had been no reason to stay.

Finn's voice startled him from his reverie. "A special order meant me and my cousin had to travel to the capital. The last time I was here, I asked a Forge Master about the metal. He'd seen it once before and said it was useless. That it was tougher than any iron he'd seen, and couldn't be smelted. So far, he's been right."

"I'm not a smith, but tell me why," said Balfruss.

"No matter how much I heat it, the metal stays solid. I've tried making it as hot as possible and still nothing."

Balfruss approached the fire and looked carefully at the furnace. It glared orange like an angry eye and even at this distance the heat against his skin was intense.

"How tough is the furnace?" asked Balfruss.

Finn raised an eyebrow. "Why?"

"How hot would the fire need to be before it melted the furnace?"

"It doesn't work that way," said Finn with an indulgent smile, suddenly becoming the teacher.

"How hot?" persisted Balfruss.

"I don't know. Why?"

Balfruss rolled up his sleeves and stared at the fire. "If the furnace starts to crack, tell me and I'll stop."

"What are you going to do?"

"Heat up the fire," he said, focusing his will, then drawing power from the Source. After such an exhausting day it came more slowly than normal, but Finn saw none of this. His eyes were locked on the furnace.

As Balfruss forced more energy into the fire, gradually trickling in a filament of power, the glow started to change colour from orange to deep red and then white. Finn put the star metal back in the forge, turning it this way and that in the fire.

"How long can you keep it this hot?" he asked.

"A while," said Balfruss through gritted teeth. In truth the strain was already starting to bite, and the sweat on his brow was not just from the heat of the fire.

A short time later Finn removed the lump of metal with tongs and put it on the anvil. At first glance it seemed as if nothing had changed, but looking closer Balfruss noticed the metal had slightly changed colour. The black had become a deep purple, run through with silver threads. Finn gave it a brief tap with the hammer and the sound of it rang differently than before.

"It's starting to become malleable," marvelled Finn, before returning it to the fire.

"This is starting to hurt," said Balfruss, wiping his face with the back of one hand.

"A little longer," urged Finn, his whole face lit up with child-like glee.

Balfruss tried to blot out the growing spike of pain inside his head, but it would not be ignored and started to blossom into something else.

"Finn," he said, but either the smith didn't hear or he pretended not to. He was staring deep into the furnace and Balfruss wondered how he could see anything. With a cry of triumph Finn pulled the metal from the fire and returned it to the anvil. It was glowing orange, but somehow Balfruss could still see silver veins running through it.

With regular, even strokes Finn began to work the metal, and this time it responded to the hammer. He only had eyes for the star metal and didn't seem aware of his surroundings. Balfruss released the power and sank to the ground, out of breath and even more tired than before. After a while his breathing returned to normal, but the pounding in his head remained. To make it worse the thumping wasn't in time with Finn's hammer. Sleep seemed the best idea to rid him of it, so he closed his eyes for a moment.

It was the silence that made him sit up. The hammering had stopped, but not the drum beat inside his head. Finn was standing by the slack tub, holding something under the oily water and smiling as if he'd received the best news of his life. With reverence he pulled the star metal from the water. Balfruss expected to see a finished weapon, but was disappointed when it was only a slightly flatter lump of grey metal. Regardless, Finn put it to one side with great care before fetching a water skin and sitting down. He offered it and Balfruss took a long drink before passing it back.

"It's never been done before," Finn said with a broad smile. "No one has ever forged a weapon using star metal. It could take me weeks."

"You're welcome," said Balfruss, struggling to his feet.

As Finn helped him up, Balfruss could feel him trembling with excitement.

"How? How did you do it?"

"You already know."

He barely hesitated before asking "Can you teach me?"

"I can. But we'll start tomorrow night, all being well," he said with a vague gesture at the army of men camped around them.

"Tomorrow night. Thank you, Balfruss." Finn's smile was so genuine that Balfruss couldn't help smiling in return.

When Eloise woke up from her nap by the fire she found herself alone with Darius. Balfruss had gone in search of Finn, Ecko had wandered off into the dark and she could hear Thule snoring in his tent.

Darius smiled when he saw she was awake, but then returned to staring into the fire. She knew that look.

"What's wrong?"

"Tell me again about the destruction of the Red Tower," said Darius, much to her surprise.

"It's still there, but after the Grey Council left, it became disorganised. Children who find their way there are trained, but it's brief and barely enough. Most of the teachers left and never returned. It's nothing like what you have at home."

In the desert any child showing any magical sensitivity was celebrated and their family honoured and showered with gifts. In every city there was a special temple devoted to the Maker, run by the Jhanidi, priests with magic. The monks trained children and adults in their temples to control their ability, but also how to control their emotions so that they were always in charge of their power. Children were not taken away to a remote location and trained in secret behind closed doors. At the end of their training all students were given a choice. Either they could return to their normal lives, or they could choose to serve their King. Many chose the latter and were bestowed with the mark of Ayilah. The tattoo they all bore was not a brand of service as some from the west believed. The mark was a badge of respect that told everyone who they were dealing with at a glance.

"Something should be done. When we return home, I will speak to the King. Perhaps children from the west could be trained by the Jhanidi. Of course I will speak to King Matthias about this as well. Do you think it's a good idea?"

"I think it's a very good idea, but it won't help us with Finn."

Darius said nothing for a while, but a scowl crept across his face. She knew her husband well enough to know where the conversation had been going from the start.

"He could have killed you."

"But he didn't," she reminded him.

"He's dangerous, unpredictable and he's putting us all at risk."

"You mean me."

"I mean all of us," said Darius, struggling to contain his anger. "Today he was tethered to you, but tomorrow it could be any one of us."

"I've taught him some basic breathing techniques. It's a foundation we can build on to help him control his emotions."

"I don't want you to be tethered to him again. I forbid it!" said Darius.

Eloise raised an eyebrow then put her arms around Darius. "If you'd wanted a compliant wife, you would have married that hag your mother kept bringing to the house when you showed an interest in me."

Darius's fond smile quickly faded. "I'm scared about what might happen. I swore on our wedding day to protect and honour you. I feel that I'm failing."

"All will be well."

Darius grunted. "You have more faith than me."

Eloise held him tight and together they stared into the fire, their thoughts drifting away like ash on the wind. Part of Eloise believed her own words, but another growing part worried about Finn and what he might do. During the battle there were three occasions when he'd held back a volcano of power with the thinnest shred of control. If he'd lost control she would have been burned to ash from being connected to him. Finn had little discipline and wielded his power without any planning or forethought, just raw emotion and brute strength. Until he mastered his abilities he would remain a threat. She only hoped that both she and Balfruss could make a difference before it was too late.

CHAPTER 15

"I'm not sure this is a good idea," said Shani, for the tenth time since they'd set off from the palace. The army were steadily retreating towards the capital but Talandra had decided to come home early with her father and Graegor. There were some things that she needed to do in person and she could do more here than in the field.

"Just watch where you're going," said Talandra, tugging on the hood of her borrowed robe to make sure it concealed her face.

"I can see in the dark, remember?" said Shani, her amber eyes glowing slightly in the gloom.

"I know, so tell me what to avoid."

Just before they'd left, Talandra had heard back from Gunder about High Priest Filbin. The seed had been planted in his mind. Now all she needed to do was make sure an appropriate letter was waiting for him when he returned home to Zecorria. The contents didn't really matter, as long as it contained several mentions of the phrase 'true faith'.

Most letters sent to the High Priest would never pass beyond the lowest circle of his priests, but one from herself would land directly on his desk. Their success on the battlefield and in keeping Perizzi free was not guaranteed, so it didn't hurt to try to disrupt the alliance from the inside with a powerful ally. It was even better that, at home, Filbin was almost as powerful as Taikon. He was also insulated by his people so he couldn't have a convenient accident or be ignored.

"There are better places to meet him," said Shani, bringing her back to the present and her next meeting. "It's not uncommon to entertain foreign dignitaries at the palace."

"We need him to stick to his normal routine. Summoning him to the palace at short notice would look very suspicious."

"You're just being stubborn. What if someone recognises you?" A hint of desperation was creeping into Shani's voice. Talandra knew she was just trying to protect her, but she needed to do this tonight. It also wasn't often that she managed to wander through the streets without guards watching her every move. She felt a strange sense of freedom simply in walking unannounced and unrecognised through the streets of her city.

"No one will recognise me, and even if they did, no one would believe them anyway!"

Shani sighed and led the rest of the way in a sulky silence.

The building looked no different to any of the others on the street. There were no discerning features, nothing hung or painted in the windows and the front door bore no special decorations or markers. They watched the building from the mouth of an alley across the street for several minutes before Shani signalled the all clear. Ignoring the front door she led her down to the end of the street and then back along the narrow lane between the row of buildings and the one behind.

"Why aren't we using the front door?" whispered Talandra.

"That's only for customers."

Talandra's boots squelched as she stepped on all sorts of things she couldn't and didn't want to identify in the dark. When they reached the back door of the right building Shani knocked three times quickly and then stepped back. A small hatch slid open at head height in the door, revealing a pair of brown eyes set in a wide face.

"Good evening, Red," said Shani. Tonight she'd dressed in worn woollen clothing in dull browns and Talandra wore the same. All jewellery and anything of value had been left back at the palace to avoid attracting undue attention. The only thing she couldn't change was her face, but she'd concealed that in a hood.

"Who's that with you?" asked Red, from behind the door. Talandra stepped forward until the man could see her face.

"What do you want?"

"We need to speak to Marissa," said Shani, taking a pouch of coins from her belt, which she held up and shook. "We'll make it worth her while."

"Wait there." The hatch closed and Talandra heard the sound of heavy feet retreating inside.

"Are they always this friendly?" asked Talandra.

"Marissa is very careful. She has to be, given her clients."

Talandra heard a loud scraping of bolts and the door opened to reveal Red, a man so tall his bald head nearly touched the ceiling. He was dressed only in a kilt that showed off hairy legs almost as wide as her. It wouldn't take much for him to snap her in two like a twig. Talandra reconsidered whether coming in person had been such a good idea. Despite being familiar with Shani the big man held a dagger in his free hand. The expression on his wide face wasn't exactly unfriendly, but his eyes watched for the slightest hint of trouble. They slipped inside and the big man relocked and bolted the door behind them.

"Can we see Marissa?" asked Shani.

"You'll see her when I'm happy," snapped Red.

"Calm down, Red," a woman said in a husky voice. "We're all friends here. Isn't that right, Shani?"

"Yes, Marissa. We are," said Shani, sketching a deep bow.

Shani had told Talandra what to expect, but she'd said almost nothing about Marissa. It wasn't an exaggeration to say she was one of the most beautiful women Talandra had ever seen. Voluptuous and curvaceous without being overweight, mature without any lines around her eyes and mouth, and with striking features that suggested a mixed heritage Talandra couldn't identify. Raven-black hair fell to her narrow waist and a single white streak ran through it that was surely an affectation. Her modest red and black dress hugged her figure, showing little bare flesh and yet revealing much of what was underneath. Talandra tried not to stare too much, but she found it difficult as she was particularly envious of Marissa's ample bosom. If she tried to wear a gown like that it would have gaped in all the wrong places and made her look like a flat-chested boy by comparison. Shani caught her staring and raised an eyebrow.

"Follow me," said Marissa with a smile that warmed Talandra.

Marissa led them along a short corridor decorated with expensive glass vases from Shael, unusual oil paintings that looked Zecorran in origin, and several carved figures made from brightly coloured crystals. The plain exterior hid an interior that spoke of extensive wealth and comfort.

At the end of the corridor Marissa gestured for them to enter a small room which Talandra expected to be an office. Instead she found herself in a bedroom decorated with silk hangings, dark wooden furniture and a desk off to one side of the room. Marissa gestured towards a table which held several bottles of whisky.

"Thank you," said Shani.

"How about you, my dear?" she asked and Talandra shook her head. With a small shrug Marissa poured two generous portions and handed Shani a glass. "You can take off the hood. Anything that happens inside the building is never made public knowledge."

As Talandra dropped the hood Marissa's eyes widened slightly but quickly returned to normal. "Do you know you look a lot like the Princess?"

Shani squirmed but Talandra just laughed it off. "I'm often told that."

"I take it you're not here about a job."

"No, we're here about one of your clients."

Marissa shook her head. "Shame. You'd make a fortune. I know of many men and women who'd love to fuck the Princess, and you're the next best thing. With the right dress and a bit of make-up, they'd never know the difference."

"An interesting offer, but I'll pass."

"If you ever feel like a change of career, let me know," said Marissa. "So, do you work for Shani?"

Shani was taking a drink at the time and started to choke. Eventually she recovered, although she was still flustered. "No, I work with her."

"So, what is this about?" asked Marissa.

"Ambassador Mabon has been a bad boy."

"That's putting it mildly."

"We meant the other way," said Shani.

"Ah. Well I meant what I said earlier. What happens inside these walls is completely private."

"We just need to speak to him for a few minutes. We're not here to hurt him or reveal any of his secrets," promised Talandra. "Quite the opposite in fact. We're here to help him."

Marissa added a small amount of water to her whisky then swirled it in the glass before taking another sip. "Is this going to affect his relationship with my establishment?"

"We hope not," said Talandra. "But I've been authorised to make sure you're suitably compensated if he decides to take his business elsewhere." Shani placed the heavy bag of coins on the table. "This is just a token of our appreciation."

Marissa didn't glance at the money, and judging by the display of wealth in the building she didn't need it. Talandra wondered what did motivate the Madame. Instead of answering straight away Marissa studied both of them intently. Talandra tried to stay calm and give away as little as possible in her body language.

"You're hiding something," said Marissa, "but I don't think it relates to Mabon. You've always been a good friend, Shani. I would hate it if this spoiled our relationship."

"It won't," she promised.

"We'll see," purred Marissa. "Mabon is upstairs in room eight. Send Kitty down to me."

Despite the thickness of the doors, Talandra heard all sorts of strange noises and groans of pleasure. Men and women's voices mixed together in cries and whimpers of pleasure and pain. A door on her left briefly opened, revealing a naked man on all fours with a bridle around his head being ridden around the room by a woman dressed in leather. The door closed but she still heard the crack of the whip as it struck his bare flesh and the squeal of pleasure that followed. As Shani opened the door at the end of the corridor Talandra realised the man being ridden was the Head of the Scribes guild.

Another unusual vista greeted her eyes in room eight where the Zecorran Ambassador Mabon hung naked from a cross attached to the wall. A web of chains held him aloft by the arms, facing the wall. A tall woman dressed in only a pair of knee-length boots stood off to one side with a whip in her hand. There were already numerous red welts across Mabon's buttocks and lower back.

"Marissa would like to see you for a few minutes," said Shani, holding open a long cloak taken from the back of the door. The woman accepted the cloak and stepped into the corridor, followed by Shani, who closed the door behind her.

"Kitty? What's going on?" asked Mabon. His restraints prevented him from turning around, but he tried to crane his neck to look behind him.

"She's stepped out," said Talandra.

"Is she coming back?" asked Mabon.

"Soon, Ambassador, but I thought we'd have a little talk."

Mabon twisted around but couldn't see, so Talandra helped him by stepping to one side of the room.

"Maker's balls!"

"They're not that impressive," said Talandra, nodding towards his shrivelling sack. "But we're not here to talk about that, or how you spend your free time."

"What do you want?" asked Mabon.

"I've been told that Taikon has imprisoned your family back home. That's he's going to cut them up, even cook them, unless you send him intelligence about our defences."

"My son is five years old," begged Mabon, tears leaking from his eyes. "My daughter is twelve. She will be thirteen in three months. Please, please. You can't put me in prison. If I don't keep sending them reports, he'll kill my children. But I don't have anything to tell them, I promise!"

"Don't worry, Mabon. I'm going to help you. In fact I'm going to make sure you regularly send them information about all sorts of things in Charas."

"You are?"

"Yes, but it will be information that I supply. It will be pure fiction, but it will sound reasonable."

Mabon heaved a sigh of relief, slumping against his restraints. "And what do you want me to do in return?"

"Nothing," said Talandra with a friendly smile. "I won't do anything to put your family at risk. I swear it."

"Thank you."

"I suspect you're being watched, so don't change your routine in any way. If you do they may get suspicious and word could get back to Taikon." The possibility of that actually happening was slim, since she knew all of the Zecorran spies in the city and regularly had them followed, but she needed Mabon to remain anxious.

"Why?" asked Mabon. Until now he'd been a loyal subject to Zecorria, but also quite moderate in comparison to some. A steady, calm voice would be useful and perhaps more influential in the future when the alternative was a rabble of noisy extremists.

"When the war ends, I expect you'll be recalled and sent home. One day, at some point in the future, you will owe me a favour. And when I collect, you will repay me in full."

The possibility existed that he would talk at the first opportunity when he returned home. It was a gamble, but he would be useful until then as his missives would be another useful source of misinformation flowing into Zecorria about Seveldrom.

Mabon heaved a deep breath. "I understand."

"Good. Then I'll let you get back to your evening's entertainment."

"You're very confident about winning the war, Highness," said Mabon. "What happens if you lose?"

Talandra had spent a great deal of time considering that possibility and making plans, just in case. She was doing all she could to make sure it didn't happen, but it always paid to be prepared.

"You'll still be sent home and I'll be the one in chains. I hope that if it does happen, you'll look kindly on your time here and how you were treated."

"Highness," said Mabon, inclining his head. The gesture was faintly ridiculous given his position, but she sketched a short bow in return.

"Ambassador."

Talandra stumbled towards her chambers, barely looking where she was going. Her head was swimming with plans for her agents and her intelligence network, tactics from the battlefield, and she was struggling to remember all of it and keep everything in perspective. Somehow her father could watch the battle, anticipate what was about to happen, and give orders to counter disasters before they developed.

Talandra considered herself reasonably good at playing Stones, but now they were at war she realised she was an infant in comparison to her father. He was able to see more than a few moves ahead, think through all of the likely outcomes, and make plans accordingly, and all within the space of a few heartbeats. The only person who'd ever been able to challenge him was her mother. Her father had not touched a Stones board since her death.

A yawn made Talandra's jaw crack as she rounded a corner and thumped into something that sent her flying. A strong hand grabbed her arm, keeping her upright.

"Careful, Tala," said Graegor. As usual the grizzled General was dressed in black armour with that wicked axe hung at his belt. He might be only a couple of years from his sixtieth summer, but only days ago Talandra had witnessed how lethal Graegor could be if needed. By the time she'd arrived, most of the assassin had been mopped up, but Graegor had been covered in gore. He'd taken no notice of the blood, as if it were just red paint adorning his face. For someone who was normally very loud, the icy stare and silence that hung around him had been unsettling.

"Sorry, I'm asleep on my feet. I'm heading to bed."

"You look awful."

Talandra was tempted to ask if he'd looked in the mirror, but such comments were never well received.

"I thought you and my father were headed back to the front?"

"We're going in the morning."

Looking along the corridor she saw Graegor was alone. Also,

for the first time in her life, she thought he looked nervous. "Are you all right?"

"I'm curious about something. Thought you could help," he said, walking beside her along the corridor.

"Of course. What do you want to know?"

"The Battlemages. What do you make of them?"

The question sounded reasonable, given that they were an essential part of the war, but she sensed something else. Talandra wasn't imagining the hesitation in his voice. The man never hesitated. If he wanted something he chased it, heart, body and soul, until he succeeded. Tact and diplomacy were alien concepts to him.

He adjusted his eye patch again, a nervous twitch. The eye and two fingers on his right hand had been lost in a brutal war eighteen years ago. He refused to talk about it, and it would have remained a mystery if Talandra hadn't begged her father for the story as a girl. For months afterwards she woke up screaming in the night.

"I think the Battlemages have done very well," said Talandra. "All major attacks have been repelled. I know it looks as if they're just standing there—"

Graegor waved that away. "I've seen what they can do. I know they don't need to jump around to fight."

"Then what are you asking?" They rounded another corner and her chambers were at the end of the hall.

"What do you know of them, personally? Their backgrounds."

Talandra raised an eyebrow. "You think one of them can't be trusted? They might be a spy?" It was something she'd considered, and one of her people was making gentle enquiries. But if the General had suspicions she might have to dig more deeply. The man had only one eye, but he saw more than most.

"No, I didn't mean that," said Graegor, starting to get

annoyed. She could see all the familiar signs that he was losing his temper. With considerable effort he regained control, which made her raise an eyebrow. He was putting a lot of effort into their conversation.

They reached her bedroom door and Graegor stared at the wooden surface, as if it would reveal the answers he sought. Talandra gave him time to find the right words. She leaned against the wall and the cold stone chilled her hands, temporarily sharpening her mind.

"What do you know about Balfruss?" Graegor finally asked. "Where does he come from?"

"I don't know the name of the village, but Vannok would be able to tell you," said Talandra, expecting that it would be enough, but the General still wore a blank expression. "They grew up together," she added.

Something seemed to click into place behind Graegor's remaining eye and he nodded grimly, as if confirming something. All traces of anxiety faded from his expression and body language until the impenetrable warrior stood before her again.

"Does that help?"

"Goodnight, your Highness," he said, stomping away before she could ask him anything further.

If she hadn't been asleep on her feet Talandra would have attempted to unravel what had just happened. Instead she decided it could wait until the morning and pushed open her door.

"I thought the old bastard was never going to leave," said Shani, sitting up in Talandra's bed. She wore only a blanket and one long pale blue and white leg poked out from underneath.

Talandra checked the corridor and then quickly stepped inside and locked the door. Technically she wasn't betrothed and could sleep with whoever she wanted. However, Talandra was fairly sure her father would think it imprudent of her to sleep with one of her own spies.

Normally Talandra felt a thrill at seeing Shani in private, and she always appreciated her energetic exertions, but not tonight.

"It's late, Shani," said Talandra, sitting down on the end of the bed and pulling off her boots. "I'm tired. Maybe another night."

"Are you serious?" said Shani. All traces of the temptress faded from her amber eyes. Her long black hair shimmered like a curtain of silk in the light from candles scattered about the room. The room smelled of jasmine, and not all of it was from the flowers outside her window. Shani knew it was her favourite scent and undoubtedly wore some of it on her skin. Talandra's libido stirred briefly at the thought, but her mind was turning in slow circles, and her ardour faded.

"If all you want to do is sleep, you're welcome to stay," said Talandra. "But I suspect you have something else in mind."

Shani had a half-smile on her face, as if she still expected Talandra to tell her it was all a joke. When she didn't oblige, all traces of humour slid off Shani's face. With stiff movements she slipped out of bed and quickly pulled on her underwear. Not for the first time Talandra marvelled at the smoothness of the white skin on Shani's pert backside. The skin on her back was a marbled mix of white shot through with seams of blue, while tendrils of colour ran down her legs and arms.

Normally she enjoyed watching Shani getting dressed almost as much as seeing her clothes come off, but tonight there was nothing sensual about it. Shani managed to dress in black breeches that hugged her shapely legs, a white shirt and black jacket in less time than Talandra thought possible. After pulling on her belt, daggers and boots, she moved towards the door. Talandra knew she would regret it later if she didn't offer something.

"Shani, wait." Shani had one hand resting on the door handle, her back towards the bed, and didn't turn around. Talandra chose her next words with great care, but was struggling to think clearly. "I need you. More than you know."

It wasn't what she'd intended to say, but she was exhausted and it was the truth. It was enough to make Shani turn, but there was still no warmth behind her tawny eyes.

"The war is pulling me in all directions and I'm just exhausted. There's so much going on. It's just not a good night." Talandra wasn't sure if her words were having any effect on the Morrin, as her expression remained neutral, but she wasn't sure what else to say.

"Get some rest. You look exhausted." Shani finally relented and moved forward to gently touch her cheek with one hand. "I'll come by in the morning."

"I do like your surprise visits, just not tonight."

"It's fine." She gave Talandra a little wave and went out the door.

Talandra stared after her for a moment, her mind whirling with emotions. Her whole body throbbed with exhaustion but something nagged at her. Was it something to do with Graegor? Or Shani? Or both?

She lay back on the bed, trying to work it through in her mind, but fell asleep in seconds.

CHAPTER 16

Vargus stayed perfectly still as the nurse stitched the wound in his shoulder. He wondered how many other men had lain in the same bed before him, staring up at the same patch of tent. All around he could hear men grunting, crying and screaming in pain. Two beds down, a dying man sobbed and called for his wife, cradled in the arms of a voluptuous Sister of Mercy.

He wished she was the one attending to his injury, not the sour-faced shrew sewing him shut. Then again, a Sister meant he was dying, and he had to admit this nurse knew her business. Her movements were precise, the stitches small and neat, and her delicate hands were steady. She'd also been very gentle with him.

"All done," she said with a brief smile. Moving slowly, he rotated his shoulder and felt the stitches pull, but only a little. Wounds from previous days were starting to heal, but the bruises around those from today were still purple and full of blood. On impulse Vargus kissed the nurse's cheek and was pleased to see her blush. The old woman hurried away before he could offer further thanks.

"There you are," said a booming voice. Hargo and the others approached as he sat up on the bed. Orran had a fresh cut on his cheek, Black Tom was limping slightly and some of the others sported fresh injuries too. He also noticed a few faces were missing from the group.

"Are you going to lie around on your back all day? Thinking of getting into a new trade?" asked Orran, gyrating his hips, and the others laughed. A trace of his old humour had returned after the death of Tan, but now his jokes were darker and more cutting.

"I considered it," mused Vargus as he pulled on his shirt and armour. "But I didn't think you'd want the competition."

"Fucker," said Orran.

"That's the idea."

Orran just shook his head in disgust.

"Curly?" asked Vargus.

Hargo's expression turned grim. "Crows did their best, but he's going to lose the arm. They won't know for a few days if he's going to make it."

Outside the air smelled clean compared to the inside of the hot and smelly hospital tent. Grey clouds threatened rain and the others grumbled about soggy clothes and rusty armour, but Vargus barely noticed. His whole body buzzed with unspent energy and a primal need.

Hargo moved in front of him, blocking out the light, and Vargus realised he'd been talking. "I said we're going for a drink. Are you coming?"

"Later."

"Do you need to lie down?"

Vargus considered a witty comment but changed his mind. "I need something else. I'll catch up."

The big man gave him a worried look, but said nothing. They moved away towards the mobile taverns and Vargus went in the other direction, towards the outskirts of the camp.

Every soldier knew where to find them. They were usually close to the supplies and the rear of the army. Somewhere with a bit of space and the chance of privacy. A couple of the more upmarket ones who serviced the officers had their own tents, dyed in dark colours which made them stand out against the standard army grey. Vargus didn't get too close at first, watching and appraising who came and went. When he'd decided, he approached a woman drinking wine by a campfire. She had brown hair, a generous bosom and kind eyes that lit up when he sat down. Her lips were full and she wore a simple, colourful skirt with a cream shirt and sandals.

Without saying a word she offered him a glass of wine, which he accepted. To his surprise it wasn't half bad, but then, from looking at her, Vargus already knew she wasn't going to ask for five coppers. Those women were rutting in the lee of tents with the worst-paid men in the army. The kind of man who didn't have a problem showing his hairy arse in public.

They chatted for a while about the war, about the city and old songs. She told him her name was Adira. Usually she served drinks in a tavern and sang one night a week if the innkeeper was feeling generous. The audiences were never large, and she didn't get paid any extra, but she liked being the focus of so many people.

Adira claimed to be able to hold a decent tune so Vargus asked her to sing something old. He kept up the rhythm, patting it out on his thighs, as her voice rose into the cool air. Her voice was low and rich, something he'd not heard from many women. It explained why she wasn't popular, but the hairs still rose on his arms at the song. Her voice stirred up old memories and wounds buried deep in the back of his mind. It was an ancient song about love and betrayal, and although the words were different to the original, the story remained the same.

When the bottle of wine was empty she asked if he wanted another, but Vargus said no.

He reached for his money but she shook her head.

She offered her hand and as dusk began to fall she led him past the sentries and beyond into the growing dark. She picked a direction at random and they walked together in comfortable silence like a pair of old lovers.

A tiny trickle of water, barely wide enough to be called a stream, ended in the lee of a small copse of evergreens. Adira led him into the shadows of the trees and laid out a blanket.

With gentle hands she explored the bare skin of his chest, pausing briefly on recent wounds and old scars. Her fingers felt cool, but her mouth was warm and welcoming. For a moment, when he stared at her face, Vargus saw another woman looking back, one with pale blue eyes and blonde hair. The mirage lasted only a second but Adira seemed to understand, telling him to close his eyes. She asked him his name and he told her the oldest one he could remember.

He explored the skin of her shoulders with his fingers, her neck with his lips. By the time she pulled down his breeches and handled his cock, it was already like a hot iron bar. As he entered her she whispered in his ear, and for a moment they were two different people, lying in a giant bed with dawn light streaming through the windows.

She dug her nails into his back, bringing him back to the present, but he kept his eyes closed. Between gasps she urged him to move faster as he quenched a need that couldn't be put into words. As their cries mixed, he didn't care about anything any more except the feel of her in that moment. Knowing that it was a betrayal of both women, Vargus opened his eyes as he came, shouting out in a wordless cry of defiance.

They lay for a while after, cooling off, and a hundred questions ran through his mind. Somehow she seemed able to predict his thoughts and asked him to tell her a secret no one else knew. Vargus considered what she would believe but instead of something personal he told her he knew the original lyrics to the ballad, then quietly sang them.

When they returned to camp Vargus bought a bottle of wine from a vendor and passed it to Adira. As she stepped into her tent to fetch some glasses, he left her money by the fire. As she re-emerged Adira saw his expression and there was a knowing look in her eyes. His armour was back in place and now he was just a warrior named Vargus again. Her smile looked a little sad, but that was probably just his imagination, or part of the wish fulfilment. Without saying another word he walked away and didn't look back.

It was very late by the time Balfruss found his tent after another tiring training session with Finn. The others were asleep and the fire had burned down to glowing embers. Despite being so tired that he couldn't summon even a spark of power between his fingers, Balfruss couldn't sleep. His body and mind were so exhausted he felt numb, but something wouldn't let him rest.

Someone moved outside his tent and he heard them settling down. At first he assumed it was Finn or Ecko, but after listening to their movements and breathing for a while he realised it was neither Battlemage.

Poking his head out of the tent Balfruss saw a plainly dressed man sat at the fire, staring into the dying embers. He looked as if he'd not seen twenty-five summers, and from the fabric and style of his clothes, Balfruss assumed he was a farmer turned army labourer. There were always some who were forced to leave their homes during a conflict to find alternate work. Unskilled workers often found themselves driving carts, carrying stretchers, working for the quartermaster, cooking meals, digging latrines, or one of a thousand other jobs that needed doing in an army on the move. He remembered the two labourers who'd pretended to be Battlemages and wondered where they were now.

Their eyes met and a startled expression crossed the young man's face. "This isn't my tent, is it?"

"No," said Balfruss, sitting down opposite.

"I must have got turned around."

"You're welcome to stay awhile."

"You look familiar," said the man, scratching at his hair as if he had lice. It was likely, with so many people living together. "Do you work for the quartermaster?"

"No, I'm Balfruss. One of the Battlemages."

The young man started to stand up, his pale blue eyes widening so much Balfruss was afraid they'd fall out of his head. "I'm sorry. I'll leave you to rest. My tent must be around here somewhere."

Balfruss waved him back to his seat and added fresh wood to the fire. "Stay. At least have some tea."

"Are you sure?"

"On one condition," said Balfruss and the young man looked afraid. "You have to tell me your name."

He relaxed with a long sigh and sat down. "My father always told me names have power, but I think he was soft in the head. My name's Torval."

As Balfruss fished out some tea he saw Torval sneaking glances at him. "Is something the matter?"

"What? Oh no. Nothing's the matter. Nothing at all."

"Do I have some food in my beard?" asked Balfruss, checking for crumbs. It wouldn't be the first time.

"No it's just—" Torval bit his lip, afraid to go on.

"Speak freely," said Balfruss. "I'm no different to you. I'm just a man like anyone else."

"You're not like anyone else though," said Torval, a distinct challenge to his words.

"Maybe not in that way, but I'm not noble born. I grew up in a village where my mother was a baker and my father a warrior for the King. What about your parents?"

"Fisherman and fishwife," said Torval, watching as Balfruss took the kettle off the fire as the water began to boil.

"Not for me. I can't stay."

"Are you sure?"

"I'm fine, thank you."

Balfruss didn't push and tipped some leaves into a mug before adding water and leaving it to stew.

From his pale hair and light eyes, he guessed Torval had a mixed heritage from Yerskania and Seveldrom.

"Do your parents still live in the same village?" asked Torval.

"Both are dead. My village was decimated by bandits." The memories were old, but the guilt of not being there to help his neighbours still burned. "My mother survived, but she died a few years later from the pox. I don't really remember my father. He was often away and only came home a few times when I was young. He might still be alive, but I doubt it."

"So you were trained at that magic school," said Torval, making it sound like a question.

"For ten years. A Seeker came to our village when I was very young and said I had great potential. When I turned eight I travelled to the Red Tower on the back of a wagon."

"Do you regret it?" asked Torval. He gestured around him at the sleeping army. "Studying and becoming a Battlemage, instead of something else."

"No. I've never regretted it," admitted Balfruss. "My choices were limited in the village. I saw it as a chance to get away from a life spent planting in the fields, or digging in the quarry. I wanted more. Even as a young boy I always asked questions that no one could answer. I saw the Red Tower as a blessing. A chance to learn about the world, as well as control my power."

He sipped his tea as Torval stared into the fire, his pale eyes distant.

"So," said Balfruss, breaking the silence. "When did you know you would become a Battlemage, Torval?" The younger man stared at him with a blank expression. "Or do you prefer your title? The Warlock, isn't it?"

Torval didn't move a muscle or blink for a few long heartbeats, but eventually a smile crept across his face. There was a faint stirring in the air and suddenly Balfruss could feel an echo of power coming from the other man. It was there for a moment and then it was gone again. He wanted to ask how Torval masked his ability, but didn't. There were more important questions.

"Why did you come here?"

"I wanted to meet you in person," said Torval. "I've heard a lot about you."

"Through your mindless slaves? Those shells."

"I'm very proud of my Splinters," boasted Torval.

Balfruss had to ask. "What did you do to them?"

"It started when I became a Seeker, travelling around the west, looking for those with potential. Sometimes I found adults that were too far gone to be saved. There were plenty of children, but they were unruly and lacked discipline." Torval waved them away dismissively. His impatience was clear. He didn't have time to waste on children. "Eventually I found those caught in between. The ones with repressed potential. It didn't take much to nudge them in my direction with an offer of help," said Torval, rather smugly.

"I touched the thoughts of a Splinter," said Balfruss with disgust. "There's nothing there. You scoured their minds clean. Why?"

Torval looked at him askance. "Because without me they would have died in pointless accidents. Blown themselves up, and their families."

"You didn't do it to save them, or innocent lives."

Torval laughed. "Of course not. I needed malleable tools. Those with an ability that could be reshaped to my purpose."

"Your purpose? Who are you to decide?"

Torval cocked his head to one side, a wry smile on his lips. Without realising, Balfruss had started to focus his will and draw on the Source. Torval would have felt it too, but he'd made no move to defend himself.

When he was a little calmer, Balfruss asked again. "Why did you come here?"

"Don't you want to know how I did it?" Torval seemed genuinely surprised when he shook his head. "How I cleared out all the shit inside their heads and replaced it with something new? I call them Splinters because they're tiny pieces of me. Simple rules and thoughts, copied from my mind into theirs. Just like the stories I heard as a boy about dancing clay golems."

"I don't care. All I know is you made them your slaves. They breathe, but they're just hollow men and women. Walking corpses that feel nothing."

"I gave their lives meaning. I gave them a purpose. Without me they were nothing. This way they matter."

This time, as Torval lost his temper, Balfruss remained calm. "Whatever you say."

Torval took a breath and a moment to relax. "Taikon needed Battlemages he could rely on, and I did it because it had never been done before. I needed a challenge."

"Challenge? Are we playing a game of Stones? Is this a test?"

"Of course. Life is a series of tests. Don't you like to be challenged? To test yourself?"

Balfruss couldn't deny it, and from his expression Torval knew the answer. If he didn't like a challenge Balfruss would have returned to the Red Tower years ago to teach new students. Instead he travelled the world, going wherever people needed his help. He didn't want to kill himself and wasn't excited by the danger. He did it because he needed a constant challenge.

"Our goals are the same. We both have a passion for life."

Balfruss met his fevered gaze. "You're wrong. You and I, we're nothing alike. There are many things I would never do. Things you've already done."

"You haven't done them, yet," said Torval with an ominous grin. "But only because you haven't been pushed hard enough."

He stood and Balfruss rose to his feet as well, not liking the idea of looking up to the man in any way.

"I have to go, but I hope we can talk again."

A witty retort rose in his mind, but Balfruss repressed it and remained silent. Torval looked disappointed, but said nothing before walking away into the darkness.

Balfruss felt sick and when he took a sip of his tea it tasted like blood.

CHAPTER 17

G under had been putting it off but now there was no way to avoid it. It was time for his annual stock check. Sabu stood in the back room calling out items and amounts, while he recorded them in a big red ledger.

The small bell above his front door rang and he moved to the counter with a welcoming smile. The woman dressed in the modest blue and gold livery of a palace servant was very familiar, but in his role as Gunder the merchant it was unlikely they would have met before.

"Good afternoon," he said with an ingratiating smile and a small bow. "How can I help you?"

"I'm here on an errand for her Majesty," said the servant. Sabu wandered in from the back, gawping with his mouth hanging open.

"Don't stare, boy," snapped Gunder, turning back to his honoured guest. "Whatever her Majesty requires, I am happy to provide."

"A guest is due to visit the palace. Her Majesty has requested a special meal be prepared in their honour. Do you have any of these items?"

Gunder took the offered piece of paper and perused the list.

He kept his expression thoughtful. His body language needed no theatre to make it apparent that he was tense.

"Rare items," he mused. "I believe I have some of these in stock in my warehouse. I would be happy to personally deliver them to the palace tomorrow."

"I need those ingredients today," said the woman, her eyebrows drawing down into a frown. "I was told you were the best spice merchant in the city. Was I misinformed?"

Sabu started to edge away, not wanting to be included in the ire of the palace servant and the Queen she served.

"No, no. I can get them. Later today," promised Gunder, wiping sweat from his brow. "I just need to fetch them from the warehouse."

The servant looked at the padded seats by the front window and sat down. "I will wait here."

Gunder turned away, his smile dripping off his face, morphing into a grimace. He crooked a finger at Sabu and then wrote down three items on a piece of paper, which he handed to the boy.

"I want you to run, don't walk, all the way to the warehouse and fetch these spices. I will take the rest from stock."

The boy opened his mouth, no doubt to complain about the distance, but then saw Gunder's expression. He flew out the door and a few seconds later Gunder heard his sandalled feet pounding down the road. When they receded into the distance, he brewed a fresh pot of tea for his guest and sat down in the opposite chair.

"What are you doing here, Roza?" said Gunder in a hoarse whisper. "Weren't we scheduled to meet tonight?" This was the first time she'd approached Gunder during the day, which worried him.

"Do you have any idea what's been happening in the palace?" said Roza. "It took me hours to get inside and speak to our people. Everyone is afraid for their lives."

"This has to do with Filbin's visit, doesn't it?"

"If only it were about him," said Roza, her voice trembling.

"Let me fetch the tea. It will look suspicious if I don't," said Gunder. If either of them were being followed, or a stranger came into the shop, they needed to look the part.

He returned a few minutes later and poured two glasses of tea, by which time Roza had composed herself. Playing the good host, Gunder fetched a plate of delicacies, spicy pastries and seasoned dates. He took a pair of dates, placing them on the edge of his plate.

"A week ago, the Queen was supposed to make a public declaration," said Roza in a steady voice. "The paper mills were working day and night. Notices were supposed to be posted everywhere in the city. Messengers were ready to be dispatched. Everything was in place, but then she changed her mind. She went against Taikon's order."

Gunder took a mouthful of tea and sucked at a slice of lemon, but it was neither which made him grimace. He knew Taikon was unpredictable and dangerous, and that was when his orders were being followed. Being ignored would normally be lethal, but even he couldn't openly kill the Queen of Yerskania. At least not yet, with the alliance barely holding together. The Queen had gambled and from the look on Roza's face it had not paid off.

"What did he do?"

Roza stared at the dates on Gunder's plate and shuddered. "High Priest Filbin arrived two days ago with a large retinue."

"I know, I met with him on his first night here."

"Did you know some of his people are Chosen?"

"Who are they?" asked Gunder.

"They're what Taikon calls his fanatics. Last night Filbin persuaded the Queen to change her mind, but he also came with a message from Taikon. She was to be punished for delaying his plan. The Chosen castrated the Crown Prince."

Gunder choked on his tea and quickly put the glass down before he dropped it. The Queen had four children, but only one son. Two of her three daughters were already married and the youngest had the mind of a small child, preventing her from ever sitting on the throne. It hadn't mattered as the Crown Prince was the eldest and the jewel of his mother's eye. He possessed her intelligence and sharp wit, and the business acumen of his late father. Everyone had anticipated him becoming an even greater ruler than his mother. The crown of Yerskania had been passed down through their bloodline for nearly four hundred years. Now that was at an end.

"They should've just killed him," muttered Gunder.

"The public declaration is going out today. Messengers are already on their way north and south." Even as Roza finished speaking, Gunder saw a unit of the City Watch nailing declarations outside shops, on the side of wagons and onto stalls in the market. Crowds of people gathered around to read them, and from where he sat their shocked expressions were clear. A group of four swarthy Zecorrans, dressed in blue and white uniforms, walked past his shop window. They seemed oblivious to the outrage.

"She's abdicating?"

"Yes, and worse," said Roza with a grimace. "She's announced Taikon as the Regent in her stead."

Gunder sucked at his teeth in shock. There was no need to hide it now that it had become public knowledge. It would be the only topic of conversation in every tavern across the city.

"Do you have any good news?" asked Roza, clearly desperate for something to lift her spirits.

"The war on the battlefield is going well. Taikon has the numbers, but they're not as disciplined. He killed another group of Generals because the army didn't meet his expectations."

"He's insane," said Roza. "How could his own people trust him? Couldn't they see his insanity?"

"He's very charismatic. Not everyone in Zecorria supported him and we're hoping Filbin will help with that when he returns home."

"Do you have any new orders from Talandra?"

"Yes, but you're not going to like it," said Gunder. "I need you to hire someone to burn down a temple of the Maker."

Roza raised an eyebrow. "Is that a joke?"

"No." He scratched at his head and made a mental note to wash the hairpiece. He was fairly sure it had lice. "So far it's only been pagan temples Taikon's followers have burned down in the north, but Talandra wants people here to fear the worst. Their Queen has been forced out and now their religion is being overwritten by his cult. We need the people of this city to get involved."

"It will be dangerous," mused Roza. "But it's possible."

"I'll leave the details up to you. If you need money to grease the axle, let me know."

"What do you want me to tell our people in the palace?"

"To do nothing that might jeopardise their position. But if they feel in danger, to get out to a safe house."

Sabu came flapping back into the shop, red faced and breathless. Gunder moved to the counter and carefully weighed out the ingredients Sabu had brought with him. He wrapped up the herbs and spices in a Drassi paper box, which he decorated with a blue ribbon.

Roza approached him and reached for her purse, but Gunder waved it away. "It's my gift to her Majesty. A pleasure to serve."

Sabu nervously hopped from one foot to the other, as if he were desperate for a piss. They both knew that approval from a palace servant by itself meant nothing, but if it became publicly known that he was supplying the palace kitchens, his shop would gain a lot of prestige.

"If the quality of your goods proves satisfactory, I will make sure you are credited," promised Roza.

"Thank you," said Gunder with a wide grin.

Without another word Roza swept out of the shop and down the street. When she was out of sight Sabu began to dance a little jig. Gunder smiled at the boy and let him have his moment.

The situation in the north was dire and seemed to be getting worse every day. They were winning the war on the battlefield, but that wouldn't matter if the west became one kingdom under Taikon's rule.

The people on the street were upset about the abdication notices being put up. He could hear them talking in loud voices and complaining about the news. They would need to do a lot more if they wanted to continue enjoying their current level of freedom.

CHAPTER 18

It seemed like only moments ago that Balfruss had closed his eyes and now someone was shaking his shoulder. He stubbornly ignored it and slapped the hand away but it came back, more urgent this time. As his groggy mind started to come awake, he slowly remembered where he was and sat up sharply, nearly hitting his head on a tent pole.

It was pitch black, and the dark figure crouched over him was hard to identify until it spoke.

"Balfruss, you must wake," said Ecko. "You're needed. It's urgent."

The little tribesman retreated outside and Balfruss could see him stoking up the fire and adding fresh wood. Rubbing the sand from his eyes Balfruss pulled on his boots and ran his fingers through his hair and beard. Both were getting long and unkempt. He'd needed to get his hair cut since returning to Seveldrom, but hadn't found the time. He'd been so tired last night he'd gone to sleep in his clothes, but now it was a blessing as he was already wrapped up against the cold.

"What time is it?" asked Balfruss, emerging from his tent and sitting down by the fire. The others were asleep, and looking around he saw no signs of alarm or distress in the camp.

"Not yet dawn," said Ecko, hanging the teapot on its hook.

"What's happening? What's so urgent?" Balfruss was still woolly headed and his arms and legs felt heavy. Looking at the sky he guessed he'd been asleep three hours at most.

At first Ecko said nothing and kept fussing with the fire. When the water began to boil he brewed some of his stinky tea and offered Balfruss a cup. He was going to refuse, but then realised he didn't know much about the customs of the First People. The last thing he wanted to do was offend a new friend. They'd spoken about Ecko's family and his home, but more often he seemed happy to listen to the others when they talked.

"They are coming. Very soon now," Ecko said eventually.

He sipped at his tea and Balfruss stared at the brew. It was made from a black root and ground leaves, and some little white bits floated on top. The smell made him gag, and the first couple of mouthfuls were difficult to swallow. Despite that, he kept drinking it and by the time he reached the bottom of his cup the fuzziness of his thoughts was beginning to fade.

A few minutes later they heard a frantic pounding of hooves as two warriors rode into their camp with a third horse in tow.

"Are you Balfruss?" asked one of the riders.

"Yes."

The man was rigid with tension and his eyes were haunted. "What's happened?" asked Balfruss.

"I'm Garrow. You must come with me. You've been summoned to the palace." He turned his tired horse around and gestured at the empty saddle. The two men must have ridden through the night, as the capital was several hours away. A cold prickle of dread crept up Balfruss's spine.

As Balfruss climbed into the saddle he glanced over his shoulder towards Ecko. The tribesman seemed deep in prayer, but Balfruss was sure one eye opened and then closed again.

The sentries made no challenge as the three of them rode out of the camp at a gallop. Balfruss asked Garrow what had happened, but he wouldn't answer so they rode in tense silence.

After a couple of hours the horses were starting to tire. They would not make it all the way back to the palace before collapsing, so the riders were forced to divert off the main road and approach one of the staging areas. They were challenged long before they saw the Morrin on duty, but Garrow called out a password and they were allowed to approach.

The Morrin sentries were kind enough to light a couple of lanterns, but they kept their backs to the light to maintain their night vision. As his eyes adjusted to the faint glow, Balfruss saw the Morrin were heavily armoured and each had a sword on his belt and a crossbow in hand. He could hear soldiers snoring, and could just make out dark hillocks of the supply dumps rising above his head. Even this far into his own territory King Matthias was not taking any risks with provisions.

They exchanged their horses for fresh mounts and climbed back into the saddle. As soon as they reached the main road they went as fast as they dared in the dark. With only a few stars to light their way, the landscape around them was a sea of grey and purple shadows. The sound of the hooves scared away any nightlife, but Balfruss heard the faint whisper of bats on the hunt.

The urgency of the summons and the closed-mouthed warriors started to prey on Balfruss's mind. He started conjuring up countless scenarios and tried to prepare himself for the worst.

They seemed to be racing the dawn, but the sun crested the horizon and had risen well above it before Charas came into view. The replacement horses were starting to tire as well and he was afraid what would happen if they pushed them for much longer, but when Balfruss suggested they slow down he was told to keep going, even if it meant riding the animals to death.

By the time they rode through the city gates they'd already

passed a dozen wagons going in the opposite direction. The city was awake with traders setting out their wares in the streets. The warriors led him directly towards the Old City and then up the winding streets to the palace. As if they could sense the end of their journey was near, the horses found a sudden burst of energy that kept them going until they reached the palace gates.

The warriors leapt off their horses, while Balfruss managed to slide off without falling onto his face. His thighs burned and he felt it as if his legs wouldn't support his weight. They didn't give him any time to rest and he stumbled after Garrow towards the front doors. The back of his neck itched, and glancing around he saw at least two dozen warriors on the walls. Every man wore a bleak expression, as if blighted by a personal tragedy. Two heavily armed guards stood either side of the main doors, their expressions a perfect match for the others. Any time he passed a servant in the halls they looked on the verge of tears and many had red eyes. Balfruss focused his will and drew power from the Source. As it filled his being the aches and pains receded, until he was striding along at the same pace as the warriors. He would pay later for borrowing energy, but right now he needed a sharp body and mind.

To his surprise they entered the royal living quarters. The number of armed guards increased, until there were at least two stationed every few paces along the corridor. Eventually they reached an area that seemed to be the centre of all activity. Vannok was sat outside a door dozing on a chair, but as they drew near he came awake with a start, drawing his sword.

"Easy, Vann, it's me," said Balfruss. Vannok slowly relaxed and eventually let go of his weapon. Balfruss was about to ask what had happened when he smelled it. All he had to do was turn his head and look into the room, but he didn't. Not just yet. From the bags under his eyes and colour of his skin, Vannok had been awake all night.

"Get some rest," suggested Balfruss, but his friend stubbornly shook his head.

"Bring the others," said Vannok and the two warriors marched away.

Sensing that the immediate threat had passed Balfruss released the power he was holding.

"When?"

Vannok shook his head. "See it first, then ask your questions."

Balfruss braced himself and turned to look properly into the room. The first thing he noticed was the door had been staved in and broken off its hinges. The stout wood had not given up easily, as there were large splinters littering the threshold.

The curtains had been thrown open and a faint breeze stirred them, but it wasn't enough to dislodge the overpowering stench of death. As he stepped over the threshold Balfruss felt a faint remnant of power. An echo of what had happened. It also told him who had been here. The seed of fear in his stomach began to sprout.

The private quarters were spacious, bigger than any he'd seen in the palace, and yet they were sparsely decorated. No riches or great works of art decorated the walls. There were only a few personal items, and none of them looked valuable. He was only delaying the inevitable by not looking at the thing on the bed, but he wasn't ready.

Hung on the back wall, above a huge stone fireplace, was a six-foot sword with serrated edges like shark's teeth. It would be impossibly heavy and totally useless as a weapon. There wasn't a man alive who could wield it, and yet he knew there would be stories of men who could. In the far corner he spotted a small shrine devoted to the Maker with an old battered stone icon.

Beside it a tarnished old helmet sat on a shoulder-high pedestal. Balfruss guessed it was either a remnant from another age or a family heirloom. On the mantelpiece he saw a small faded painting of a beautiful blonde woman, but he didn't stare. It was too personal an item and he was starting to feel like a grave robber searching the pockets of the dead. No doubt all of the items had enormous sentimental value, and even a cursory glance told him there would be many myths and legends surrounding them. They were alive with history and pulsating with energy that enriched them, making them invaluable.

Unable to ignore it any longer, Balfruss walked through the open doorway into the master bedchamber. A large four-poster bed framed a bloodbath that he knew would haunt his nightmares for a long time. The shredded remains of a man's body lay spread out across the sheets. At first he thought there must be two victims as there was so much blood, most of which had dried and turned a ruddy brown. Pink flesh and stark white bones protruded where none should be showing. Bright purple and rich red innards spilled out of the torso, like scattered treasures tossed out of a chest of dead flesh. Purple coils of human rope were strewn around the floor, staining the rugs with filth. The stench of dead flesh filled his nostrils, working its way down into the pit of his stomach.

And the eyes. Unmercifully they remained intact in a face permanently marked with horrific pain. King Matthias's corpse stared at Balfruss. Bile rose up and seared the back of his throat. He struggled to swallow and was forced to turn away and take a minute to catch his breath. He had seen death and brutality before but this was something else. This murder had been conducted with malice and the victim had been terrorised. This was worse than anything he'd seen in an abattoir. The butcher showed mercy for the cattle, killing them as quickly and cleanly as possible. None had been shown here. The King had died in horrific agony.

"How?" someone asked. Balfruss didn't turn around as he was still trying to think it through. "How was this done?"

Balfruss waved the question away, struggling to believe what he was contemplating. "A moment, please."

He scanned the floor by the bed, but saw only faint scuff marks and the same indentations from heavy footprints in the rug over and over. No one but the King had walked in this bedchamber in a long time.

Someone grabbed his forearm, breaking his concentration. Acting on instinct Balfruss spun his wrist in a circle, broke their grip and shoved the person away. His time in the east had not just been about protecting the Desert King and learning local customs.

Balfruss turned to see Prince Thias stumbling back, his face haggard and etched with grief. Vannok was stood behind him, Talandra in the doorway. She seemed unable, or unwilling, to cross the threshold and enter the room.

"I'm sorry, Highness, I was lost in thought. I didn't see it was you," said Balfruss, adding a deep bow to his apology.

"Tell him," said Thias after a moment's pause. He was definitely cut from the same cloth as his father. Another man would have made more of the slight. The corpse at Balfruss's eye corner continued to torment him.

"The door was locked from the inside and the windows were sealed," explained Vannok. "Guards were posted at the end of the hallway and they came running when they heard the screams. When they couldn't open the door they broke it down."

"Are there any secret passageways in the palace? Any false walls?" asked Balfruss. He wanted to eliminate the obvious, before he considered the alternative.

"None," said Thias with confidence. Behind him Talandra's expression told a different story.

"There are none in this part of the palace," said Talandra. The others looked at her with surprise but she just shrugged. As the head of intelligence it was her business to know such things.

"Do you know how this was done?" asked Thias.

"I can guess," hedged Balfruss. "I'm certain magic was involved, and I know who is responsible; beyond that I cannot be sure."

Thias seemed lost in thought, but eventually he asked, "Was it the Warlock?"

"Yes, Highness."

"Tell me your theory."

Balfruss wondered if he should, but from their expressions, half an answer wouldn't be enough. "It's a myth, from a different time when magic users used to be called Sorcerers. It's said they could Dreamwalk. Leave behind their flesh and travel great distances as a spirit."

"In their sleep?" asked Talandra, finally coming into the room.

"Something more like a trance, brought about with drugs and music to focus the mind."

"And while, dreamwalking," said Thias, stumbling over the new term, "these Sorcerers could hurt people?"

"I believe the King was asleep and the Warlock entered his dreams. In the King's mind he may have fought something monstrous, maybe a huge beast, and it tore him apart. Somehow the Warlock was able to make it real. That would explain the wounds."

Thias stared at him and Balfruss saw something shift behind his eyes. "Can you do it? Enter dreams and kill people?"

"No," said Balfruss. "I wouldn't even know where to begin."

"So any one of us could be murdered in our sleep," said Talandra.

"To do something like that would be incredibly taxing, physically and mentally. A lot of power would be needed. Any nearby Battlemage would be able to sense the build-up of energy."

"What do you propose to prevent further attacks?" asked Thias. Balfruss didn't even realise he'd come up with a plan until Thias asked the question.

"A Battlemage must be taken off the front lines and brought here to guard you," he said to Thias, as the successor to the throne. "One would be enough to keep watch while you sleep and prevent it happening again."

It was a gamble. Not only because his proposal was built on a theory, but taking someone off the front line would increase the pressure on the others. They also had no idea if the Warlock would try something similar in the future.

"See that it's done," Thias said to Balfruss. Without another word Thias walked out, followed closely by Vann and Talandra, leaving him alone with the body of the dead King.

Balfruss wondered if the mind link would work over such a great distance, but even as he considered it Thule's voice came into his mind.

"*I am here, brother.*"

CHAPTER 19

Balfruss was ready to collapse from exhaustion. A few hours' sleep the night before had not been enough, and the long ride through the night had sapped his energy further. He desperately needed sleep, but before he could lie down there were arrangements to be made with the other Battlemages. It took a while to organise, as he was communicating over a long distance through Thule, but eventually they came up with a plan.

For the next three nights he would remain at the palace and guard the royal family from further attack. After that the Battlemages would take turns on the front line and at the palace. He was needed on the battlefield, for his strength and control, but he knew the others would be able to manage without him against the Splinters. Apart from Finn, all of them were experienced and accomplished Battlemages in their own right. In three days Darius would replace him and then Eloise after that.

Although no one had said it, they planned to exclude Finn from rotating away from the front line. For all his power, he couldn't effectively protect the royal family and no one wanted to take the risk. Balfruss guessed that the awkward conversation about this would be left to him. It was something to worry about another day.

There might come a point in the war when this method of

protecting the royal family wasn't necessary, if the army was pushed back as far as the city. Again that was something beyond his control, so Balfruss focused on the immediate problem.

He'd been given generous accommodation with spacious rooms, but the only thing that drew his attention was the bed. If he needed to be up all night, then he had to get some rest. It was early evening when someone woke him and he was summoned to dinner with the royal family.

Even before entering the room Balfruss heard raised voices and walked into the middle of an argument around the table. The Generals had returned from the front line with what sounded like disastrous news. Graegor was shouting at Vannok, while Thias and Talandra were unsuccessfully trying to calm them down.

"You were wrong to give the order," said Graegor.

"Please, sit down," said Thias, but both Generals ignored him. Vannok angrily shook his head. "You'd advocate genocide?"

"What are you talking about?" scoffed Graegor. "You're exaggerating and you panicked."

A thick vein began to pulse in Vannok's forehead. He seemed seconds away from punching the grizzled General in the face.

"I recognise that look. Step back Vann," said Balfruss, stepping in front of his friend.

"Stay out of this," snarled Graegor. "It doesn't concern you."

"I fight in the war every day, so it does concern me," said Balfruss, facing off against the old General.

"You know nothing of war, boy," sneered Graegor.

Balfruss laughed, a dry bitter sound. "Have you ever travelled abroad? Ever seen what else is out there?"

"What does that mean?" asked the old General.

"It means there's more to the world than your country and your wars," said Balfruss. "You stare at the horizon and think only of Seveldrom. You're blinkered and ignorant."

"We need to talk this through, calmly," said Thias, but it wasn't enough.

"What did you call me?" snarled Graegor.

"Graegor," shouted Talandra, her voice echoing off the walls. She patiently waited until the General looked in her direction. "You knew my father for more years than I've been alive. I know it hurts, but picking fights here won't honour all that he accomplished. We need your wisdom and your strength, now more than ever."

Graegor still seemed poised on the verge of violence, but Balfruss ignored his bluster. It took Balfruss a moment to realise Graegor's rage was misplaced anger at the loss of his oldest friend. Rage was the only way he knew how to express himself. If not for his friends, Balfruss knew he might have ended up the same. Thankfully his rage had been tempered. But what would the General become without the King?

"I suggest we eat and then talk about this after," said Thias, and no one disagreed.

The dining room was not one of the larger banquet halls for visiting dignitaries, but a space for ten to sit comfortably around a table. The heirs took after their father, as the meal was modest fare compared to some feasts Balfruss had seen. Not one single platter was overladen, and the food was simple, roasted beef from the south with local vegetables. The only departure was the unusual spices, which were not from Seveldrom. To Balfruss, who had been eating lamb and goat for years, the beef tasted delicious. He soaked up the thick gravy with crusty flat bread that fell apart in his hands. The sweet greens, sliced potatoes and redshoots were incredibly filling and the spices made his tongue tingle.

They ate in silence, unanimously agreeing without speaking that they wouldn't interrupt the meal with talk about the war. When everyone had eaten their fill, the silence stretched on until Balfruss's ears hummed.

"Perhaps," suggested Talandra when the strain was making everyone fidget. "We could try this again. More calmly this time." She gestured towards Vannok to start.

"We were following the King's orders," said Vannok, "waiting for them to attack and engage with our infantry, while archers and then cavalry cut into their flanks. It was going as planned, until we saw their foot soldiers."

"You shouldn't have changed the order," said Graegor, but Talandra laid a hand on the General's arm, calming him.

"What was different?" asked Balfruss, preferring they focus on him than each other and get into another argument.

"At first I thought it was some sort of trick. Another illusion like the leviathan, but it wasn't." Vannok swallowed hard and shook his head sadly. He hadn't quite finished eating, but he pushed his plate away. "They were using prisoners, Balfruss. Prisoners from Shael, armed with paltry weapons and driven forward with whips."

Graegor opened his mouth to speak again, but Talandra held up a hand and the General snapped his mouth shut.

"They were malnourished, filthy, barely able to walk, never mind fight. I think they were sent just to tire our men. We couldn't attack them. It would have been a massacre. There were men and women too, but you could barely tell them apart, they were so skinny. I couldn't give the order to kill them," said Vannok.

"Morrin warriors are men and women. Same as the Vorga," Graegor said stubbornly.

Vannok's anger seemed to have evaporated. His response was calm and deeply troubled. "The people of Shael are academics, scholars and sailors for the most. You know that, Graegor."

It was the first time Balfruss had heard his friend use the old warrior's name, and he had the impression Vannok didn't use it often. It also reminded the older man that they were both

Generals, despite the difference in age. It took the wind out of Graegor and surprisingly he nodded in agreement.

"What I don't like, and I hate saying," Graegor muttered slowly, forcing the words out between his teeth, "is it looks as if we don't know what we're doing. As if your father was the only one of us with any knowledge of war. It wasn't a real victory. They only gained ground because we pulled back, but it's the first day they've not left the battlefield beaten and bloody. It will fire them up."

"But they won't try the same tactic again tomorrow," said Thias and Talandra nodded.

"They can't."

Balfruss was missing something. "What happened?"

"It was one of yours, the big lad, that sorted them out," said Graegor and Balfruss knew they were talking about Finn. "He put up some kind of a wall so the Shael prisoners couldn't attack us while we . . . pulled back." Graegor might have conceded that it had been necessary, but he wouldn't say it had been a retreat.

"The men say he was like a Titan from the old stories," said Thias, a note of wonder creeping into his voice. "One man against an army, and he just held them there. They tried pushing the Shael prisoners forward, but none of them could move. Arrows couldn't go through or over his barrier. I have two separate reports that say he caught fire at one point." A nerve twitched in Balfruss's face, but he said nothing to deny it as impossible.

"Once we pulled back he let down the shield, but they just left the Shael prisoners and withdrew," said Vannok.

"We've set up a refugee camp east of the city, in the town of Tormandan. It will be a long march for the refugees, but they can't stay here," said Thias.

"Why not?" asked Balfruss.

"The city is stocked for a siege, and we've already moved out as many people as we can to the country," said Talandra. "If the army gets pushed back here, the quartermaster has made preparations. The siege would be over in three days if the refugees stayed. We'd all starve to death."

"How many?" asked Balfruss, wondering if Thule could hear this conversation. "How many refugees are there from Shael?"

The two Generals looked at each other and Vannok gestured for Graegor to answer.

"Maybe five thousand. Just thrown away like they were gristle and fat."

They talked a bit more about the war, but eventually they couldn't ignore what everyone had been carefully avoiding.

"There will be a state funeral," said Thias in a lull between conversations. "Preparations are being made, but the people already know. We couldn't stop the news from spreading."

Balfruss considered asking about when Thias would take the throne but changed his mind. It would happen, but not until King Matthias had been given his final rest in the flames in keeping with the traditions of the Maker.

Graegor and Vannok planned to return to the front line in the morning, while Thias would stay in the city for the time being. Hyram was notably absent, but Vannok waved it away when asked. Unable or unwilling to accept that his father was really dead, Hyram had chosen to stay with the men. There were rumours that Hyram had been fighting and Balfruss thought it very likely.

It was early when Balfruss received a summons to take up his post outside the royal chambers. He suspected they'd not slept the previous night and were feeling utterly drained, physically and emotionally. Even without a draught from the apothecary they would sleep, which also put them at their most vulnerable.

At first Balfruss patrolled up and down the corridors, but soon he became bored and sat for a time, reading a book he'd taken from the palace library. The broad chair left for him was extremely hard and uncomfortable, perhaps to help keep him awake, but a kind servant had left him a selection of plump cushions. He filled the chair and sat on them all to stop his backside from going numb through the long hours of the night. The book was a history of modern religions written by an impartial academic. Normally it would be an incredibly dry and tedious subject filled with names and dates, but the author kept it interesting with wit and humour. Having spent some time in the far east and seeing how far back their religions stretched, Balfruss was keen to discover the roots of the modern faiths in the west that had crept into Seveldrom. Three hundred years ago no one had heard of the Lord and Lady of Light, and yet no one could tell him the origin of the Church of Holy Light. He hated mysteries, and for the first time in months, there was time to investigate.

Something light brushed at the edges of his mind and Balfruss was immediately alert, focusing his will and drawing power from the Source. The book fell to the floor as he stood up, amplifying his senses to identify who approached. A shield of energy crackled and formed around him, a blue shell that made his ears hum. A familiar presence drew closer and even before he saw who it was, Balfruss knew their identity.

The Warlock slowly walked towards him, holding up his hands in surrender. "I only came to talk."

"What do you want?" asked Balfruss, refusing to lower his shield.

"To say I'm sorry."

"Sorry?"

"For what happened to the King." Torval shook his head sadly. "I know he was a great man. I didn't want to do it, but we all have our orders."

"You're not sorry at all," said Balfruss. "I think you enjoyed it, because it was something you'd never done before. Dreamwalking is supposed to be impossible. No one has been able to do it for centuries. I doubt even the Grey Council could've managed it." Balfruss shook his head. "No, you're proud of what you accomplished. The murder of the King was just an unfortunate by-product of your experiment."

Torval stared at him with an unreadable expression for a long time. The only sound Balfruss could hear was the rapid beating of his heart. Sweat beaded in his hairline and began to run down the sides of his face, but he ignored it. He ignored everything and focused. He checked his shield and mentally prepared for the fight of his life.

Slowly a grin spread across Torval's face.

"I told you. We're two of a kind," he said with a delighted laugh. "You understand me so well. It was amazing, Balfruss. I've achieved so much!"

"We are nothing alike," said Balfruss in a cold voice.

Torval shook his head, but still wore a smile. Balfruss almost lashed out to wipe the smug grin off his face, but thought better of it. "One day they will be afraid of you too. One day they will ask you to leave, to make it easier for them."

"They wouldn't do that. I'm needed here."

"But for how long?" asked Torval, tipping his head to one side. "Consider this. If you win the war, if you somehow manage to defeat Taikon's army and me, then what? Do you think they will welcome you into their homes? Ask you to stay and protect them?"

"This is my home. They have no reason to fear me, or send me away."

"Don't be stupid. I know you're smarter than that," snapped Torval, his mood rapidly switching in the blink of an eye. "Don't talk to me like I'm one of them. The soldiers and Generals. They're worms. Maggots in a rotting corpse. I could wipe them all out if I wanted. Just like that." The Warlock slapped his hands together, but it didn't make a sound. His eyes were feverish, his whole face filled with a desperate hunger.

"We are the new Gods of this world. Forget the churches and their faceless stone idols. They should be building temples to our glory. We can do anything we want. We're only limited by our imagination, but you don't believe me, do you?" He was ranting now and his eyes showed white all the way around. Not trusting himself to answer, Balfruss shook his head.

"Then answer me this. You were taught at the Red Tower, yes? How long did it take you to realise the teachers were lying?"

Balfruss considered the question. "They taught me and the others as best they could. They didn't lie."

The Warlock pursed his lips, one eyebrow raised. "Really?" His mood quickly shifted again and just as suddenly he was smiling again. "I think you're being modest. I think you played the same games I did as a boy in the dormitories. Ah, I see you did," laughed the Warlock, reading something from his expression.

They were not supposed to do it, but just as warriors sparred to test their skills, students at the Red Tower tested their strength against one another when no one was watching. Rumours were rife about pupils burning out their power in unauthorised duels, but he never saw or heard about it actually happening to any students while studying there.

"You noticed it during the fights in the dormitories, didn't you?" said Torval, and when Balfruss didn't reply his expression turned sour again. "Didn't you?" he shouted, spittle flying from his mouth. Balfruss was so startled he almost lost grip on his shield. The guards at the end of the corridor should have heard Torval yelling, and yet seconds ticked by in silence as they stared at each other. Somehow the Warlock was muffling all sounds, maybe even silencing the whole corridor so that their conversation remained private.

"I noticed after three months," Balfruss said finally. "At first I thought it was a mistake. They were the teachers and I was just a boy. I was there to learn. I didn't have their experience, so I trusted them."

Torval nodded encouragingly and smiled. "You asked them, didn't you?"

Balfruss cast his mind back to his days at the Red Tower. "The teachers said I was mistaken. That I hadn't been concentrating properly the first time."

"It's one of the first tenets laid down on the first day you arrive. Every student is told the same thing." The Warlock was getting worked up again, but this time his rage was directed at their teachers who were missing and presumed dead. "We're all different. We're all special." His tone was mocking and nasal, like one of the instructors Balfruss remembered. "And we all have different levels of strength."

"And a Battlemage's strength will never change over time," finished Balfruss.

"Exactly," said Torval, jabbing a finger towards him. "And it's the biggest lie they ever told."

It was dangerous, deadly in fact, for a Battlemage and anyone nearby if they lost concentration, but it was possible to keep reaching for more power from the Source and stretch what you could wield. Push it too far and the power would surge through you, burn out your mind and scour away all ability to touch the Source as it melted the flesh from your bones.

But if you pushed just hard enough, if you walked the razor's edge long enough, you could hold on to a little more each time. A trickle. A drop. But over time those drops added up. And if you practised every day for months, or even years, it could make a huge difference to your strength.

During his first term at the Red Tower, Balfruss had duelled a second-year student called Pyson. Balfruss was thrown the entire length of the dormitory and pinned to the wall. The bruises from his beating stayed with him for weeks. His opponent had been just too strong. Six months later his strength surpassed Pyson's and he'd taken great pleasure in thrashing the older boy. He didn't know why, but Balfruss found himself telling Torval the story.

"The same happened to me."

"Why do you serve Taikon?" asked Balfruss, finally releasing his shield. If Torval intended to kill him he would have done so by now. "Surely you can see how insane he is?"

"He is mad," admitted Torval, "but he keeps pulling back only to skirt across to the other side. Recently he's spent more time over the line, but that's partly my fault."

"Was he just another experiment, like the Splinters?"

The Warlock sat down on a window ledge and looked up at the night sky. He seemed completely at ease. Balfruss wondered if he could catch the Warlock unawares and kill him before he could defend himself, but his instincts told him he would be too slow.

"It was an experiment of a kind," conceded Torval. "I gave him the artefact to help him unite the west. The Zecorrans and Morrin in the north needed a bauble to make them believe he was their prophet." Torval laughed at that. "I didn't think the idiot would swallow it. He's more paranoid than I thought."

"And now?"

"It's changed him in ways I never anticipated." Torval seemed genuinely puzzled, which was probably something rare, because for once he didn't have all the answers. "But I'm making the best of it. We both get something from our arrangement."

"Why did you come here tonight?" asked Balfruss, quickly tiring of Torval's rambling and rapid mood swings. "What do you want?"

Torval's smile showed far too many teeth. "I want you to

realise that the others mean nothing. I want you to admit that we're better than all of them. That we're superior."

Balfruss shook his head. "I'm the same as every other man."

"Hold on to your false modesty a while longer," said Torval, getting to his feet. "But it won't last. The day will come when you realise we're far beyond these mortal men. On that day, I will face you on the battlefield and we will shake the very foundations of the earth. The sky will split and mountains will tumble into the sea. We will bend the world to our will and we will show them exactly what we are capable of." Torval's eyes were fevered. "And even if you win, they will hate you and fear you like no other man in history. Because they will know, deep down in their hearts, that Gods walk among them."

The Warlock started to walk away down the corridor and with each step he faded like a desert mirage. Before he reached the end of the corridor he'd vanished.

CHAPTER 20

Normally Talandra sought out the peace and quiet of the royal chapel when she needed a moment alone. She came to sit quietly and think, although not for the usual reasons. If the Patriarch asked, she would lie and tell him her thoughts were of a spiritual nature, rather than espionage and politics. Today she didn't have to lie.

At any moment she expected her father to come blustering through the door, make his way down the row of pews and sit down beside her. If she closed her eyes and focused she could almost smell him. His presence still echoed along the corridors of the palace.

It would be a long time before she stopped looking for him.

Everyone in the palace and the city grieved with her family, but all of them had only known the monarch, not the man who wore the crown. Talandra would never claim that her father had been perfect, but he'd been a steady and encouraging force her entire life.

The chapel door creaked open but Talandra didn't turn around. Shani sat down beside her and together they stared in silence at the stained-glass windows that depicted creation at the hands of the Maker. She'd grown up hearing the stories all her life. The seven wonders, the seven early races of mankind, the seven oceans and the seven sins that mark the fall of humanity. Despite not being deeply religious, and even after she learned about other faiths, she always felt most at ease in a church of the Maker.

As a child, Talandra had questioned the Matriarch, a skinny woman with a shrill voice, who had grown increasingly exasperated by her endless questions. Eventually she'd resorted to avoiding Talandra or quoting scripture when she didn't know the answer. It was one of the most disappointing moments in her life as a child. The sudden realisation that adults didn't know everything and that no one had all of the answers. The skinny Matriarch had died a few years ago and a more patient priest had taken her place.

Shani's hand crept into Talandra's, startling her.

"You shouldn't," said the Princess.

"It's not unseemly to offer comfort to a grieving friend," said Shani, giving Talandra's hand a squeeze. After a moment she returned it, glad for the warmth and contact of another person.

"Did you pray to the Maker for your father?" asked Shani in a hushed voice. The chapel was large enough for twenty people but they were alone. A door at the back to the priest's quarters stood open, but Talandra thought she was elsewhere today.

"Yes I did," said Talandra, her voice muffled by the thick blue and grey curtains that covered the cold stone walls. "And I prayed for the Prince of Yerskania."

Talandra felt Shani stiffen beside her. "Why didn't the Queen fight?"

"She can't take the risk."

"The risk of what?"

"That her country will become another Shael," said Talandra. It seemed apt to be talking of sorrow and death in the chapel. The Maker's scripture was full of stories of warring brothers, duplicitous Kings and Queens and savage armies that clashed to claim countries of their own before the land had names and boundaries. "Most of Yerskania's warriors are fighting here, with the rest of the western army. There aren't enough members of the Watch to stop an invasion into Yerskania. Her country and people have already suffered, with thousands of her warriors dying for her disobedience, and now this. A personal attack on her family."

The same family had ruled in Yerskania for generations and now her son would never father any children. One of her daughters could take the throne, but only if Yerskania were free. Thinking about the succession of Yerskania reminded her it was time to begin the process of finding Thias a wife. She had a few names in mind already, those who would be useful allies in the future.

"I've just received a report from Zecorria," said Shani. "High Priest Filbin has returned home and he's started making some noise."

"That's good news at least," said Talandra, turning her hand over and looking at the grey veins beneath the skin on Shani's hand.

"There are rumblings about blasphemy, pollution of the faith, even a story of him flagellating himself in public."

Talandra raised an eyebrow. "Is it true?"

Shani shrugged. "Perhaps. Filbin has yet to speak out in public against Taikon, but it will happen soon. It's a shame the people of Yerskania are so divided among different religions."

"Then we need to unite them around something else. Most people think the Yerskani care only about profit, but they're incredibly patriotic."

"The Queen," said Shani and Talandra smiled.

"Right now the people are angry. They were grieving for their loved ones who died in the war, and now many feel personally slighted. They loved the Prince and they love their Queen. He was the future of their country and now it's been taken from them."

"Perizzi is a city full of merchants," said Shani, shaking her head, her tawny eyes narrowed in frustration. Talandra couldn't help staring at her lips as Shani thought it through. "Surely you don't want to arm them?"

"No. They wouldn't survive more than a day. But a city full of merchants means a lot of money and goods that need to be protected. The Drassi are supposedly part of the western alliance, and yet we've not seen one of them fighting on the battlefield."

"Because no one was paying them to fight," said Shani.

"The merchants have the money to hire their own army. It will have to be done carefully and with some subtlety, so the Yerskani still believe it's their rebellion, but it will be the Drassi who free Perizzi from Taikon's stain."

"They'll need to unite behind someone charismatic," mused Shani, lightly running a finger across the back of Talandra's hand in a way that she found very distracting. "Someone eye-catching and bold."

"A fat merchant with a toupee won't inspire anyone," murmured Talandra, closing her eyes as Shani's delicate fingers moved across the skin of her forearm.

"How about a bold blonde beauty from Yerskania?" asked Shani.

"That sounds perfect."

With obvious reluctance Shani stood up. "I'll get in contact with Roza. See you tonight?" she asked.

"I'd like that."

The chapel door opened and a royal guard entered.

"Sorry to disturb you," he whispered, staring at the altar with reverence. "But Prince Thias asked to see you."

Shani walked past the guard, who barely looked at her as he'd become so familiar with her presence. He had no idea of her value or importance to Talandra. If recent events had taught her anything, it was that she should enjoy every moment because tomorrow it could all end. Once Thias had taken the throne she could look to her own future. With the feeling of Shani's touch lingering on her skin, Talandra hurried out of the chapel.

CHAPTER 21

The Sheepdog and Whistle wasn't the nicest tavern in Charas, but the food was decent, the owner seemed honest and the beer wasn't watered down. It mostly catered to locals rather than travellers, but a lot of people had already left the city in readiness for the siege. Without the local warriors it would have been empty, so the owner voiced no complaints.

The crowd was probably louder than his usual, but there were a couple of big lads lurking, just in case anything got out of hand. As Vargus came through the front door most heads in the room turned his way and everyone waved or smiled. He didn't know more than a dozen by name, but they all knew him. Vargus tried his best to ignore the tingling across his skin from so many people staring.

A locally brewed pale ale was on tap, but there was also imported dark ale from Yerskania for those with a hankering. In the current climate the portly owner kept the barrel out of sight, but he was happy to fetch Vargus a pint when he asked.

Hargo and the others were already well into their cups by the time he sat down. The mood in the tavern was sombre, as it was across the whole city, and he doubted these were the only people in Charas tonight that were toasting the late King. Orran was absent from the usual crowd and there were some new faces, lads who'd recently joined the squad. There were also a few noticeable absences, Tan, Curly and, more recently, Rudd. The skinny man had died horribly, gurgling and gasping for breath, as blood pumped from a savage wound in his throat. It took him less than a minute to die.

"There you are," slurred Hargo, his eyes red rimmed and bloodshot. "Was jus' telling the boys about you spearing that fucker in the throat."

Vargus approached the table and a seat was cleared for him.

"Tell them. Tell them what he did," insisted Hargo, his head lolling forward as if he might fall asleep at any second.

"He just kept walking round and round," muttered Vargus. "Like a headless chicken. Took him a long time to die."

"Funniest thing I ever saw," said Hargo, but he didn't laugh and didn't look even slightly amused. A few smiled to indulge the big man, but no one laughed. It wasn't something any of them thought was funny. Not any more.

The war was taking its toll on all of them. This break from the front line was overdue for the squad, but he wondered if there would be another.

For a time Vargus sipped his beer and let the conversation wash over him. The streets outside were wet from a recent shower, and he was tempted to take off his boots and leave them by the fire. He'd avoided losing any toes on the campaign so far and didn't want to start now. After a few minutes he realised that while the others were still talking Hargo was staring.

"Are you all right? Because you look like shit," said Vargus.

Hargo grinned. "I feel it."

"You should do that in your tent."

This time Hargo's laugh was genuine. "Not that. The thrill. The thrill of being alive."

Vargus noticed he wasn't slurring his words as badly as before.

Looking down at Hargo's half-empty glass, he suspected it was the big man's first. It didn't even count as a warm-up for him.

"What's brought this on?"

"When we're up to our balls in it, the mud and the blood, there's no time to think. It's just hack and slice and chop," said Hargo, touching the Yerskani cleaver at his waist. "All I can do is try to stay alive." He stopped suddenly and looked away, wiped at his face and took a minute.

Vargus rested a hand on the other man's shoulder. "We're all scared of dying. Me more than most."

When Hargo turned back, his eyes were still red, but they were dry. "The Brotherhood, or whatever you want to call it. I know it's changed me, but I never believed the other stuff you said. About being glad to be breathing. I thought it was religious shit you were spouting."

"I'm not a priest, you got that, you big bastard?" said Vargus, digging his fingers into Hargo's shoulder. He relented when the big man nodded. "I told you about it, but the idea was passed on to me from someone else. I didn't start it. So don't go making me into some kind of saint or leader."

Vargus sat back and slowly sipped his beer, forcing himself to calm down. Hargo hadn't taken offence at being knocked on his arse in public. He wouldn't take offence at being called names.

"Well, you said it, and the words took root. I didn't want them to, but they did," said Hargo, breaking the strained silence between them. "Some of the lads wouldn't have made it this far without your words. That's all I wanted to say."

Vargus looked closely at the man who'd fought beside him every day in the war. His face was harder and leaner than when they'd first met, and his eyes burned with a hunger that hadn't been there before. Scars and cuts marked his thick arms and a piece of his right ear was missing. To look at him, most would only see a thick-headed brute, or maybe a good soldier. But

Vargus could see there was a lot more going on behind his eyes than he let on.

"One day, some bastard will get me," said Vargus in a whisper. "Could be a lad on his first day, just about ready to piss himself. Could be some big Vorga bitch, all sharp teeth and claws. But I'll bleed and die just like any man." Hargo shifted uncomfortably in his chair but didn't interrupt. "You saw what happened the other day?"

"Three Drassi blades came straight for you. Went past everyone else on the line."

"You know why?"

Hargo shrugged, playing ignorant. Vargus waited and eventually he answered. "I can guess. They probably know about the Brotherhood by now, and wanted to get rid of you."

"Just like they did with the King," said Vargus. "They think cutting off the head will kill it. So you've got to stop using my name. I can't be tied to the Brotherhood any more. If any new lads ask, then tell them about it, but don't mention me. It can't end when I die. I barely stopped those three, and still ended up in hospital. Next time they'll send ten, or twenty. Even if it's not them, my luck will fail one day."

"I'll tell the others," said Hargo. "But I still owe you."

Vargus drained the last of his ale and held out the empty tankard. "Then you can buy me drinks until I pass out and piss myself."

"Sounds good," said Hargo with a grin.

The front door banged open and a few men flinched at the noise. Orran came strutting in as if he'd just found out a rich uncle had died and left him a fortune. He sat down at the table and waited until Hargo returned before sharing the joy.

"You found your whore then," said Hargo, passing them both a drink.

"The Blessed Mother, she was not," said Orran, slurping at his drink. "I asked her to do something I'd not tried before. Something new."

"I don't want to hear it," said Vargus, turning away.

"If this story ends with her shoving a finger up your arse, I don't want to know either," Hargo warned him.

"So I closed my eyes," continued Orran, ignoring them both. "And all of sudden there was music and this weird tingling."

Vargus raised an eyebrow at Hargo, who shook his head. "Don't. Ask."

Hargo couldn't resist. "All right. What was it?"

"She had one of my balls in her mouth and was humming a tune," said Orran. "It was amazing. I came so hard I almost blinded myself."

"Gahhh, we don't want to know," spat Vargus.

"I feel so alive!" Orran drank the rest of his beer in a couple of long gulps and headed back to the bar. "Come on girls, try to keep up," he called back.

When the door flew open again Vargus didn't look around until a peculiar silence fell on the room. A haggard man dressed in torn clothes stumbled in, coughing and gasping as if he had the damp lung. His wide eyes were ringed with purple shadows and he was desperately searching the crowd for someone. When he saw Vargus a spasm passed through his body.

"Hey, no beggars in here," said the owner, nodding to one of his lads with a cosh.

"Wait," said Vargus, approaching the ragged man. "I'll take care of him." The last vestiges of the stranger's energy drained away and he fell into Vargus's arms. The man was just skin and bone. Every drop of fat and muscle had been leached off his frame. His cheeks were hollow and his breath was sickly sweet. An unnatural warmth radiated from his body and Vargus knew he was close to death.

The man's clothes were caked with mud and dust from the

road, and there were brown stains down the front of his thread-bare shirt. As Vargus helped him into a chair the stranger began to cough so violently his whole body shook with vicious spasms. After a few minutes the coughing subsided and there was blood around his mouth.

"It's the pox!" shouted someone. "The red pox is back!"

"Maker protect us."

"Get him out of here," said the owner. "If he's sick, I don't want him in here."

"Who is he?" asked Hargo. All traces of the drunken act were gone.

Vargus wasn't sure how to answer. In the end he went for the simplest of truths. "He's my brother."

"Then he's our brother," said Orran.

"You don't understand," said Vargus as the stranger started coughing again. "He's a . . . blood relative."

"I didn't know you had any," said Orran.

"I'll take care of him," said Vargus, pulling the stranger to his feet and putting a bony arm across his shoulders. The man was leaning on Vargus with all of his weight, but he barely noticed the difference. "He just needs some rest and a draught from the apothecary. It's not contagious."

"Do you want some help?" asked Hargo, holding open the front door.

"We'll be fine. Go back to your drinks."

Vargus could feel the others watching, but he didn't turn around. When they were a few streets away he lowered the stranger to the ground, propping him up against a wall. He was barely conscious and his eyes kept rolling back in his head. Blood dripped from one nostril and the skin at the corners of his mouth was cracked and peeling. Gripping the stranger's face in one hand Vargus repeatedly slapped him until he came awake.

"Kai? Is that you?"

"Help me, Weaver," gasped the dying man.

"What happened?"

"They're gone. All gone," sobbed Kai. "They burned down every shrine, raped and slaughtered my priests. All my followers were purged. Those who wouldn't convert were drowned or burned. Some are just playing along, but now they're being forced to mouth prayers to that Lantern fuck. I'm finished."

"Where is this happening?"

"Everywhere!" said Kai, grabbing at him with grubby hands. "Help me."

For a brief moment Vargus considered leaving him to die in the street. No one besides him would know the truth, and Kai wouldn't last the night without help. Someone would find him in the morning, think him a beggar and that would be the end of it. If their positions were reversed, he knew it's what Kai would do.

"Just be glad I'm not you," he said, picking up Kai and putting him over one shoulder with ease.

They received a few curious glances, but no one paid them any real attention. A pair of drunks was not uncommon, especially with warriors on leave in the city. Vargus passed a few groups of warriors in a far worse condition, sleeping or vomiting loudly in back alleys. Units of city militia were already seeing to the worst of them. Scooping up those warriors who had passed out, and herding others who could walk back to their lodgings for the night.

Intimate noises from alleyways caught Vargus's ears and almost every shadowy doorway and dark corner seemed occupied. The working boys and girls in the city were making a fortune. Nothing fired a man's passion like walking on a knife edge and courting death, day after day.

The long walk into the Old City became more difficult as they moved uphill. Kai kept drifting in and out of consciousness, muttering to himself and occasionally farting, but Vargus ignored him and kept walking.

Warm light spilled onto the street at regular intervals from taverns, and bursts of laughter and music made Vargus pause in his lonely trek. More than anything he wanted to step inside one of the inns, spend the night enjoying himself and forget about his responsibilities. A few drinks would numb the pain and a dozen more would help him forget his own name. It was tempting and once again he considered putting down his burden.

At the end of the street loomed the Cathedral of the Maker. As was traditional, lanterns and candles burned inside throughout the night. The candlelight shone into the street in a dozen colours through stained glass, painting the damp stones in hues of red, gold, yellow and blue. The huge church was a reminder of what could be accomplished, and how worship could be sustained over the long centuries, even when its deity was absent.

With a sigh he turned off the main street, walked past a large temple devoted to the Blessed Mother, and stopped outside a run-down old building. A dozen people were waiting outside the shrine, strangers to one another, and yet all of them had been called here by an instinct they didn't understand. Most of them were locals, but one was a Morrin and two were Drassi women, rich merchants dressed in demure but expensive silk robes.

As Vargus forced open the warped doors and went inside, Kai stirred and then came awake. A small cloud of black specks swirled in the air around him, even though he'd not disturbed any of the rotting food and filth that littered the ground. Once inside the old building, Kai regained a little vigour. Vargus propped him up against the back wall where he managed to stay on his feet unsupported.

The twelve strangers came inside and as one they knelt before the ragged man. Vargus moved to one side. He didn't belong, but was unwilling to leave just yet.

"Master," said one of the locals, and the others echoed him.

"My faithful children," said Kai, wiping the blood from his mouth with the sleeve of his ragged shirt. "I'm glad you're here. I didn't want to die alone."

"Give me a command, Lord, and it shall be done," said one of the Drassi merchants. She bowed towards Kai, her forehead brushing the filth, but she didn't seem to notice the dirt or the stench.

"Ask any boon of us," said someone else, and the others were quick to agree.

"There is little that can be done." Kai's smile was sad, and he seemed to have accepted his fate.

"Surely there must be something. We will do anything."

"Anything, Lord. Just ask."

A sly look crept across Kai's features.

"Don't do it, Kai," said Vargus. The faithful were shocked at his informal address, but he ignored their disapproving looks. "Go in peace. Leave them alone."

Kai sneered. "When your end comes, brother, let us see if you're so accepting."

"I could stop you," said Vargus, but they both knew it to be an empty threat. He wouldn't interfere.

"Command us, Lord," said one of the faithful.

Using what must have been the last reserves of his strength, Kai stood and held out his hands above his congregation, as if warming himself in front of a fire. "Do you offer yourself to me? All that you are. All that you will be, from this day forward. Heart, body and soul."

"Yes, Lord," they said in unison.

"Swear it. Swear it on your immortal souls."

"We swear it, Lord," they chanted, without hesitation or a moment's thought about the consequences.

A cold blue light began to burn behind Kai's eyes, something ancient and malevolent.

"Do you have any coins?" he asked. One of the Drassi merchants offered him a heavy purse from which he selected a dozen small silver coins. Holding them in both hands Kai held them to his lips and whispered. "This is my body, this is my blood."

Kai placed a coin on the tongue of each of his followers, repeating the mantra before moving onto the next.

He switched language and began speaking in an ancient tongue that had been dead for centuries, but Vargus could still understand it. Kai's mouth was moving, but the noises didn't match the shape of his lips. They were sounds no man had ever made, hissings and clicks interspaced with shrill notes like a bird. The air in the shrine grew heavy and still, as if they'd been plunged deep underwater. Pressure built up against Vargus's ears and he backed away from the congregation until his shoulders brushed the far wall.

Kai crooked a finger at one of the women. She stood up and eagerly approached. Her face was rapt with ecstasy, as if this were a moment she'd always dreamed about. With trembling hands Kai embraced her like a lover, his arms hugging her close to his chest. The woman melted against him, completely at peace as she rested her head on his shoulder and closed her eyes. As a result she didn't see the long teeth that began to protrude from Kai's mouth, or the horrified expressions on the faces of the faithful. The woman managed a faint mewling noise as he bit down into her neck, but that was her only protest. Blood began to jet from the wound, but Kai quickly covered it with his mouth and began to drink from her throat.

Master and servant sunk to the ground as the strength left the woman's body, flowing into Kai, and when her heart began to slow he started taking bites instead, gobbling down lumps of flesh. His face was already changing, the nose shrinking away and his mouth growing wider and wider. The top lip stretched and tore. The skin peeled back to reveal something orange underneath that started to protrude further and further from his face.

The fire behind Kai's blue eyes began to grow brighter and the back of his shirt began to ripple as something stirred beneath. A long shadow swelled behind him, a swirling pulsating mass that covered everything in a terrible darkness. Even from where he was standing, Vargus felt a chill against his skin.

The sound of snapping bones echoed around the shrine. Vargus didn't know if it was Kai's human shell breaking apart, or the sound of him gnawing lumps out of the woman's shoulder with his beak. His shirt came apart and six churning dark blue tentacles burst out, swelling and fattening as they stretched across the ground. With a monstrous cry Kai finally pulled away from his feast, his unearthly voice echoing in the night. The skin on his face split in two and his skull burst apart like an egg as it could no longer contain his mass. Two dark red eyes became four, then eight, then more than Vargus could count as fresh tentacles erupted from what was left of Kai's human body.

Some of the faithful were frozen, others were praying and crying, and the rest were staring in terror at the true form of their ancient Lord and God, the Eater of Souls, the Pestilent Watcher.

As his body grew and tentacles split and multiplied, some of Kai's limbs tore apart what remained of the woman, which he gobbled down in a few bites. Even as the last of her was being crunched inside the gaping maw, fresh tentacles pulled two more people forward. They managed a scream, short and shrill before they too were consumed, bones grinding and juices spattering the ground as they were eaten alive. One man's nerve failed and he ran for the door, wailing in terror and shouting for help. Faster than a striking snake he was pulled from his feet by a tentacle. His mouth was covered with another, and his arms ripped from his torso by two more. A hundred red eyes blinked in unison, seeing everything and all places, as Khai'yegha fed on the last of its faithful.

There were a few more screams, the Morrin briefly begged, and then he too began to shriek as he was torn to pieces and gobbled up. It took only a few more minutes and then there was nothing left, not even a scrap of clothing or a stray shoe. A long pink tongue combed the floor, lapping up the last of the blood, tears, piss and other juices that had spilled out from the faithful as they were consumed. With nothing else to eat, it sighed and the endless eyes closed in a semblance of rest, but the countless arms never stopped moving.

Slowly its body began to unravel, shrinking and wilting away, piece by piece, until eventually a man dressed in rags was all that remained. The pressure against Vargus's ears lifted and the sounds of the city returned. Somewhere nearby he heard a woman laughing and could just make out the sound of a violin playing a jaunty tune.

"I feel much better," said Kai.

If Hargo or anyone else in the tavern saw Kai now, they wouldn't think it was the same person. Here was a man at the peak of physical fitness. His body toned with muscle and his face round from good living. Lines at the corners of his mouth spoke of a happy life full of joy, and the fire behind his eyes was warm and welcoming.

"It won't last," warned Vargus, "but then, you already knew that."

"It was the only way," said Kai, looking around at the ruins of the shrine. He shook his head sadly and stared up through the gaps in the ceiling at the night sky. "Help me, brother."

"I think I've done enough."

Kai's expression was one of reproach. "They would have found me on the street if you hadn't brought me here. You carry no blame for what happened."

"What do you want?"

Kai looked at him with bemusement. "I want to survive. You are one of the oldest. You know how it's done. I want you to teach me."

"I don't have time for that."

"Yes, you're caught up in their war." Kai's tone implied he was beyond such tedious concerns.

"And so are you," Vargus reminded him. "Otherwise you wouldn't be here."

Kai conceded the point with a nod. "What would you have me do?"

"Nothing. I'm going to put you somewhere safe, but close enough that I can call on you, should I need help before the war is done."

"And what am I supposed to do while I wait for it to end?" asked Kai, sounding incredibly bored by the idea.

"Nothing. I want you to stay out of trouble. Can you do that?"

Kai's only response was a grin that showed lots of pointy teeth.

CHAPTER 22

By the time Gunder had descended the steps of the aviary he'd read the latest coded message from Talandra. He paused on the bottom step and considered potential locations to host the covert meetings of the rebellion. Even from down here he could still hear the faint cawing of the ravens.

It would need to be a large space to host a crowd and somewhere easy to get to without it looking suspicious. He had access to several buildings, one of which was a warehouse not far from the docks. The last time he'd been in there had been to interrogate Filbin and set him on his path. This new plan to mount a rebellion would require someone eye-catching and he agreed with Talandra's assessment. It wouldn't be difficult for his Gunder identity to disappear and someone more verbose to start a rebellion, but the fat merchant still had a role to play; getting the others on board for starters. Roza was the perfect choice and when she spoke with passion people tended to listen.

He stopped off at a tavern and left a note for Roza behind the bar with another agent, before setting off for The Lord's Blessing. On the way he passed familiar faces and occasionally a customer, but none of them smiled or waved at him. They made eye contact and there were curt nods, but it went no further. The streets were far quieter than they should have been at this time of night.

Given the recent news about the Queen's abdication, and the uncertainty about what lay ahead, it was not unexpected that her people were subdued.

A common misconception was that the people of Yerskania stood for nothing. That they were just greedy merchants and middlemen. That their only loyalty was to money, and their real places of worship were the banks. In truth, there was a deep-seated national pride and loyalty to the royal family, who had transformed them from a nation of fishermen and miners into shrewd business people. They were a rich nation compared to some, and while their wealth might be envied, their open stance on religion was not. Now their freedom was under fire and Gunder felt it was time to stir the ancestors.

Six men dressed in bulky mail, with blue and white tabards over the top, marched towards Gunder. People gave them plenty of room on the wide streets, trying their best not to draw any attention to themselves. The Chosen were the new religious foot soldiers of Emperor Taikon, Overlord of the West.

Two of the six black-eyed Zecorrans stared at Gunder as they marched past. One touched the heavy mace at his waist, but made no move towards him. A week ago there had been few of them in the city, perhaps fifty at most. Now their numbers had swelled and new recruits joined their ranks every day. The Chosen received three meals a day, a uniform, money, weapons and power. All they had to do was swear allegiance to the new Emperor. Most of those who had already signed up were the worst of the worst. People who enjoyed inflicting pain, power-seekers, the greedy, the desperate and the insane. There were only a few natives in their ranks, but Gunder thought it would only be a matter of time before more joined up to take advantage of what was on offer.

He'd also seen the temple being erected on the site of the old pagan shrine. Something told him it wasn't the first of these being constructed. A place of worship devoted to God-Emperor Taikon, the man who could not be killed.

The burning down of the temple of the Maker had angered the locals, but without some military backup to support them, any rebellion was doomed to fail from the start against enemies both within and without.

As he stepped into The Lord's Blessing, Gunder was surprised to see all tables were occupied. Every face in the room turned in his direction, but, his face being familiar, they quickly went back to their conversations. Masson, the enforcer, sat near the door and beside him were two bulky men with scarred faces. Both were armed with swords and metal coshes, and from the way they held themselves they were not street toughs. They stared at his walking stick for a moment, but after seeing how much he leaned on it, they disregarded it. Masson nodded in his direction, but then went back to watching the street through the window.

Gunder joined his friends, who had saved him a seat at their table. The grim and nervous expressions around the room told him he'd missed something.

"Out with it. Before you burst."

"A group of Chosen tried to arrest someone," said Zoll in a quiet voice. "A sailor."

"What did he do?" asked Gunder.

Zoll shrugged. "Nothing. They made something up about smuggling. I think they wanted to commandeer his ship. Parrick's a good man," he said, gesturing with his chin towards one of the men by the fire. Parrick was a hook-nosed man with a shaven head, broad hairy arms and a stocky build. From the way those nearby deferred to him, Gunder guessed he was the ship's Captain.

"Every man and woman in the room stood up to defend him," said Iyele with more than a hint of pride. He glanced briefly around the room at the crowd, which was the usual mix of locals and a spattering of Morrin and Zecorrans.

"The Chosen. They will try this again," warned Ramalyas, "and someone else will not be so lucky."

"I may not have been born here, but this is my home now. We should drive them out of the city," declared Gunder.

"How?" asked Zoll. "The army is fighting abroad and every day more Chosen are recruited. Already the Watch is outnumbered."

"These are troubling times," agreed Gunder. "My spices come from the four corners of the world and are often hijacked by bandits or pirates. Extra protection at my warehouse would help me sleep at night. Perhaps a couple of Drassi Fists would be enough. Perhaps five or six, just to be sure."

As ever there were always a couple of hundred Drassi warriors for hire in the city and many more nearby.

Iyele was quick to catch on. "Some of my wine is very expensive. I wouldn't want to see it stolen. A few Drassi would secure my business."

"This will cost," muttered Zoll.

"Then let it," snapped Iyele. "I will give up every coin and become a beggar on the streets if I must."

"It will take more than a few Drassi to drive them out," said Ramalyas.

"I've heard of several groups that support the Queen and her rightful place on the throne," said Gunder.

"Pah," scoffed Zoll. "I have seen these people. Shouting slogans and marching up and down in front of the palace. They are nothing but sheep. One Drassi Swordmaster could scatter them."

"At least they show willing," said Iyele.

"They make a lot of noise, but they're not the group I'm talking about," said Gunder with a vague wave of his hand. "There is another group. True patriots who aren't afraid to get their hands dirty."

"I've heard nothing of such a group," said Iyele with a frown.

"They're very secretive," said Gunder. "Some of them are business people, like us, and they take few risks. Their next meeting is tomorrow night."

"I will attend," said Iyele.

"As will I," promised Ramalyas.

When Zoll hesitated to show support, the others looked at him. "The Chosen. I do not agree with their methods, but what if Taikon *is* a prophet?"

"Even if that were true, now he proclaims himself to be a God. He will replace all other religions with his own," promised Gunder. "He's already burned down one temple of the Maker."

"That was an accident," said Zoll.

"When did you ever hear of a stone temple accidentally burning down?" asked Gunder. "And now he's building a temple of his own."

"Taikon—"

"Promotes a perversion of your faith," said Gunder, stabbing a finger at Zoll. "In your heart, you know he's not a prophet. The people know it too, but they're too scared to say it. Alone, we're vulnerable, but together, supported by an army of our own, we cannot be stopped. We can reclaim this city from the Chosen and restore the Queen to her rightful place."

A heavy silence settled on their table as his words sunk in. The talk in the room flowed around them. Gunder caught snatches of conversations and most of them had the same tone. People were angry and tense. They felt personally slighted but couldn't see a way to disperse the poison that had infected their city.

Gunder let it sit with the other merchants for a while then moved the conversation on to other matters.

Roza and the rest of the network would spread the word to

other merchants and people of influence in the city. Tomorrow night the rebellion would begin to free Perizzi from Taikon's corruption before it was too late and they were all bowing to his idol in church.

CHAPTER 23

The sun was barely over the horizon, but Vargus and the others stood ready, waiting in the growing light for the enemy. Not one man spoke or even whispered. Every face was tight with concentration and a murderous rage burned in every heart. Normally many took strength from seeing him on the battlefield, but today they all had something to prove to someone else.

Spaced out along the front line stood only five of the Battlemages, shoulder to shoulder with the warriors. If they were nervous about Balfruss's absence they didn't show it.

The magic users had come to Seveldrom from all over the world, and yet each had proven themselves sufficiently that they were as much a part of the Seve army as any soldier. The smith, the one some called Titan, stood clenching his scarred fists over and over. The heavy muscles in his bare arms jumped up and down, the air around him charged with energy. Vargus could see that Finn was impatient to begin, and he could feel the smith drawing heavily on the Source.

More worrying was the implacable and calm expression on the face of Thule. He didn't move, barely seemed to breathe, and if not for the slow blinking of his eyes, most would think him dead. There was a lot of empty space around him and the smith, just in case. Eloise and her husband looked relaxed, their body language showing two people at ease, but Vargus could sense their nervousness. The little tribesman, Ecko, stood ready, his eyes scanning the land in all directions.

It felt like hours before the enemy arrived. A sea of shaggy faces with horns from Morrinow, swarthy Zecorrans, and this time even the savage Vorga had come. Green coastal, brown marsh and even some of the smaller blue-skinned hill tribes were there. A sea of swords, pikes, axes and shields caught the first rays of sunlight that broke through the choppy clouds.

The enemy's hopes of a surprise attack were quashed as they saw the Seve army stood ready. Nearby a great horn rang out. A single clean note that shattered the silence, with a purity that made the heart soar. Seconds after came a horrendous roar of voices that destroyed the moment of beauty in a guttural cry for blood. Thousands of warriors joined together in a wordless cry of anger, rage and hatred.

No ground would be given on this day. No mercy shown and no prisoners taken. The earth trembled as the Seve army marched towards the enemy, on the offensive for the first time since the war began.

The clouds thickened overhead and a storm rolled in from nowhere. Thunder rumbled, but no rain fell in its wake. Taking long and slow deep breaths Finn tried to calm his mind and control his emotions, just as Eloise had taught him. He drew heavily on the Source, shaping and carefully manipulating thick cords of power into a gigantic hammer forged from his imagination. The grey clouds turned black and, reaching out with one hand towards the sky, Darius brought down lightning, directing its raw power into the face of the enemy.

One bolt struck close to their front line, and their charge faltered. The second strike landed among the ranks, as did the third, sending them tumbling into the air, cooking men alive in their armour and blowing others apart, creating a rain of blood and body parts.

Finn could feel every single hair on his body. The faces of the dying and the dead were etched in his mind with such clarity he thought he would never forget them. The blood rushing through his body sounded like a river in his ears. Every heartbeat within a mile echoed in his thoughts like drums in a monstrous orchestra, all clamouring for attention. And with each death the music receded and the call of the Source grew. A siren's song that was so strong it made him ache right down to the core of his bones.

The enemy soldiers began to look so small, as if he were growing taller or floating above them like a bird. He could see their tidy lines and units, hear the rattle of their armour, taste the fear that coursed through them. The Splinters were nowhere in sight, and the cost of their absence began to show. For every westerner cut down by a sword or axe, ten or a dozen were killed by the Battlemages.

To his left Finn saw the little tribesman, Ecko, weaving his magic with brutal efficiency against a group of soldiers. It spread out from his hands like a spider's web. An intricate and invisible net of wires that he laid over their heads. At first glance it looked harmless. Finn looked closer and this time he could see the hooks, spikes and blades hidden in the weave. With a twist of both wrists Ecko pulled the net tight, drawing it towards him like a fisherman reeling in his catch. A dozen men were split apart and sliced into gobbets of meat. Heads flew off and fountains of blood erupted from gaping mouths as invisible blades tore into their bodies. At first he thought Ecko was dancing with glee, but watching closely he saw his feet weaving patterns in the dirt. Even as he slaughtered the enemy, he wove a protective shield against surprise attacks.

Darius's expression remained utterly calm despite the storm

that raged around him as he continued to strike at the enemy with summoned lightning. With a sweep of both arms, Darius brought the wrath of the storm down into the enemy ranks. They didn't even have time to scream. Men vanished in bright white flashes, and chunks of blackened, scorched meat tumbled to the ground. The control and precision he wielded made Finn feel clumsy. Balfruss had taught him some control during their nightly lessons, but it was still meagre compared to the others. Finn used raw force like a giant hammer, to smash the enemy into a pulp, while they wove power into lethal weapons with great skill.

The calm expression on Eloise's face helped him focus and control his breathing. Despite what they were facing, the screams of the dying and the din of so many warriors, she remained serene and at peace.

A horde of savage Vorga broke off from the rest and ran straight towards Darius. They whooped and clicked their teeth together, their bone armour rattling. As Eloise raised a hand towards them, a shiver ran across Finn's body and his breath began to frost in the air. A vortex of swirling sparks began to gather in her outstretched hand, growing in size and spinning faster and faster. Heat continued to be leached from all around, and soon Finn lost the feeling in his toes. His bones began to throb as if he stood naked in the heart of a terrible winter storm.

With a flick of her wrist, Eloise released the energy and a massive streak of fire rushed from her hand towards the Vorga, roasting them alive in a conflagration. The flow of fire kept pouring from her hand, as if it were hidden up her sleeve, and she swept the unnaturally sticky flames back and forth, setting more soldiers alight like dry stalks of wheat.

As the flesh melted from the Vorga's bones, the smell reminded Finn of his mother's fish stew. Their high-pitched war cries quickly turned into gurgles and wet plopping noises as they dissolved. The oily black fat from their bodies sizzled and the fire swelled with new fuel, catching more warriors unawares, who burned to death in their armour.

A stocky Zecorran pointed a crossbow at Darius, whose attention was focused on the storm. While controlling the fire with one hand Eloise pointed a finger at the crossbowman and made a twisting motion with her hand, snapping his neck.

Furthest away in the line, and silent as ever, Thule faced the enemy soldiers with an icy detachment. With him there was no slow gathering of his will, no build-up of pressure or even a gesture with his hands. Groups of men simply dropped dead when he stared at them.

Finn felt a shifting in the air. A change in pressure, as if he'd climbed into the mountains where the air was thin. His stomach lurched and for a moment he felt dizzy. There was an echo in his blood, a familiar calling from far away. He lost his concentration and the hammer he'd forged with his power dissolved. The warriors around him had no idea what was about to happen, but the other Battlemages felt it.

"They're coming," shouted Eloise. Finn didn't need to be told who they were. The Splinters. He'd been waiting for this moment since the last time they'd fought. The others had been horrified when Balfruss explained what had been done to them, but he knew the truth.

They were prisoners. Slaves to a terrible power they didn't want and hadn't asked for. It had ruined their lives, and what little remained had been stolen by the Warlock. Their memories had been stripped away until they were nothing more than ghosts with a heartbeat. In truth they were already dead and just didn't know it. Finn intended to give them peace in the hope that, one day, someone would grant him the same.

As the five Splinters drew closer, Finn realised he could feel something different about them. A new heartbeat and a pulse he'd never felt before.

"It's him. He's here," whispered Eloise. The Battlemages exchanged a look and even the enemy soldiers hesitated in their advance. Somehow they could feel it too. The Warlock was taking to the battlefield for the first time.

CHAPTER 24

The dying man raised a hand to cover his face and hide his terror. Moments ago he'd been cursing Vargus, promising torture and death. With one swift thrust Vargus's sword pierced the man's chest, straight through the heart. Stepping over the staring corpse Vargus dragged his sword free and saw that there was an unexpected lull in the battle. Those around him were looking for the cause, but he could feel it. The Splinters were approaching from the west, and each was drawing heavily on the Source. His skin tingled in response and his mouth felt dry.

"What is it?" asked Hargo, cleaning his cleaver on a piece of cloth torn from one of the many corpses.

"The Battlemages are coming."

"Theirs?"

Vargus nodded. "And someone else." He knew he'd said too much. There was no way to see them from where they were standing. Vargus moved away to help one of the surgeons before Hargo could ask how he knew.

The crows were taking advantage of the lull, treating men where they lay or pulling them onto stretchers and dragging them back to the hospital tent.

"Give me a hand," snapped a fat, red-faced surgeon. He was

trying to press down on a man's stomach and reach into his bag at the same time. Vargus pushed down on the warrior's gushing wound with both hands, making the man wheeze and his eyes bulge with pain. There wasn't any breath left in him to scream. The ragged wound was deep and the blood flowing from it was dark and smelly. They'd cut into the man's bowels and he was slowly poisoning himself. The surgeon took out a small purple vial, held it to the man's lips and almost immediately he started to breathe easier. He closed his eyes and all of the muscles in his body relaxed.

"You can stop now," said the surgeon, taking a dagger from his bag. He sliced the man's right leg on the inner thigh, severing the artery. In a few seconds the warrior was dead. It wouldn't look like it to some, but Vargus knew it was mercy. No man could survive a wound like that. It would fester and the pain would become unbearable. After a few days of horrendous agony, the man would die screaming, covered in shit, coughing up blood and crying for his mother.

Vargus offered his hand, still slick with the dead man's blood, and the surgeon took it, coming to his feet with a grunt. His clothes hung off him as if they were borrowed from a larger man, but Vargus guessed what had happened. The war was taking its toll on the surgeon and the weight was dropping off him. If the man lived to see the end of the conflict he would be as thin as Orran.

Vargus heard the heavy crunch of familiar footsteps approaching.

"Something's happening," said Hargo, glancing between Vargus and the dead man.

The black clouds above their heads started to pull together. An unusual smell began to wash away the stench of the dead, and this time even Hargo could feel the difference in pressure. The hairs stood up on the back of his forearms and the big man shook his head. They'd already seen what the Battlemage they called Titan could do to the enemy.

"Reckon we'll see Titan?" asked Orran.

"I'm just glad the big bastard is on our side. He's the most dangerous one out there," said Hargo. Beside him Orran nodded, tightening the straps on his shield.

Vargus had a different opinion, but didn't say anything. Not far away, enemy units were pulling themselves together into a semblance of order. All around him Seve warriors started getting ready, locking their shields together, while bowmen winched back the arm of their crossbows. Behind them archers took up position and the surgeons pulled back out of range, away from the worst of the fighting.

Vargus picked up his bastard sword, rolled his weary shoulders and cast a quick glance at the sky. Beyond the magically drawn clouds, the sky was clear and the sun still high. It wasn't even noon and yet it felt as if he'd been fighting all day. Looking at the others he saw the same weariness in their movements. Their respite from the front line had given them a boost, but it had quickly eroded in only a few days. The memories of pleasure and home comforts had been ground out in the dirt, blood and carnage. Without another rest they would all die, veteran and fresh recruit alike, face down in the mud.

There was no signal this time. No horn summoning them to battle, not even a roar of angry voices. The enemy just marched forward at a steady pace, weapons at the ready.

"Let's show these pig-fuckers what we can do!" shouted Vargus, trying to fire up the men. It roused them a bit, a few yelled insults, but not nearly enough showed any real passion. "And remember what they did to our King!"

That caught the attention of every warrior in earshot. Those out of range had the message relayed to them. The same eerie silence that had settled on the men in the morning returned. The

King's murder was still a fresh wound and Vargus had just stuck his hand in and twisted. Now they were ready.

There were only a few minutes until the Splinters and the Warlock arrived on the front line. After a lengthy discussion Ecko had volunteered to stay outside of the Link. The others would defend the army and he would keep an eye out for trickery and separate attacks.

Ecko watched as the two huge armies crashed together again. There was no ocean or shore here, only two monstrous waves of flesh and metal. Even if the sounds of their chaotic embrace hadn't reached his ears, he would have felt it. The earth shook with the pounding of thousands of feet, rattling his teeth and shaking leaves and berries from the few trees on the plain. The din shocked a flock of small grey birds into flight. They fled and then circled back, no doubt staring down at the armies with agitation.

The blood of the dying and dead was already nourishing the soil, sinking deep into the land. More would follow soon enough. And from all of this death and carnage, new life would blossom.

In this place, thick grass and tall golden crops would rise and the bodies would be gone, turned to bones and then dust. Red and blue flowers would spring up in dense patches, and no one would know where the seeds had come from, or why they grew here and nowhere else.

As Ecko looked out across the battlefield, he didn't see thousands of men fighting for survival, but an endless sea of green moving in the wind like waves on the ocean. And rising up from the middle of the land was a shining obelisk, sometimes black, sometimes amber, glowing in the sunlight like a sword from the heavens. An endless number of people journeyed to see it, a line that stretched to the horizon, coming from lands in the east and the west. Each came to look for names they recognised, searching for a way to put down the pain they carried inside.

For all of their learning, the people of this land had forgotten much. They built towers of stone, wore thick boots and covered themselves in metal, severing their roots, cutting themselves off from the land. But the First People remembered. Despite their exile and being forced to begin again in a foreign country, they endured and still remembered. They remembered the past, they honoured the land, and in return it gave them many rich bounties. But most of all they honoured Elwei.

"Lord, I am far from your embrace," said Ecko as he knelt on the ground, digging his fingers into the rich black earth. "I beg you, do not forsake your humble servant. Give me the strength to face what must be. I'm afraid. I'm so afraid, Lord."

As he bowed his head in silent prayer a wondrous calm fell over him like a heavy blanket. His whole body tingled and his scalp prickled because he wasn't alone any more. Elwei was with him, even here in this distant land, so far from home. Ecko felt a hand on his shoulder and tears of joy fell from his eyes.

The others were already linked together, creating a huge barrier only those able to touch the Source could see. It pulsed and shifted as if it were alive and had a spirit. Flowing from each Battlemage into the barrier he could see threads of power in a variety of colours. There were too many to count and some he could not name, but they all spoke of life and passion, joy and love, and a terrible sorrow.

From across the battlefield they came, black spots amid a sea of life. They were husks without spirits. Pits of darkness that moved like people, but they had not been individuals for a long time. Ecko could see narrow threads of power flowing into them, pulsing blue and grey, feeding the tiny spark of life that kept them moving. Sat at the centre of the web, like a fat spider, was the one they called the Warlock. He was a thousand colours by himself but mostly a deep, volcanic red. A mountain of anger and pain drove him forward, and where his heart should have been there was nothing at all. If they were stood facing each other Ecko thought it possible he might see through the hole in the Warlock's chest. The Source endlessly fed and nourished him, and yet the Warlock was as hollow as his Splinters. No matter how much he learned, no matter how many lives he took, no matter how great his accomplishments, he was empty and would forever be.

The Warlock directed the Splinters to attack with the barest trace of power. Ecko's siblings reacted, blocking the first of many deadly strikes which would continue until the Splinters died or were told to stop.

The warriors around him knew the hooded figure. His blood-red robe made him stand out amid the sea of black, grey and silver. The western warriors gave him room, and the Warlock walked unopposed through their ranks until he was standing on the front line. Normally it would be impossible to see inside the hood, but Ecko let the Source flow into him and his eyesight sharpened. The Warlock was younger than he'd expected, but behind his eyes Ecko sensed something ancient. All of his accomplishments were not his own. Someone, or some thing much older, had been schooling him.

As soon as Ecko embraced the Source, the Warlock's eyes scanned the sea of opposing faces until they were staring at one another. The Warlock grinned and Ecko smiled in return, but he wasn't smiling at the boy.

The first attack came so quickly Ecko barely reacted in time. The tip of it lashed his face like a whip, cutting a deep gouge in his left cheek. The taste of blood wasn't new, but it still came as a surprise. Before the second strike came, Ecko drew more heavily on the Source as his feet sketched patterns on the earth. With a shower of sparks the whip-attack shattered against his shield, dazzling his eyes and filling his ears with a faint buzzing.

Far away someone was calling his name, but Ecko couldn't risk looking away from the Warlock. The boy was still grinning, enjoying a new challenge and the promise of something he'd not faced before. Someone with power and control. A worthy adversary to test himself.

The Warlock started to concoct something unpleasant, weaving together a nightmare with threads of malice. Tilting his head to one side Ecko touched the construct with a small filament of power, unravelling it in a heartbeat. The Warlock tried again and then again, but each time Ecko was able to pass the smallest thread of power through any shield and tug the nightmare apart, before it became fully formed. The Warlock met his gaze and this time Ecko was smiling at the frustrated boy. Eventually he would work out how it was done, but for now his complex shield only extended above the ground. He didn't see Ecko reaching into the earth and coming up between his feet. A simple child's trick and yet the boy still fell for it. While he was distracted Ecko wove a net with his other hand and cast it at his feet.

Instead of trying to work out how it was done the Warlock showed his age and lack of discipline. With the impatience of youth he gave up with his weave and lashed out with brute force. A monstrous hammer thundered into Ecko's shield, cracking his defences and making him stumble. Pressing his advantage the Warlock sent a shower of searing darts that would burn holes straight through his flesh. Even though his ears were ringing, Ecko sketched with his toes, reinforcing his shield, and the darts bounced away.

The Warlock's eyes widened as he realised how his shield had been breached. With a snarl of rage he sent his power deep into the earth to rise up underneath Ecko. A shrill scream of pain split the air as he became tangled in Ecko's net. The weave, laden with traps and invisible blades, tore into his arms and legs. The pain was so intense the Warlock's concentration broke, his shield collapsed and even the faint threads of power flowing into the Splinters stopped. As he fell forward onto his hands and knees Ecko sensed the flow of the battle changing around him.

His siblings drew more deeply and began to lash the enemy soldiers with lethal strikes. The Splinters remained utterly immobile, unaware of the fighting all around them. When a stray arrow hit one of them in the shoulder the man didn't react. In fact he showed no signs of life at all.

Finn was right. Or at least, he dared where the others valued caution. The worst of this could be brought to an end in a day.

The Warlock was still on his knees, wiping blood from his mouth, when Ecko made a short stabbing motion towards him with one hand. The incision must have hurt, but the boy didn't show it until Ecko made a scooping gesture with his out-stretched hand. The Warlock's scream changed in pitch at the gesture, becoming strangled.

Ecko sensed something hurtling towards him and barely had time to sketch a shield before it crashed into him. The force of the blow knocked him off his feet and black spots danced before his eyes. When he regained his feet the Warlock was standing, one hand pressed to the wound in his chest. Blood oozed from between his fingers and a darker patch of red was spreading across the front of his robe.

His threats were lost in the noise of battle, carried away on the wind, but the boy's hatred was clear. Ecko expected more tricks or a complex weave to rip him to pieces, but instead the Warlock drew heavily on the Source. A river of power flowed into him, more and more until it seemed as if he must surely burst. The air around him crackled with pent-up energy, blue flames danced along his arms and shoulders, and his eyes began to glow. And yet, he channelled more power, as if he were dying of thirst.

Too late Ecko realised what was about to happen. He sketched out a shield on the earth and crafted another with his hands, but part of him knew it would not be enough.

Fire fell from the sky and the world turned white as the earth rose up to meet him. Every bone in his body throbbed and it felt as if his skin was on fire. Blood dripped from his mouth from where he'd bitten his tongue. His shields had stopped the attack, but as he watched they started to fracture and fell apart.

His fingers were weaving a second shield when something hit him again, hard enough for his feet to leave the ground. At that point all of his aches and pains, all of his worries about his people and the future, didn't matter any more. They belonged to someone else. His hands twitched and he thought they were weaving another shield, but he couldn't be sure.

Ecko knew he was lying on the earth, as he was staring at the clouds, but for some reason he couldn't feel his body. It should have worried him, but he was so tired and comfortable that it didn't seem to matter any more. Above his head the sky was growing dark as dense grey clouds pulled together with unnatural speed. Thunder rumbled, distant and then much closer, and he felt a build-up of energy in the air that came before a lightning strike. There was a flash and then he saw nothing.

CHAPTER 25

Roza timed it carefully so that she was the last to arrive at the warehouse. Officially it was empty and currently available to rent, but unofficially Gunder owned it and several similar properties across the city. It was a good location for the first of the rebellion's clandestine meetings.

She slipped on the mask, pulled up the hood and then boldly stepped into the building. Normally the warehouse was cool, but with more than a hundred heavily dressed bodies inside, the air felt sticky. Every person wore a mask of some description, although some had gone for a much simpler approach of a hood with a scarf tied across the bottom of their face. She spotted Gunder in the crowd and had to repress a laugh at the ill-fitting peacock mask stretched across his face. The costume shop she'd bought her mask from had no idea as to the sudden cause of its good fortune, but the owner wasn't complaining. Almost every mask in the shop had been sold in a day, and the masquerade for the summer solstice was several months away.

Despite their disguises, people had made it very easy for her to identify them by not changing their clothes. Many were dyed very specific colours and others wore their family crests. None of them had removed their jewellery, which were mostly unique and priceless items. More obvious were three Morrin in the crowd who wore exceptionally tall hoods in a poor attempt to hide their horns. Amazingly no one was laughing at them.

As she passed through the crowd Roza felt eyes lingering on her and waves of raw emotion radiated from the people. The whispered conversations ended as she jumped onto the raised platform at the far end of the warehouse. As she turned to face the crowd Roza cast back her hood to reveal blonde hair. This, combined with her pale skin, marked her as native to Yerskania.

"My name is Petra," a name as fake as her blonde wig, "and you've all come here for one reason. There are other gatherings out there. Those that prefer to talk endlessly, so if that's as far as you're willing to go, leave now." She waited a few seconds, looking over the crowd expectantly, but no one dared move. A few had probably come along for the thrill, thinking it was exciting to play rebel, but they had no intention of actually lifting a finger to help their own country. They would slink away after this meeting and not come to the next one. Those who returned would form the heart of the rebellion. "I want to take back my country from those who have crippled it," she declared passionately.

"We should kill all the Chosen. Send a message!" someone called out.

"Some of the Chosen are my countrymen. But, for a moment, let's pretend we did kill them. Then what?" asked Roza. "How does that help us? Taikon will send his soldiers south, or the Vorga north to deal with us. He will focus his attention on Yerskania instead of Seveldrom."

"The Chosen arrest people for no reason," someone complained. "The City Watch and Guardians of the Peace are outnumbered. We have to do something."

"We will, but it must be done at the right time and with great care, because the stakes are high. And I don't just mean your lives, or those of your families. If we make a mistake, Yerskania will become another Shael."

She let that sit for a while, her words soaking into the crowd. They'd all heard the horror stories. Death camps led by the bloodthirsty Vorga who relished slaughter. Funeral pyres that burned day and night. Experiments being conducted on live victims. Mass graves filled with rotting corpses. The entire nation had become a country of slaves who were being worked to death. Those Yerskani who spoke out against Taikon were executed or they disappeared, and many believed they were sent south to Shael. If the Yerskani rebellion became public knowledge too soon everyone would suffer.

"Then what do you suggest?" asked a man with an oversized hood.

"The alliance is a fraud. We were all lied to." Roza made sure her voice carried a hard edge, as if she'd personally been deceived by Taikon. "It's time others knew what you all know. The Morrin are not evil butchers, but misguided people turned away from the Blessed Mother. The Zecorrans are not black-eyed devils. Their leaders have been deceived by the Warlock and his black magic. He manipulated them into believing Taikon is a prophet of the Lord of Light, twisting their faith."

"Lord of Light save us," muttered someone and a few others repeated the blessing.

"Yes, let us hope He will save us," agreed Roza. "And the Maker, and the Blessed Mother too, because we've become idolaters. Taikon and his pet wizard have made a mockery of all faiths. Claiming one thing to our faces and laughing at us in private. We helped raise up a man who is not chosen of any God."

Again she paused for dramatic effect, letting her words sit with the crowd, and a faint murmur of conversation swept through them. In Yerskania people were free to choose their own faith. You were not spat at in the street, or treated as if you had the pox like some in the north. Those who didn't give lip service to the Blessed Mother in Morrinow and the Lord of Light in

Zecorria didn't last very long. Atheists and those who didn't conform chose to live elsewhere before they were banished or worse.

Despite the freedom offered in Yerskania, the majority of the population were deeply religious and there were several large temples devoted to the Blessed Mother and churches devoted to the Great Maker and the Lord of Light.

"You said others should know the truth," someone shouted, cutting through the noise. "After all of your talk of action, you want us to use words?"

"No," snapped Roza, silencing the whispers. "That is the work of others. We all know the truth about what Taikon has become. A man that does not sleep or eat. A man who drinks the blood of children. His own people in Zecorria will tear him down when they realise the truth. I want you to protect your home when the time is right."

"How?" asked a bold man, stepping forward from the crowd. Roza made a note of the way he stood, his height, build and the tone of his voice. The mask he wore was modest, but the cut of his clothes hinted at much greater wealth. There were also several bulges under his leather gloves, suggesting he wore several expensive rings. A man with a big ego to match his deep pockets. He probably belonged to one of the more wealthy families.

"I can tell that most of you are not without privilege, and these are dangerous times. Hazardous times for honest merchants." Roza waited and a few heads picked up on her meaning. The bold man nodded briskly and stepped back, but a few others still looked towards her expectantly. "You will hire as many Drassi mercenaries as you can afford. Keep them close and keep them hidden. Your lives depend on it. When your Queen calls on you, I expect you to answer."

"The Queen?" asked more than a few people.

Before anyone could ask any more questions she quickly stepped down from the platform and slipped out the back door.

Roza pulled off the mask and set a brisk pace across the city, taking an indirect route away from the warehouse to her next appointment. The last thing she needed was anyone following her.

This time when Gunder entered his house and sensed he wasn't alone, he didn't reach for the nearest weapon. As before, Roza was sat in his kitchen, this time rubbing at her face from where her mask had pinched the skin on her nose. His cheeks were still red, but it would fade in another hour.

"Not very subtle," said Gunder, "but I suppose it was necessary."

With a sigh Roza pulled off the long blonde wig, laying it on the table between them. She unwound her red braid and scratched at her scalp. "I don't know how the idiots make a profit. They've no guile."

"The Yerskani are very straightforward people. It's why I like them. You always know where you stand."

"Usually behind them with a spear, prodding them towards the bear pit," said Roza.

Gunder raised an eyebrow. "Something bothering you?"

Roza waved it away. "I also heard a rumour from several sources about King Matthias being assassinated and Taikon dancing in the streets in celebration."

Gunder grimaced. "All true. I received a message last night from Shani."

A heavy silence settled on the kitchen. Roza always had a witty retort and Gunder maintained that her most dangerous weapon was her tongue. But now she sat in silence, lost in thought.

"Any word on what they're doing?"

Gunder shook his head. "I expect we'll hear about the succession soon enough. Prince Thias is solid, like his father. I think he's ready."

"Let's hope so," said Roza. She shook herself and seemed to throw off her melancholy as if it were a blanket. "It's going to take a bit of time to trickle the Drassi into the city. How about we have the next meeting in a week's time?"

"If not sooner. We don't want them having second thoughts, or thinking it's just talk. I'll start passing the word around."

He would have to make some new friends in the Watch. Even if the Chosen were too busy or stupid to notice an influx of Drassi, the locals were far more astute. Their straightforward approach made the idea of offering bribes a difficult and touchy subject, especially with soldiers who had sworn an oath. It would require delicate work, walking the line between telling them the whole truth and revealing just enough that they wouldn't ask too many questions.

Roza stood up to leave.

"Do you have time for a drink?" He felt the need for some companionship, and to be with someone where he could just be himself, not the merchant.

"Another time." Roza moved to the door, but turned back before leaving. "The next story I want to hear about Taikon is one where he's weeping and pissing blood in the streets."

"I'll see what I can do," Gunder said with a vicious smile.

CHAPTER 26

The day ended in a rough stalemate. The two armies sullenly withdrew from the battlefield, each knowing the conflict was far from over.

The sky was a dull grey and a light wind blew in from the west, bringing with it the stench of death and enemy campfires. A little drizzle fell continuously, sitting on eyelashes, soaking into clothing and trickling down the back of necks.

One of the field surgeons, checking for survivors, found Ecko's remains. At first the crow thought a young boy had snuck onto the battlefield and been killed by accident. It was only when he saw the bone charms, and a few untouched patches of skin, he realised who it was.

Huge chunks of flesh had been completely burned away, right down to the bone. Any remaining tissue was charred and black. Somehow the skin on his face remained intact, while the rest of his head was a bright white skull, washed clean in the rain. His hands were curled up into twisted claws, and his empty eye sockets were filling with rain.

Finn and Darius wrapped the body in a blanket and carried it from the battlefield back to their camp. Despite not being Linked with Ecko, they'd all felt the moment of his death. Everyone on the battlefield saw the column of white fire fall from the sky like a signal from the Gods, but all of those connected to the Source had felt it in their bones. Hours later the air was still charged with energy, and Eloise's skin tingled as if she'd been sitting too close to a fire.

The others Battlemages were stood waiting by a spitting fire, silent and soaking wet, but no one complained. They would rather be alive and catch a chill than the alternative.

"I'm not familiar with his customs," said Darius, looking at the others for help.

"We have to bury him, deep in the earth," said Eloise. "Return him to the bosom of Elwei." Finn started to reach for the Source, but Eloise shook her head. "It has to be done by hand."

They found a secluded spot at the edge of the camp beside a copse of trees. A few warriors came to watch, but when they saw nothing more than Battlemages digging a grave they kept their distance. Plenty of others were doing that tonight or burning bodies on funeral pyres.

Soon after they started Eloise's clothes were stuck to her body, her skin flushed. Mercifully the earth, normally tough from a long winter, had softened with the rain.

They took it in turns, digging in pairs, but it was hard work and none of them, except Finn, were used to prolonged physical labour. After a day of using their power they were already drained, and this sapped their remaining energy. Only Finn seemed immune. Eloise could see he was relishing the physical exertion, often taking over from others before it was his turn. His rain-soaked clothing revealed the heavy muscles of his arms and upper body. Perhaps it reminded him of his old life, working in the forge all day.

Thule looked ready to collapse, but his indigo eyes burned brightly in the growing dark. After hearing what Thule had endured to reach them, Eloise knew him to be a lot tougher than he looked.

When the grave was six foot deep they gently lowered Ecko's body into the hole.

"Merciful Elwei," said Eloise, turning her face towards the sky with arms stretched out. "Bless and keep your faithful servant, Ecko. Embrace him into your bosom and look kindly on any misdeeds. He was a noble, kind and generous man who suffered greatly for others. He travelled a long way by himself to protect the lives of strangers. Grant him eternal peace." Eloise turned towards the others expectantly. "It's customary for all of us to say something about our time together."

To her surprise Darius stepped forward to speak first. He hated speaking in public and being the centre of attention, but he looked determined. This was something he needed to do. "His love for the land was infectious," said Darius with a faint smile. "I shall not take the gifts it gives us for granted. The bounty of the earth, the sea and the sky." He opened his mouth and tasted the rain.

Eloise looked at the others and Finn stepped forward.

"He showed me how clumsy I was compared to him," said the smith. "He was always in control. If he was afraid, he never showed it. I wish I could be more like him." The words were simply put, although they also touched on something Eloise had sensed, but was struggling to put into words. Something tugged at a corner of her mind.

The others were so focused on the grave they hadn't noticed the large crowd that had gathered at a discreet distance. The warriors knew they owed their lives to the Battlemages, and hundreds had come to pay their respects.

Eloise looked at Thule, who started to speak in a hoarse whisper. It was all that his ravaged throat could manage, and the effort was great, but he needed to say the words.

"He loved the earth and his family, but he loved his homeland even more. One night I found him weeping. He told me it was because he was homesick. He was born on this side of the Dead Sea, and yet he wept for the memory of home. The First People were exiled long before his birth, so he suffered for a crime he'd not committed. As a boy his father told him stories of their homeland's majesty and the endless forest, and some nights it haunted him that he would never see it. I found in him a kindred soul. Someone who loved his country as much as me."

Eloise thought of her own homecoming weeks ago and how difficult it must have been for Ecko to know that he could never go home. She had left Seveldrom in search of adventure and a new life and had stayed away because there had been no reason to return. The thought of having that choice taken away hurt more than she had realised.

"He taught me about love," said Eloise. "Love for all things, but mostly for my family." She smiled at the others and felt a kinship with them all. They were connected to each other and the world in a way that few experienced. If they sunk deep enough into the Source they could hear the very heartbeat of creation, the ebb and flow of life in the land. As Eloise thought about the web that joined all things, something clicked into place.

"Ecko was braver than any of us," she said. "Sometimes he spoke of other places and other times, but there was always some ambiguity. As if he couldn't quite remember, but that wasn't it. I think part of him knew this would happen."

"He knew he was going to die?" asked Finn.

Eloise shook her head. "I think he knew this day would come, and that he'd face a powerful enemy, but the outcome wasn't clear."

"He had imperfect Sight," said Darius, shock and awe warring on his face. "He was an Oracle."

"Of a sort," she said, hating that word, but unable to think of another to describe Ecko's Talent. "He knew that he might die, and yet he volunteered to remain outside the Link. I wonder, how many of us would be as brave in the same position?"

There was little else to say. As they moved to pick up the shovels some of the warriors came forward to help. The hole was filled in quickly and soon only a small bump in the soil showed where Ecko was buried. In keeping with his customs, no stone or symbol was left to mark the grave. He was returned to the earth and the final embrace of Elwei, naked and anonymous, as he had come into the world.

It wasn't often that Talandra drank, but tonight she felt justified in drowning her sorrows and indulging in a bit of self-pity. The reports from the battlefield were still coming in, but on the whole it had been a bloody and costly day. More so for the loss of one of the Battlemages. She knew it was callous. Warriors could be replaced, but a Battlemage could not.

Hours before a messenger arrived with news from the battle-field, Balfruss had stumbled into her office, hair mussed and eyes bloodshot from just waking up. With tears streaming down his face he'd told her that Ecko was dead, slain by the Warlock. Through his mental link with Thule he'd felt it and shared in his brethren's grief. With help from her apothecary they'd put him to bed with a sleeping draught. He'd wake in a few hours and hopefully would have rested long enough to stay awake through the night and stand guard.

Battlemages were a dying breed, and Talandra knew that if they lost any more, the army would be overwhelmed. At that point it wouldn't matter how many warriors Seveldrom could muster. The Warlock and his Splinters could tear every warrior in two, burn them with fire, or call down lightning and destroy the army in less than a day. After that it would be child's play for him to tumble the city walls and let Taikon take the throne.

The most recent report from Gunder gave her some hope, as

the rebellion had begun in earnest in Perizzi. If they could scour the city clean of Taikon's influence and get rid of the Chosen, the Queen would retake her throne from a position of strength. The growing unrest in Zecorria with High Priest Filbin was also drawing the eye of many people in the west. Added to that, she'd been sent stories from contacts in Morrinow about division among its leaders. All of these combined could be enough to destabilise the alliance. Western leaders might withdraw troops from the battlefield and refocus their efforts at home, which could end the war and prevent further bloodshed.

Talandra knew such things did not happen overnight and that much could go wrong with such plans. But slim hopes were all she had. The battle itself was nothing more than a delay tactic, as they were horrendously outnumbered.

Papers with all the gory details from the battlefield lay scattered across the dining table in front of her. Talandra couldn't ignore them, although she desperately wanted to. The remaining scraps of her evening meal still looked tempting. Despite everything that had happened, she'd managed to retain her appetite.

Instead she poured herself another mug of ale and stared out the window at the night sky, thinking of other times and places. The night was cold and heavy bursts of rain swept across the sky followed by the occasional rumble of thunder, but no lightning. The unusual storm was the result of Battlemages summoning lightning earlier that day. She had reassurances that the storm would dissipate by itself, so there was nothing to do but watch and wait.

The open windows made the room chilly, but it was the closest she'd been to being outdoors for three days and she liked the smell of the rain. There was so much information and so many reports coming from the battlefield, and her spies in the west, that she barely had time for sleep.

At moments like these she would normally seek her father's counsel, but those days were gone. More than anything she wanted to lose herself in oblivion. Bury her misery in a layer of fog from the ale, but she couldn't even manage that. Her mind would always reassert itself and point out the futility of what she was attempting before she was drunk.

So, she drank, and stared at nothing, lost in a tedious stupor while being irritated by her own brooding.

Her brothers came into the dining room, their faces united in misery, but somehow they also looked refreshed. Thias frowned at the windows and immediately pulled them closed, shutting her off from the rest of the world.

Their father's body still lay in state and the three days of greeting people who came to pay their respects wasn't over yet. She felt utterly exhausted but her brothers seemed to be riding high on something.

"What is it? Good news?"

Thias and Hyram sat down on either side of her at the head of the table. At first neither of them spoke. Eventually Hyram gestured at Thias, who cleared his throat.

"When the three days are over, father's body will be . . . consumed by fire," said Thias, stumbling a little. "At which point it's customary to announce his successor."

Talandra had been thinking about it a great deal over the last few days. "We need to make it a spectacle. Right now our people are hurting. They need something to look forward to. They need reassurance and a confident leader. We have to make sure they understand that nothing will change when you take the throne."

"But it has changed," said Hyram, ever the pessimist. He was still dressed for battle, and his face was criss-crossed with tiny scars and fresh cuts. He also stank as if he'd slept in his armour, which was likely. "Some aren't sharp enough to know we lost the fight today, and more than one Battlemage, but they'll work it out soon enough. We can't keep going as we are."

"What are you suggesting?" asked Talandra. Her surprise turned to shock as Hyram smiled and then laughed until tears ran down his cheeks. Talandra slammed her tankard onto his hand, but it only made him laugh even harder.

"What's so funny?"

"You don't see it. Thias may look like him, but you're his true inheritor."

"What Hyram is trying to say is that we've discussed this at length, and you will succeed father," Thias said with a warm smile. "You will be crowned Queen of Seveldrom."

Talandra stared at her brothers, searching for something that would suggest it was a joke. She wouldn't blame them. Right now they needed to laugh, but both of their faces had turned solemn.

"Why?" gasped Talandra.

"Many reasons," said Thias. "I've been preparing for this all my life, but now that the moment is here, I know I'm not the right choice."

·"I don't understand. Did father leave you a letter?"

"No, but I think he knew." Thias smiled sadly. "You know your own strengths and weaknesses, and so do I. There's still much I need to learn before I can rule, but there's no time. Our country needs someone now. Someone to inspire them with the right words. You may not be a warrior, but when you lead, others follow. I've seen it. Countless times I've looked to you for advice, as did father. My mind is set, Talandra."

Talandra turned towards Hyram. "And you?"

"You are calm where I am rash. You ask for counsel from all and listen to advice when it's given, whatever quarter it comes from. I have little patience, and have even been known to brood on occasion."

"On occasion?" said Talandra, earning a smile from both of her brothers.

"Your mind is far more agile than mine as well. I put my strength in my arm, in the Generals who lead, and in the Maker," said Hyram. "It was never going to be me."

"But I'm no General, or battlefield tactician. Father could read a battle and predict its movements with only a glance."

"It wasn't always that way," said Graegor from the doorway. None of them had heard his approach, but he'd obviously heard enough to understand what they were talking about. He came striding into the room, a spectre of death, dressed as ever in black mail and armed for battle with axe and sword. If time was taking its toll on him beyond a few lines on his face, Talandra couldn't see it. He still moved like a man twenty, even thirty, years his junior.

Graegor came around the table to stand at Talandra's left shoulder, just as he'd done for their father for years as his body-guard and then advisor.

"He learned over time. He was coached by his elders until he surpassed them and saw what even they missed. It will come to you as well, but until then, the Generals will guide you."

"You have no qualms about this decision?" Talandra asked the grizzled General.

Graegor had been a surrogate uncle all her life, an unwaver-ing constant, and like some family members, he wasn't someone she would've picked if there'd been a choice. There were times when she couldn't stand the sight of him. He was rude, blunt, racist, always angry and they had little in common. Their longest conversations had taken place in the last few months, and all of them had revolved around the war. Graegor was a valuable ally in a conflict, but without a war, Talandra wondered what he would become. She wondered if he even knew who he was with-out an enemy to fight.

"You've never been one to hold your tongue, so don't start now," said Talandra.

"I see your father's strength in you," said Graegor, briefly gripping her shoulder. "He was decent with a sword. He couldn't best me of course, but he was good enough. You wouldn't last an hour on the front line compared to your brothers."

"Well thank you for pointing out the—"

"But," interrupted Graegor, holding up a meaty hand. "It was never your father's skill with a blade that helped this nation prosper. He didn't cut his neighbours into chunks and force them to bend their knee. He brokered peace between nations in the west, arranged marriages, exchanged ambassadors and a hundred other political games I've no patience for. What you lack in experience on the battlefield, you make up for in other areas."

Talandra wasn't sure what to say. It was the closest thing she'd ever heard to a compliment from the old General.

"One day, this war will end," promised Graegor, "and my job will be over until the next one, but yours will begin in earnest. You will have to build something better from the ashes. That's not something I envy, but I know you can do it."

Never one for labouring a point, Graegor turned on his heel and was walking away before Talandra could thank him.

"We'll always be here to help you," said Thias, "however we can."

"Do you accept?" asked Hyram.

Talandra's thoughts whirled and were slow to settle. She struggled for an answer, but in truth she'd already made her choice.

She poured two mugs of ale and they drank to the memory of their father. They told stories about his life, crying and laughing until the flagon of ale was empty. Hyram fetched two more, and much later Talandra was surprised to see both of those were empty too.

The ale dulled some of the shock and took the edges off their shared grief, but always in the back of her mind was the mountain. The weight of responsibility that came with governing a nation. For one more night she was able to put it to one side, and all of the problems that came with it. And for a time, they were just three siblings enjoying each other's company.

A strong gust of wind made the tavern walls shudder as another heavy blast of rain hammered against the tent canvas. None of the patrons paid it much attention. They were too busy celebrating, drowning their sorrows and mourning friends lost in the day's fighting. The air was filled with a steady hum of conversation, and clouds of blue and grey smoke from cigarettes and pipes. Buckets of sand and water sat in three corners of the tent, just in case there were a fire.

In the fourth corner sat a pair of musicians playing jaunty tunes on a fiddle and drums. They were trying hard to raise people's spirits and lift the depressed mood hanging in the air. Working girls and boys circled throughout the crowd looking for business and free drinks, but they weren't having much luck because of the storm. Most were happy to stay indoors and flirt where it was warm and dry.

Staring into the bottom of her empty glass, Eloise wondered if she could have done more to prevent Ecko's death. On the other side of the table Darius looked equally glum, sipping the last of his ale and grimacing.

"Still hate the taste?"

"It seems to be the only thing to drink around here, and tonight I need something."

Silence settled on their table for a while.

"It was my idea. I should have remained outside the Link," said Eloise.

"I cannot even begin to imagine that," said Darius, gripping her right hand in both of his. "So do not make me."

"I'm sorry."

"I wish he were here with us, but we cannot change the past."

"I just keep seeing it in my head," said Eloise, gulping down some more ale in a desperate attempt to blur the images in her mind. The column of white fire descending from the sky. The terrible echo of pain filtering through the Source and her connection to Ecko.

"The Warlock is more powerful than we imagined," said Darius, but then he laughed and slapped the table. "Despite everything, Ecko nearly killed him. I wish I'd known him better."

"A few more seconds and Ecko would have succeeded. Then all of this would all be over," muttered Eloise, struggling to throw off her melancholy. "I wonder how he did it?"

"Who?"

"The Warlock. How did he become so powerful? I don't believe he did it by himself."

"Who could have helped him, and why did they do it?"

They sat in silence for a while, each pondering the questions. Long before she'd travelled to the desert and been tutored by the Jhanidi, she'd been a student at the Red Tower. It was there she'd first seen Balfruss, already well known among the students and teachers. They'd never spoken of course. The oldest students, those almost ready to go out into the world, did not socialise with the youngest.

But even then she'd seen how members of the Grey Council had looked at him. With a mix of awe and possibly a hint of fear.

Perhaps the mystery surrounding their disappearance wasn't as complex as some claimed. Perhaps they'd gone in search of their Chosen One, but instead they'd found the Warlock, who squeezed them for every bit of information then cast them aside. Worse still, perhaps some of the Splinters were all that remained of the Grey Council. A shiver ran through her at the thought.

"It doesn't matter who helped him," said Eloise, a flush of anger rushing through her. "It only matters that we kill him."

"That is not all that matters. I would not see you consumed by hate. Let the anger fuel you, but do not let it be your master."

Similar words had been spoken during one of her first lessons with the Jhanidi, where she had been educated for a second time about her power. Taking a deep breath she pushed the anger away, but let a small coal of it remain, burning in the back of her mind for when it was needed.

"Let's go to bed," said Eloise. "I want to celebrate life, because tomorrow could be our last."

She thought Darius would wince and tell her that everything would be all right, but he remained silent. He'd mastered his emotions a long time ago, but she could read him easily and knew how deep his worry travelled. Instead he smiled, pulled her into his embrace then kissed her fiercely. Tonight was for the living. They would worry about tomorrow with the dawn.

The royal apothecary woke Balfruss a short time before he was due to guard the royal family. The sleeping draught had mercifully allowed him to sleep without dreams, but now that he was awake the pain of Ecko's loss hit him anew. More than anything Balfruss needed to speak to someone about this who would understand, but all of the other Battlemages were hours away with the army. He thought about talking to Vann, but knew his old friend wouldn't truly comprehend the loss, as he had no concept of the Source.

"You are not alone," said Thule's voice, as crisp as ever in Balfruss's mind despite the distance. *"I am here."*

"I should have been there with you," said Balfruss, moving to the window.

"If you had, the royal family would have been defenceless."

"I could have stopped the Warlock," persisted Balfruss.

"*How?*" asked Thule.

Balfruss stared at the uniform streets of Charas below him for inspiration. "I don't know, but if I'd been there, two of us could have left the Link to fight him. The Warlock wouldn't have stood a chance against two Battlemages."

"*True, but we both know the Warlock is extremely cautious, even in his private meetings with you.*"

Balfruss was stunned. "How long have you known?"

"*Since the first time he approached you by the fire.*"

"Why didn't you say something?" asked Balfruss, as fresh waves of guilt washed over him.

"*Normally I would never have known, if not for this joining. So I was waiting for you to tell us.*"

He shook his head. "How do I tell the others? What do I tell them?"

"*Balfruss, I've heard every word of your conversations with him. If I had any concerns I would have told them myself by now. Just be honest.*"

"Thank you, Thule."

"*You're welcome, my friend. I am always here if you need to talk.*"

Thule's presence faded from his mind and Balfruss rushed to get ready for his nightshift. He may not have been able to stop the Warlock from killing Ecko, but Balfruss wouldn't let him touch the royal family. He would die before he let the Warlock hurt them or another of his brethren.

CHAPTER 27

The vast banqueting hall was cold and featureless one moment, then welcoming and familiar the next. The bare stone walls became huge slabs of white marble veined with gold which glowed and were warm to the touch. At intervals along the walls were huge fireplaces and a roaring blaze in each heated and lit the room, creating long shadows that pooled in the corners. The wood crackled and snapped, and yet no ash littered the immaculate red carpet. Above each fireplace was an ancient tapestry depicting battles from centuries ago. Every detail and thread was impeccable, the colours impossibly bright, as if they'd been perfectly restored or woven only days ago.

At the far end of the room sat a loom, a collection of flags from nations long turned to dust, and a battered wooden chest strapped with black iron. Vargus didn't approach it and couldn't bear to think about what lay inside. Mementos from previous lives and all the memories that came with them. Names and faces of countless people, all of whom were now dead.

All of the furnishings seemed too good to be true, which they were. The room had been empty until his arrival. The only feature not of his making was the long black wooden table and chairs. None of the seats were marked, and yet he instinctively knew which belonged to him.

The others began to arrive soon after and Kai was one of the first. Vargus didn't want to know what he saw when he looked around the room. To his surprise Kai still looked in good health, but it was probably an act. What he had done would not sustain him for very long. No one wanted to show weakness in this place. Mercy might be asked for, but rarely was it given. And one person's mercy was murder to another. Vargus shied away from that particular memory and concentrated on the present.

The others arrived in ones and twos, each looking so ordinary and everyday in their robes, leather armour and gowns of silk or wool. Some were dressed for war, others looked as if they'd just woken up, and one or two wore almost nothing at all. Some resembled farmers daubed with dirt, while others were slathered with oil until their skin shone like polished metal. No two people were the same and their facial features didn't belong to any one nation.

Nethun slapped Vargus on the back in greeting as he moved towards his chair. The big man's bald head shone in the firelight and damp impressions showed on the carpet in the wake of his bare feet. The old sailor swayed from side to side as he went, bellowing greetings, clasping hands and waving at others. Those who found him uncouth smiled and pretended it didn't bother them. Nethun was practically eternal, and it didn't pay to offend him.

Kai put on a good act but was clearly nervous. He politely returned any greetings from others, but stayed close to Vargus, just in case.

A barefoot woman with pale white skin and long black hair down to her waist swept past leaving a rich aroma in her wake. Vargus smelled wild flowers, fresh grass, ripe berries and a hundred other scents he couldn't name, and yet all were tantalisingly familiar.

As ever there were a few new faces in the crowd and it was

they he surreptitiously studied, while pretending not to be interested. In return the newcomers tried not to gawp and point at some of the others, including him. Just as they all knew Nethun, Vargus was old enough to warrant a few stares.

One of the newcomers almost dropped to his knees when Nethun walked past. The wiry youth was pulled to his feet by his companion, a lithe woman dressed in leather and armed to the teeth with knives.

"We don't need to bow," she hissed. Her companion nodded but didn't look convinced. The woman's bravado wavered when Nethun looked in her direction. She took an involuntarily step back, but he just smiled and moved on.

The last few were arriving and as anticipated some were waiting to make a grand entrance. Not far away, a large cluster of people stood around the loveliest woman Vargus had ever seen in all his long years. There were a dozen beautiful women in the hall, but underneath they were all something else. In this place everyone hid their true face, except her. She was radiant and glowed with an inner fire that made her more desirable than any other woman. Vargus also felt incredibly protective of her, and somehow he was also comforted by her presence, as if she were his elder. All of the emotions were jumbled, but at their core they were all feelings of love in different guises. The Blessed Mother was almost as old as the Maker and twice as lovely.

Somewhere a bell started to toll. A small crisp note that sounded so pure. Vargus didn't smile or feel cleansed by it. No bells existed in his version of this place. He knew the others must have heard it too, and no doubt they were also feeling a violation of their space. A few muttered quietly, some simply bit their lip while others pretended it didn't bother them.

The Lady of Light came into the room first, moving slowly as if walking to a death march, trying to draw every eye in the hall. The white gown was supposed to be demure, and yet was so tight around her breasts and hips it was almost transparent. Something that resembled a nun's wimple was tied around her head like a scarf, bright golden hair spilling down her back. In one hand she held a white lantern that burned so bright every shadow in the hall receded. A few people twitched and winced in discomfort. There were some who thrived in the dark.

Nethun's only complaint was to raise an eyebrow and sit down, which prompted everyone else to follow suit. Vargus moved to his seat, beside Nethun and opposite the Blessed Mother. The Lord of Light hurried into the room looking flustered and annoyed. His attempt at making an entrance had been ruined and no one paid him any attention. The hood of his robe fell over his face as he scrambled into his seat and he threw it back with an annoyed flick.

At the head of the table sat an empty chair much larger than the others. Vargus had never it seen occupied. Nethun inclined his head towards the empty seat before standing to address the crowd. As one of the eldest it was his right to conduct the meeting.

"I probably don't need to ask, but who called us here?" asked Nethun. He was used to shouting orders and his voice easily carried to the far end of the long table.

The Lord of Light stood up and started to thank the others for being there, scattering around praise and compliments like grains of rice. Vargus found his nasal voice annoying and blocked out the words until he saw only the gaping of his mouth. It flapped open and closed, reminding him of a drowning fish on a river bank. It was the only way he knew to make the tedious speech a little more bearable.

Tired of seeing the mask of a handsome young man, Vargus looked deeper into the Lord of Light. The room shuddered and everyone's true faces were revealed. The man in white was replaced by a boy with a candle, trying not to draw attention to himself and yet remain useful to his elders. Beside him sat a girl in rags whose face was smeared with soot. The Blessed Mother looked the same and yet her appearance constantly wavered between lover, mother, sister and crone. Summer resembled a collection of golden crops and berries wrapped around the constantly shifting bodies of brown, grey and red furry mammals. Nethun became a vast crustacean wrapped in chains of seaweed, a saw-toothed monster gobbling down ships like minnows in his whirlpool mouth, a school of purple, red and blue fish swimming in perfect unison. The images kept changing and there were so many it started to make Vargus's head spin.

The room flickered again and returned to normal just as the boy finished talking. It was only then that Vargus realised the others were looking at him expectantly.

"What?"

"Were you listening to a single word I said?" asked the boy.

"No, and I've more interest in listening to a donkey fart all day," said Vargus. The Lord of Light tried to appeal to Nethun, but the old sailor just laughed in his face.

"Vargus, please," said the chimney sweep, but he ignored the girl.

"What do you want, boy?"

"In a rush, are we? Keen to get back to building an army of followers?" asked the Lord of Light.

"We all do what we need to in order to survive," said Vargus. The Lord of Light screwed up his face in confusion, missing the point, but a few of the others nodded in understanding. The youngest and the new faces around the table looked equally puzzled. They would learn in time or perish.

"That's why I asked everyone here," said the boy, trying to include them all with his toothy smile. "To see if we can work together and direct the affairs of our followers, not be subject to their whims. We all want to exist for as long as possible."

Vargus sneered, but the Blessed Mother spoke before he could respond. "We have not done that in a long time and it is forbidden."

All eyes turned to the empty seat at the head of the table. It was the last edict the Maker had passed down before disappearing. Many believed him dead, but only Vargus knew the truth.

The Lord of Light licked his lips carefully before speaking. "Maybe it's time we changed that . . . tradition."

"It's not a tradition," said Summer, her rich voice filling the room with its vibrant warmth. Her time was approaching. She was blossoming and growing stronger by the day.

"Who heard him give the order? Were any of you present at the time?" asked the Lord of Light.

He looked up and down the table, but no one chose to answer. Vargus said nothing, pretending that he'd also been told about it from someone else.

"If you're keen to face oblivion by interfering, then go ahead. I won't stop you," said Kai from halfway down the table. "For all we know, you've been doing it already."

"I had nothing to do with your little mishap," said the Lord of Light.

"You fucking child!" screamed Kai, the whole room shuddering under the swell of his monstrous voice. "You're nothing but an abortion. You're not even supposed to exist!"

The Lord of Light didn't flinch at the insult. He calmly rose to his feet and a sneering grin slowly spread across his face. Vargus wanted nothing more than to slap it off, but it wasn't his place to interfere. As Kai realised what he'd done, his anger faded and was replaced by a look of wary caution. To his credit, he didn't sit down but stood his ground. Everyone knew his power was fading while the Lord of Light's was growing exponentially. It wouldn't even be worth calling it a fight if the two of them clashed.

"I see nothing has changed," said the Blessed Mother. As ever she was the voice of reason. She gestured at them both and eventually they sat down, although the Lord of Light was still grinning like an idiot. "If you choose to break with what has been laid down, then the risk will be yours and yours alone. You will not coerce any of us into sharing your punishment." Her voice brooked no further argument, and although he looked as if he wanted to push it further, the Lord of Light remained silent. "Is there anything else we need to discuss?"

"Actually there is," said Winter. Her voice was crisp and edged with a hint of anger that made Vargus's ears hum. "These Battlemages, as they name themselves. They disturb me." Many people around the table made sounds of agreement. "All of you must have felt it. The power some of them can wield is like nothing I've seen in a long time. They are capable of disrupting the natural order of so many things."

"A few of them are more powerful than some of us," complained a new face from further down the table. He sounded scared, and rightly so. "How is this possible?"

"One of them, the Warlock, has delved deeply into the past. He unearthed something that came from beyond the Veil," Nethun said.

"But who told him where to look for it?" asked Winter, the air cracking and frosting in front of her pale blue lips. "Such items were buried deep and the knowledge lost to all mortals."

"And so we return to pointing fingers," said the Blessed Mother with a sigh.

"This is not the first time something like this has happened," said Vargus. "Other Sorcerers were just as powerful once."

"They are lost without their teachers. Their numbers dwindle and many die as children before they come into their power," said the Blessed Mother with regret. "The problem will attend to itself. Their star is waning."

"True, but I'm more interested in who taught the one called the Warlock? If it wasn't one of us, then who guided this man?" asked Winter.

No one had an answer. Glancing around, Vargus saw many worried faces. Those that worked in the shadows would look for answers in their own way, but he had an idea of his own about where to start. The camp was full of stories about the Warlock, but all of it was third-hand information. He needed to get closer to the truth. One day the Warlock would be defeated, either during the span of this war or from old age, but after he was gone they needed to make sure the knowledge and artefacts he had uncovered stayed buried.

There was one other question that no one had asked, which plagued the remaining Battlemages. Why had their teachers abandoned the Red Tower? Looking around the table Vargus wondered if someone here had manipulated the Grey Council, and if so, for what reason?

With no answers, and little else to discuss, they began to disperse. There would not be a grand alliance as the Lord of Light had hoped. The time of ruling over their followers was gone and would not return, no matter how much some might wish it. For good or ill, the future of mankind was their own to make, and in the long and endless struggle, some of those around this table would die. No one was eternal.

CHAPTER 28

The roar of the crowd was still ringing in Talandra's ears as she walked along the empty corridors to her chambers. Thousands had turned out to see her ride through the streets after the coronation. With her father's body turned to ash and carried away on the wind, the people had expected a spectacle, and from the noise they'd not been disappointed. Talandra had witnessed the sight of the armies spread out on the battlefield through a spyglass, but this was different. A sea of faces close enough to touch, all of them screaming for her attention, was a different experience. It made her more aware of how many people were relying on her decisions to be the right ones. The mountain felt particularly heavy today.

Lost in thought Talandra got her long cloak caught between her legs, nearly tripping her. Thankfully there was no one around to see their new Queen stumble and right herself against a wall. When she nearly tripped a second time Talandra realised King Taikon wouldn't need to send assassins. She was more likely to die from falling and breaking her neck because of a stupid ceremonial cloak. Hers would be the shortest reign in the annals of Seveldrom, and the only note left to her in the history books would be in relation to a moth-bitten garment.

As she entered her room Talandra yanked it off and hurled it across the bed. Staring at her reflection she still thought she looked like an idiot, despite the compliments she'd received during and after the ceremony. Her silver gown was very tight, particularly across the bust where the seamstress had done her best to show off Talandra's limited assets. She was convinced that if she sat down too quickly it would split across her arse. The dress was soft and it did feel nice against her skin, but it was so thin it held no real warmth. The frilly collar and cuffs would also make it impossible to eat without dipping them in her food. The dress had apparently been made by the finest tailor in the city.

With a snort Talandra stripped and threw all of the clothes across the room. Getting rid of the stinking cloak wasn't the only tradition she was going to change now that she sat on the throne. Her son or daughter would not be forced to wear it when they eventually took over.

The thought made Talandra pause and sit down heavily on the end of the bed. She'd not been crowned more than an hour and was already making plans about how to change the kingdom. A family. Normally it was the last thing on her mind, but right now it seemed more important than ever. Her thoughts drifted to Shani and that took her down a path she didn't want to explore.

After slipping into clothes that were more comfortable and much warmer, Talandra made her way to the War Room where her Generals and advisors would be waiting. Vannok Lore had been present for the coronation, but he was waiting with fast horses to return to the front line. Everyone stood up as she entered the room, even Graegor, but Talandra waved at them to sit. Her father had never been one to stand on ceremony in private and there were many of his traditions she intended to honour.

"What's the latest?"

"No movement. They've had scouts out, same as us, but

showed no signs of an attack," said Wolfe. His only concession to the coronation was a new green cloak on top of his leathers. Talandra noticed he'd enough common sense to wear a cloak that ended at the waist. No chance of him tripping over it in a hurry. As ever Wolfe was armed with daggers and a short sword, even in the presence of his Queen. An empty quiver sat on his opposite hip and his unstrung longbow rested in a corner of the room.

"Keep me posted. I'll send orders shortly," said Talandra. Wolfe picked up his bow and went out the door. By the time he and Vannok reached the front line the decision would have been made and orders waiting, sent via pigeon or raven. "Is this because of what happened with Ecko?" asked Talandra, turning towards Balfruss.

"I think so," said the Battlemage. He seemed withdrawn, no doubt mourning the loss of his friend, but as he spoke the distant look faded from his eyes. "Ecko might have been defeated, but not before he nearly killed the Warlock."

"I'm tempted to suggest withdrawing your protection at the palace," said Talandra but she quickly held up a hand before anyone could protest. "But I suspect you would counsel against it."

"The Warlock is unpredictable, more so than Taikon. It's unlikely he'll try to kill you in the same way as your father, but the risk, however small, isn't acceptable," he said in a voice that brooked no argument. Graegor grunted in agreement, which was practically a compliment.

"Can you defend the army with one less Battlemage?"

"I don't know." It was a brutally honest answer and not the one Talandra had been hoping for. She expected Graegor to make a comment or argue with Balfruss, but for once the grizzled General remained quiet. She doubted he'd developed any form of subtlety, but perhaps he was not a stranger to loss and could see Balfruss was in pain.

"We need to discuss what happened yesterday," said Hyram, ever the pessimist, but she knew there was a reason their father had listened to counsel from everyone. He always wanted to hear all of the options before making a decision, not just the ones he liked.

"Tell me," said Talandra, getting comfortable.

"Despite our sacrifices, we were nearly defeated. Taikon's numbers are starting to tell." It was a bold statement and again she expected Graegor to argue, but the old General said nothing. Eventually he met Talandra's stare and slowly inclined his head.

"We've done everything we can," said the old General. "Used every trick, fold of the land and scrap of local knowledge to our advantage. It's helped, but now we're on the plains and there's nothing between the armies. They've also got nothing to plunder to slow them down. All the villages between us were abandoned weeks ago, so there are no distractions."

"What would you advise?" asked Talandra, gesturing at everyone to offer their opinion.

"Father created the staging points for this moment," said Thias. "I'd hoped it wouldn't come to it, but it seems inevitable. We should pull back."

"He's right," said Graegor, but Talandra could see the sour twist to the old General's mouth. It probably sounded a lot like running away to him. "The city is our next line of defence."

"It's our last line of defence," Hyram reminded them.

"And what would happen if we dug in and fought? What would our chances be?" asked Talandra.

"You're not seriously considering it?" asked Hyram, aghast.

"It would be brutal, bloody and horrendous," said Thias. "Our men would fight bravely, and while greater discipline gives us the edge, it wouldn't be enough. They'd fight to the last man, because they believe in us. But eventually we would be defeated."

"And your assessment?" Talandra said to Balfruss.

The Battlemage looked as if he'd swallowed a lemon. "I don't disagree with anything that's been said."

"But?"

"Although the city's defences are strong against traditional weapons, there is a greater risk of damage from magic. The Splinters don't need to target me or the other Battlemages. They can crack the gates with lightning, or sap the stones, or a hundred other tricks to bring down the walls in a short amount of time. On the other hand, we wouldn't need to split our focus being in two places at once."

"And what are the risks of a siege?"

"The usual," said Thias. "Disease from so many people living together in a confined space. And if the siege went on longer than we've prepared for, food and water will become an issue. But, the western army will face the same problems. They've already picked the land clean like locusts, scouring it for every drop of food and fuel. The longer it goes on, the more desperate they will become."

"We've been lucky so far. There's been very little of the usual health problems in the camp," said Hyram. His tone told Talandra he didn't expect their good fortune to last.

"How long would it take the army to reach the city if we started a staged withdrawal?" asked Talandra.

"Five days," said Graegor without hesitation.

"One final question. If we pull back into the city, can we win?"

No one rushed to answer her question this time. Their odds were much better because their defences were strong, but the city had never been besieged by such a large army before. The others looked to the most experienced in the room for an answer. Graegor thought on it for a while before finally answering.

"I don't know."

The others probably expected him to say something more, but she knew with so many elements to consider it was almost impossible to judge. If the western army hadn't had any Battlemages of their own then it would be a different story. If Gunder's plans to destabilise the west were successful and the alliance broke apart, then it would be a different situation. A sudden drought, or bout of disease in the enemy camp, could change it again. There were too many factors to predict what might happen. All that they could do was try to limit the damage and prepare for the worst.

"Send the order to the front. Pull the army back into the city," said Talandra. "We'll hold the line here."

After the order was given they discussed other details that needed finalising, but the important decision had been made. Talandra just hoped it was the right one.

Almost two hours later she retired to her chambers, her head whirling with numbers and details about the city and army.

"You should move into the King's chambers," said Shani. Talandra wasn't surprised to see her. In fact, she'd been expecting her for some time. For once she was glad to see Shani fully dressed. She sat perched on the end of the bed, a glass of wine held loosely in one hand.

"I will, but not yet. His ash is still on the wind," said Talandra, fetching a glass for herself. A five-year-old white from Shael. Although common in the past it was perhaps one of the last they'd see in many years. Perhaps ever. There were stories about the Vorga burning vineyards. Everything changed. She needed to prepare not only herself for the future but also her own country.

Shani raised her glass in a toast before taking a sip. "To your health, Majesty."

"I didn't see you at the ceremony," said Talandra, making small talk and delaying the inevitable.

"I was there." Shani put down her glass and crossed the room. "What's wrong? Aren't you happy to see me?"

Talandra forced a smile. "Yes, of course I am."

Shani raised an eyebrow, but still kissed her. "It doesn't seem that way." Talandra moved away and went to stand by the window. "What's wrong?"

Talandra's laugh was bitter. "There's a long list."

"I meant with you."

"I have a lot on my mind. There's much I need to deal with."

"But you're not on your own," said Shani, moving to her again and hugging Talandra from behind. Talandra took comfort from the feeling of Shani's arms around her and forgot everything for a moment. "Now that you're Queen, you can do whatever you want. Change the rules."

"I'm just one person. I can't do everything by myself."

"I'm here to help you, however I can. We all are. You know that."

Talandra turned around to face Shani, still within the comforting circle of her arms. "Do you really mean that? Would you do anything to help me? To help Seveldrom?"

"Of course I would," said Shani, her gaze never wavering. "It's my home."

"There's so much to do. More than I ever realised."

"What are you saying?"

"I can't be selfish and think only of myself. Not even for a moment."

"Answer the question," pressed Shani.

Talandra moved to the far side of the room before speaking. "I cannot be Queen and head of intelligence. You will run the network for me."

A big smile started to creep across Shani's face, but then froze halfway. A heavy silence settled on the room, stretching out between them. "What about us?" she asked. Talandra's silence spoke volumes.

Talandra started to turn away but Shani crossed the room and slapped her hard across the face. Talandra just stared and said nothing.

"Say something."

"What do you want me to say?" asked Talandra.

"That this isn't the end!"

Blood rushed to Talandra's face but the anger quickly faded, leaving behind only disappointment and regret. "Would you really be happy as a concubine?"

"What?"

"My father had three children. Three heirs. The people expect me to have a family," said Talandra. "My position, my responsibility to the future, demands it. An unbroken royal bloodline would secure the succession. But maybe you could lurk in the shadows for the nights when I'm alone." The look on Shani's face spoke volumes about that idea. Even though it felt as if she were driving a spear through her heart, Talandra pressed on. "One day I will marry a man and have children. It's the right thing to do for my country."

"That's very noble and selfless, but don't pretend it's the only reason, yes?" said Shani, falling back on her old way of talking.

Talandra smiled, unwilling to lose her temper again. "You're right. It's not the only reason. I've always wanted children, but you knew that. It's why we never spoke about the future. Did you know my father knew about us?"

Shani's mouth fell open. "You never said anything."

"He never mentioned you by name, but he told me that one day I would have to make a choice."

"What choice?"

"To live for the moment, or to build something and create the future. I've made my choice." The words had an ominous sound, like a door closing. Talandra's posture shifted as she slouched off the unofficial part of their relationship and adopted a neutral expression.

"Shanimel, I am formally offering you the position as head of the intelligence network for Seveldrom. If you do not feel able to fulfil these duties then I expect your resignation, together with the names of three replacements, on my desk by tomorrow morning."

"Tell me one thing. Answer one question truthfully," said Shani, and Talandra gestured for her to continue. "Do you love me?"

They stared at each other for a long time, saying nothing. She desperately wanted to answer, but couldn't and had to work hard to stay calm and hold back the tears. Her throat tightened and she forced her breathing to remain slow and even. She wondered what Shani saw when she looked at her. Would Talandra even recognise her own face in a mirror?

In those final intimate moments together she tried to memorise every line and curve of Shani's face. She tried to fix in her memory the passionate nights they'd spent in her room. A part of Talandra knew that quiet moments, and time devoted to personal pleasure, would be few and far between in the future.

Shani crossed the room and for a brief moment Talandra thought she was going to kiss her, but the spark of hunger in her eyes faded. Instead she walked out without saying another word, leaving Talandra alone with her duty and responsibilities.

CHAPTER 29

After four days of guarding the army's withdrawal to the capital, Balfruss felt physically and emotionally drained. He'd spent each day on edge, in a constant state of readiness, expecting an attack at any moment from the Warlock and his Splinters. So far there'd been no sign, but none of the Battlemages dared relax. They all knew the Warlock to be extremely dangerous and unpredictable. The unusual murder of the King and recent loss of Ecko served as constant reminders of the Warlock's power and abilities.

During the withdrawal, Darius took his turn guarding the royal family at night, so at least Balfruss didn't need to sleep through most of the day any more. When he had, finally, slept at night he'd been so tired that mercifully there had been no dreams. Balfruss didn't know how long that would last. Thule had shared with him what he'd seen and felt from Ecko's final moments and already a seed of guilt was starting to flower in Balfruss's stomach. If he'd been honest with the others from the start and told them everything about the Warlock, then perhaps it wouldn't have happened. Or if he'd stayed in the field and someone else had protected the royal family at night, his strength might have made the difference. The mix of guilt and regret made his stomach ache and left a sour taste in his mouth. The Warlock would pay dearly for Ecko.

As well as Battlemages, Seve cavalry scouts maintained a constant watch, but the western army didn't pursue them. They seemed content to rest and regain their strength, while the Seve warriors slowly crawled home through a river of churned mud. A steady downpour on the second day limited their ability to see the enemy, making the scouts' task much more dangerous, but fortunately no men were lost. The rain didn't affect the Battlemages, as they relied on other senses to detect the presence of magic, but it didn't stop them being as miserable as everyone else. After a day spent riding in soggy clothing that clung to the skin, a dry set of clothes, a warm fire and a hot meal were cherished blessings.

On the third day the western army began to follow. If both armies maintained their current speed, and there were no surprises, the Seve army would have a few days in the city before the siege began.

At the end of the fourth day the army was only a few miles from the city, but still stopped for the night to set up camp. There wasn't enough daylight to move warriors into the city, a laborious task that would take up most of a day.

As soon as he'd pitched his tent Balfruss lay down on his bedroll. He expected to fall into a black pit as he'd done on previous nights. Nothing happened, even though it felt as if his eyes had been scrubbed with sand he couldn't sleep. Instead his mind came awake, his thoughts sharpening with unusual clarity. Stripped of all distractions the silence bred fear. All of his worries and doubts about the war came to the surface. He persisted for a time, determined to get some rest, but none of the meditation techniques he knew were working.

Frustrated and annoyed Balfruss left his tent and was surprised to see it was dark outside. He must have fallen asleep at some point, but felt no better for the rest.

Although some warriors were still awake, sat around fires not far away, he didn't feel as if he could intrude. Many of them had lost family, friends and brothers in arms, and were in mourning. Heaping his misery about Ecko on top of theirs wouldn't help anyone.

Instead he watched their shadows pass back and forth in front of the flames and when the smell of cooking meat reached his nose his stomach grumbled in complaint. His last meal was a distant memory and his mouth began to water. He was about to start building up the fire when a shadow fell across him.

He came to his feet and was only slightly surprised to see the Warlock. As before, he wore plain clothes to suggest he was nothing more than a common labourer with the army. He might be powerful, but he was also wise enough to avoid a fight when it wasn't necessary. For a few seconds Balfruss considered raising the alarm. Torval might be able to stop the first few swords and arrows, but Balfruss wondered how he'd manage against fifty, or a hundred warriors. In the end he decided it wasn't worth the risk. It was very likely Torval would kill them all and their deaths would be on Balfruss's conscience.

Balfruss gestured for him to sit down as he built up the fire. Torval seemed completely at ease in the middle of the sprawling camp, making Balfruss glad he hadn't warned the others. As he stacked the kindling Balfruss noticed Torval's face was pale and drawn, his cheeks hollow and dark smudges circled his eyes. His shirt was loose and Balfruss could see a bandaged lump on his chest from where Ecko had wounded him.

"He nearly tore out my heart," said Torval with a smile. "It's taken me days to recover."

He looked a long way from recovered, hours away from death in fact, but Balfruss didn't say it. Perhaps he should take a risk, try to kill the Warlock and put an end to this conflict. The thought drifted in and out of his mind as he weighed up the potential risks and benefits.

Balfruss lit the kindling with flint and tinder, added small twigs and gradually built up the blaze. There was leftover stew in the pot, which he set to warm on an iron tripod over the fire. He offered a bowl to Torval, who declined with a wave of his hand. Even that small movement made him wince in pain. His smile didn't look nearly as smug or arrogant as a few days ago.

"I know why you're here," said Balfruss, stirring the stew with a thick wooden spoon.

"Really?"

"You're going to try and convince me that we're the same. That we're alike because we both have a thirst for knowledge."

"Power," said Torval, holding up a finger. "Power is everything. That's what you want, just like me."

Balfruss shrugged his shoulders and looked around at the vast camp spread out around them. "Power for what? To rule? Lead an army? I don't want either of those things."

Torval dismissed those suggestions with a shake of his head. "Neither do I. Blinkered bureaucrats and morons with sharpened steel."

"Then what do you want?"

"To create the future," hissed Torval. His eyes burned with a peculiar, unsettling light. Staring into them Balfruss saw a hint of madness and something he hadn't expected. Loneliness.

"The future?"

"Religions come and go. Wars move the borders a little this way, a little that way. They cull the population for a generation, but nothing is built, nothing created of value that lasts. It's all a distraction."

Balfruss did nothing to hide his sarcasm. "Instead of fighting we should be working together."

"Exactly!"

Balfruss shook his head. "You didn't unite the west for that. You have no interest in peace, or helping people better themselves. You put a madman in charge of an army. You're partly responsible for every life that's been lost."

Torval ignored the barb and wouldn't be taunted. "Do you know why the Sull refuse to deal with us?"

"The Sull? No one has spoken to them in over a hundred years."

Torval ignored him. "It's because we're so primitive compared to them. We're savages, rolling around in the mud, fighting over scraps of land. They've moved beyond such petty rivalries."

That only confirmed what Balfruss had suspected for some time. The Warlock was insane. No one was in contact with the Sull. No one. "You think you're special. Better than everyone else, but the truth is, I pity you."

Something he'd said finally caught Torval's attention. His mouth gaped a few times before he regained control. "You pity me? Please," said Torval, gesturing expansively, "enlighten me."

"Once you and I were alike," admitted Balfruss. "When I was a boy I dreamed of escaping the daily hardship my mother endured. It was selfish and ungrateful, but I was just a boy. She seemed to work all hours of the day and some nights too. She was always tired and never at peace. Once I asked her if she dreamed at night. She told me she didn't have time for dreams. For her, sleep was a release. It was her only time to rest and put down her burdens. I wanted something more. When I found out about my ability, I saw the Red Tower as my one chance. I absorbed everything they taught me, but it wasn't enough."

"It was the same for me. What they taught was so narrow. The teachers and the Council promised much, but they hoarded their knowledge."

Balfruss guessed what happened next. "So you travelled in search of something more. Something worthy of you."

"You went into the west and the deserts of the east. Did you find what you were looking for?" asked Torval.

Balfruss ignored him this time. "But then you began to change. Your magic became a crutch. You used it to bully and control others. If someone didn't agree, then you found a way to change their mind, sometimes literally, with magic. You've spent so much time by yourself, listening only to your own counsel, that you can't accept what other people think any more. They must be wrong, because you are strong and they are weak, and only the strong deserve to survive. You've never met anyone that's challenged you."

"Are you going to challenge me?" asked Torval. All humour had steadily drained from his expression and now he looked on the brink of violence.

"If I must."

The Warlock's voice was very quiet, but Balfruss heard every word. "I've seen more than you can imagine. I've crossed the Dead Sea and walked through the endless emerald jungle. I was the first outsider to speak to the Sull in over three hundred years. I've discovered ancient temples devoted to religions from a thousand years ago. My skills and knowledge are beyond the Grey Council. How are you going to challenge me?" The question was dripping with scorn and yet Balfruss felt utterly calm.

"Because you're weak," he said. "You're weak because you're incapable of change. Everyone else grew up, but you're still a scared and stubborn little boy. You're desperate to convince me because you're lonely. You need affirmation. You need someone else to tell you that what you're doing is right."

"You have no idea," snarled Torval.

"Are you having doubts?"

Torval continued as if he hadn't spoken. "You have no idea what I can do. I could kill you in a hundred different ways."

"Threats. How original," Balfruss said with a smile as he stood up. "You seem to forget that I was also trained at the Red Tower. And even if I don't know how something is done with magic, I can easily disrupt the flows."

Too late Torval realised what was about to happen. Balfruss focused his will and reached for the Source. With the speed of thought a giant hand grabbed Torval's body, yanking him into the air. The illusion flickered, and for a few heartbeats he could see through the image of Torval's body dangling off the ground. Narrowing his eyes Balfruss saw faint threads of power running away from the projection into the distance, like the strings of a puppet. As much as he struggled there was no way for Torval to break free without Balfruss releasing him.

"I know this won't kill you, but it will hurt a lot," said Balfruss. He imagined a short sword being driven through Torval's forearm and it became a reality for the projection. Torval screamed and thrashed about, but no blood dripped from the wound and no one came running. No one else could see or hear him.

"I will—"

Before Torval could finish his threat Balfruss drove another sword through his other arm. The Warlock's mouth stretched wider and wider in a silent scream until it looked as if he would dislocate his jaw. His eyes rolled back in his head and he thrashed about but it made no difference.

"I'm ashamed to say that when I first heard that one man had united the west, I admired you," said Balfruss. "I imagined the Warlock to be a great man to have accomplished so much in such a short space of time. Now, I just pity you."

"I thought you had vision," said Torval between gritted teeth, "but you're just like the rest. Narrow minded, focusing only on tomorrow. The next sunrise, the next meal. With our power we could do anything, go anywhere. We could live forever as Gods and create a new world."

"I don't want any part of that."

"I will make you beg for death," promised Torval. "I will strip you of every friend, kill everyone you care about one at a time, until there's no one left. Then I will show you who you really are."

He released the Warlock and, instead of falling, the illusion remained hovering in the air. "Don't come here again."

Balfruss thought he would make another threat. Instead the Warlock just snarled and vanished.

The stew was bubbling in the pot but Balfruss had lost his appetite. The next time they met it would be as implacable enemies. His knees wobbled, but he managed to sit without falling over. His doubts resurfaced anew and, for the first time in years, Balfruss prayed to the Maker for strength and courage.

CHAPTER 30

Gunder was sat in his kitchen looking over the accounts when someone started pounding on his front door. Although it was late, he had been expecting a visitor, but they never usually came through the front or bothered to knock.

"Open up! In the name of the Emperor!"

Gunder grimaced as he realised who stood outside, and what was about to happen. He considered running, but knew it would only convince them of his guilt. As a humble merchant he had nothing to hide. He couldn't risk them finding out about the other part of his life.

Leaning heavily on his cane he limped to the door. Six members of Taikon's Chosen were standing outside. All were armed and one held a lantern that left their faces in shadow. It gave them a villainous look, but Gunder could see it was more than just a trick of the light. These men were recent recruits and not true believers. Their leader, marked with white epaulettes on his uniform, was the only one who didn't resemble a thief or former street tough. He was a broad-chested Zecorran and had the rigid bearing of a soldier.

"Stand aside, fatty!" said one of the men, barging past Gunder and nearly knocking him over. The others followed, leaving the officer on the doorstep.

"You're accused of spying and being an agent of foreign powers working against Emperor Taikon," said the officer. His black eyes revealed nothing but his bushy eyebrows waggled as he spoke, giving him a comical appearance. "We've received a report about suspicious activity."

"I'm just a spice merchant," said Gunder, wobbling and nearly falling over again. The officer put out a hand to steady him. "I don't know anything about spying. I swear it by the Lord of Light. May he strike me down if I'm lying."

Gunder put his hand over his heart and the officer's hand twitched in response as he started to copy then stopped himself. Long years of habit were hard to break. The officer still believed in the Lord of Light, but it wouldn't do for one of the Chosen to be seen making gestures to an old religion.

Behind him it sounded as if the soldiers were rummaging around in his kitchen and throwing objects on the floor.

"If you're just an honest merchant then you'll have no issue with us searching your home."

"Of course not," said Gunder, stepping back to create space. "Please, come in. Would you like a drink? Tea, or wine perhaps?"

The Zecorran gave him a strange look before stepping inside. He was probably more used to people hurling abuse in his face than engaging him in polite conversation and offering him a drink.

"No, thank you."

A heavy object hit the floor and shattered, making Gunder wince.

"Watch what you're doing!" roared the officer, hurrying towards the kitchen. Gunder followed at a more sedate pace, as befitting an overweight man with a bad knee.

As expected every cupboard and drawer had been opened and their contents scattered across the table and heaped on the floor.

A couple of glasses had been broken and the shards were being ground underfoot by the thugs.

"We've got to be thorough, Sir," said one of the men with a grin that showed uneven yellow teeth. He pushed past Gunder and went into the front room. Taking out his sword, Yellowtooth pointed at a delicate black vase sat on the mantle above the fireplace. "Anything you want to tell us?" he asked, tapping the point of his blade against the vase.

"I don't understand," said Gunder. With a sad shake of his head Yellowtooth pushed the vase off the mantle. It shattered against the tiled floor with a loud crash and the other men cheered from the doorway. Next Yellowtooth pointed his blade at the watercolour hung above the fireplace. It was a simple painting Gunder had picked up from one of the local markets. It wasn't expensive and the artist wasn't famous, but there was something about it that he liked. It depicted a busy day in port, with ships jostling for space on the docks and sailors swarming like ants as they unloaded cargo. His favourite part was the sky. A single white gull soared in a cloudless sky, high above the noise and the rush. It spoke to him of freedom and peace.

"Anything to say?" asked Yellowtooth, pressing the tip of his sword against the canvas. "Favourite of yours, is it? Expensive, maybe?"

Gunder was about to protest, but then stopped himself. He realised he was genuinely concerned about the painting. A cheap object that had no worth other than sentimental value. From his eye corner Gunder caught sight of his reflection in a decorative mirror, another local handicraft he'd picked up on a whim. A fat merchant stared back at him.

"Anything you want to tell us, fatty?" asked Yellowtooth, getting impatient.

"No," said Gunder. The man slashed the painting while the others continued with the search, moving into other rooms of the house. The loss of the painting stung, but Gunder pushed away the feelings as other personal items around the house were broken.

The officer looked puzzled when Gunder sat down and ignored the continuing destruction. A few minutes later the men returned from the other rooms looking annoyed and dejected. Sticking out of Yellowtooth's pocket was a small white marble statue taken from Gunder's sacred corner. One of the other men had suspicious lumps in the pockets of his breeches.

"We didn't find anything. No papers or nothing."

The officer pointed at the barely concealed icon. "What's that?"

Yellowtooth grinned as he pulled out the statue, a representation of the Lord of Light. "Illegal, innit. It's not Taikon, the one true God, just that Lantern prick."

The officer snatched it away from Yellowtooth and backhanded him across the face. "Get out!"

For a second it looked as if Yellowtooth was going to reach for his weapon. Then he saw the officer's hand already resting on the hilt of his sword and changed his mind. "All of you. Empty your pockets then get out!"

Looking suitably cowed the Chosen dumped several items by the front door and shuffled out. Once he'd regained his composure the officer carefully put the religious icon down on the table with a touch of reverence. "I apologise for my men and for any damage they've caused. I'll make sure you're compensated."

"Nothing important was destroyed," said Gunder, in a hollow voice. "It can be easily replaced."

"Well then," said the officer. He clearly wasn't sure what he was doing any more and seemed at a loss for words. With a vague shrug he went to the front door. Just as he was about to step outside, Gunder spoke.

"I would offer a blessing, but I wouldn't want to break any

new laws." The officer froze on the threshold and Gunder thought he would apologise again. With a sigh he went out, carefully closing the door behind him. Gunder sat down and stared around at the wreckage of his house.

The silence that filled Gunder's ears was so complete it made his ears hum.

"I take it you heard everything?" he said to the empty room.

"Most of it."

Roza came into the room from the kitchen. She was dressed in a long black cloak, but as she approached, Gunder caught a brief glimpse of her clothing underneath. The short black leather skirt, knee-high boots and black corset with red lace wasn't her usual attire.

He raised an eyebrow and she pulled the cloak tighter. "Should I ask?"

Roza shook her head and he let the matter drop. He was aware she had several aliases, but this was the first time he'd seen one of her costumes. The clothes were very much at odds with Roza's nature. Then again, who was he to comment? He barely knew where the fat man in the mirror ended and he began any more.

"Do you want to change our plans?" she asked, gesturing at the front door with her chin.

"No. I'll just have to take more precautions from now on." Gunder picked up the icon of the Lord of Light. The sculptor had been very careful not to commit sacrilege. The face inside the hood remained totally blank, without any human features, not even a shadow of a jawline or nose. A faceless man. It seemed quite apt. "How did your last meeting go with the local rebels?"

"Good. Mercenaries from Drassia are continuing to trickle into the country and city in small groups. They're being lodged in warehouses and walled estates that the Chosen wouldn't dare approach. In a few days we'll have enough men to hold the city and more close by. Enough to stop an invading army, perhaps."

"Good."

"Are you well?" asked Roza, taking a few steps closer.

Gunder ignored the question. "I've spoken to several senior officers in the Watch. It's painstaking and slow work. They're being very careful with everyone, given recent events."

"I don't blame them. Has something else happened? You seem ... different."

"I'm fine," he said, forcing a smile. "I've received word from several contacts in the north. Civil unrest is continuing to mount in Zecorria with High Priest Filbin speaking out in public against Taikon. A few of the Emperor's fanatics have even been attacked in the streets of the capital. There have also been some protests and demonstrations at Taikon's new temples. But did you notice building has recommenced here on Taikon's temple?"

Roza grimaced. "I thought we'd done enough to sabotage that."

"Apparently not. The Seve army is withdrawing to Charas. They're claiming it as a victory, which helped morale. As a result they've swelled the local ranks of the Chosen with thieves, thugs and pickpockets. Useless in a pitched fight, but a large group of men will intimidate anyone."

"What do you want me to do?"

Gunder turned the icon over before seizing it by the base and smashing it down on the edge of the table. The head snapped off and rolled away under his chair.

"Our orders are to push forward with the rebellion as fast as we dare. Strengthen Yerskania and free Perizzi."

"Is the war going that badly?"

"No, but the siege is about to begin. Any birds or bats leaving the city might be shot down, so we may not receive orders very often going forward. Talandra also gave me one more order." Gunder paused and thought about how best to phrase it.

"From your expression it's not good."

"We're to prepare for the worst."

"Meaning what?" asked Roza.

"That if Seveldrom should fall and the west wins the war, we're to stay in character and continue working from the shadows."

Despite the bleak scenario he'd just laid out Roza was still looking at him with concern. He found it touching, and smothered that emotion too.

"You have your orders. Keep me posted on the rebels."

She studied his face, looking deep into his eyes and probably read a lot more than he was used to sharing with others. Breathing deeply Gunder relaxed his facial muscles and shoulders until his body language became unreadable and his expression blank.

She nodded slowly, and went out the door without another word.

CHAPTER 31

It was well past midnight when Balfruss stumbled towards his room in the palace. After a long day the army was finally inside the city and the gates were sealed. The western army wasn't expected to arrive for another two days, but that didn't mean there was time to rest during the interim. His first day in the capital had been filled running drills with warriors and endless meetings with the Queen and her advisors. He hoped that after such a tiring day he would fall asleep the moment he closed his eyes, and mercifully rest without dreams.

As his bedroom door came into view Balfruss came to an abrupt halt. Crouched in front of the door was a man. For a split second he thought it was the Warlock, but realised his eyes were playing tricks on him. The warrior looked nothing like Torval, a tall man with a grizzled face, deep blue eyes and shaven head. He was thick across the chest and his arms were criss-crossed with old scars. Most surprising was the sword on his back and the heavy daggers on his belt. No one apart from warriors guarding the royal family were allowed to carry weapons in the palace.

"I'm Vargus," he said, offering his hand. Balfruss shook it and took further measure of the man. His grip was firm but not crushing, suggesting a man of strength who didn't need to prove it. There was also a careful, measured look in his eyes that spoke of wisdom and an instinct for survival.

"I need your help with Finn," said Vargus.

Balfruss leaned against a wall and closed his eyes for a moment. "What happened?"

"He's in The Tin Whistle. It's a warriors' tavern."

Balfruss rubbed the bridge of his nose where a headache was forming behind his eyes. "Has he caused any trouble?"

"Not yet, but he's been drinking for hours and he won't leave."

Everyone in the army knew who the Battlemages were and what they could do, and although no one had said it, Balfruss knew a lot of people were afraid of him and his brethren. The old folk story about angering a wizard and the explosive consequences was deeply ingrained in the general psyche.

"Show me," said Balfruss.

The Tin Whistle was located in the New City and the long walk from the palace in the cool air helped Balfruss wake up. On the way Vargus didn't speak unless spoken to and he seemed watchful for danger.

"Expecting trouble?"

Vargus spoke without turning around. "You never know. They closed the gates, but didn't flush out all the rats first."

Balfruss heard noise from The Tin Whistle long before he saw the tavern. Music from fiddle and drum, surprisingly in tune, drifted along the streets, and he could also hear a crowd of people stamping their feet in time to the music. As the tavern came into sight the music reached a crescendo and the noise from the crowd increased. Rich golden light spilled through windows onto the street, and Balfruss was surprised to see a few tables outside. Given the current circumstances, rules about drinking on the streets must have been eased.

Thankfully it looked as if there hadn't been any trouble, as the mood of those drinking outside remained friendly. Most were leaning into the tavern through the windows, singing along with everyone else. Not far away Balfruss spotted two enforcers keeping watch, but tonight they had little to do except tap their feet to the rhythm. The music swelled one final time and the tavern erupted in a huge round of applause.

Vargus led the way through the packed room, filled with warriors drinking away their wages, and valiant barmaids trying to keep up with the thirsty crowd. The room was warm from so many bodies pressed together and the musicians were dripping with sweat from their exertions. Every tavern was experiencing its best trade in months and this would continue until the siege ended. If the war didn't end soon the warriors would drain every barrel in the city.

Every chair and space in the room was filled, except for one table against the far wall with only one occupant. Balfruss went straight towards it and was surprised to see a long sword on the table in front of Finn. A dozen empty glasses were lined up beside the blade and the smith was nursing another half-empty glass. His eyes were bloodshot and there was a dangerous gleam behind them. He was desperate for a fight.

People carried on talking and laughing as if nothing was wrong, but Balfruss noticed a few glanced nervously in their direction. Vargus sat down beside him and touched the hilt of the long sword with reverence.

"That's beautiful," said Vargus. At first glance it looked exactly like every other sword Balfruss had seen, until he tilted his head to one side. The steel had a green tinge one second and then shifted to pale blue the next. It was an elegant blade that bore no fanciful decoration or unnecessary adornments. A simple weapon created with its purpose in mind over style. Nevertheless, the sword was the work of a master smith.

"You'd think so," slurred Finn. His voice was rough and cracked as if he'd been shouting, or perhaps crying for hours.

"What is it?" Balfruss was keen to get Finn talking. A fight in the tavern with magic would kill everyone and bring down the building on top of them.

"It's what I've been working on at night," said Finn. He stared at the sword with a mixture of hatred and despair. Balfruss reached out a hand towards the blade before pulling up short. "It's safe," Finn reassured him.

The metal felt cool to the touch but Balfruss could sense something stirring beneath the surface. A faint prickle of energy danced across his fingertips. He pulled his hand back as if burned, but the skin was unmarked. Finn smiled but it quickly became a grimace, painting his face with misery. He downed the last of his ale and waved the empty glass towards one of the serving girls. She keenly avoided making eye contact and he growled.

"This was forged from that weird lump of metal?" asked Balfruss, trying to distract the smith.

Finn nodded. "Star metal. No one has done it before. Ever," he said, thumping the table, and all of the glasses jumped and clinked together. "I took it to the Forge Masters in the Old City."

From the corner of his eye Balfruss could see Vargus staring in wonder, or perhaps fear, at the sword. "What happened?"

"At first they didn't believe me. They thought I was a fraud until I showed them how." A tiny spark of blue fire danced along Finn's fingertips and over his knuckles like a coin before disappearing.

"And then?"

"They didn't want to know," snarled Finn. His hands tightened around his glass until it cracked. "They were scared of me and *Maligne*, for she is truly spiteful. Forge Masters, scared of a sword." Finn's laugh was harsh and bitter. It rattled in his chest until he started to cough violently. He raised the glass to his lips, remembering at the last second that it remained empty. A dangerous glimmer crept back into his eyes and Balfruss quickly lowered Finn's hand.

"I'll get us a drink," he promised. Balfruss waved at a barmaid, who was slow to approach. From her expression he could see she'd rather stick her head into a wasps' nest than come too close. At first he thought she was just afraid of Finn, but then he realised it wasn't only the smith.

"Three ales please," he said before leaning close to whisper. "Water his down. He won't be able to taste the difference."

The girl nodded, took his money and disappeared into the crowd.

"I told you this power was a curse," muttered Finn. "Doesn't matter what I can do, or how many times I save people, they're still afraid of me. Everyone is afraid of me."

"I'm not afraid of you," said Balfruss.

"The rest are," said Finn with a vague wave of his hand at the crowd, "and they should be. This power, it's not something we're supposed to have. I can kill hundreds of people with just a wave of my hand. No one should have that power over others."

"I'm not afraid of you," said Vargus. Finn laughed but then just stared at the warrior with a puzzled expression. Their drinks arrived but the staring contest between the two men continued. The barmaid tapped the rim of one glass before leaving. Balfruss pushed it across the table towards the smith.

"You're not afraid," admitted Finn with a grunt. "Why?"

Vargus shrugged and took a sip of ale. "I've been around people with magic before. I know roughly how it's done. Most people are scared because they can't share what you can do."

"What do you mean?" said Finn, reaching for his ale. He took a drink and didn't seem to notice anything unusual about the taste.

"All of my stories are about stopping someone from hacking me to pieces at the last second. About muscles burning, my heart pounding and going blind from blood running in my eyes. I talk about nearly drowning in the mud after being stepped on and not knowing which way is up or down. I've been in a hundred battles, and in the end they all come down to a bloodbath in the mud. Do they sound like your sort of stories?"

Finn shook his head.

"Every warrior is afraid of dying," said Vargus, gesturing at other men in the room. "If it comes at the end of a sword, it's a tragedy and all, but it's not surprising, given what we do. The risk comes with the work. I don't like the idea of dying, I don't want it to happen, but I can understand it." Vargus paused then shook his head in bemusement. "But what you do, tearing people apart with a wave, calling down lightning, setting people on fire with just your mind, they don't understand that. It makes you different, but you're still just a man. Flesh and blood, like the rest of us."

Finn sighed and stared down at the sword on the table. He seemed lost in thought so Balfruss left him alone, enjoying the rest of his drink in silence.

Not far away the tired musicians were having a well-deserved rest, but despite the hour the crowd showed no signs of going home. The landlord was urging them to play again and people all around started cheering them on. A slow clap started to get them moving and soon almost every person in the room was applauding. A third musician, carrying a set of bamboo pipes from Shael, joined the other two on the little stage. They let the noise from the crowd build before the lead musician finally agreed with a florid bow. The crowd roared then fell silent in expectation. The trio launched into a fast-paced tune that Balfruss remembered hearing as a boy. It was about reading the future and finding true love from the pattern in a rug, or some such nonsense. Within a few minutes everyone was clapping and singing along and he couldn't help smiling at the buoyant mood.

Vargus tapped him on the shoulder and he turned back to see Finn had fallen asleep. The warrior reverently put Finn's sword in its leather scabbard and then slung it across his back alongside his own blade. Working together they managed to get Finn to his feet. The smith was a massive dead weight and they struggled to keep him upright, but thankfully the crowd made space for them. No doubt they were glad to see the back of the Battlemages.

Outside the air was cooler but their burden no lighter. It was going to be a long walk back to the palace.

"Do you think he really heard any of what we said?" asked Vargus.

"I don't know. The wound is deep and he hates what he's become," huffed Balfruss. "Fucking Grey Council."

If they hadn't abandoned their posts, the Red Tower wouldn't have become so disorganised and Battlemages wouldn't be so rare. Seekers would have identified Finn's ability years ago. If they'd done their job Finn would be the most powerful Battlemage alive. He might have been able to stop the Warlock by himself and save thousands of lives. Maybe he could have ended the war before it began.

"You don't blame the Warlock?" said Vargus.

"I blame him too, but a lot of people would still be alive if the Grey Council hadn't deserted us."

The noise from the tavern faded as they shuffled Finn towards the gates of the Old City. Not for the first time Balfruss wished Finn was a much smaller man. As his muscles began to burn he considered using magic to carry the smith. Gritting his teeth against the pain they pressed on.

"Is it true what they say about the Warlock?" asked

Vargus. "We hear stories in camp, but I don't believe most of them."

Eager for a distraction to keep his mind off their burden, Balfruss was happy to talk. "What have you heard?"

"That Taikon is dead and the Warlock controls his corpse like a meat puppet."

"Sadly that's not true. Taikon is still alive, but he's completely insane."

"I heard he was always mad, but the Warlock made him worse," said Vargus.

They paused to catch their breath, leaning Finn against the side of a building. Balfruss took a moment to stretch his back and rest his aching shoulders.

"The Warlock gave Taikon an artefact, some ancient relic."

"Magic?" asked Vargus, rolling his shoulders.

Balfruss nodded. "Taikon was paranoid about it being stolen, so he swallowed it. No one knows what it is, but it made him worse. Drove him over the edge."

"If I had a magic stone in my belly, it would probably do the same," mused Vargus. "Ready?"

They pulled Finn to his feet again and resumed their long walk. A few minutes later Balfruss was glad to see the gates of the Old City.

"Do you know where the artefact came from?" asked Vargus as they passed through the gates. The guards had seen them pass the other way so they just waved them through.

"There are rumours, but I have a theory," said Balfruss.

For a few minutes they shuffled along in silence. The muscles in Balfruss's arms and shoulders were screaming at him to put Finn down and yet he kept smiling at the pain in his joints.

"I've got time," said Vargus. He sounded out of breath and Balfruss realised his own breathing was getting loud.

"I think it might be a relic from one of the old religions.

There are stories about priests healing wounds and bringing the dead back to life."

"A priest of the Twelve?"

Balfruss peered curiously at Vargus but the warrior was staring straight ahead, watching their path for obstructions. Not many people knew about the Twelve. Most thought religion started with the Maker.

"No. I was thinking of those that came before the Twelve. The Triumvirate." This time Balfruss felt Vargus's stare and their eyes met briefly.

"I'm surprised you know about them."

"I could say the same thing."

Looming over the top of nearby buildings stood the palace at the heart of the Old City. The upward sloping streets were more pronounced and the muscles in Balfruss's legs began to pull more fiercely.

After what seemed like the longest hour of their lives, they stumbled through the front doors of the palace. The guards recognised Vargus and knew all of the Battlemages on sight. Although their presence made some servants in the palace nervous, the guards also saw the wisdom of keeping them close. After what had happened to the King no one was taking any chances with protecting the Queen.

Finn was still completely unconscious and had started to snore. As they manhandled him along the corridors and up the stairs he didn't stir, not even when they accidentally knocked his head against a wall.

Eventually they reached Finn's room and after shuffling sideways through the door they dumped him on the bed. He fell in a heap and continued to snore, lying face down. Balfruss stretched out his back, working out the kinks before taking a minute to catch his breath. He was slick with sweat, even more exhausted than when he'd seen Vargus waiting at his bedroom door, and yet he was glad. It felt good to hear his heart pounding and his whole body throb with tired muscles. Vargus was winded but he recovered quickly.

They rolled Finn onto his side, pulled off his boots and covered him with a blanket before retreating into the corridor.

"I'm glad you came to get me," said Balfruss.

"I'm just glad it didn't end in violence," said Vargus. "Magic or otherwise."

Balfruss's headache had returned with a vengeance and he was practically asleep on his feet. Vargus left in search of his own bed and when Balfruss lay down he fell asleep almost immediately. But his dreams were not peaceful. His mind's eye swarmed with images of burning cities in Shael where charred corpses walked through the streets, beseeching him to end their suffering.

Balfruss came awake with a start, bile rising in the back of his throat but he pushed it down. One man was responsible for everything that had happened. Rage worse than any Balfruss had ever felt before burned inside. His hands began to shake and blue fire spread along his arms until he was completely engulfed in flame. The Warlock would pay for what he'd done.

CHAPTER 32

It was a cool day and a gentle wind blew in from the west, bringing with it an array of smells and the distant sound of voices. The combined army of the west lurked at the edge of her vision, slowly and inextricably marching towards Charas, her city, her home. Talandra tried not to look too hard at the assembled army, or attempt to count the men. There were simply too many and she'd already spent an hour studying them through her spyglass after running through strategies with her Generals.

She took a deep breath and forced the muscles in her face to relax until she looked calm. Breathing slowly and evenly she put one hand on her sword, to prevent it tangling her legs, and stepped out onto the battlements.

It was the first day of the siege. Others had reassured her it was their best chance to beat the enemy, and Talandra believed them. She trusted their experience and the plans they'd made together, but that didn't stop the nerves.

Her warriors were in place, spaced out along the wall, armed to the teeth, and at their feet lay various tools and implements of war. Pronged and notched iron spears to repel ladders, heavy axes and maces, spare arrows, rations, medical kits, water canteens, unlit torches, and in the courtyards and streets below, huge cauldrons full of bubbling oil. The courtyards nearest the western wall had been cleared and piles of rubble sat beside six catapults. Each could throw huge stones twice as big as a horse. The engineer had been as good as his word, and despite several field tests, he raced between the six engines making final checks.

Nearby the reserves sat in neat lines, talking and gambling, trying to distract themselves from what was about to happen. Surgeons, nurses and stretcher bearers lurked in doorways, smoking, dozing quietly and staying out of sight as much as possible. No one cursed or wished them ill, but no one spoke to them either. No one needed them yet, but they would. Buildings were set aside for what must inevitably happen, where Sisters of Mercy and more surgeons waited with sterile tools, a mountain of bandages and priests for last rites.

The mood was tense but only a few men seemed anxious. Their collective fear was being eased by the men that passed through their ranks.

Graegor stalked through the streets and then up to the battlements where he glared at the enemy before spitting over the wall. As ever he was dressed in black mail over ragged furs, a plain short sword on his belt and a shield strapped to his right arm. In his left hand he carried the lethal axe that was already infamous for saving her father from an assassin. Wherever the black General went, men stared at him with a mix of awe, fear and respect. A few brave men asked what he thought of the enemy and the response was always coarse and to the point. Graegor swore, spat and made vulgar gestures. The men laughed and relaxed at his dismissive attitude towards the invading army. He gave them strength and hope that they might see tomorrow, if they just held on to the shreds of their courage.

Walking through the men in the opposite direction was Vannok Lore. Like Graegor, the younger General had earned his position the hard way. Having no friends in high places and being common born, he'd received no preferential treatment in his career. Vannok had started in the front line and risen up through the ranks due to skill, hard work and sheer determination. He was tough, slow to anger, intelligent and a damned good fighter, which always helped. Men shook his hand, clapped him on the shoulder and offered him toothy grins. They were ready and didn't want to let him down.

Thias and Hyram moved through the reserves and the response from those warriors was no less awed. Talandra wondered what would happen if she went to meet the men. Would they smile or just stare? Would they even recognise her? Would they think her a foolish girl playing dress up as a warrior?

Each man down there knew how to wield their sword and had used it many times to defend their life. The blade at Talandra's side had not been drawn in years and had been gathering dust until two days ago. Her father had insisted all of his children learn how to fight and, ever the dutiful daughter, Talandra had complied with his wishes. She knew all the basic forms and understood the principles, but she wondered if she could actually kill someone. She would never be anywhere near the front line, so would never find out. Thias and Hyram had asked permission to fight but Talandra had refused their request. There might come a time when the men needed something to inspire them. A symbol that all hope was not lost, but they were not that desperate yet. Talandra put the thought to one side and focused on the present.

She wasn't here to fight on the wall. That wasn't why her brother had given up his rightful place on the throne. Talandra thought on that for a moment, on what it must have cost him and why she was here in his place.

As she stepped onto the battlements a few men turned in her direction. Much to her surprise a cheer went up that spread as far as she could see. The roar of the crowd became deafening as men stamped their feet, rattled blades against their shields and chanted her name.

Talandra remembered how her father would act in these situations and struggled to do the same. She kept her expression calm, acknowledged a few with firm nods and smiles and tried to appear relaxed, even though her heart was pounding.

Vargus sat with eyes closed, resting his head back against the stones of the battlements. In the distance he could hear the steady tromp of thousands of marching soldiers and the rattle and squeak of siege engine wheels. The acrid stink from the oil below stuck in his nose and wouldn't leave him despite a breeze. All around him hundreds of men made last-minute preparations for the coming battle.

"You should take a look at this, Vargus," said Orran. His voice held a mix of awe and fear. Curly whistled and nearby he could hear Black Tom's endless chewing. "They're huge. They got more than a dozen horses pulling each one."

"It's not the towers I'm worried about," came Hargo's reply from somewhere above his head.

"I'm fine where I am," said Vargus.

There was a pronounced silence and Vargus knew the others were staring. "What are you doing?" asked Orran. "Don't you want to watch?"

"What for?" asked Vargus, cracking open an eye. Orran opened his mouth to answer but didn't know what to say. "Are they still marching towards us?"

"Well, yeah."

Vargus closed his eyes and got comfortable again. "So tell me when they get here. Until then I'm going to rest and finish digesting my last meal. I'm still a bit stuffed, but I'm going to need it. Every single mouthful. Because make no mistake lads, this is going to be the longest day of our lives."

A hush spread over the men immediately around him and Vargus knew his audience had grown. Opening both eyes he spoke directly to the men in his squad, to the faces he knew, but his voice carried beyond their ears to other men on the wall.

"When they finally arrive, when they climb up here on their ladders and towers, they'll break against this wall like the tide, over and over again. There'll be so many of them you won't believe it. Time won't matter and the sun will stop in the sky." Vargus took a deep breath and looked away. His mind was once again caught up in a memory from another war and a similar speech he'd made a long time ago.

"That's what it will feel like. That we're outnumbered and that it's hopeless to even try fighting. Looking at them will turn your knees weak and make you piss yourself," he said with a gesture over the wall. "But, remember, you're not alone. The only way any of us will live to see tomorrow is by trusting our brothers. You can't fight ten men by yourself, but you don't have to. I'll be there with you, and so will Hargo, Orran, Black Tom and a hundred others. I might die today, but that's all right, because there's ten of my brothers who will take my place and kill the bastard that got me. You know that anyone here will guard your back and step into the breach, because we are one. It's the only way we'll win."

Vargus settled down again and just before he closed his eyes he saw a few men stand a little taller. Some leaned against the wall and one or two copied him and sat down to rest and wait for the enemy to arrive. He hoped they were ready, because this was the ultimate test and for many it would be their last day alive.

Balfruss was the last of the five Battlemages to step onto the crowded western wall, but the warriors made room. He leaned forward against the stones and stared at the approaching army less than a mile away. Voices carried on the wind and he could hear officers shouting orders, the grunt and whinny of horse teams pulling the enormous siege towers, and the rattle of weapons and armour.

Despite the proclamations of unity, the western army was split into distinct squads from different nations. To the right were the Morrin, clad in black leather with short stabbing spears and tall oval shields painted gold and red. Naked Morrin berserkers took up the front two ranks, their pale skin daubed with orange and yellow paint, each carrying a weapon in both hands. Many were already chanting, screaming and breaking rank, only to be beaten back in line by officers with whips and quarterstaffs. Beside them were the steady Zecorrans, clad in mail painted with white lanterns and armed with a mix of swords, axes and pikes. A small unit of Yerskani militia held the centre, and on the left came the savage Vorga, dressed in little or no armour, but each carried an array of vicious weapons. Their rubbery skin was so thick it could deflect an ill-timed blow. The Drassi were absent from the army and Balfruss was pleased there were no golden-skinned prisoners from Shael being forced to fight.

Balfruss spent only a short time looking at the soldiers before his eyes were drawn to the robed figures spread throughout their ranks. The five distinct figures were a part of the army, and yet they marched with space all around them in pools of silence. The Splinters carried no weapons, didn't cheer or make threats, sang no songs and gave no signs they were alive. If not for the tiny spark of life fed into them by the Warlock they would be rotting corpses. They were nothing but husks. Shells of men and women.

"*We will release them,*" said Thule.

Balfruss nodded and wondered again how someone could do that to one of their own. It would be worse than death, to be utterly powerless and trapped in a prison of your own flesh, unable to resist or lie down and die. How self-aware were they?

Did they even know what they were doing? Did they have any memories, or were they without thoughts? What happened when they slept? Did they dream?

"*I pray that they remember nothing of who they once were*," said Thule, answering his thought.

He hoped Thule was right, but felt certain the Warlock wouldn't care and had never thought about it.

Although they couldn't see him, Balfruss knew the Warlock was out there somewhere, controlling the Splinters. He scanned the colourful ranks of soldiers but saw no more people dressed in robes. This close to the walls a stray arrow or crossbow bolt would kill the Warlock just as easily as any other man. He considered the entire war beneath him, nothing more than an entertaining distraction, and yet he wasn't brave enough to wear his red robe. Perhaps the Warlock's brush with death had shaken him up more than Balfruss realised. Red rage started to creep in around the edges of his vision and Balfruss took a deep breath to calm himself. Soon, but not yet.

"Will the Splinters attack first?" someone asked. Balfruss turned to address the warrior and saw a vaguely familiar man dressed in the blue and grey uniform of a quartermaster. The man was busy passing out quivers full of arrows. It took Balfruss a while to place him, even though their first meeting had only been a few days ago.

"Sam, isn't it?" asked Balfruss. The former charlatan Battlemage bobbed his head but didn't make eye contact. "The Splinters won't attack for a while."

"Why not?" asked Sam.

Balfruss had spent time thinking about the most ruthless and bloodthirsty tactic the enemy could use in the siege. When the answer came he knew it was the right one because it was exactly what the Warlock would do. He would wait until the Seve defenders were tired and worn down after a long day of fighting.

At that moment the Splinters would attack, try to break down the gates, or perhaps breach the walls and flood the city with soldiers.

In a few hours many of those stood around him would be dead or dying, and the rest would be tired and slow to respond. Hitting them when they were at their weakest would result in the highest number of casualties. It was utterly brutal and efficient.

Balfruss's stomach clenched as he thought about those who would die, but he forced himself to stare at the opposing army in its entirety for the first time, and to appreciate its scale. He forced a smile and slowly felt the fear pass through him.

"They won't attack because they're afraid," said Balfruss, clapping the nearest warrior on the shoulder. It wasn't the truth, but they needed to hear it. "We'll win this day together. With steel and magic."

The enemy were steadily drawing near. It wouldn't be long before they were in range.

A sword whistled through the air with enough force to cleave Vargus's skull in two. With no room to manoeuvre he had to block with a two-handed grip. The jarring impact up his arms nearly made him drop his weapon. Gritting his teeth against the pain he twisted his enemy's blade to one side, exposing the ribs. Orran obliged, stabbing the Zecorran warrior twice in the side before they pitched the dying man over the wall together. The falling warrior struck several others on the ladder coming up and they all tumbled to their death with bone-crunching impacts.

There was another loud crack from nearby but they'd grown so used to the sound that no one even flinched. Huge stones sailed overhead before plummeting down beyond the walls, crushing men into sticky red paste.

Bows still hummed all around Vargus, and occasionally the

twang of a crossbow, but already the fighting had degenerated into a vicious melee. The muscles in his arms were throbbing and his shoulders burned, but a part of Vargus knew the fight was only just getting started. Perhaps two hours had passed since the first arrow had killed one of the enemy, but no more than that. Hundreds were already dead, three breaches had been stopped with horrific losses on both sides, and still they came in their thousands.

On his left Hargo continued to chop away at the enemy like a butcher dicing up cuts of meat. His blade came down on a Zecorran's shoulder, splitting his collar bone and sinking deep into the meat below. Blood spurted out, splashing across Hargo's face. He already wore a brown mask of the stuff and didn't bother to wipe off his latest victim's. The Zecorran screamed in agony and started to topple backwards, taking the cleaver with him, but Hargo kicked him in the face, knocking him off the blade. He fell out of sight to his death without a sound.

"Tower!" someone screamed above the din. Another siege tower had slowly rolled up to the walls. Several flaming arrows swept towards it but they bounced off canvasses that had been doused in a greasy material making them fire-proof. One or two archers managed to embed their arrows in the wood itself, but the flames spluttered and died. Inside the tower they heard screaming and thrashing, as if some monstrous creature were being strangled to death.

"Oh shit. Morrin berserkers," muttered Orran. Black Tom spat but Hargo just grunted and loosened his neck in anticipation.

"Crossbows!"

"To me! To me!" shouted several officers, shoving and pulling men away from their posts, propelling them towards the tower.

"Help me," someone shouted. Nearby a rangy southerner with black hair was struggling against two Zecorrans. With a hoarse cry Vargus charged, feinting high before switching and sweeping his blade in an upwards arc. The Zecorran swayed backwards but the point of Vargus's blade sliced a deep channel in his sternum and jaw, spraying teeth into the air like hailstones. Kicking and spitting, stabbing and slashing, Vargus and the ranger overpowered the other Zecorran. The bodies slid off the wall, landing in the street below with wet smacking sounds.

"Hargo, Orran, give me a hand," snarled Vargus as he picked up one of the pronged spears and pressed it against the ladder. The top of another Zecorran's head showed above the battlements. Vargus punched him in the face and the man sailed backwards off the ladder. Hargo stepped up beside Vargus and together with the ranger the three of them pressed their combined weight against the spear. Vargus felt his feet skid on the bloody battlements before he finally dug in and the ladder started to wobble.

"Fucking push!" screamed the ranger. An arrow flew towards them and Orran leaned over the wall and quickly loosed an arrow in return. Someone screamed, the ladder shuddered again and then felt a little lighter. Orran swore and ducked back a second too late with a crossbow bolt buried in the meat of his forearm. His short bow fell over the wall and he stumbled back, pale faced, trying to stem the bleeding.

Vargus's hands were slick with sweat and blood. The others were having the same difficulty maintaining their grip, but somehow they managed to hold on. It felt as if his fingers were on fire, but he held on and continued to push with everything he had.

If they didn't finish this quickly they were all dead. With both hands on the spear they were defenceless if someone reached the top of the ladder before it toppled. A ranger, called Eviss, and Black Tom came up beside him, lending their weight to the ladder.

Finally, it started to move. It rattled against the stones and began to slide sideways but they all gave the spear one final shove. For a moment the ladder remained perfectly upright, balanced like a spear on its point. Men were poised all along its length, with three very close to the top. A few more seconds and the defenders would have been killed.

The soldiers started screaming before the ladder toppled backwards. Ten or eleven men fell to their death, landing on top of their comrades far below, impaling themselves on weapons, spears and armour. The falling men crushed those too close to the wall and it all became a tangled mass of torn flesh and gushing red innards.

Further down the wall the door to the siege tower burst open and naked Morrin berserkers spilled out, screaming and foaming at the mouth. The first few died instantly, impaled with arrows and crossbow bolts. Behind them several more rushed forward, lashing out wildly, injuring some of their own men in the hurry to kill the enemy. The two sides slammed together with a deafening screech of metal, sprays of blood and keening yowls of pain.

Several berserkers impaled themselves on weapons and kept fighting, unaware that they were already dead. A tight knot of five Morrin attacked the Seves with such fury that they managed to breach the defenders' line. Men staggered back with gushing stumps, chunks missing from their faces and limbs, heads split, bellies torn open by sword, axe and even bare hands.

To Vargus's surprise a black-clad figure stepped forward to meet them. Graegor's axe split one Morrin right between the horns, cracking open his skull like an egg, revealing a dark purple brain. His shield caught another in the face, severing his jaw as Graegor kicked out at a third, roaring like a wounded lion. Beside him fought eight grey veterans, their bodies crisscrossed with faded scars and their skin tough as old leather. With methodical precision they gutted and sliced the Morrin soldiers, giving them no openings, turning aside wild and vicious blows with almost casual ease. Against the veterans the berserkers died quickly, but loudly, and the breach was closed.

The old General was breathing hard from the exertion, but he didn't seem to care. The blood fury was upon him. Graegor spat on the corpse of the nearest Morrin and started to move forward when one of the veterans put a hand on his arm. With obvious reluctance Graegor stepped away from the front line to wait in reserve in case he was needed again.

With a high-pitched ululating scream, a group of green-skinned Vorga made it to the top of the wall. The Vorga shook with rage, wide ears flapping, spiky teeth clicking and bulbous eyes swivelling in all directions as they took in the enemy around them. One of the Vorga barked an order in their native tongue and the group split in two. With those around him caught in other struggles Vargus suddenly found himself facing two Vorga armed with curved swords and axes.

"All right, you fish-head fucks. Come on," he said, rolling his shoulders.

The gangly form of Eviss stepped up beside him on his left as Hargo came up on his right. With no signs of fear at the odds the two Vorga charged.

Vargus managed to block the curved sword but the force of the blow drove him back and he stumbled to one knee. The Vorga whooped but didn't press its advantage. It dodged around Hargo, moving far more quickly than Vargus had expected, then came at him again. A group of men busy fighting their own battle slammed into both of them and Vargus was crushed almost face to face with the Vorga. It bit and snapped at him, trying to rip out his throat as he struggled to keep away from its teeth. When it leaned forward to bite him Vargus surged forward, slamming his forehead into its wide face. He felt his skin split from the impact, but the Vorga hissed in pain as well. Locked together they both resorted to kicking and biting, clawing and kneeing each other until the group of warriors thinned.

A little space opened up around them and Vargus took the offensive, dropping his sword and using a dagger in each hand. The Vorga charged and he managed to score a long gash down one of its legs before it backhanded him. His heel caught something and he fell backwards, smacking his head against the stone. Black dots danced in front of his eyes and when they cleared he saw the Vorga stood over him, sword raised above its head.

Just before the steel came down an axe severed one of the Vorga's arms and a sword erupted from its stomach, spraying Vargus with white and green intestinal juices. The Vorga shrieked in pain, but even as it died it managed to tear out one man's throat who ventured too close.

Eviss offered him a hand and Vargus was pulled to his feet. He wiped the slime from his face and spat, trying to clear the taste of sour fish and bile.

"Thank you," he wheezed.

"You're welcome, brother," said Eviss with a feral grin. The enemy came again and they fought back to back, desperately trying to ignore the pain and fire in their joints. The day wasn't done yet.

CHAPTER 33

They pushed the western army back one more time before they finally retreated. In their wake they left a wave of broken, bloody and dead bodies. All around Balfruss, men were screaming, pleading, begging and dying. Broken weapons and shattered men lay everywhere. There was more blood splashed and pooled on the walls than he'd ever seen before in one place. Red blood from men, deep green from the Vorga and white from the Morrin was all mixing together, creating pools of muddy brown.

The moment the enemy withdrew a murder of black-capped crows moved onto the battlements, followed closely by stretcher bearers, a group of priests from different denominations and Sisters of Mercy.

Not far away a stocky surgeon knelt down beside a screaming man who was clutching his bloody stomach with both hands. The surgeon pulled the warrior's hands away, revealing a bulging mass of torn purple and pink intestines. Blood that was almost black pumped from the jagged wound and it showed no signs of slowing. With a quick shake of his head the surgeon moved on to the next injured man. A priest of the Maker knelt down beside the dying man to give him the last rites.

Several times the enemy had withdrawn in a similar fashion,

but all too quickly they regrouped and attacked again. The surgeons moved as fast as they could, taking seconds to decide the fate of men, gauging with a glance if they thought a warrior would live or die. At any moment the western army would come again and the surgeons would have to wait for the next lull before they could tend to the injured.

Those with a chance of surviving were quickly bandaged or sewn up, just enough to hold the pieces together until they reached the nearby hospitals. One by one, stretcher bearers took them off the wall and slowly the din from screaming men began to recede.

Warriors still able to fight finished off the dying enemy soldiers, showing no mercy to the injured, tossing the dead over the wall. Nurses clad in dark grey moved among them, tending to minor wounds, sewing and sealing wounds with glowing metal brands. It was fast and painful battlefield medicine, but they needed every able-bodied man to fight. The only way to leave the wall was on a stretcher or as cold meat.

When horns began to sound a warning along the wall it took Balfruss a few seconds to realise the signal was different. Three short blasts. It was what he and the other Battlemages had been waiting for and dreading all day. The Splinters were coming.

Warriors started moving away from the wall, streaming past Balfruss on both sides as he grimly walked towards it. By the time he reached the front, most of those able to walk had pulled back and the rest were on their way, leaving only the dead behind to keep him company. On either side of him he felt the other Battlemages take up their positions. They were a thin line spaced out along the western wall, five souls to protect thousands, but the next part of the battle would not be won with blades and armour.

To Balfruss's left a siege tower still rested against the battlements. Morrin bodies were strewn around the entry ramp and the battlements directly in front were awash with gore. It was partially blocking Thule and Darius's view of the battlefield.

"*We should destroy it*," suggested Thule. "*They can rebuild, but it will take time and help our warriors.*"

"Agreed," said Balfruss. He reached for the Source and felt its power flow into him, easing the aches from his body with its touch. The retreating figures of enemy soldiers swung into focus as all of his senses became more acute. The westerners were running as well, trying to put as much distance as possible between themselves and the five robed figures walking towards the city. It would only be a few minutes before the Splinters were in range, which didn't give the Battlemages much time to destroy the siege tower.

He considered burning it to ash, then realised that would expend too much energy. Every drop would be needed to face the Splinters and he had no idea how long the fight with them would last. A simpler solution was required.

With a grinding of wood and a loud sucking noise, the wheels came free of the gore-soaked mud as the siege tower rose into the air. It felt so light Balfruss briefly considered throwing it at the Splinters on the off chance he could kill one or two of them. They might not be aware of the danger and their surroundings, but the Warlock was out there somewhere, and there was nothing wrong with his reflexes. Instead Balfruss lifted the tower higher and higher until its shadow fell over him, the wheels rising above the top of the city battlements. With a small push he moved it away from the wall and then let go. For a few seconds there was an eerie silence as the tower fell, then it hit the ground with a massive crash. Balfruss heard the timbers snap and shatter, then a huge cloud of dust rose into the air.

The Splinters paid no attention to its destruction, continuing to march towards them in silence. Because of their mind link Balfruss felt Thule's stare from along the wall.

"What's wrong?" asked Balfruss but the golden-skinned man didn't reply.

"We need to form a Link," said Darius, and the others agreed. "You should lead us, Balfruss."

Balfruss was surprised his Blood Brother didn't want to control it himself, or that Finn didn't disagree. Their expressions were a mix of anxiety and wariness, but all of them were willing to place their power and trust in his abilities. In some ways this fight would be a battle between him and the Warlock, with each channelling power from other people. What if he became addicted to the power? What if this was what happened to the Warlock at the beginning? Was this the first step to madness and destruction?

"*You should have more faith in yourself,*" said Thule. "*We freely lend you our strength and we trust you. He controls mindless slaves with no free will, not people. Trust in yourself.*"

Power from Thule flowed into him and this time Balfruss was ready for it, mentally bracing himself against the rush. It was a lot easier than the last time and after a few seconds he waved towards Darius, who added his strength to the Link. When all of them were joined Balfruss stepped forward and rested his stomach against the battlements, leaning slightly against the wall for support.

This time he didn't need to concentrate to see the black wires of energy connecting the Splinters to the Warlock. Several floated in the air behind each robed figure like threads from a spider's web. In the distance he could just make out the seated figure of the Warlock. Even this far away Balfruss could tell that for all of his boasting, the Warlock had still not completely healed. His brush with death had been a lot closer than he claimed. A few more seconds and Ecko would have ripped out his heart and changed the course of the war. If the opportunity arose today Balfruss swore he would not hesitate. Far too many lives had already been wasted because of the Warlock.

The first attack came from the cloudless sky, a rain of green fist-sized stones that sizzled and popped. Balfruss covered all of them in a shield, wrapping it around the top of the wall, encompassing the battlements for a hundred paces in either direction. The poisoned hailstones crackled when they struck the shield and evaporated, but where they fell on the battlements, each left behind deep pockmarks as it ate into the stone. A few hailstones bounced and hit nearby rooftops inside the city, melting stone and metal alike. One struck an unfortunate warrior who was resting against a wall. He didn't have time to scream. It melted half of his skull and continued down towards the ground, dissolving portions of his torso as it went. A few warriors moved even further away from the wall on the off chance that another hailstone bounced and caught them unawares.

It was a twisted idea the likes of which Balfruss had never heard or read about during his time at the Red Tower. The melting rain fell for a few more minutes, scarring the walls and buildings, but because of the shield, the damage was minor and only one warrior died.

Balfruss could practically feel the Warlock snarling and gnashing his teeth. This was not going to be a battle of wills. The Warlock was finally getting a chance to test all of his most unpleasant ideas and experiments. The single goal of each seemed to be a painful death for him and the other Battlemages. He knew the Warlock didn't care about the city, or the outcome of the war any more, if he'd even cared in the first place. Now it was personal. He wanted to punish Balfruss for rejecting him, for exposing him to the truth and making him feel small and weak. Being the most formidable Battlemage in hundreds of years, the Warlock would not be used to such feelings.

The sky turned black and then everything else vanished into a featureless void. Balfruss blinked a few times to make sure his eyes were still open and that he was awake. Waving his hand in front of his eyes made no difference. The cloak of darkness was absolute. Sounds carried as normal and he called out to the other Battlemages, to reassure them as much as himself, even though he could feel their presence through the Link.

The unending darkness was disorientating and for a few seconds Balfruss thought the ground was moving beneath his feet. His stomach was still pressed against the stone and reaching down he gripped the wall to maintain his balance. The world tilted one way and then the other, as if they were on a ship in the middle of a storm.

Windmilling one arm slightly he focused his will on the air around him and fed power into a small cyclone. At first nothing happened so he drew more heavily on the Source and for a few seconds he saw spots of daylight in the black.

Pressure against his ears increased and the world seemed to shift under his feet as if he was experiencing an earthquake. Gritting his teeth against the disorientation he increased the size and speed of the cyclone. Gradually the darkness began to fade in layers, like peeling an onion. As more sunlight crept in, the dizziness started to recede.

A feral grin crossed Balfruss's face as he sent cyclones in both directions along the wall, warning his brethren to hold on to something via the Link. Blood, forgotten weapons, loose stone chips and even severed body parts were swept up in the cyclones' wake until each contained a deadly array of objects. The darkness faded until it was just a small cloud hanging over the wall and then it vanished. Bringing his hands together Balfruss sent the raging cyclones past the city wall, down towards the Splinters. He made sure each had built up a lot of momentum before he suddenly severed the connection. It was good to be on the offensive for a change.

From what she thought was a safe distance away, Talandra watched the battle rage between the Battlemages and the

Warlock. On more than one occasion the spells launched against the city spilled over, exposing her and all the warriors nearby to their effects.

Nightmares from her childhood that she thought held no power over her any more became real. Horrendous fleshy monsters with gaping mouths and teeth as long as her arms waddled towards her. A winged beast with a woman's face, bare breasts and a lion's claws dove towards her out of the sky. Rotting skeletal hands grasped at her ankles as a decaying corpse tried to pull her into the ground. A hundred old memories that she thought were locked away forever resurfaced and were made flesh.

The terror was so overwhelming she struggled not to claw out her eyes to stop the images. The fear clogged her throat, stifling her breathing, making her heart stutter and beat erratically.

Sirens called out from just beyond the wall. Their ghostly song flowed around and then into her mind, pulling provocative images to the surface, stirring her loins, connecting with her in a way no man or woman had ever achieved. Desire for Shani made her sweat and she struggled to control her raging urges.

The Warlock and his Splinters launched an endless stream of attacks that tried to tear down the walls, shatter the minds of the Battlemages, or make them kill themselves. Talandra and those around her were catching only the smallest of ricochets, and already a dozen men had thrown themselves from the walls. One man had cut his own throat just to escape the conjured nightmares.

Without warning the battle came to an end and Talandra saw all five Battlemages slump against the battlements. Thule collapsed and Darius stumbled to his knees before sitting down heavily. The rest looked utterly drained, their clothes drenched with sweat and their faces drawn and haggard. Even the big smith looked on the verge of collapse.

"Did you see—" asked Hyram, but their brother cut him off.

"I don't want to know," said Thias. "Whatever it was, keep it to yourself. My own nightmares are company enough."

Both of her brothers were badly shaken, their eyes haunted from images locked away inside the deepest corners of the mind.

On wobbling legs Balfruss approached the Queen, leaning heavily on the wall to keep himself upright. When the Battlemage stumbled, Vannok held him up on one side and he offered a weak smile as thanks.

"It's over," gasped Balfruss. "One of the Splinters is dead. Burned out from being pushed too hard. Another collapsed. I'm not sure if it will live."

"Will they attack again today?" asked Talandra.

Balfruss shook his head. "Not tomorrow either. Maybe not for two days. It will take all of us time to recover."

"Get some rest, we'll talk later."

"Someone still needs to keep watch over you tonight," said Balfruss. "Just in case."

Talandra wasn't sure any of the Battlemages would be of any use but she didn't argue. Vannok helped his friend down from the wall as the other Battlemages were attended by surgeons. Darius and Thule were carried away on stretchers but the others managed to leave without support.

Graegor approached, his black armour splattered with gore, and more caught up in his beard. Despite wading into battle on a few occasions to fill a breach, the old General looked no different from this morning. In fact, he looked more invigorated, as if hacking up the enemy gave him strength and restored his youth. He moved like a man twenty years his junior. No one was born a warrior, but stripped of any familial attachments or emotional baggage, Graegor had become what many boys dreamed about. If only they realised what the grizzled General had sacrificed along the way.

Talandra had merely watched the fighting all day, dressed in armour and sword, standing by doing nothing more than give orders. The blade around her waist felt as heavy as a grown man, but she tried not to show any signs of discomfort.

"They're withdrawing," reported Graegor, unstrapping his shield with what Talandra thought was disappointment. "A good first day." The General nodded to himself and stumped away, no doubt in search of beer or a fight. Talandra knew she was being unfair to Graegor, but after all that she'd witnessed since morning, she wasn't feeling in a generous mood.

"How can he say it was good?" muttered Hyram. "Look at the dead."

Talandra had seen men butchered and hacked to pieces in more ways than she thought possible. Childhood daydreams about becoming a surgeon were squashed after seeing countless brightly coloured innards exposed to sunlight and smelling the open bowels of dying men. Blood was spattered and pooled as far as she could see along the wall beside bits of skin, scalp and chunks of meat she couldn't identify. At least she'd managed to hold on to the contents of her stomach.

"Look over the wall and look at their dead and dying," suggested Thias. "This was a victory."

The screams of a thousand wounded men still rang in her ears and Talandra knew they would haunt her in the darkest hours of the night. She'd given her agents orders to kill in the past, but had never seen so many dying in one place.

In a way she was responsible for every death. She might not have swung the sword, but her decisions had led them here. Rationally she knew nothing could have prevented the siege, and even surrender would have resulted in some bloodshed, but part of her refused to accept it. A stubborn seed of guilt burned in her belly.

"We held the city."

"But at what cost?" asked Hyram.

"I'll find out soon enough," said Talandra. They would already be counting the dead and wounded. A report that stated the facts and nothing more would be added to the pile on her desk. Numbers, but no names or faces. It was easier to deal with it when she didn't have to see them die or hear their pleading screams.

Talandra forced herself to look closely at the broken corpse of a nearby warrior. She fixed every grisly detail in her mind in case she forgot, even for a second, what her decisions cost other people. It would never be her, always others that would suffer in her place. As Queen she was now responsible for every single life in her kingdom. The weight of her responsibilities threatened to crush her.

"This is only the beginning," said Talandra. Without looking she could feel the surprised stares of her brothers. "It's going to get a lot worse. A day of vicious fighting and yet it still ended in defeat for the enemy. Tomorrow they will come back twice as hungry. They want this to be over as quickly as we do. No one wants this to turn into a long siege."

As ever Talandra tried to calm the emotional parts of her mind and focus on the war as a whole. It was what her father would have done. He would have looked at today as a step in the right direction, but also assessed what today had cost them. It was the first of many such bloody days, but they could not continue in this way for long.

It had been important that the men see her standing with them on the first day, but tomorrow she would be elsewhere. The Generals knew what to do better than her, and she would be kept well informed. They would fight the war on the battlefield and she would continue to fight in more subtle ways. After seeing the enemy horde, and despite the reassurances that a siege was their best chance for victory, Talandra knew they were only delaying the inevitable. Now more than ever she was certain that the war would not be won with steel and magic alone. With a surge of energy she hurried from the battlements, eager to get back to work.

As Talandra had anticipated, the horrors of the day caught up with her as she tried to sleep. A dying man, his throat torn open to the bone, reached towards her beseechingly while a Vorga ripped him open from groin to navel with its claws. Another warrior, one of his arms completely torn off, stumbled around in a daze looking for his missing limb. Over and over, these and other atrocities she'd witnessed ran through her mind in a seemingly endless cycle of blood and death.

She came awake covered in sweat, her heart pounding loudly in her ears. Slowly her fear ebbed away and in its place a void of despair threatened to swallow her whole.

Slipping out of bed she stripped out of her soggy clothes and used a towel to scrub the sweat from her body. With a rough bar of soap she washed her skin until clean, losing herself in the familiar rhythm while her mind wandered. The others would always be there to offer her counsel on matters of the crown, but it was times like this during the longest hour of the night that she wished her bed wasn't empty.

Dressing in fresh clothes she tied her hair into a loose plait and stepped into the corridor. At the far end of the hallway a figure rose from its chair and came towards her.

"Is everything all right, your Majesty?" asked Eloise.

"Fine, thank you," she said but then let the fake smile slide away. "Actually no, I'm a long distance from being fine."

"Nightmares or worry keeping you awake?"

"A little of both," said Talandra with a wry smile. "I think some air might help me sleep. Will you walk with me?"

"Of course," said Eloise. As they set off down the long corridors Talandra glanced at Eloise's tattoo, wondering how long it must have taken to ink. The design looked simple, but being so close allowed her to see complex weaves and knots hidden in the script.

"It didn't hurt," said Eloise without looking around. "I drank a hideous-tasting brew that numbed my face."

"When did you leave Seveldrom?" asked Talandra. Although her spies had already pieced together some of the information it was always better to hear it first-hand.

"Like many students at the Red Tower, once my training was complete I felt the call of the road. We saw so little of Shael during our time there, and I wanted to see more. It's a beautiful place. At least it was," said Eloise, a frown briefly creasing her brow. They rounded another corner and Talandra pushed open a door that led outside. Judging by the colour of the sky, dawn looked to be several hours away. A chill in the air made goose bumps rise on the flesh of her arms, but Eloise seemed unaffected by the cold. They descended several flights of stairs to the inner courtyards and started a circuit of the palace grounds.

"Where did you go after that?"

"All over the west. The Drassi welcomed me into their homes, but I always felt they were keeping secrets. Hiding a part of themselves from me because I was an outsider."

"They're a very private people," agreed Talandra. "I've known one of their ambassadors since I was a girl, but even now, I don't feel especially close to her."

"Have you ever visited the desert kingdoms, Majesty?"

"Please, call me Tala. And no, I've never travelled that far east."

Eloise paused beside a green bush with red berries that had started to flower. She bent down to inspect one of the small white flowers. After living here all her life Talandra thought she should know the name of it, but didn't.

"You wouldn't think anything this green would grow there,

because it's so arid. When you first arrive, the cities look barren and dull. High stone walls, heavy squat buildings with few markings on the outside, but they've learned from centuries of experience. A bad sandstorm will strip the flesh from a man in seconds, so you can imagine what it will do to a city without walls. Once they trust you, and let you into their homes, it's very different to Drassia. They're a warm and generous people, and many have gardens, lush oases in the middle of the desert."

"Was it hard? Leaving Seveldrom for the desert?"

Eloise left the flower and they resumed their walk. "May I ask you a question first, Tala?"

"Of course."

"Have you ever been in love?"

The question caught Talandra by surprise and immediately her thoughts turned to Shani. She took a deep breath, tried to answer but just nodded instead.

"My father died years ago in an accident when I was twelve, but he lived long enough to see me start my training at the Red Tower. My mother blamed a Morrin for his death, although he was innocent. She became bitter and distrustful of foreigners. Once I'd explored the west, I came home to Seveldrom to see my family. I started to tell her about all the wonders I'd seen, but she didn't care. She had no interest."

They came to a small garden and sat down on a bench surrounded on all sides by lush grass, blooming flowers and jasmine vines. The air hummed with the sound of insects and Talandra's nose filled with a rich floral perfume that bordered on being overpowering.

"That must have been upsetting."

Eloise shrugged and her expression remained neutral. "At the time, but now I'm just disappointed. When I travelled to the desert I found a new family who were loving, generous and kind. Then I met a wonderful man who made me feel special and beautiful. I sent my mother a letter when he proposed and to my surprise I received one in return."

Despite Eloise's calm expression, Talandra's instinct told her the story didn't end well.

"She disowned me, told me she had no daughter; that I'd shamed her and my father would be cursing me from his grave."

"I'm sorry," she said, not knowing what else to say.

Eloise smiled and gave her hand a brief squeeze. "It's all right. You didn't know. So, as much as I love Seveldrom, the green spaces, the music and the people, it was actually very easy to leave. I hadn't been back, until now."

"Because my father asked King Usermeses for aid."

"What about you? Now that you're Queen, will you be able to travel?"

It wasn't something that she'd thought much about. The war seemed to be consuming all of her waking, and sleeping, thoughts. As Queen she would occasionally be required to go on a state visit, but she would never be free to simply ride out on a whim by herself.

"You should think of the future," said Eloise. "Think about tomorrow beyond the war. It will help with the nightmares."

"This isn't your first war?"

Eloise shook her head. "What started out as small raids on merchant caravans in the desert turned into something else. Something organised and dangerous. It was Balfruss who helped us shatter the enemy. We killed many men. I still see their faces, but they don't haunt me like they used to."

"What will you do after the war?" said Talandra, not wanting to be too negative. She tried to keep in mind everyone's reassurances about the siege being their best option for victory. "Settle down and have children?"

"We've talked about it, and one day we will, but not yet. There's still so much to see, so many places to explore. Now is the time, before I've grey hair and my bones ache in the cold."

"That sounds nice," said Talandra getting up, and they resumed their walk, arm in arm. "If I ever make it as far as the desert, I'll come visit you."

"I would be insulted if you didn't call on us," said Eloise. "Well, my husband would be, although he'd never show it. Of course, behind closed doors, I'd hear all about it for days."

Talandra laughed and although the horror from her nightmares still lingered in her thoughts, they didn't seem quite as oppressive. Instead of focusing on all that had been lost, she tried to turn her mind to what came next, what she would build in the future.

By the time they made it back to her quarters she was starting to feel tired.

"Thank you for the walk," she said, embracing Eloise. "Perhaps we could do it again."

"Whenever you like, Majesty. Sleep well."

This time when she closed her eyes and the horrors came, Talandra had something to fight back with. The idea of tomorrow and what happened when she stepped beyond the reach of her nightmares.

CHAPTER 34

Nirrok, the Emperor's body-servant, wrinkled his nose at the stench emanating from Taikon but he said nothing, made no sound and remained perfectly still. Being silent and still was the best way to go unnoticed. Being seen meant he would be called upon to fulfil a bizarre, and often impossible task, and that led to a greater chance of being butchered for his inevitable failure.

Yesterday the rotting corpse of the former palace herald had been decorating the throne room but this morning it had disappeared. It wasn't Nirrok's place to ask, so he'd said nothing and made very sure he didn't stare at the brown stain on the floor where the body had been sitting in a pool of blood.

Emperor Taikon was busy staring at himself in a long ornate mirror that the Chosen had recently discovered. Until a few days ago the mirror, and the large house it resided in, had belonged to one of the most powerful families in the region. Now they were either dead, decorating the city walls, or had gone into hiding to avoid the wrath of the Emperor's Chosen, his most devout followers and brutal enforcers.

The powerful families had been less than enthusiastic about Taikon's recent announcement to increase the size of the temple, devoted to him, currently being built in the heart of the city.

He'd unveiled the latest scale model to a carefully selected crowd, consisting of his most loyal followers and those with considerable wealth to finance the project. Instead of cooing and applauding with the others, the attending members of the families showed no interest and then left the celebrations early.

Soon after, or so it was claimed, they'd begun scheming to murder the Emperor and had engaged in several meetings with foreign powers. There had been no trial, no chance to plead their innocence, nor even any evidence of guilt. It wasn't required any more when it came to a living God whose word was law. Those members of the Great Family too slow to escape were murdered in their beds and all of their possessions, property and wealth now belonged to the Emperor.

Roggo, the Chosen in charge of the raid, had taken great pleasure in describing in detail how he'd butchered the traitors. Nirrok had never thought he had a weak stomach, but some of the methods Roggo had used were very inventive and quite revolting. It was while one of the children had fled to a dark corner that he'd discovered the mirror and presented it to the Emperor.

"I'm not sure about the cuffs," mused the Emperor, tugging on the long triangular sleeves that trailed on the floor. As he turned from side to side, making his robe swish, it gave Nirrok the perfect view of the Emperor's profile. Something moved beneath the skin on the Emperor's face, across his forehead and then down his right cheek. The lump disappeared, only to reappear on the side of his neck and then slowly creep up the back of the skull. Two more bumps started to move independently, as if there were insects or rats crawling beneath his skin, trying to find a way out. As their eyes met in the mirror Nirrok froze, held his breath and waited for the Emperor to look away. Instead he turned around and stared straight at Nirrok, an unreadable expression on his face. The lumps had stopped moving and just as suddenly they all disappeared beneath the Emperor's skin. In their wake they left faint black marks beneath the skin, like charcoal lines.

"What are you staring at?"

"The mirror, Most Holy," blurted Nirrok, averting his eyes and bowing low.

"It is pretty," said the Emperor, turning to run his hands over the golden frame that depicted dozens of people being torn apart and fed to a series of hideous monsters. Things with too many eyes and tentacles, gaping beaks and mouths lined with daggers for teeth, arms that ended in claws and pincers, winged bloated bodies with tiny heads or creatures with no head at all. No wonder the mirror had been gathering dust in an attic.

A loud knocking on the door preceded an out of breath and red-faced herald who bowed so low his floppy hair brushed the floor.

"Most Holy, you asked me to inform you the very second we received word from your Generals on the front line."

The sweaty-faced herald held out a scroll in both hands, which he presented towards the Emperor. Somehow he managed not to shake.

"Did I?" he said, looking bored. As Nirrok watched, another lump erupted on the back of his right hand before inching its way up his sleeve and disappearing from view.

"Yes, Most Holy," said the nervous herald.

"Did anything special happen today in the war?"

The herald hesitated before answering. Saying too little could prove to be as dangerous as saying too much. "It was the first day of the siege of Charas, Most Holy."

"Ahhh," said the Emperor, suddenly interested again and coming forward to take the proffered scroll. He broke open the seal and quickly scanned the contents. The smile on his face ebbed away bit by bit until his whole body sagged. On seeing the Emperor's reaction the herald started to creep backwards. He'd almost made it to the door when the Emperor threw down the scroll and screamed, his voice echoing off the stone walls over and over. The herald turned on his heel and tried to run but the Emperor grabbed his head with both hands and yanked it around to face him. Nirrok heard a crack and the herald's body dropped to the floor.

Still in a rage and howling like a wolf, the Emperor stomped on the herald's face over and over. Nirrok took a risk and closed his eyes, but could still hear cracks, snaps and squelching amid the screeching and rhythmic pounding. When something hot and wet landed on his fingers Nirrok instinctively shook it off but didn't open his eyes. Sometimes it was better not to know. Eventually the Emperor's rage faded and an eerie silence filled the room.

Nirrok risked opening his eyes and screamed involuntarily as the Emperor's blood-spattered face was almost nose to nose with him.

"Bring me some clean clothes," he said, wiping the gore off his face with Nirrok's shirt. "And be quick about it."

Trying his best not to stare at the red and grey pulp where the herald's head had been, Nirrok scrambled to his feet and ran from the room. His sandals slipped on blood and crunched over bits of skull, but he didn't slow down. He pulled several pairs of trousers, shirts and three robes at random from shelves before sprinting back to the throne room.

He skidded back into the room and the Emperor immediately stripped off and stood naked with his arms held out. As Nirrok helped him dress, he noticed the herald's body had been removed. The guards were becoming very proficient at ignoring the screams and then quickly dealing with the aftermath.

"Follow me," ordered the Emperor, marching away down the corridor as he fastened the last of his buttons. Four members of the Chosen fell in behind Nirrok but didn't make eye contact or acknowledge his presence in any way. If he were to stop abruptly, he suspected, they would just keep walking and step on him in order to remain close to their saviour.

As he hurried after the Emperor down a long corridor, Nirrok heard the distant roar of many voices. The volume swelled until he could feel it in his bones and his teeth started to ache. The Emperor threw open a set of double doors and stepped out onto a balcony overlooking Lachim Square where a crowd of thousands had gathered to hear him speak.

Nirrok kept himself busy mixing the Emperor's drink, getting the perfect blend of wine, water and fruit juice, so he didn't look at the crowd until he crept out onto the balcony. Crouching down to one side beside the Emperor, he peered out at the people and nearly dropped the cocktail jug he'd prepared.

Instead of thousands of adoring people he saw a giant mob of angry faces, cursing, spitting, shouting and throwing rotten fruit and eggs towards the balcony. The front of the crowd was being kept back by hundreds of Chosen so that even those with the best arm had no chance of hitting the Emperor with any projectiles. Even so, several very enthusiastic people with eggs came very close. Nirrok watched in horror as they were beaten and dragged away while the Emperor continued to laugh and wave at his people, totally oblivious to the hate pouring off the crowd towards him.

When the Emperor failed to respond or even notice any of the insults hurled at him, the mood of the crowd turned nasty. It started with shoving the Chosen, trying to force them back, and when that failed Nirrok saw something flash in the crowd. One of the Chosen staggered back, a dagger in his neck. The screams became more high-pitched, the insults stopped and more people started producing weapons from underneath their clothes. One of the Chosen had his head bashed in with a blacksmith's hammer, while the two men on either side of him were stabbed to death with kitchen knives.

The crowd forced their way through the first rank, scrambling forward in victory as they sensed a chance to get their hands on the Emperor. A volley of arrows cut into the fastest runners at the front and two dozen people fell to the ground, crying and screeching in pain. A second volley followed and then a third, at which point the crowd began to break up, the fighting clustering into pockets. Groups of Chosen were cornered, slashed open and their weapons taken and passed on to others in the crowd. Soon afterwards, it devolved into a pitched battle.

All the while the Emperor sipped his drink, looking down on the crowd with a benevolent and slightly bemused expression.

A rogue thought entered Nirrok's mind about pushing the Emperor off the balcony and seeing what would happen. He'd seen him heal from small wounds, but Nirrok wondered how the Emperor would manage if he were torn into a hundred pieces and his skull ground under someone's boot, as he'd done to the herald.

"I'm bored," declared the Emperor. "I'm going to have a bath. You, bring my drink."

He flicked the empty glass towards Nirrok and he fumbled twice but then caught it before it hit the ground. One of the Chosen heaved a sigh of relief on his behalf before shoving him after the Emperor.

As he walked down the corridor, long before he reached the bath, the Emperor began to strip. Nirrok did his best to pick up the clothes while juggling the empty glass and jug. When the Emperor reached the royal bathing chamber the Chosen took up their position outside but Nirrok hurried inside where he started to light a fire under the huge copper tank of water.

"Don't bother," said the Emperor, sliding into the huge tiled bath that someone had already filled. "Give me the jug and get out."

Nirrok passed across the jug and graciously accepted the dismissive flick of the Emperor's hand as permission to leave. He briefly glanced at the murky water, wondered why it looked almost black, but didn't linger or let it worry him. Just before he reached the door, something fell on Nirrok's face but he ignored it until he was backing out of the room, pulling the doors closed. With the Emperor's back turned he wiped his face, saw it come away red and glanced up at the ceiling.

Above the bath at least a dozen bodies hung from the ceiling on hooks like slaughtered cattle. Dangling arms stretched towards him, pale faces with empty eye sockets, some bodies without heads, or limbs, and each was covered with dozens of cuts. Where a body had a head, the throat had been cut wide open, leaving behind a pale white husk. Nirrok glanced at the dark water in the bath, quickly closed the doors and ran.

CHAPTER 35

A terrible sense of foreboding disturbed Balfruss's much-needed sleep and he came awake with a start. Stumbling to the window he looked up at the sky and saw it was already past noon. He'd slept much longer than he anticipated. Ten hours, maybe more. Why had no one come to call for him? Had the fighting started again on the walls? Where was everybody?

"*Relax, Balfruss,*" said the soothing voice of Thule in his mind. "*The western army has not attacked today.*"

"The Warlock?" gasped Balfruss, trying to get his legs to work but they wobbled and barely seemed to hold him upright. He slumped down in a chair and pulled a blanket around his shoulders.

"*No sign of him, or the Splinters. He must be feeling the same as us. He will need to rest. The army is on stand-by just in case. We'll be called on if needed, but until then, get some rest. Go back to sleep.*"

Thule's voice had a peculiarly hypnotic quality, or perhaps the idea of sleep was so appealing Balfruss just surrendered to it. His head dipped towards his chest and he slept.

The next time he woke it was mid-afternoon and the smell of fresh bread tickled his nose. He'd fallen asleep in the chair and as he started to move, pain lanced up his neck. Wincing and massaging the muscles he shuffled across the room towards the covered tray and the enticing smells coming from underneath the cloth.

Despite sleeping for the better part of ten or twelve hours Balfruss still felt hollow and cold. His body was wracked with spasms of pain and he felt light-headed. Under the cloth sat a large bowl of stew, a huge chunk of warm crusty bread, a crock of butter and a jug of water. Beside that was a slab of cheese, three apples, two sweet pastries and some hard-boiled eggs. Balfruss tucked into the stew with vigour, shovelling it down and dipping the bread into the rich stew. As he gulped it down it brought back early memories of his mother cooking by the fire. His earliest memories of home were good, but she'd always looked a little sad.

As if he hadn't eaten in weeks Balfruss ate everything on the tray. Whether it was the stew or just the quantity of food, it warmed him up a little, but he still felt a bit chilly. He washed and dressed in warm clothes, despite it being near the end of spring, and then went in search of the others.

"Thule?" he said, trying to project the thought.

"*I'm in the gardens. The rest are asleep or eating,*" came the response.

"Are you all right?" asked Balfruss, hearing a strange tone in Thule's voice.

"*I'll tell you in person,*" said Thule.

Balfruss made his way down to the palace gardens, stopping off first at the kitchen to grab another lump of cheese and some more bread. The servants directed him to the food then quickly got out his way and went back to their chores.

Finn was asleep in a chair by one of the fires, an empty bowl at his feet. Someone had covered him with a blanket and despite the food and warmth his face still looked pale. The fight had sapped all of their energy reserves and then had started to leach the life from them. Another few minutes and one of his friends could have burned themselves out like the dead Splinter.

By the time Balfruss found his way to the right door and stepped out into the garden the sun was already starting its descent towards the horizon. He found Thule sat on a bench in a high-walled secluded garden at the heart of the palace. There were no flowers in the garden and the air was unusually still and quiet. A few bees bumbled about in search of nectar, but all of the plants in pots or narrow beds were unusual. A gravel path led to the far end of the garden where a five-foot stone disc dedicated to the seasons was surrounded by the melted lumps of old candles. Six fresh white candles sat before the disc and with considerable effort he saw Thule light them with a tiny summoned flame.

Balfruss sat down beside him on the bench and leaned closer to a curious squat plant with thick purple vines.

"Don't touch it," warned Thule, in a dry rasping voice that startled him. He'd become so used to hearing one voice in his head that it surprised him to hear a different one out loud. "All of the plants in the garden are possibly poisonous. It belongs to the royal apothecary."

"Charming," said Balfruss, rolling up the cuffs of his long sleeves so they didn't brush against the plants. "Why did you pick this spot?"

"Because I knew I wouldn't be disturbed," said Thule.

"I can go elsewhere," said Balfruss, starting to get up, but Thule laid a hand on his arm.

"I wouldn't have told you where to find me if I didn't want your company."

They sat together in comfortable silence for a while. Balfruss felt his eyes drift towards the disc. Long before organised religion, perhaps since the first days of mankind, people had given thanks for the changing of the seasons. People prayed for a mild winter so the cattle didn't freeze and they'd starve to death. People prayed for a long warm summer for growing crops and a cool autumn for the harvest. People prayed for rain and sun, even wind on the days when the air was so still and warm that even a faint breeze felt like a blessing.

Despite all the changes and the centuries that had passed, the discs could be found in every country and people still gave thanks. Whether they prayed to the Blessed Mother, the Lord of Light or the Maker, no one could ignore or forget the power of the seasons.

"My brother is dead," said Thule, the words hanging heavy in the air.

"I thought he was still in Shael."

"He is, but I'm connected to him," said Thule, tapping the side of his head. Balfruss felt sympathy for the Battlemage, but he was also amazed. Speaking between minds over any distance was something that had been a myth until Thule had shown him. It was another forgotten Talent, one that had the potential to change many aspects of daily life, even warfare. There were so many possibilities Balfruss doubted he'd thought of them all.

Unfortunately, from what Thule had told him, the Talent was almost impossible to teach. Despite being joined to Thule he had no idea of how it had been done and wouldn't know how to connect to someone else. From the way Thule described it, the process involved giving a part of yourself to the other person.

Until now Balfruss thought speaking to someone a few hours' ride away was miraculous. Thule had communicated with his brother in Shael, over a thousand miles distant.

Thule broke the silence first. His smile was sad and knowing. "My brother was not a kind man. He was greedy and quite often selfish. But he was my blood and if I ever needed help, I knew he would give it, until his dying breath."

"How did it happen?"

"He was a prisoner, held in one of the many camps since the invasion. He let me know that the Zecorran guards disappeared and recently the Morrin returned home. He thought the war might be over, but I told him we were still fighting. With only the Vorga still guarding the cells a revolt began. My people broke out and attacked their captors."

Thule had told him about the appalling conditions in the camps where hundreds of his people were stuffed into cells and were often the product of cruel games and experiments. The population had been decimated, whole cities turned to rubble and many of Thule's people were dead or starving to death in filth.

"Are you sure he's not just asleep or unconscious?" asked Balfruss.

Thule's smile was sad and knowing. "No, I felt the sword enter his body. He's dead, but at least he died a free man."

"We will free Shael," insisted Balfruss. "The King swore it and the Queen will uphold his promise."

"I know."

For a time they were both lost in thought. For the first time since the war had started, Balfruss considered what he might do after it. The war wasn't over, even if the alliance was falling apart, and they still had the Warlock and his Splinters to deal with. However, before this moment he hadn't even let himself consider where he might go when it ended.

He'd been travelling for a few years now, moving from place to place, criss-crossing the world, going wherever someone with his ability was needed. Even before the war had begun he'd been tired and in desperate need of a rest, but he'd kept pushing himself longer and harder.

"You'll go home, then," said Balfruss.

"To free my people, to see what remains and to rebuild."

"Without the Warlock the western army would crumble,"

said Balfruss. "We could scatter them and retake your country together."

Thule was quiet for a long time before he spoke again. "I don't have Ecko's vision, but I know that one day soon the Warlock will be defeated."

"You sound so sure," said Balfruss.

"I am, because you were right about him. He's weak. Here," said Thule, touching his forehead. "And here," he said, touching his heart.

"But he doesn't seem afraid of anything," said Balfruss.

"That's because he has nothing to lose. There is nothing he values or cares about." Balfruss could hear the pity in Thule's voice. "Every day we are tested in battle. We fight as hard as we can, because we must to preserve what we cherish. There is no other choice. When the Warlock faces something difficult, or grows tired, he just stops or sends in his Splinters to deal with it."

"Ecko was his first real challenge," said Balfruss.

"And he nearly died. Stripped of everything, the Warlock relied on brute force and still it almost wasn't enough." Thule shook his head. "My people have been starved, beaten and left for dead. They fight for their freedom and one day they will succeed, because there is no force more powerful than the desire to be free."

Since he had no family Balfruss thought about what he would do to protect his friends. He thought about Vann and his family, Eloise and Darius, his city and all of the people he didn't know. Every day he fought for them because Charas was his city and his only real home. But for his friends, there was nothing he wouldn't do to protect them. He would push himself to the edge and keep going because there was nothing more important. Against that the Warlock would always lose, and with a dwindling number of Splinters to cower behind, Balfruss knew it would happen one day soon.

CHAPTER 36

These visits to the hospital were happening too often. It seemed only moments ago that Vargus had been on his back with everyone gathered at his bedside. Now another of his lads had died, crying in the arms of a Sister of Mercy at the end, his insides ripped into shreds that couldn't be mended.

Only three of his original squad remained: Hargo, Orran and Black Tom. None of them had made it this far unscathed, and they'd lost many others along the way. Benlor had been the first, gone back south, a leg shorter than when he arrived, and most recent was Curly, sent home with one less arm. Thousands followed the code of the Brotherhood, but Vargus knew only a handful of them, and his name was no longer at its heart. He had been the beginning but wouldn't be the end.

Vargus paused at the entrance. The room stank of blood and fear and sweat, but he didn't smell what he'd expect in a hospital with so many wounded. There were scented burners to try and drive away the smell of rot and festering wounds, but today he couldn't smell it at all. Maybe the surgeons were doing a better job than he gave them credit for. He took another deep breath but only came back with the smell of unwashed bodies.

As he ran a hand over his scalp, Vargus realised where part of that smell was coming from: him. He needed a shave, a bath and a fresh set of clothes, but they would have to wait. Food and sleep were all he had planned for the next six hours, anything else was a luxury. He cast one last curious look around the room, then went out after the others.

The surgeon kept his head dipped forward, chin almost resting on his chest, as the grizzled warrior scanned the room one last time before walking out.

"Is it bad?" asked the injured man. For a moment the surgeon had forgotten all about him. It wouldn't do for Vargus, or any of the others for that matter, to find out what he was doing. Not yet anyway. Not until he was ready.

Returning his mind to the present, the surgeon leaned closer to the man's wounded leg. The fresh bandages were already soaked through with blood. There was also a strong smell, not too dissimilar to old cheese, coming from the wound. Pulling off the warrior's boot he saw some of the toes were discoloured, two were yellow and black, and it was spreading to the rest of the foot.

"Great Maker save me," said the man on seeing his ruined foot. "Will I lose my leg?"

"I'm afraid it's worse than that," said the surgeon, bending his head again, this time in prayer. When the warrior saw him clasping his hands together he started to weep. "If you're a religious man, now is a good time to offer a prayer to your God."

As the surgeon leaned forward a pendant fell out from between the folds of his shirt.

"What's that?" The warrior was staring at his pendant and the surgeon quickly tucked it away.

The surgeon glanced around in case anyone else had noticed, but no one was looking in their direction. "Nothing. Forget you saw it."

The warrior's eyes narrowed in suspicion. "That wasn't the Maker's symbol, or the Blessed Mother's."

"Course it was."

"That wasn't for the Lord of Light either, was it?"

"You're just confused, because of the infection," suggested the surgeon with a weak smile.

"What was it? Let me see," insisted the man, grabbing the front of his shirt with desperate strength.

The surgeon reluctantly took the pendant out and showed it to the warrior. It was simply made, fashioned from iron to look like an open eye at the centre of a triangle.

"It's the symbol of Akharga," he said in a whisper. "It's an old God. One for medicine and healing. He's supposed to be able to cure plagues and infection. I can't do anything to save your leg, so I thought a prayer wouldn't hurt."

"I'll take whatever help I can get," said the warrior. He released the surgeon's shirt and fell back.

"Will you pray with me?" asked the surgeon.

"I've got nothing to lose."

The surgeon guided him and together they offered a prayer to the old God of pestilence and plague.

After whispering a few words he sketched the symbol of Akharga on the man's forehead, then covered the wound with both hands.

"My leg feels warm."

The surgeon concentrated on the wound, picturing it free of infection and the blood circulating through the lower leg and foot.

"My toes are tingling."

A few more seconds and then it was done. The warrior's skin was paler and his heart was racing, but when the surgeon took his hands away the wound didn't smell any more. The skin on the man's toes was pink and all signs of the black toe were gone. Energy flowed into him, bringing a flush to his pale cheeks.

"It's a miracle!" gasped the warrior, on the verge of unconsciousness. A few seconds later he passed out. The surgeon took the chain from around his neck and put it over the man's head, tucking it away under his clothing.

His back made loud cracking sounds when he stood up, but the surgeon ignored the pain. Glancing around the hospital he inhaled deeply; not a single tasty infection or any delicious diseases.

He left the hospital, moving deeper into the New City. Walking along Monstad Street he passed in front of the biggest church in the city devoted to the Lord of Light. Pausing in front of its open doors he spat and sneered at the edifice.

"One day, you bastard," promised Kai.

CHAPTER 37

Every day since the siege began, the Battlemages rose at the same time as the warriors. By sunrise they were standing on the walls in case of an early attack. Now it was well on its way to midday and still no sign of the enemy. This was the second day they hadn't attacked, and although the respite was welcome, everyone knew it wouldn't last. The majority of the Seve warriors were taking advantage, staying out of the sun and catching up on their sleep, but they were still on alert. Whether or not any of them could actually get any sleep with an army camped outside was another matter.

The Battlemages gathered in an abandoned tailor's shop, one street away from the city walls. Afraid of having the business destroyed during the siege, the owner had stripped it bare and left. All that remained was a table, four chairs, a couple of wooden dummies, and an old bolt of moth-eaten grey cloth. The bee-hive racks for storing cloth were fixed to the back wall, but every single cell was empty. The front door had been left wide open, and with nothing worth stealing there had been no damage. Perhaps the owner would return once the war was over and carry on as if nothing had happened. Balfruss doubted it would be that simple.

Spring was starting to wane, summer was on the rise and

already it felt as if today was going to be another hot one. All of the Battlemages were sitting inside enjoying the shade, apart from Finn, who kept watch outside the door. The smith stared at the city walls and Balfruss didn't know what he expected to see. The Warlock and the remaining Splinters would not come flying over the top, but Finn's concentration never wavered. It was almost as if he expected trouble at any second.

"The western alliance is crumbling," said Thule in a rasping whisper. There were no soft furnishings to muffle sounds and his voice echoed off the walls, making it easier to hear. Even though the swelling on his throat had gone it still pained him to speak, but the Queen's surgeon had told him it was necessary to strengthen his damaged vocal chords.

Balfruss had already made a report to Talandra on Thule's behalf about the revolt in Shael, but he didn't mind hearing it again. It gave him hope for the future. By now new orders would be on their way via raven and pigeon, spreading the good news across the Queen's network of allies and spies. The war wasn't over, not even close, but the alliance was rotting at its core like a tainted apple. The centre would have to collapse and spill forth the wriggling maggots before the enemy outside the walls would listen to reason and think about returning home. He reminded himself again that it was good news, but also knew that it would not prevent further bloodshed for at least a few days. Hundreds, perhaps thousands of warriors could die in that time and their lives would've been wasted for nothing.

"What about the Morrin and Zecorrans in Shael?" asked Eloise.

"Gone. The Morrin have returned home. There are rumours of violent outbreaks between opposing religious groups in their country."

Talandra had briefly mentioned receiving reports that supported the rumours. The Morrin nation was also in turmoil, but so far they had not seceded from the alliance, or given the order to withdraw their troops.

"The zealots persuaded the rest of the Morrin Council to join with Taikon. Now the traditionalists are fighting back and a large portion of the population supports them. There have been riots and a temple of the Blessed Mother was destroyed."

"Good news for us," said Darius.

"However, despite growing unrest in Zecorria, their troops are not going home as well. They're coming here from Shael to bolster the army."

"Which explains the pause in fighting," said Eloise.

"But I've heard stories about fighting in the streets of Zecorria. It's all coming apart," said Darius, hugging his wife and she smiled.

Balfruss let the conversation wash over him, splitting his attention between the discussion and Finn. Every muscle of the smith's body was tense and he stood poised on the balls of his feet.

"What is it?" asked Balfruss.

"Something's happening," said Finn. He took a few steps into the street then stopped, looking at the surrounding buildings in alarm.

"What is it? What did you see?"

"I felt something," said Finn, scenting the air like a dog. "I think it's the Splinters."

All along the wall Balfruss could see warriors stirring at their posts, nudging others awake and readying their weapons. More were trooping up the stairs to the wall, blinking rapidly in the bright sunlight. A horn blared, a long low note that went on and on, until Balfruss felt the sound in the pit of his stomach. The noise seemed to pass through his skin and then settle inside, like an angry knot of fear and dread.

A grinding sound cut across the din as the engineers started winding back the winches on the catapults. Balfruss didn't need to be on the battlements to know what was happening.

The other Battlemages followed Finn out into the street, shielding their eyes against the sun. The horn came again, insistent and urgent, a call to arms for all those able to fight. Groups of men hurried past him, pulling on armour and strapping on weapons, their expressions a mix of fear and excitement. Stretcher bearers, doctors and nurses carrying stacks of bandages and satchels bulging with medicine trailed after them like an unwelcome cloud of flies on a corpse. Behind them came runners, skinny teenage boys and girls with long legs, clutches of priests and an assortment of tradesmen carrying additional supplies.

Then came the sound of hundreds of feet marching in unison and a flood of bodies flowed past the Battlemages on both sides. The sea of armoured men seemed to be endless, with rows and rows of them heading for the walls. It seemed as if the entire army had concentrated on this one street. Eventually the flood of men slowed to a trickle. A few latecomers ran to catch up with the rest, some rubbing sleep from their eyes. One man was half dressed, wearing only one boot and no armour. He hopped along, trying to pull on his other boot and don his armour at the same time, but lost his balance and fell over onto his face. Sat on the ground he took a moment to pull on his other boot, rearrange his breastplate and surreptitiously rub his sore nose before getting up.

When Balfruss sensed someone else approaching from behind he paid them no attention, waiting for the straggler to follow the others. When no one moved past he turned around, eyes widening in surprise.

The Warlock was standing next to his friends, grinning from ear to ear.

Time slowed to a crawl. Every frantic beat of his heart stretched out further and further apart. Even as Balfruss summoned power from the Source and opened his mouth to warn the others, it was already too late. The dagger caught the sunlight at its zenith, glinting maliciously before it plunged down into Darius's back. It came away with a red trail of gore. The Warlock stabbed him one more time before dropping the blade. Darius's mouth stretched wider and wider, a scream surging up from deep inside, but no sound came out. His knees buckled and he started to fall. Eloise screamed as she reached for her husband, but Balfruss couldn't hear her any more. Either the world had fallen silent or he'd been struck deaf. Somewhere in the distance he could hear something, screams and voices, but the sounds seemed to belong elsewhere.

Darius collapsed into the arms of his wife, who gently bore him to the ground, blood pumping from the wounds in his back. Balfruss froze in terror, horrified at what he was seeing, his mind unwilling to accept that it was real and not a nightmare.

A hammer forged of power lashed out towards the Warlock, but he casually sidestepped the blow and retaliated with a flick of his wrist. A loop of energy snagged Finn by one ankle, picked him up and sent him headfirst into a nearby wall. Thule's attack hit the Warlock next but he fared no better. The thin wires he'd conjured met an invisible barrier a hand's breadth from the Warlock's skin, dissolving on impact. Thule managed to erect a shield but the blunt force of the Warlock's riposte sent him through the nearest shop and out the back of the building in the street beyond.

All sound returned in a rush, and as the air around him began to crackle with energy, Balfruss realised he held a huge amount of power.

"I told you this would happen," shouted the Warlock over the din of the assembling army and the roaring in his ears. "I'll kill them all and then you'll be just like me!"

With a roar Balfruss finally retaliated, but the Warlock had already danced out of the way and the building behind him bore the full brunt of the attack. The entire stone edifice cracked and was compressed under an enormous amount of pressure. The building started leaning to one side and then the walls collapsed inwards, followed by a huge cloud of dust which spread into the street and up into the air. With a snarl Balfruss summoned a fierce wind that blew the yellow cloud away in seconds, but by then there was no sign of the Warlock. All that remained was the destruction he'd left in his wake.

Finn had made it back to his feet, but leaned heavily against a wall as blood trickled from his scalp. There was no sign of Thule and Eloise cried as she held the bloody figure of her husband. The sight of his Blood Brother drained the rage from him in an instant.

"He needs a surgeon," said Balfruss, but he wasn't sure anyone heard him.

A runner came pounding into view, a sweaty teenage boy with a red face. He skidded to a stop in front of Balfruss, his eyes widening at the sight of Darius lying in the street, before he refocused.

"General Vannok," gasped the runner. "Said you have to come now. Splinters. Attacking."

Seizing the boy by the shoulders Balfruss bent down until they were at eye level. "Find a surgeon. Now!"

He waited until the runner nodded before releasing him. The boy set off at a sprint, his long legs eating up the distance. Balfruss could hear the boy shouting for a surgeon as he went.

He wasn't sure if it would be in time, but he had to hope there was something that could still be done. For all of his power, Balfruss didn't know how to use any of his abilities to heal. The city still needed defending against the Splinters. If he did nothing, even more people would die.

Balfruss approached Finn. "Can you fight?" The big man was dazed and his eyes wandered a little until Balfruss slapped him across the face. "Can you fight?"

His eyes settled on Darius and then drifted to Balfruss's face. "I can fight."

Thule stumbled into the street with blood trickling down his face, but the cuts on his cheek looked shallow.

"Thule, can you fight?"

"*Yes*," said Thule. Even that one word, sent through their link, seemed a struggle, but at least he showed willing.

The runner came around a corner, dragging a tall surgeon by the hand towards them. She was struggling to keep up and stop her satchel from bouncing around and damaging its contents. Although he was loath to do it, Balfruss approached Eloise.

"Don't ask me," she said without looking up.

"I don't want to."

"Then don't."

"We're dead without you. Then all of this will have been for nothing."

Finally, Eloise looked up at him. Her expression of grief was one that he knew would stay with him for the rest of his life. The sum of every moment of anguish, every drop of sorrow he'd ever experienced, was nothing compared to the look on her face. It had become etched into the lines around her eyes and mouth, where laughter once lived. Now they had become something else, a testament to her grief and anguish. The total loss of something priceless that could never be replaced.

The surgeon dropped to her knees beside Eloise, made a quick assessment of Darius and then laid him out face down on the ground.

"Press here," ordered the surgeon, guiding Eloise's hands over a wound. Darius's skin looked pale and waxy and his face composed as if sleeping, but one eye remained open. For a second Balfruss thought his Blood Brother was still awake and trying to tell him something.

"Eloise," he tried again. "We need you."

"No." The word was said quietly but there was a finality to it. "Without him, I don't care. About anything."

The surgeon pulled bandages and several small vials from her satchel, while directing the runner to fetch a stretcher.

"We can't fight the Warlock and his Splinters without them," said Finn. "It's suicide."

"We must at least try," whispered Thule.

The Warlock had attacked one of his friends. He'd sneaked into the city like a coward and knifed his Blood Brother in the back. The undercurrent of rage started to surge towards the surface, making his fingers tingle.

"Take good care of him," said Balfruss. It seemed like a weak and inadequate thing to say about an old friend who had given him so much. The sort of careless comment a stranger might offer to someone they'd seen fall over in the street. The surgeon nodded, but didn't look up from her work. Balfruss felt the urge to say something to Eloise, but he lacked the words to communicate all that he was feeling.

"*She already knows*," said Thule in his mind.

A roar went up from the walls. A wordless shout of defiance from thousands of throats directed at the approaching enemy. An echo of it thrummed in Balfruss's veins and his whole body began to shake. His hands curled into tight fists and his shoulders hunched up.

Thoughts of Darius were pushed to one side as he and the two remaining Battlemages ran towards the city wall. By the time they'd ascended the stairs and reached the battlements, Balfruss saw the enemy soldiers would soon be at the wall. The scream of the warriors enveloped him, flooding his senses with noise. As his mind went over the last few minutes, his blood began to boil.

The fear and worry melted away until he was enveloped in a cocoon of rage. Balfruss summoned power from the Source and the air began to crackle all around him. Pressure built up and the charge caused the hair of his beard to bristle. The power, or maybe it was the beat of his heart, hummed in his ears, an angry drum that needed release.

Stood less than a mile from the walls were the four remaining Splinters, faceless and silent as ever. Although he felt no anger towards them, for they were nothing more than mindless puppets, Balfruss still hated them because of who held their leash.

As he drew more heavily on the Source, Balfruss thought about all the lives that had been lost in the war. The warriors and the innocents, the refugees from Shael, Ecko and maybe his Blood Brother, Darius. Someone was talking, but Balfruss couldn't hear them. He pulled even more power into him until it pressed against the back of his eyes and he felt it deep down in his bones.

Reaching towards the sky, Balfruss added his voice to the throng of defiant warriors on the battlements before unleashing all of his hatred, rage and frustration at the closest Splinter.

There was a loud cracking sound and a fat bolt of lightning split the sky, slamming down into the cowled figure. A fountain of earth and stones were thrown half a mile into the air at the point of impact.

Finally, when the dust cleared, only a deep fissure remained and not a single trace of the Splinter.

CHAPTER 38

Talandra insisted the conversation take place in the dining room, so that it didn't look like an inquisition, and yet she felt it still resembled one. She sat at one end of the table with Graegor stood behind, armed to the teeth as usual. Her brothers sat to her immediate left and right, and beside them her two Generals, Wolfe and Vannok Lore. Graegor had asked that Vannok be excused because of his personal connection, but she'd refused and then reminded Graegor this wasn't an inquisition, formal or otherwise.

It was late and Talandra was already struggling to stay awake after another long and busy day. In truth she could have done without this. She already knew much of what had happened, and she could make a reasonable guess about what she was about to hear. Unfortunately procedure needed to be observed. The others needed this ritual and she hoped it would at least clear the air, allowing them to put it behind them and move forward together.

Two guards escorted Balfruss to the door where they left him and took up their posts outside. Looking at his face Talandra was once again reminded of his recent losses. First Ecko and now his Blood Brother. By the time Darius reached the hospital it was already too late. Shani's report from the surgeon detailed the stab wounds. One had pierced the Battlemage's heart and the other a lung. Nothing could be done and now she'd lost another irreplaceable weapon. Part of her recognised it was a cold and calculating way to look at it, but every warrior in the army could be replaced. The Battlemages could not. Without them the war would already be over, and all of them would be dead or enslaved. This faux inquisition seemed like a poor reward for all that Balfruss had done to save lives in her service.

Somehow, Balfruss, Thule and Finn had managed to hold the line against the Splinters while the battle raged around them. She'd heard that Balfruss had destroyed one of the Splinters in the first minute of fighting, but there was no way to prove it. Talandra considered it a possibility, especially as minutes before the battle started Balfruss had seen his Blood Brother dying in the arms of his wife. From what little she knew about how their power worked, emotion played an important part, and Balfruss could certainly have used it as an outlet for his rage.

King Usermeses IV would have to be informed about the tragedy and the death of Darius as soon as possible. She didn't want the Desert King finding out about this news from unofficial channels ahead of any formal missive. Talandra's next task after this meeting was to draft a letter to the King, extending her deepest condolences and sympathy.

Talandra offered Balfruss a friendly smile and gestured towards the only available chair in the room at the other end of the table. For all intents and purposes this could have been just another meeting of the War Council, if not for the fact that Graegor was standing behind her seat and there were no papers or maps scattered across the table.

The war was affecting everyone, but as Balfruss sat down she thought the Battlemages seemed to be showing it the most. When he'd first arrived Balfruss had been a little plump with round cheeks and a mischievous twinkle in his eyes. Now his red-rimmed eyes were shadowed by deep purple slashes, his face was lean and his skin a little grey. His long beard and shaggy black hair gave him a wild look. Despite his obvious exhaustion after another day of brutal fighting, his mind still worked quickly. Talandra saw him glance around the room, making a note of the dour faces, then finally at Graegor standing behind her chair.

Balfruss also looked at the closed door and was perhaps thinking of the guards posted outside. All guests were escorted inside the palace, but had they been any less friendly with him than usual? How much did they know? Would they try to stop him leaving if he stepped outside the room? These and a hundred questions must have been running through his mind.

To Talandra's surprise Balfruss leaned back in his chair, adopting a blank expression to match her own. It seemed pointless to leave him to stew, since he clearly knew why he'd been summoned.

"Tell me about the Warlock," said Talandra, breaking the heavy silence.

"What do you want to know?" asked Balfruss.

Without looking around Talandra reached out and put a restraining hand on Graegor's arm. She could feel the old General shaking from head to toe, seething with rage. Graegor was on the cusp of doing something reckless, but violence was the last thing she wanted. Steel was useless against a Battlemage. After a second's thought Talandra corrected herself; it was useless if they saw it coming. The thought felt unworthy after all they'd given to protect Seveldrom and yet she couldn't ignore it.

"When did you first meet with him?"

"He approached me a few weeks ago. It was late at night, and I was the only one awake in our camp. At first I didn't know who he was, but after talking for a while I realised he was different."

Talandra raised an eyebrow. "Different?"

Balfruss sighed. "His tone was challenging. He claimed to work for the quartermaster, but he was used to giving orders, not taking them. He pretended to be nervous, but it soon fell away."

"I see," mused Talandra, working it through in her head.

"When did you start conspiring with him?" roared Graegor, shattering the calm. His voice echoed off the stone walls and faded away. Talandra rolled her eyes and was about to discredit the remark when she saw the expressions of everyone else at the table. All of them looked uncomfortable at the idea, but she noticed a hint of something else. A notion that, perhaps, such an idea was possible. Talandra looked at Vannok, who met her gaze steadily. No doubt lingered in his eyes. His faith in Balfruss was absolute.

"I wouldn't have put it that way, but . . . " Talandra trailed off and left the unspoken question hanging.

Balfruss snorted. "After everything I've done, how can you ask me that?"

"You didn't answer the question," said Talandra, not unkindly.

"I've never conspired with him," spat Balfruss, staring at Graegor. The two men were locked together in a glaring match, neither willing to back down. Talandra suspected it would go on for days, weeks even, unless someone intervened. Both men were stubborn and totally unyielding.

"You said he was different," said Vannok, perhaps the only person in the room who could disrupt the staring match. "Did you know who he was at your first meeting?"

Balfruss hesitated only briefly before answering. "Yes, and I confronted him."

"Why didn't you tell someone afterwards?" asked Vannok. "If you knew, why keep it a secret?"

There was a note of betrayal in Vannok's voice, enough to make Balfruss look away from Graegor. The Battlemage's eyes widened in surprise as he stared at his oldest friend. "You think I'm a traitor, Vann?"

"No. But it's unusual to keep this a secret."

"I don't know why. It didn't seem important."

Graegor snorted in disbelief.

"What did he want?" asked Talandra, steering everyone's focus back to her before another staring match started.

"To gloat, to find out what sort of a man I was."

Talandra raised an eyebrow. "That's all?"

"That was all at our first meeting."

"Great Maker!" swore Graegor. Talandra slammed both fists on the table to distract Graegor before he did something stupid. She shouldn't have done it. It hurt a lot more than expected, and the sound wasn't as loud as she'd hoped. She wasn't heavy enough, but even so the pain gave her something to focus on. Anger stirred inside beneath the surface, especially when she thought about the shredded remains of her father, but she wouldn't let emotion be her master.

Her father had always remained calm during tense discussions, whereas Graegor often swore and shouted. She realised that was one of the many reasons her father always included the grizzled General. He remained composed and dispassionate, but Graegor could rant and rave, sometimes on his behalf. He was a handy surrogate for one's rage and useful misdirection. It amazed Talandra that even now, after more than thirty years, she was still learning about her father.

"How many times have you met with the Warlock?" asked Thias.

"Maybe half a dozen. Each time he wanted to boast and challenge me. I also think he met with me because he was lonely."

"Lonely?" scoffed Graegor.

Balfruss clenched his hands into fists and the ridges in his furrowed brow deepened. He must have known how ridiculous it sounded, as he slowly relaxed and took a few deep breaths.

Talandra noticed that Graegor relaxed his grip, but didn't move his hand away from the axe on his belt.

When Balfruss spoke, his voice was ragged. "In many ways, he's like a child. He's more powerful than any Battlemage I've ever met. Maybe stronger than one of the Grey Council, and yet he's constantly seeking approval. He wants me to admit that we're alike, that we're the same, so he's not alone any more."

"Why?" asked Talandra.

"For years he's been doing whatever he wants, and no one can stop him. He has almost unlimited power and there are no consequences for his actions. Can you imagine what that's like?" said Balfruss, shaking his shaggy head. "Helping Taikon form the alliance, creating the Splinters, murdering your father, even the war, none of it means anything to him. People mean nothing to him. They're all just toys to be played with and broken."

"He sounds insane," muttered Hyram.

"Perhaps," admitted Balfruss.

"Why you?" asked Vannok. "Why has he fixated on you?"

"Found a kindred spirit, has he?" sneered Graegor.

Talandra expected more anger, but instead Balfruss remained utterly calm. He tilted his head to one side as if listening to something before speaking. "No. We're nothing alike," he said finally, with a faint smile.

"Then why?" said Talandra.

"Because he needed a new challenge and I won't yield. He's threatened to kill all the other Battlemages, one at a time, until it's just the two of us. He wants me to lose control, drive me over the edge, until we're the same."

One incredibly powerful and unstable Battlemage had manipulated nations and drawn almost the entire world into a war. The idea of two such beings working together was a terrifying thought she didn't want to consider. Not even for a second.

"He doesn't want to kill you. He wants you as an ally."

"Failing that, he will try to turn me into another Splinter."

That thought disturbed Talandra even more. She saw the same unbridled fear in the faces of those around her.

"It doesn't change the facts," said Graegor. "You've been meeting with him in secret. How do we know you're not one of his puppets?"

"Because I have free will."

"I don't believe you."

Giving Graegor's anger free rein was useful. It kept people off balance and allowed her to see how they coped under pressure, but Talandra was quickly realising there were times when she needed to rein him in before he went too far.

"Graegor," she said, trying to interrupt the General, but it was too late. The rage he'd been holding in check started boiling over and it would not be put aside so easily. The meeting was not going as she'd planned.

"Everything we've been told about the Splinters came from you, not the other Battlemages. I think it's all been lies. Mind games to distract us, because you're working for him. You're a traitor!"

As Balfruss surged to his feet Graegor drew his axe. The others quickly leapt to intervene, keeping the two men apart before there was any bloodshed. Talandra remained seated, letting it flow around her. Her brothers were struggling to restrain the big General despite the differences in age, while Vannok and Wolfe kept Balfruss at arm's length. He could have drawn on his magic and turned Graegor into a red spot on the wall, and yet he didn't. Perhaps, on some level, he already knew.

"Where were you?" shouted Graegor. "When the King was murdered. Where were you?"

"I've fought every day of this war, while you sit around on your fat arse!" roared Balfruss. "You're a fucking coward!"

Graegor stopped thrashing about in Thias's grip and all colour drained from his face. With an inhuman scream he surged towards Balfruss. Both of Talandra's brothers were pulled six feet across the room before their combined weight managed to stop the General's forward motion. The door to the dining room burst open and her royal guards came in with their weapons drawn. She waved them back and they retreated but stayed inside the room.

"Traitor!" snarled Graegor, unwilling to leave it alone.

"He's not a traitor," shouted Talandra, her voice cutting across all noise. "He's your son."

The silence that followed was so deafening it made her ears ring. Somewhere outside she could hear the repetitive strike of a hammer against an anvil. Even at this late hour the smiths were still hard at work when most were in their beds. She wondered if Finn laboured alongside them, trying to beat a piece of twisted metal back into something useful. She knew the smith wished someone could do the same to him. Remake him anew.

Talandra felt everyone's eyes on her. All strength seemed to drain out of Graegor as he dropped his axe, and would have fallen if Thias and Hyram hadn't held him upright.

Balfruss looked between her and the old General in open disbelief. But then his expression changed as he saw something familiar in Graegor's face. There were some similarities around the eyes, but not enough to make it obvious they were related. The rest Talandra had put together over the last few weeks. Graegor was always angry, but recently he'd been particularly irritated about something personal. Everyone knew the man had no family, but that hadn't always been true. Talandra's father had mentioned it once or twice, but it had taken recent events for her to remember the tragic story of Graegor's family being killed by raiders.

Another clue had come during her unusual conversation when the General had walked her back to her quarters. At the time she'd only known a little about Balfruss's background, and in a tired daze she'd sent Graegor to speak with Vannok. Two days ago the pieces of the puzzle had started to come together in the back of her mind. A little more digging and a few discreet questions from Shani confirmed her suspicions.

She had intended to discuss this with Balfruss and Graegor in private to give the Battlemage another reason to stay in Charas after the war. She knew he'd also reconnected with Vannok and his family. Combining that with suddenly having a father, she'd hoped it would make it difficult for Balfruss to walk away. Now her plan was ruined, and she didn't know what would happen next.

Thias and Hyram were struggling with Graegor's weight, so they shuffled him towards a chair. He collapsed in a boneless heap and, for the first time in her life, Talandra thought the General looked defeated. The seemingly bottomless pit of rage that burned in his eye had been extinguished. He stared at the surface of the table, lost in thought.

"I thought you knew," Talandra said gently.

"I suspected," said Graegor, without looking up.

"You're not my father," said Balfruss, slowly getting to his feet. Talandra caught a brief glimpse of something before the Battlemage recovered. Behind his eyes she saw an abyss filled with terrible pain and so much anger it took her aback. "You're nothing to me." Balfruss turned and walked out of the room.

CHAPTER 39

Roza waited a few minutes in an adjacent street to make sure she was the last to arrive at the warehouse. As before at previous meetings, those gathered in the warehouse wore disguises and masks. The numbers in the crowd had dwindled slightly, but those that remained were real patriots. Those willing to do more than just talk and attend clandestine meetings for a bit of fun.

Although none had removed their masks, she knew all their identities and they believed they knew hers.

A few days after the first meeting, each of the activists received a personally addressed letter from Petra with their first set of orders. As expected this scared away the thrill-seekers chasing the latest craze, and the cowards only willing to mouth off behind closed doors about what needed to be done. The rest were willing to do whatever was necessary to retake their country, starting with the capital city.

For almost two weeks wealthy landowners, merchants and figures from high society had been frequenting a flower shop in the Trade Quarter to purchase floral arrangements from a familiar-looking woman. With each bouquet they bought from her, they also received orders about the number of Drassi they were expected to hire, and where to station them.

So far everything was going to plan, but experience had taught Roza never to take anything for granted.

As she passed through the crowd Roza felt a familiar heat coming from the stares of some of the men. Perhaps one or two remained for a different reason, but they would be sorely disappointed in that regard. It was also too late to back out now. They were committed, and anyone trying to withdraw at this stage would have to be silenced to minimise potential risks. Although with so many Drassi in the city, it would be obvious even to a half-witted operative that something was happening.

"It's time to take back our country," she said without preamble. "Just as we planned, there are five hundred Drassi in the city and another four thousand nearby." She tipped her head towards a group of masked men dressed in custom-made finery and gold-edged masks.

Some of those in the crowd owned country estates that remained empty for most of the year, except on those rare occasions when they felt a whim to live as country folk. That is, country folk who were surrounded by opulence and waited on by servants, of course. Now their manicured gardens and colourful flowerbeds had been trampled underfoot and were the temporary barracks for Drassi warriors. They could reach the city in less than half a day's march. Those inside the walls were more than enough to take care of Taikon's Chosen, but it was what they couldn't plan for that Gunder worried about. It was why he'd insisted she tell them to bring in so many Drassi, just in case the Chosen had been busy with unofficial recruitment.

"When?" someone shouted. "When do we get to fight?"

"Very soon," she said. "I'm making final preparations. I have new orders for all."

The orders all said the same thing but she made a show of carefully selecting letters from her satchel before passing them out to individuals. Each masked activist quickly hid it inside the fold of their robes, or shoved it in a pocket, to read later in private. They would not meet again like this. The liberation of Yerskania would begin in three days.

"It is almost the right time to strike," said Roza, moving back onto the raised platform. "The war is not going well. The Seves continue to stall and defeat the west. The alliance is crumbling. The Morrin are fighting among themselves and the Zecorrans are divided and want to overthrow Taikon. Shael was crushed, but now even its people are fighting back."

The Zecorran reinforcements had gone directly through the southern pass to Seveldrom, for which she was grateful. If they'd attempted to take Yerskania it would have turned into a bloodbath in the streets. The plan with High Priest Filbin had proven incredibly successful. His Holiness had become a leading figure now who spoke out in public against the rebels and even Taikon.

Elsewhere the Morrin had abandoned Shael, sailed north and returned home. Every day she heard stories about fresh tragedies and outbreaks of violence committed by the extremists. The Morrin were too busy fighting to free their own country to care about anyone else. All of this, combined with so many troops engaged in Seveldrom, made it the right time to shatter the remaining pieces of the western alliance. Events were finally moving in the right direction and what they were planning in Yerskania could be the tipping point.

"Yerskania will be free," she promised. There was a brief cheer and a sporadic round of applause before the crowd began to disperse. Groups began to leave, a few minutes apart to avoid attracting too much attention. She spotted Gunder in the crowd who moved to the rear of the warehouse to wait for everyone else to leave. When they were alone she made a brief circuit of the warehouse before coming back inside and locking the door.

"What didn't you tell them?" barked Gunder, which made

her raise an eyebrow. Normally he maintained a firm grip on his emotions.

"Nothing. We're ready. Do you have any news?"

"The Watch is still being cautious. I've done all I can. Now it's up to the rebels," he said with a sneer.

"Meaning what?"

"Either they help with the rebellion, or you make sure they don't interfere. The Drassi won't care if their targets are Chosen or local citizens. They'll kill whoever they're told, as long as it's within the time limit of the contract."

Roza shook her head. "That's not a good idea."

"We can't afford for word of this to leak. Eliminate anyone who gets in the way, even members of the Watch."

Something had him rattled. He'd become a lot more unsteady, which she'd not seen happen to him before. Perhaps he'd been playing the game too long.

"What's happened to you?" she asked but Gunder ignored the question. He started to turn away until she put a hand on his arm. "Talk to me."

From beneath the Gunder mask of flabby flesh and gaudy clothes, Regori the butcher glared back at her. He glanced briefly at her hand and she pulled away as if burned.

"You have your orders."

Adopting his usual friendly mask, Gunder waddled out of the warehouse.

Without thinking about it, Gunder took an indirect route home from the warehouse through the winding city streets. Once he was a few streets away he peeled off his pheasant mask and threw it into an alley. The red marks on his face would fade in less than an hour, leaving no trace behind. He wondered how long it would take to cast off the remnants of the fat merchant when this mission had run its course.

He criss-crossed Perizzi, passing over the River Kalmei several times, ever watchful for shadows. It was only when he came abreast of The Lord's Blessing that Gunder realised he was being followed. After a few minutes it became clear they were very inexperienced. Despite the person's attempt to muffle the sound, he heard faint scraping from their shoes. They were also following too closely, as twice he saw movement at the corner of his eye when he turned his head.

Ducking into a narrow alley that ran behind a row of shops, Gunder dashed ahead, jumping over broken boxes and crates of rotting fruit. His boots squelched and stuck to the ground, but he didn't stop to look at what he'd stepped in. Not far ahead the alley opened onto a street that was quiet at this hour. Instead of running any further Gunder ducked into a doorway beside the mouth of the alley, pressing himself into the shadows as much as possible.

A few minutes later he heard someone coming towards him at speed. At their current pace his pursuer would go right past and he could slip away before they doubled back. It had been a long night and he was tempted to let them go, but changed his mind. It was the easy and generous option and not something he would ever have done before coming to Perizzi.

As the shadow came abreast of his hiding place Gunder burst into the alley, knocking them against the far wall. All he had time to see was a small figure dressed in blue and white. It was some kind of uniform, but unlike any he'd seen before. Before they had time to recover Gunder lashed out with a boot, catching his pursuer in what he thought would be the stomach. The resulting cry of pain was too high pitched for his pursuer to be a man.

Gunder pulled his pursuer upright, shoving them against the far wall. Light from the street lanterns fell on the figure's face and Gunder stepped back in surprise.

"Sabu?"

The boy was wheezing and holding one hand to his chest, but it was the uniform Gunder found the most startling. It resembled the uniform of the Chosen, except for the red badges sewn onto the sleeves. Three decorated the right and two the left. Each had a different symbol at its heart, indicating some kind of achievement.

"Why are you dressed like that? What are you doing?" he asked quietly, keeping one eye on the street.

"I'm doing my civic duty to protect the civil liberties of the nation," said Sabu. His intonation was off on certain words, suggesting he'd learned them through repetition.

"Do you even know what that means?"

"I'm doing my duty."

Gunder raised an eyebrow. "How?"

"I find traitors. I've already helped get five arrested," he said, gesturing at the red shields on his uniform.

Even though he already knew, Gunder needed to hear it. "Who do you work for?"

"His Holiness, Emperor Taikon, Overlord of the West."

The sinking feeling in his stomach deepened. "You stupid boy. You've no idea what's really going on."

Sabu shook his head sadly, as if Gunder was the one being misled. "I know enough."

He tried to dash into the street but Gunder grabbed him by the neck, flinging him deeper into the alley. Sabu landed in a pile of mud and something that was decomposing, which roused a cloud of fat angry flies. As he got to his feet the boy looked more horrified by the grime on his uniform than his predicament. He tried to wipe the crud off, but only smeared grey and brown sludge down the front of his breeches.

"Why were you following me?"

"You're a traitor," said Sabu. "Just like the other one."

Sabu looked over his shoulder as if considering trying to run back the way they'd come. Gunder grabbed him by the arm before he made an attempt to escape. "What other one?"

"The Zecorran jeweller. I saw him sneaking into your house the other night."

Ironically Zoll's visit had been a social call from a lonely man who hadn't wanted to drink by himself. But if Sabu had given the Chosen his and Zoll's names then it would explain why they'd raided his home. Gunder had not seen the jeweller for a few days, which meant he was still in custody, in hiding, or likely on a ship back to the north.

"Did you tell the Chosen I was a traitor?"

The boy squirmed and looked as if he'd swallowed a lime. "I was going to, but I needed proof. They gave me the lash last time I guessed and it turned out wrong."

Gunder sighed in relief. There was still a risk that Sabu could compromise the rebellion, but if he took extra precautions they would be minimal.

"Why did you—" Gunder started to ask and then stopped as he noticed the hilt of a dagger protruding from his stomach. It was simply crafted and bore the boy's name and an inscription on the hilt that read 'Initiate'.

Sabu's eyes widened with terror as he realised what he'd done. He tried to run, but Gunder maintained a firm grip on the boy's arm. After a few seconds, Sabu's panic faded and he stared at the wound with suspicion.

"It's not bleeding."

The blade, barely longer than Gunder's index finger, was embedded in the padding he wore to resemble a fat man. A normal dagger would have cut him, but the boy's blade had not even pierced his skin.

"I really wish you hadn't done that," said Gunder, letting a dagger drop from his sleeve into his empty hand. Sabu saw the blade and frantically tried to pull free.

"I won't tell anyone. I promise!" he babbled, then started to cry when Gunder pulled him deeper into the alley. When Sabu realised tears were having no effect he lashed out, kicking and punching Gunder. He opened his mouth to scream, but the dagger flashed by his throat and his voice faded to a gurgle. A curtain of red enveloped his neck and he crumpled to the ground, gasping and choking for breath. Gunder waited until the boy stopped breathing before wiping the blade on Sabu's stained uniform and walking from the alley.

CHAPTER 40

It was just after dawn and yet there were over a dozen people sat or kneeling inside the cathedral. Despite having travelled throughout the west, and as far as the court of the Desert King in the east, Balfruss still experienced a deep sense of awe when entering the oldest surviving church of the Great Maker. For almost a millennia countless people had come here to pray to the oldest of the Gods. In that time a hundred wars had ravaged the world, nations had come and gone, but this site had remained devoted to the Maker throughout.

There was something profound and calming about the atmosphere in the church, its familiarity and consistency. After only a few years away from Seveldrom, Balfruss noticed small changes in the city. The latest fashion was to grow a moustache, whereas full beards had previously been the norm. People's clothing seemed more colourful, and yet also more conservative than he remembered. Food in taverns was now commonly flavoured with spices from the west, which was a blessing as it had always seemed bland to him before. He'd noticed these and a hundred other changes but here, in the house of the Great Maker, time stood still.

The huge arched ceiling, wide stone pillars, stained-glass windows and heavy wooden furniture were exactly the same. Down one wall was a procession of paintings of former Patriarchs from centuries ago up to the present. On the opposite wall, landscapes that had been donated by local artists to raise money for the church. One change Balfruss did notice was a gallery of brightly coloured crude paintings, stuck to an area on the back wall. On closer inspection he realised they were drawings made by local children of King Matthias, together with simple messages of condolence.

Eloise was sat four pews from the front. Her eyes were open, staring straight ahead but they were distant. Balfruss sat down nearby but said nothing, enjoying the soothing peace and quiet.

With no distractions his thoughts turned to recent events. There were no more secrets between him and the others. The Queen and her Generals knew everything about the Warlock and so did his brethren. He'd even told the other Battlemages about Graegor, although he was still struggling with it.

"Have you spoken to him?" asked Eloise, as if she'd read his thoughts.

Her face was pale and drawn, her eyes red rimmed and blood-shot from crying and lack of sleep. The black robes of mourning made her look gaunt, and for a second she reminded him of a Splinter. A spark of life remained in her eyes, but she'd buried it beneath a mountain of grief.

"No."

"Is he your father?"

As much as he wanted to deny it Balfruss knew the truth. Vannok had known for a while and had been trying to find the right moment to tell him. "Yes," he said finally.

"Then you should talk to him soon," insisted Eloise.

"Why?"

"Because tomorrow one of you could die." The words were spoken gently but he knew they must have hurt a great deal. Balfruss gripped one of her hands in a vain attempt to offer a meagre form of comfort. He kept his eyes on the altar, afraid that looking at her would bring all the emotions he'd buried in the desert back to the surface.

A part of him still didn't believe Darius was really dead. It just didn't seem possible. Any moment he expected his bluff friend to casually wander into the church and sit down beside them. It seemed like only days ago that he'd walked into the distant city of Korumshah as a stranger. It was Darius who had made him feel welcome, taken him into his home and taught him the local customs. It was through him that Balfruss had met Eloise, and later earned his place at court by impressing the Desert King. His impact had been so significant the King allowed Darius to make him a Blood Brother. Dark thoughts of what that meant, now that Darius was dead, swam to the surface. Balfruss looked around for a distraction but there were none. A part of him felt that the church had been designed that way on purpose, so that no one could avoid the truths they would not speak aloud.

"I can't promise anything," said Balfruss.

"Why?"

"He abandoned us." Even after all this time it surprised Balfruss how much it still hurt. "I was just a boy when he left, but they'd been married for years before I was born. Once he'd been gone for a couple of years I didn't really notice, but sometimes I'd hear my mother crying at night. I didn't know why until I was old enough to understand. She never gave up on him and she never recovered."

"He never tried to get in touch?"

Balfruss sighed and took a moment to gather his thoughts. "Just before she died I found a few letters. He always mentioned coming home, but was vague about when." The Red Tower had given him leave to visit his dying mother in her final days. By that time he barely recognised her. The pox had robbed her of any beauty and stripped the meat from her bones, leaving behind only a grey-skinned wraith. For as long as he could remember there'd always been sadness in her eyes, but in her final days the last spark of hope had been extinguished. She'd died broken-hearted and in pain, but proud of his accomplishments.

"It was too little too late," said Balfruss, gritting his teeth. "He made his choice. He has to live with the consequences."

"Don't turn your back on family," Eloise urged him.

"I'm here for the family that matters," he said, unwilling to yield on this matter. "I'm here for you."

"Have you come to claim your property?" asked Eloise, offering up both wrists in a gesture of supplication.

"What are you doing?" he asked, trying to keep his voice low.

"Didn't he tell you?"

"Tell me what?"

"As his Blood Brother you're expected to marry his widow." Eloise adopted an expression of docile servitude. "How can I serve you, my beloved?"

"Stop it."

"Should I get on all fours and bark like a dog? Or do you want me on all fours for another reason?" she asked, giving him a dirty look.

"Don't!" His voice echoed off stone walls, drawing curious and hostile looks.

As he walked out of the church Balfruss heard someone following, but didn't turn around.

"Wait!" said Eloise, but he ignored her and pressed on.

A hazy orange sun cast long shadows down the streets. Balfruss maintained a fast pace, passing through sunbeams and icy pools of shadow that made spots dance in front of his eyes. When he was a few streets away from the church he came to a market square where vendors were unpacking their wares and setting up for the day. Many of them were preparing food and delicious smells came from several of the stalls. Balfruss approached a baker's table and picked out a couple of cinnamon pastries. The merchant recognised him and Balfruss had to insist on paying, but even then the man looked deeply troubled. He was afraid of incurring the anger of a Battlemage. A lot of people gave him nervous glances when they thought he wasn't looking.

In the centre of the square he discovered a small abandoned fountain. The statue of the woman was so old and corroded he could make out little of her features. She could have been an idol to an ancient God or a famous Queen. Either way no one remembered who she was or why they had erected a statue in her honour. Balfruss sat down on the stone lip surrounding the fountain, munching on his pastry and enjoying the banter of the merchants.

A few minutes later Eloise sat down. He passed her the other pastry and they ate in silence, soaking up the morning sun. After a few minutes Balfruss started to sweat but the heat barely affected Eloise, despite her being dressed in black. Compared to the desert this was probably a cool winter's day.

"I'm sorry."

"You've nothing to be sorry about."

"But—"

"It's forgotten."

The silence returned, but this time he felt no awkwardness between them. Taking a deep breath he inhaled the familiar and heady aromas of the city as it came awake.

Balfruss watched as a young boy helped his father slice up fruit with uncanny speed, his knife flashing in a silver arc like a ritualised dance. The diced pieces were skewered and dipped into a pot of honey, sugar and herbs and then left to dry in the sun. One day the boy would inherit the business, his father's legacy to him. He wondered what his legacy would be and how he would be remembered by others in years to come.

"He loved you so much and would want you to be happy."

"I don't know how to do that without him," said Eloise.

A long silence settled on them for a while and once again Balfruss wondered who would mourn for him if he died.

"Will you go back east?" he asked eventually. Eloise was also watching the boy, her eyes full of terrible longing.

"I don't know if I belong there, or here. I'm of both countries and neither. I just can't think about any of it now."

"If I can do anything, you only need ask." Balfruss dusted the crumbs off his fingers and stood. "I have to go, they think the first attack will come early."

"I'm ready."

"Are you sure?" asked Balfruss.

"No, but I can't lock myself away while other people are dying. I'm needed, and can do something to help. I can prevent other husbands and wives from feeling this way."

Balfruss wanted to comfort his friend, or tell her how lucky Darius had been, but he didn't feel that he could do either. Instead he said nothing, leading the way towards the walls where the Warlock and his Splinters would be waiting.

The fighting started an hour after dawn with the western army bolstered by the arrival of the Zecorran troops. The fresh soldiers seemed to invigorate the others, as fighting on the walls was frenzied and savage. Rivers of blood ran down the battlements and the endless screams of the dying carried to Balfruss's ears on the easterly wind. His arms were red to the elbows from helping field surgeons stem bleeding wounds. Most of the warriors he assisted with died regardless of their efforts. One died while he still had a hand inside the man's abdomen, pinching shut a gushing artery.

It was approaching midday when the enemy soldiers finally withdrew. At first it seemed like a brief pause, but then the warriors started looking expectantly in his direction. By the time Balfruss reached the battlements the western army was pulling back, while four cowled figures walked through their ranks towards the city.

"*We must end it. Today*," said Thule in his head.

Thule was better at concealing his grief and anger than most, but after sharing his thoughts for so long Balfruss could sense his emotions. Finn's expression was grim, and although he'd recovered from his night of heavy drinking, the experience with the Forge Masters and his sword had irreparably changed him. He seemed equally determined to put an end to the Warlock, once and for all.

To his left Eloise threw back her black hood. The tattoo on her face seemed livid against her pale skin, more like a fresh brand than a mark of honour, and he would not have been surprised if blood had run from it. Her grief could not be measured, weighed or balanced. Nothing would ease it. Not even victory.

"It has to end today," said Balfruss, echoing Thule's thoughts, and the others gave signs of agreement. He called for a runner and a few minutes later all of the Seve warriors started scrambling off the battlements. They didn't stop until they were a couple of streets away. They'd all seen what had previously happened to an unlucky few caught in the crossfire.

As he stared out over the walls of his city, Balfruss knew that somewhere out there the Warlock would be watching. He was controlling his puppets from a distance, making them fight in his stead while he looked for weaknesses. Ecko had outsmarted him once and Balfruss knew the Warlock would not allow himself to be tricked in the same way a second time.

"Coward," he muttered.

"We should attack them," spat Finn. "We shouldn't wait and just defend."

Balfruss took a deep breath and drew on the Source until it

infused every fibre of his being. His senses sharpened exponentially and the rotting faces of the Splinters leapt into focus. Despite the spark of energy that kept their bodies moving, the decay was worse than ever. Their skin had turned purple and green in places. One Splinter had empty eye sockets and another had bitten clean through its tongue. It was no longer possible to tell which had once been men or women. All were bald and little more than shambling skeletons wrapped in a cloak. A cloud of flies followed in the wake of each, and none of them tried to stop themselves being eaten alive. They would not hold together for much longer. It would be a mercy to destroy them.

"He's right. We must take the fight to them," said Balfruss.

"*Are you sure?*" asked Thule.

"Do you see another way?" he asked, but no answers were forthcoming. A defensive posture would protect the city, but there was no guarantee any of the Splinters would die. That would only happen if they were overpowered. "Then we fight."

"*Whatever happens, I want you to remember you're nothing like him. Whatever words come out of his mouth, they are always one part truth and two parts lies.*"

Balfruss looked along the wall, trying to catch his eye, but Thule was staring towards the Splinters. With a faint smile Thule drew on the Source and his golden skin seemed to shimmer as power infused his being.

"You don't think we can beat them?" whispered Balfruss. He didn't need to speak out loud, but still wasn't comfortable communicating mind to mind.

"*Not without paying a price.*" Thule finally met his gaze, and in his eyes Balfruss saw deep sadness and a terrible sense of knowing. "*The Splinters have no will, except that which he gives them. They will not stop because they are tired or in pain. They will only stop when they are dead. You know there is only one way that we can win. We must destroy them utterly.*"

As Balfruss stared at his friends the weight of what must happen settled on his shoulders. His concentration wavered and he almost lost his grip on the Source. Gritting his teeth Balfruss focused on steadying his will as he swallowed the bitter taste of bile. This is what Ecko had faced in his final moments, and yet he'd managed to marshal his courage and fight. After having travelled so far and already lost so much, Balfruss couldn't imagine the loss of another friend. Now he faced losing three more. There was so much he still wanted to say to them, but there was no more time.

"Eloise," he said, trying to find the words. She turned towards him and fresh tears were already running down her face.

"I know," was all she said.

"Here they come," shouted Finn. Energy crackled in the air around him as blue fire ran across his bare arms. With a cry of rage he unleashed something red and black towards the Splinter nearest him. It spiralled down from the walls towards the cloaked figure, gathering speed and size as it went. The meteor shattered against a shield with a shower of angry red sparks. Finn continued his assault, battering away at the Splinter, over and over again like a smith hammering at a piece of metal. The Splinter was driven to its knees by the force of his blows but its defence never wavered.

Thule didn't move a muscle, but Balfruss felt a surge of power, then a narrow fissure opened beneath the feet of another Splinter. Without a sound it fell into the hole, disappearing from view. Thule didn't hesitate and threw a pebble towards the crevice. Ice crystals formed around the stone as it fell until an unstoppable icy boulder was hurtling towards the Splinter. Just as the skeletal figure climbed out of the hole it was struck full in the face and knocked backwards.

Eloise was faring just as well against her opponent. It was being driven backwards under the blunt force of her will, as if being squeezed by a giant hand. The Splinter was on its knees, arms crossed in front of its face, as white and blue sparks sheared off its shield as she tried to crush it.

The last Splinter remained immobile and had made no aggressive moves. No doubt the Warlock was already having great difficulty fighting three separate battles that he'd forgotten about the fourth Splinter. Looking down the line Balfruss expected to see Darius beside his wife and for a few seconds he forgot why he wasn't there. With a bestial roar he threw a black spear forged from his hatred of the Warlock at the last Splinter. Before the Warlock could raise a shield the spear struck the Splinter, burying itself deep in the creature's chest. No blood ran from the wound and if the Splinter noticed the injury it showed no outward sign. A blue egg-shaped shield flickered to life then turned opaque, shearing off the spear. Balfruss's next projectile shattered on its surface, but it left behind a spider web of fractures that were slow to repair themselves.

The battle had only just begun and already it was turning in their favour. All of them kept hammering away at their opponents, driving them back, making them work harder and harder to maintain their defences. Even though the Splinters were not really alive any more and incapable of feeling pain, a faint murmur of life remained within them. None of their wounds bled, but when an arm was broken by one of Thule's boulders, it stayed bent at an impossible angle and the Splinter's shield became unsteady.

A stray thought entered Balfruss's mind, and for the briefest moment he thought they could win without any more losses. As if the Warlock were capable of reading his thoughts as easily as Thule, all of the Splinters dropped their shields at the same moment. Everyone's attacks faltered, but only momentarily before resuming with renewed fever. Even as their magical weapons struck the decaying shells, fire blossomed in the palms of all four Splinters. One of them was thrown onto its back by one of Finn's blows, and another was impaled by one of his spears, but it seemed to make no difference. Blue and yellow balls of flame became cherry red, flowing across the Splinters' bodies before flying out towards the Battlemages. Eight streams of flame joined together into one monstrous cloud, rising higher and higher on a phantom wind. Even before the fire drew close, Balfruss could hear it crackling and feel an intense heat. The walls of the city shuddered and the battlements moved under his feet. This was no ordinary inferno, but something far beyond his understanding of firecrafting.

At the source of the flame the Splinters' robes started to smoulder, black greasy smoke drifting up from two of them. The one lying on its back was writhing and arching its back as if in its death throes, but the Warlock would not relent. More and more power was channelled through the Splinters into the fire, even as it consumed what little remained of their minds and bodies.

A huge wall of blood-red fire rose above Balfruss's head, then hung in the air for the count of three heartbeats. In that moment, as he stared into the heart of the fire, all of his hope evaporated. And with the loss of the future came acceptance of his fate. A peculiar calm settled over Balfruss and his fears drained away, leaving behind only the deepest of regrets.

Even though a part of him knew it would be too late, Balfruss stretched forth with his mind and drew heavily on the Source, drinking deeper than he'd ever dared before. Weaving a shield made of layer upon layer of the hardest substance he could imagine, he took a wide stance on the battlements and braced himself against the onslaught.

Something heavy slammed into him with enough force to drive the air from his lungs. A blistering heat wrapped itself around his shield on all sides and the air inside became unbearably hot. He gulped in a deep breath and felt the air burn all the way down his throat and then settle into his lungs. As he struggled to breathe, Balfruss fell to his knees gasping and choking. In his desperation he considered lowering the shield for some fresh air, but part of his mind knew it would be madness and would kill him instantly.

The stone beneath his feet began to blister and crack. Even through the protective layer of his shield the stone scorched the skin on his hands and knees.

A high-pitched scream split the air, drawing his attention along the wall. It was a sound he didn't know another human being could make.

Thule was burning.

Somewhere inside his mind Balfruss felt something flicker and then ignite. Echoes of Thule's agonised thoughts ran through his head, sending fresh jolts of pain lancing around his skull. Somehow it felt as if the fire was inside his head. His eyes began to water, his thoughts turning sluggish as if his brain were melting into grey sludge. The flames outside his shield were still raging, but this was more than just magically conjured flame. It was a fire of the mind, and through his link he shared in Thule's agony.

The coarse stones of the battlements pressed into Balfruss's cheek. He didn't remember falling, but now found himself looking up as a screaming comet flew off the battlements into the street below. The air inside his shield was almost gone and he was losing consciousness. Flames licked at his clothes, singeing his hair and beard and yet something inside him refused to yield.

Somewhere nearby a woman started screaming, then Balfruss saw a second blazing figure fall from the battlements. His will began to crumble, darkness pressing in on all sides. In the street below a group of men were throwing their cloaks on top of the burning figures, trying to smother the flames. It didn't matter. Everyone would die very soon. With the death of the

Battlemages the city would be left without any defence against the Warlock. Taikon would rule and the Warlock would tear the world apart with his experiments.

As Balfruss started to lose his grip on the last shreds of consciousness, his hold on the Source wavered and then evaporated. His shield disappeared and, much to his surprise, cool air washed over him. Taking deep wheezing breaths he gulped it down and the darkness slowly began to recede. Although the stones against his face were cool, he could still hear the crackle of flames. When the feeling came back into his limbs Balfruss pushed himself upright, leaning heavily on the wall.

Beyond the city wall lay two smoking piles of charred bones. Beside them were two human torches, burning with yellow and blue flames, but neither person made a sound as they burned to death. Without reaching for the Source Balfruss could feel a river of power flowing into the dying remains of the Splinters. All of their attention and the unnatural fire was focused on one point on the battlements.

A wall of white flames, the height of a man, standing atop the battlements. Staring at the fire felt the same as looking directly at the sun. Balfruss had to avert his eyes or risk going blind. Just before turning away Balfruss thought he saw a figure moving in the fire. The light sputtered and the flames died to reveal Finn.

He emerged from the fire unmarked and naked as if it had given birth to him. Finn glowed with so much power from the Source his skin shone like burnished steel. He strode along the battlements and came to a stop, staring at a particular point somewhere in the distance. The amount of power he wielded was so great, it made Balfruss's back teeth ache and his skin prickle.

"You would burn *me*, with fire?" roared Finn in a huge voice. His words rolled out across the plains, echoing over and over.

Finn put one foot on the battlements and stepped off the city wall. Balfruss made a desperate attempt to grab him but was too slow. With a cry of desperation Balfruss pulled himself upright and peered over the wall, expecting to see the shattered remains of the smith's body. Instead a naked, glowing figure streaked towards the ground, wrapped in a shell of blue fire like a blazing comet. Finn struck the ground with enough force to shake the walls, but seemed unharmed from the fall as he stomped towards the burning Splinters. With a casual wave of his hand and a twisting motion, the nearest Splinter exploded, scattering body parts in all directions. Balfruss could feel the Warlock's grip on the Source lessen as another of his puppets was destroyed. Only one remained, and with a snapping motion Finn separated the Splinter's head from its body. The tiny spark of life animating the body was extinguished and the last Splinter was finally allowed to die.

"Face me!" shouted Finn. Balfruss felt the ground shift beneath his feet again and looking closer at Finn he saw the reason. The smith was drawing even more heavily on the Source. The blue and white flames dancing over his body were now spreading, scorching the land around him in a growing circle. The grass burned to ash in an instant, the mud started to melt and then bubble, creating a sludgy quagmire. A black cloud of burning mud started to build up as Finn walked towards the enemy ranks.

"Show yourself, coward!" he screamed at the western army, but the Warlock did not come forward. Snarling and gnashing his teeth Finn kept walking forward until he was within range of their archers. Roaring like a wounded lion he lashed out, sending a wide bar of fire into a section of the army. The fire burned hotter than any flame and men were instantly incinerated. Flesh and metal were turned into greasy smears in the blink of an eye.

"Face me!" shouted Finn, before hitting another section of the army with fire, carving another chunk out of their ranks. More than a dozen men died, and with every passing moment that the

Warlock failed to appear, Finn killed dozens more. The power coursing through him was immense, the breadth of his attacks was getting wider, melting more and more warriors.

Archers attempted to end his rampage as a shower of arrows descended towards him. Finn gave the deadly rain a casual glance, then flicked one hand towards it. All of the arrows were burned to ash in an instant. The western army started to withdraw, first in formation and then running for their lives as Finn continued to turn men into slag. Even though Finn was moving away from the city, the build-up of energy in the air was so strong that Balfruss felt the hairs stand up on his arms. There was also a change in the air, a tang and sour smell, and he felt warm air on his skin.

"No, no, no," shouted Balfruss as he realised what was happening. With his eyes on the flaming figure of Finn, he tried to reach for the Source. Something red and painful lanced along his veins and he fell to his knees, gasping for air and vomiting on the stones. Once his stomach was empty Balfruss tried again, but every time the result was the same and he experienced a violent physical response.

The river of power flowing into Finn was growing, and any attempt to reach for the same energy felt like sticking his hand into a furnace. The Source was an endless pool of power. Every teacher had always told Balfruss this, but now he wasn't sure.

Finn wasn't tapping into the Source; he was channelling it.

The flames around Finn's feet spread even further, scorching the earth black and then blistering it until it cracked and melted. The clouds started to thicken, then swell until they turned grey and black. Thunder rumbled and a light rain began to fall, but no echo of lightning followed.

The western army was in full retreat, but they couldn't run fast enough to escape Finn's reach. There were so many men they kept falling over each other in their desperation. Men were trodden underfoot and left in the mud by their comrades. Finn swept both arms wide and a wall of fire rolled towards the soldiers. The fire quickly gathered momentum, easily outpacing them. Their screams and cries for mercy went unnoticed as entire units were consumed by the flames. Balfruss heard a brief fizzle, a snap and a hiss, as fat was burned up in the fire and a hundred men were obliterated. Flinging his arms left and then right Finn effortlessly killed scores of men before they had a chance to scream.

The sky blackened and the rain became heavier but it felt warm. Thunder continued to crack and rumble again and again, but still there was no flash, even a spark of lightning. When the rain landed on his face Balfruss tasted something bitter and greasy like ashes.

Something flickered at the corner of his eye and turning his head towards the source, Balfruss saw the flames rising from Finn's body were reaching higher and higher. The fire turned white and the clouds started to churn above his head.

Finally, a red-cloaked figure emerged from the shattered ranks of the western army. The concentric rings of fire spreading out from Finn immediately disappeared, leaving a blackened swathe of land in his wake.

Despite the distance between them, Balfruss heard the cry of pain and anger Finn directed at the Warlock. It was the sum of all his loss and rage at having his life irreparably changed by a gift he didn't want. He should have been living a quiet life, working in a forge during the day, going home to his loving wife at night. Instead he was standing naked on a bloody battlefield, bathed in living fire. Despite everything Balfruss had told Finn about it being a gift, he knew the smith still resented his power and would've done anything to be rid of it.

Behind Finn's scream came a river of power, forged into a single hammer blow that slammed into the Warlock. The force against his shield was so strong the Warlock was thrown backwards through the air. The flames rising from Finn's body swelled until they touched the clouds above, setting them on fire. The sky turned purple, then black as thunder snapped and thumped like an erratic heartbeat. The Warlock was just picking himself up when another strike hit him. This time the force drove him down into the earth and he disappeared from view. The land cracked for fifty paces on either side of the impact point, opening a giant fissure.

A terrible scream ripped across the plain as Finn stumbled to one knee, still wreathed in fire. Gritting his teeth against the destructive energy rampaging through his body, Finn forced himself to stand. He wobbled and it looked as if he would fall, but with grim determination he slowly walked towards the Warlock. But every step became increasingly difficult. Channelling an enormous amount of power from the Source was always hard, but Finn had pushed himself beyond the limits of any man. Balfruss had no idea how he'd managed it for this long, but Finn was losing control.

The muddy figure of the Warlock clambered out of the crater and dragged himself onto the ground. He lay there breathing heavily and seemed utterly exhausted. The sight of him spurred Finn on as he took another step forward, even as his flesh began to blacken and then crisp. Tiny pieces blew away like leaves on the wind and immediately were drawn upwards towards the clouds bunched together overheard.

The pressure in the air increased and Balfruss could hear a faint whine amid the drumbeat of thunder. Finn refused to surrender, taking another step forward although the pain must have been agonising. The Warlock was prone and defenceless with Finn only a few steps away. Even as he dropped to his knees Finn reached out with one hand towards the Warlock, but it wasn't enough. All of Finn's flesh turned black then began to blister and peel. Cracks appeared across his whole body and a blinding light shone out from inside. The smith turned his face towards the heavens, there was one final rumble of thunder, and then the lightning finally came. Finn's scream was lost as bolt after bolt of raw elemental power struck the ground where he was standing. The sky split with purple and red forks of energy and it kept falling over and over again, dancing on the area where Finn had fallen. The Warlock was thrown clear of the blast and Balfruss lost sight of him. The lightning storm continued, a wholly unnatural barrage on the same area, as the built-up energy was finally released.

Slowly, the lightning began to ease and the rain slackened with it. The thick knotted clouds started to unravel and a small patch of blue appeared amid the black. After a few minutes the thunder and lightning had stopped, the clouds drifted apart and the rain tailed off completely.

Balfruss stared at the spot where he'd last seen Finn, hoping to see something of the man. The lightning had ripped up the ground, blasted holes and scorched the earth, but nothing remained of the smith. The Source had consumed him.

CHAPTER 41

That evening when Talandra met with her Generals the mood in the room was very sombre. She knew the events of the day would be spoken about for many years. The bravery of their warriors and the heroics with steel and muscle were already being forgotten in the wake of what had happened with the Battlemages. No one spoke about the lives saved or the tragedies averted on the walls by their warriors through skill or sheer luck. All talk had become of magic.

Two of the Battlemages had fallen from the battlements completely aflame. Even now Talandra couldn't dislodge the images from her mind. They'd reminded her of straw effigies burned at the end of autumn to give thanks for a bountiful harvest. But these had been flesh and blood, not corn and wheat.

Beyond those tragedies all talk was about the man everyone now called Titan, the Battlemage once known as Finn Smith. She remembered seeing him for the first time in the throne room a few weeks ago. Her first impression had been of a large and clumsy man out of his depth, unfamiliar with court politics, being thrown into a position of power. Now, when people spoke about him it was with a mix of awe and fear.

Outside the city walls the land in all directions was burned and broken for miles. Even those who had not peered over the walls had witnessed the unusual storm and heard the endless thunder. It had seemed to roll for hours before the lightning finally came, with tragic consequences. Some claimed the white light that fell from the sky was not lightning, but the fire of creation.

Ultimately there would be a lot of questions about what it meant to the war, to the western alliance, and what her warriors should do tomorrow morning. She knew part of her responsibilities to the people was to come up with answers. Over the years her father had faced many challenges and been forced to make many difficult decisions. Even so she was confident he'd never been required to have a conversation such as the one she now faced. Once again she turned to the wise counsel of her Generals to help her decide what they should be doing next.

Vannok Lore had been the last to arrive and before they began discussing their plans, she turned towards him.

"How is he?"

Vannok looked exhausted, and she knew not all of it was from the physical hardships of the day. "He's barely spoken since they fell."

Talandra hated to ask, but needed to know because thousands of lives depended on it. At present, Balfruss was the only Battlemage who could still fight. Whether it was a blessing or a curse she didn't know, but, unlike Thule, Eloise had survived her fall from the battlements. "Is she still alive?"

"Barely," said Vannok with a long sigh. "The surgeons don't know why or how. Her burns are severe and cover most of her body. They don't expect her to last through the night and Balfruss won't leave her side."

Talandra wished she had something wise to say, some words of condolence to offer, but she didn't know where to begin. Grief for her father still filled the forefront of her mind and thoughts of him still caused her physical pain. Any words she might conjure up in an attempt to offer some comfort would be a hollow lie. She had no idea how to come to terms with her loss and would not presume to tell others. Grief was not a standard measure a person could squeeze into a cup. In a way the war was a good distraction as it gave her no time to sit and think about what she had lost. There would be time for mourning later. Right now she needed to focus on protecting the city and the people depending upon her.

Clearing her throat she turned to Graegor, but he didn't seem to hear her. Physically the one-eyed General sat in the room, but his mind remained elsewhere. He'd barely spoken a word since sitting down and had not even poured himself a drink.

"How are our defences?"

It was Vannok who spoke up, filling in for Graegor's silence. "The city is still secure and the walls will hold. There are fractures in places, but they're not severe. They will need close attention in the future."

"And the men? Are they able to fight?"

Vannok shrugged. "Before the fight between the Battlemages there were casualties, but nothing we weren't anticipating."

Talandra raised an eyebrow at Vannok's reluctance. "What is it? What's wrong?"

"Many of the men are asking if the war is over. They want to know if they still need to fight."

"The western army is still out there," said Talandra. "All they need to do is look over the walls."

"The news about Shael has reached the front lines," said Thias. She hadn't anticipated that. Officially trade channels with the west were still closed, but one or two of the messages she'd received via her network had not been by raven or bat.

"There are stories about the people of Shael butchering the Vorga who held them prisoner," said Hyram, somehow making it sound like a question without trying.

"I've seen a couple of reports to that effect," said Talandra, trying not to let her thoughts linger on Shani. She was performing her job admirably as head of intelligence and Talandra didn't have any cause to complain. However, Shani had been distant while delivering her reports, talking as if they were strangers. Despite being the one who had ended their relationship, Talandra still had feelings for her, but it appeared as if Shani didn't any more. Either that, or she was better at hiding them.

Talandra shook herself, bringing her mind back to the problem at hand. "The western alliance is crumbling. Shael is fighting for its freedom and my agents in Yerskania have been orchestrating an uprising. Any day now I expect to hear from Gunder about the liberation of the capital, Perizzi. Once the Queen is safe, the rest of the nation will follow. Zecorria is teetering on the brink of civil war and the Morrin are turning their gaze inwards. All of this is good news, but none of it changes the facts. Tomorrow the sun will rise and the western army will still be sat outside our walls. Even if an order were sent to disband the army, it would not happen immediately. We need to make preparations for tomorrow as normal."

"We will see to it," said Vannok, exchanging a look with Hyram.

"We've received a few requests for sanctuary through unofficial channels," said Thias. "I've also witnessed units of men deserting the western army."

"Now is the time to show mercy," said Talandra. "We can't open the gates, but pass word to those who have asked. Anyone who doesn't fight tomorrow will not be attacked. Make sure the order is clearly understood by every man in our army. I won't have anyone who seeks sanctuary being cut down. That kind of behaviour will not be tolerated and the punishment will be severe. We will need as many friends and allies in the west as we can get, not blood debts and vengeance. The fewer bodies we have to fight, the quicker this will be over."

"Is it over?" asked Hyram.

She knew what he was really asking, but didn't answer. No one had mentioned the Warlock and the threat he still represented, even without his Splinters. It wasn't an obstacle she or anyone else could really understand or oppose. The only person capable was sat at the bedside of a dying friend.

"Was there anything else?" she asked and the others shook their heads. "Get some rest."

As they started to file out of the room Graegor finally came back to the present, but she gestured for him to stay. She waited until they were alone before speaking.

"A few nights ago you sought me out. You asked a lot of questions about Balfruss."

Graegor looked up, finally meeting her gaze. His eye was troubled, but she didn't know if it was guilt, grief or something else. "I had suspicions, but I didn't admit the truth, not even to myself. He was part of a different life I left behind a long time ago."

"Was your life so unpleasant in those days?"

Graegor heaved a long shuddering breath that somehow seemed to diminish the big man. "No, it was everything I thought I'd always wanted. A quiet life away from cities with a woman who loved me. Then the village had a bad year, crops were blighted and there was a collapse at the quarry. We were running out of money, so I enlisted in the King's army. It was hard at first, being away from home so often, but we managed. I had no choice and needed to provide for my family. For a time, being apart made the moments together that much sweeter. But something was happening to me. I discovered I wasn't just good at being a warrior, I enjoyed it."

"There's no shame in that."

Graegor shook his shaggy head. "No, but after a while I started to resent my time at home, and we argued. When my son was born I stayed in the village for a few months, tried to be a good husband and father. I left the army and worked in the quarry, but it wasn't like the old days. I'd changed."

Talandra squeezed one of Graegor's hands in both of hers, but he didn't seem to notice. "After six months I returned to the army. I sent money home, so they were never without, and I visited every six months. But whenever I went back I felt out of place. They were coping without me. I didn't add anything to their lives when I was there. After a few years the visits became once a year, then I stopped visiting and just sent letters with the money. The last time I saw my son I think he was seven years old. It was so long ago I can barely remember his face."

Talandra withdrew her hands and this time Graegor noticed as she leaned back in her chair. He offered her a pained smile, one that said he was fully aware of what he'd done. Although he'd broken no law the scars of his actions were still visible today. Both he and Balfruss bore them, and only now was she beginning to understand the grizzled General. The rage that had driven him for all of these years was fuelled by guilt.

"Then the war broke out," said Graegor, holding up his maimed hand and tapping his eye patch as a reminder of what he'd done and what it had cost him. Talandra shivered, remembering the story her father had told her, against his better judgement. The nightmares had worn thin over the years, but occasionally they still had the power to wake her covered in a cold sweat.

"Three years had passed before I realised. I'd sent letters home when I could, but it wasn't often. The King insisted I take some time to recover from my injuries so I went back to the village. When I arrived all that remained were scattered piles of rubble. A local farmer told me the village had been attacked by raiders and most of the locals slaughtered. Those who survived didn't want to start over in the ruins and went elsewhere. I tried to find out if my family had survived, but no one knew."

Talandra wanted to say something, to offer some small comfort, but her mind was reeling as she tried to contemplate the burden Graegor had been carrying all these years.

"I returned to Charas and buried my past. A few years later I heard a rumour about my wife and went to investigate." Tears ran down Graegor's face unnoticed. "An old neighbour told me she'd survived the attack and left to build a new life, but he didn't know where. No one had any news of my son, so I assumed he was dead. When I finally tracked down my wife it was too late. She'd died a year earlier from the pox."

Graegor sat back on his chair and stared into the distance, into the past. When he next spoke Talandra didn't know who he was speaking to.

"I've never been a spiritual man. Everyone says theirs is the one true God, but new ones appear all the time. Those Lantern fuckers think we're all born for a reason." Graegor laughed bitterly and shook his head. "As if it were that simple. That easy. As if a child run down by a cart was always meant to die that way. It's all horse shit. We're not made for one purpose."

"Then why are we here?" asked Talandra.

Graegor shrugged. "I don't know, but I know what I can do and what's beyond my abilities. I wasn't a very good husband or father. It's just not in me, but I am good at killing. I'm good at training and leading warriors. I'm good at winning wars. That's who I am."

"I think you're wrong," said Talandra with a faint smile. "I wasn't just raised by my father. You've always been there for me and my brothers."

"That's kind, but it's not the same," said Graegor with a smile that quickly slid off his face. He sighed again and scratched at the scars on his maimed hand as if the ghosts of his fingers were still haunting him. "I wouldn't know what to say to Balfruss. I can't even try to explain, and there's no reason he should listen. It's better if we don't speak."

"Better, or easier?"

Graegor's grin seemed out of place until he spoke. "You're so much like her."

"Don't change the subject."

"Don't you want to know about your mother? About how she could take a man apart with words, far better than I can with a blade. How she used to laugh so hard sometimes she'd snort like a pig. And by the Maker, she had a dirty sense of humour. Sometimes she'd put me to shame."

Graegor wiped away a tear and Talandra frowned. "You know the war isn't over yet," she said, but Graegor didn't react. "Tomorrow your son must face the Warlock. Alone. It's likely he will die." It was only with the last word that she managed to get a reaction as a nerve twitched in the side of his face. "Talk to him, while there's still time."

The tavern was a riot of noise with people singing, clapping and dancing to the slightly off-key musicians. The atmosphere was one of celebration, as many thought the war was over and they'd already won. Balfruss knew differently, but said nothing to quell their merriment. The dawn would sober them all.

The music and joy of the others didn't touch him, or the two men sat opposite. A collection of empty tankards and a row of shot glasses covered the table. Black Tom was already asleep, snoring quietly with his face in a pool of ale. Vargus was still conscious, but his eyes were glazed and he seemed lost in thought, wandering the hallways of the past. His expression looked haunted, and Balfruss knew he would see the same in his eyes if he stared in a mirror.

Counting the glasses, Balfruss was amazed he was still conscious, never mind able to speak. But the terrible ache in his heart kept him awake and far from the comforting oblivion of sleep. Every time he closed his eyes he saw them falling from the wall, burning on the inside and out. Being consumed by the Warlock's unnatural fire of the mind. He could see every grisly detail. Smell the burning hair, see their flesh crisping up and turning black as they screamed.

Grabbing the nearest tankard Balfruss tipped its contents down his throat, gulping down the frothy ale until it was gone. He quickly followed it with a shot of rum but barely felt it. When he slammed the glass down he noticed his hand was remarkably steady, if a little blurry.

Almost everyone he'd ever loved was dead. Ecko, Darius, Thule and Finn. Eloise was still alive, if it could be called living, but the blackened wheezing husk that tenaciously held on to this world would soon let go. Whatever torments Balfruss thought he was enduring, her agony was far worse. She had lost her husband, the love of her life, only to be consumed by fire, but it had not snuffed out her life as it had done with Thule's. At least he wasn't in pain any more. When he'd last visited her, Balfruss had made several attempts to end her life with a quick stroke of a blade, but his nerve had failed.

"I just couldn't do it," he muttered. "I'm a coward."

"Coward?" slurred Vargus, coming out of his own stupor. "Why'd you say that?"

"I should have faced the Warlock by myself. He warned me. He said he'd do this. Kill everyone and take everything from me. If I'd faced him earlier, then the others would still be alive."

Vargus looked around the room at the revellers, his head wobbling alarmingly, before resting his forearms on the table and leaning forward. He beckoned Balfruss to lean closer and the old warrior's expression hardened.

"I'm going to kill everyone in this room," he whispered. At first Balfruss thought he was making a joke, until he saw what lay behind Vargus's eyes. Balfruss leaned back in shock and a moment later the terrible hunger he'd seen was gone. "Just because I say something, doesn't mean I can do it, or that it will come true. There's no way to know what would've happened. Let's say you had faced him alone, and he'd killed you. Where would we be now?"

"I don't know."

"You don't," said Vargus, stabbing a finger towards him. "You don't know. That's the fucking point. The truth of it. The future isn't set because it hasn't been written. The Warlock might be powerful, but everyone can be beaten. He's a child." Vargus dismissed the Warlock with a wave of his hand, as if he were nothing more than a minor irritation.

Balfruss grunted. "We agree on that at least."

"A child playing with fire," said Vargus, "and he will get burned. It could be you that snuffs him out, but if not, there'll be someone else. Nothing and no one stays in power forever. Time robs us all of everything. I've seen brutal kings and tyrants turned into withered husks that can't stop shitting themselves. I've seen Sorcerers lose their minds and cut their own throats, because they couldn't cope with the awful truths they uncovered. I've seen honoured warriors cry like children for their victims, while people sing about their heroism."

"Sorcerers?" The word struck Balfruss as peculiar. No one had used that name for magic users in centuries. "You've met Sorcerers?"

"I don't know. I can't remember. All of my memories are jumbled up and back to front. I must have read it somewhere." Vargus burped and then sat back trying to gather his thoughts. "What was I saying?"

"Sorcerers."

"Sorcerers were truly powerful magic users. They knew more than any Battlemage. A Sorcerer was a servant of the people who could do terrible and amazing things. A Battlemage is nothing more than a tool made for war. The mysteries the Sorcerers uncovered make the Warlock's tricks look like sleight of hand."

"I'd give anything to know just a few of those mysteries," said Balfruss, clenching his fists in frustration. Unbidden he summoned blue fire and it danced along his arms to settle on the back of his hands. "I have all of this power, but all I can do with it is destroy. I can summon storms, shatter mountains and kill hundreds of men in a heartbeat. And yet Eloise is dying and I can't do a thing to help her."

His voice broke and Balfruss choked back a sob. He cast around for another drink but all of the glasses were empty. He tried to catch the attention of a flustered barmaid battling her way through the crowd, but she didn't notice.

Vargus was quiet for a moment, reflecting on what he'd said, or perhaps lost in his memories again. Balfruss twisted around on his seat and gestured at another barmaid passing his table. She nodded briefly in his direction. "Have you tried?" said Vargus.

"What?" said Balfruss, swinging around.

"Have you tried to heal her?"

Balfruss noticed the fire on the back of his hands and immediately severed his link to the Source, snuffing out the flames. The fire made bile rise in the back of his throat. "I tried for hours. I spoke to the King's surgeon and picked apart what Ecko had told me. I scoured the palace library and went over every conversation I had with the Grey Council during my training. I even channelled power from the Source into her and sat like that for hours, trying to will it to help her in some way. Nothing happened. She's still dying and I can't help her."

"What about Taikon? I heard he can heal himself."

"So I've been told," said Balfruss with a bitter laugh. "But I don't think he'd be willing to share."

"It's true then?"

"The Queen told me he's swallowed some artefact and any wound heals instantly. I think it was another of the Warlock's discoveries that he gave to the Mad King."

Balfruss was too busy staring at the barmaid to notice the furious expression that flickered across Vargus's features.

"So what else do you know about Sorcerers?" asked Balfruss, as the barmaid set down three tankards of ale. She stared at the collection of empties on their table but said nothing and quickly hurried away.

"Not much. It was an old book. Mostly stories about how Sorcerers used to serve the old religions, the Great Maker, Nethun and the Watcher. This was long before they built the Red Tower."

"I've not heard of the Watcher."

Vargus dismissed it with a wave of his hand, nearly spilling his ale. "This was hundreds of years ago. Most of the old religions died out over the centuries, apart from that of the Maker. One day the new faiths, like the Lord of Light—"

"Lantern fucker," cursed Black Tom, before dozing off again.

"They'll be nothing but stories told by a few old men and something else will have taken their place."

Balfruss mulled it over for a while before asking, "If everything is eroded over time, why do anything?"

Vargus sighed. "Everything changes. You need to think about the day after the war. One way or another, it will end. Who do you want to be when it's over? What do you want to do? Where do you want to go?"

Balfruss tried to come up with some answers, but his mind was too muddled. Since the war had begun, all of his thoughts and effort had been focused on the next day, the next battle. He'd never once looked to the horizon and thought about what he would do after it was over. Leaving the desert and coming home to fight had felt like the end of his story, not another chapter. Now he wasn't so sure any more. There were still reasons to stay, but also so many painful memories were now attached to the city. Perhaps it would better be if he did leave, assuming he lived through the war.

After helping Vargus carry Black Tom to the barracks and putting him to bed, Balfruss made his way to the palace. By the time he lay down, his mind was whirling with a host of questions with no answers. When sleep finally claimed him the nightmares came, but beneath the guilt and the pain of his loss, something else stirred. A feeling that despite everything that he'd seen and achieved, he was still hungry for more.

CHAPTER 42

For the first time in two years Gunder felt alive. The padded suit, felt cap, wig and garish clothes were hung up for his eventual return, but for the next few hours he was free of the fat merchant.

The specialist tailor had done an excellent job. Staring at himself in the mirror he couldn't tell the difference between his uniform, and that of the real Watch. He was pleased to see three blue bars sewn onto the jacket's shoulders and over his heart, giving him the rank of Captain. The only continuation from his previous persona was the white make-up, liberally applied to his face and hands, giving him the same skin tone as a local. It was unlikely in the forthcoming chaos that anyone would notice the colour, but tonight he would not take any chances. There would be plenty of risks outside of his control. It seemed foolish to push his luck further than necessary.

As well as the uniform Gunder paid special attention to everything he carried on his person. He'd made sure the sword was plain and without decoration, so as not to draw attention, as befitting his rank. The blade itself was good Seveldrom steel and he'd spent hours sharpening it, as well as the daggers concealed about his person. Daggers were not suitable weapons for a Captain of the Watch. They were weapons only employed by

thieves, cut-throats and other members of the criminal under-
world. Gunder had a feeling they would be needed and that very
few of his forthcoming actions would be deemed appropriate.

Even though he didn't need to read it again, Gunder looked
at the latest missive from his agents in the palace. The Crown
Prince had finally come out of his chambers with a thirst for
revenge. More than that, he'd gone straight to his mother with
a plan, partly of his own making. It was all that they'd hoped for
and more.

Officially the status quo in the city was the same as yesterday,
with Taikon acting as Regent of Yerskania. Unofficially the
Queen had retaken control of the palace and was preparing to
remove the stain of the Chosen from her city. When Gunder had
passed information to one of her agents about their plan she had
been delighted. Receiving the Queen's royal seal of approval had
eliminated any doubts among the rebels.

Gunder placed the coded letter on the fire, waiting until it
had burned to ash before leaving the house through the back
door.

He stuck to narrow alleyways and quiet streets, sometimes
pausing until one of the few people abroad had moved on before
proceeding. Those with any common sense were already locked
indoors. Only the insane and the ignorant were abroad on the
streets, totally unaware of what was about to happen. That
included many units of Chosen, who were ambling about, staring at the deserted roads with gormless expressions.

When he was a few streets away from home Gunder moved
onto the main roads and boldly walked towards the Rotamph
quarter in the south-eastern part of the city. On the way there
he passed several squads of the Watch, and they all gave him
a nod or salute, which he crisply returned. One or two touched
the hilt of their swords or cleavers and he mimicked the gesture, but didn't stop to talk. Everyone had somewhere very

specific to be and time was short. It took him another thirty minutes to get into position, but there was still a little time to play with.

Just as Gunder reached the end of the street and stepped into the doorway of an apothecary, two Fists of Drassi warriors came trotting down the road. All ten men were roughly the same height and build, although the man at the front was slightly broader than the rest. As ever each warrior was dressed identically in padded grey armour and white masks that showed only their chin and mouths. Most of them carried one or two swords across their back, but two had pairs of short scythes on chains tucked into their belts.

As they reached their designated position the men stopped in unison. Gunder stepped out of the doorway and approached the leader, noticing his beard was flecked with grey.

"I'm Captain Gerall," he said, handing over the hexagonal token Roza had delivered the previous evening. The surface of the disk was inlaid with swirling black, red and blue script, the words intertwined and utterly unreadable to anyone but the Drassi. Gunder wasn't the only one with secret codes. The leader took the offered disk and produced its identical twin from a pouch on his belt. He studied them closely before pocketing both and all ten men immediately snapped to attention.

"I am Xhan gi Koto. We are yours to command until sunrise."

Gunder grinned. He wouldn't need them for that long. "Let's go. I have a list of targets."

"As you command," said Xhan.

The first two people were not on the official list assigned to him, but Gunder knew he wouldn't have a better opportunity to settle a few old scores. Two streets away he led the Drassi to the mouth of a narrow alley between a row of run-down shops. It was littered with broken boxes, bits of rotten food and scurrying rodents. On either side were sets of narrow stairs that led up to small apartments above the shops. Without hesitation Gunder walked through the filth, soiling the pristine trousers of his uniform. The Drassi followed without complaint, stopping when he did at a narrow staircase halfway down the alley.

Gunder pointed at the pale yellow door at the top of the stairs. "You'll find two men inside. Both are to be eliminated. There shouldn't be anyone else inside, but if there is, we can't afford any witnesses if this coup is going to work."

The Drassi didn't need to know any of that, and wouldn't really care, but since he was dressed as a local, he needed to play the part of patriot to the hilt. His contract with them would be annulled if they suspected he was lying, or trying to manipulate them for his own ends. Drassi spies were famous, and their ability to tell when someone was lying was equally impressive. He didn't want to be on the receiving end of their displeasure, so carefully schooled his facial muscles.

Xhan nodded and issued a series of whispered commands in his native language. Two men jogged down the alley, no doubt going around to the front of the building in case those inside tried to escape via a window. It was unlikely they would throw themselves out, but desperate men might try anything.

Two Drassi crept up the stairs with swords drawn, while the rest fanned out and kept watch. The apartment was small, so any more than two Drassi would just have got in the way of the others. There was a faint crash as the first man kicked open the door and the second leapt inside. Gunder heard a short cry of pain that was quickly cut off, then a couple of thumps as heavy objects hit the floor. Less than a minute later the two men returned and the pair from the front came back. None of them were out of breath and the night was still young.

"Our next target is a group of Chosen," Gunder informed Xhan, leading the way out of the alley and back onto the main streets. He set a brisk pace, stretching his legs and using his height to make up for lost time. All of the Drassi kept pace without complaint.

"How many?" asked Xhan.

"Six. Most of them are thugs and former criminals. Their weapon skills were learned on the street. The leader is different. He's a soldier."

Xhan nodded thoughtfully and passed this information on to his men. They were two streets away from the tavern where he'd been told they were drinking, when they came across a trio of Chosen.

One man was pissing just inside the mouth of an alley, while the other two were meandering about and swaying from side to side. The Drassi leader glanced in his direction for guidance. Gunder responded by drawing his sword and walking towards the Chosen. It was only when he was almost on top of them they finally noticed. Even then he wasn't sure they realised he was flanked by ten lethal warriors.

"Wass thisss?" slurred one of the men. "Whass hap'ning?"

"Drop your weapons, swear fealty to the Queen and we'll let you live. Surrender or die," said Gunder in a voice loud enough to penetrate their alcoholic fog. "This is your only warning."

The other man had finished pissing in the alley and came up behind his friends. All three stank and were having trouble standing up.

"Who do you think you are then?" asked the new arrival, oblivious to the danger. "We're in charge around here."

"Not any more," said Gunder, putting the point of his sword against the throat of the speaker. "Last chance."

Perhaps it was the alcohol, or their belief that as Chosen they were untouchable, but two of the men reached for their weapons. Gunder jabbed the Chosen in the throat, opening his windpipe. He quickly stepped back as blood gushed out and the man began to choke to death. The other two were cut down in seconds. One was run through and the other beheaded. They left the bodies in the street and pressed on towards the tavern where their next targets lay.

Normally at this hour the everyday noises of the street, and those around it, would have made it impossible to hear what was happening elsewhere. The unusual quiet across the whole city allowed Gunder to hear that the cull had already started. In the distance he heard shouting, the sounds of breaking glass and then a few brief screams. Gunder was about to barge into the tavern when Xhan grabbed him by the arm, pulling him up short.

"A moment, please."

Four of the Drassi sprinted away down an alleyway parallel to the tavern to secure the back door. Given the calibre of the men they were hunting, he knew they wouldn't run, but he said nothing and waited. Xhan waited a short time then released his arm, gesturing for him to go ahead. The few locals drinking in the tavern were initially alarmed, but when he pointed at the group of six Chosen they relaxed. Remarkably, most of the customers decided it was the right moment to go home for the night, leaving in a great huddle. The Drassi let them go, and by the time the Chosen realised what had happened they were alone. The man cleaning glasses behind the bar stared at the back when four Drassi came in through it.

The group of Chosen were as Gunder had described. Ugly, brutal men with ill-fitting uniforms and lumpy, scarred faces. Their weapons were a mix of axes and short swords, but each of them would be carrying several daggers. The squad leader was easy to identify, as he'd recently had a wash. He also resembled a real soldier, unlike the others who were former thieves and killers. While the other Chosen carried on talking among themselves, unaware or uncaring of their predicament, the officer turned pale.

"Surrender or die." Gunder's voice echoed off the wooden floor, cutting across their conversation. This group were some of the worst. The lowest form of street scum that other criminals despised. Desperate greedy men who brutalised their own people, in the name of an adopted God and emperor, just for the money.

"That's not much of a choice," said a broad man with a grin that showed crooked yellow teeth. He was the same bald-headed yellow-toothed man who had searched and smashed up the home of a fat merchant in the name of justice. As Yellowtooth stood up Gunder noticed his hand stayed on the hilt of a dagger.

"Maybe we should give up our weapons—" said the officer, but he was promptly cut short when one of the men sat with him slit his throat. As the officer gasped his final breaths, the thugs drew their weapons and spread out. They'd obviously been waiting for an excuse to do that and now had nothing to lose.

As soon as Gunder threw a dagger the Drassi leapt into action, moving in unison against their opponents. Gunder pretended to aim for the big man at the front, but as anticipated he moved to one side. The blade buried itself in the back of another man, who squawked in pain, stumbling forward in surprise. The Chosen fought as he'd expected, with ruthless and brutal skill, but the Drassi were disciplined warriors who trained every day, using techniques that had been developed over centuries. They were untouchable.

Xhan danced to one side of a vicious strike, took the arm and then the head of the nearest Chosen with two moves. His sword effortlessly cut through skin, muscle and bone. One of the thugs had somehow managed to disarm the Drassi facing him, but he didn't anticipate one of his own weapons being turned against him. In less than two heartbeats the Drassi took a dagger from the thug's belt and stabbed him in the chest four times. The strikes seemed excessive until Gunder realised each had pierced a vital organ. The Chosen was dead before his face hit the floor.

It took a little longer to deal with the ringleader, but once he was sliced in two the inn fell silent. One of the Drassi had a cut on his arm, but the others were unharmed. The wound was quickly wrapped and once Xhan was satisfied it wasn't serious, he declared them ready to continue.

For the next two hours Gunder led the Drassi against groups of Chosen and several individuals on his list who were, apparently, collaborators. Even if any of them recognised him or realised what was really happening, it didn't matter. He gave them no warning and no one escaped. Each target was killed without hesitation, and when the river of blood eventually dried up, several nations would find themselves blind, deaf and dumb in Perizzi.

On occasion Gunder was forced to offer a Yerskani who had become Chosen a chance to surrender. None accepted, perhaps because they realised their time was over, and even if they escaped prison they would be pariahs. Some of the Drassi picked up wounds, but none were serious enough to prevent them fulfilling the contract.

Across the city, ranking officers and Guardians of the Peace led units of City Watch and Drassi warriors against targets, all of which had been coordinated by Roza. The local citizens had played their part in the conspiracy, hiring the Drassi and keeping them hidden until tonight, but they were not allowed to lead. Few of them had any military experience, and eliminating all of the Chosen in one night was too important to gamble on good-intentioned amateurs.

Several times they encountered other squads carrying bloody weapons, and as the night progressed he saw more and more dead bodies lying in the street. A few hours previous the city had been unusually quiet, but now the streets rang with the sounds of battle and the heavy tramp of the City Watch on the march.

"What is our next target?" asked Xhan, as Gunder led them towards a seedy-looking establishment in a very run-down neighbourhood. Gunder had been here twice before on business but never set foot inside.

Gunder stopped at the mouth of an alley and pointed towards a large two-storey building that had light showing in every window. "That's a brothel."

Xhan's mouth twisted in a puzzled fashion. Until now none of the Drassi had commented on the targets. It was not their place or their business. They were weapons, nothing more. His hand guided the Fist, at least for the duration of the contract. Even so, they were not stupid men and they knew what tonight was about.

"They smuggle in girls from across the west. Even as far as the desert kingdoms," said Gunder.

Xhan's puzzled expression remained in place. Sadly, kidnapping women from abroad and forcing them into prostitution was nothing new. It was even worse when the slavers got them hooked on venthe or black crystal to keep them compliant and desperate for their next fix.

"I said, girls, not women."

Gunder didn't need to elaborate as Xhan's mouth tightened into a hard line. Many considered Drassi culture to be archaic and stagnant, but certain crimes, like child prostitution and slavery, were not tolerated on any level. While some countries claimed them as problems that could not be eliminated, the Drassi made no such excuses. Any such criminal would be killed in front of the entire town, with the perpetrator's family made to watch. The criminal's home would be burned to the ground and the land salted. Honour was at the heart of Drassi culture and it bound people more tightly than any law. Entire families had been known to kill themselves out of shame.

"What are your orders?"

"No one leaves," said Gunder.

"A moment, please." Xhan turned to his men and quickly explained the situation. One was sent to scout the building and surrounding streets while they waited in silence. When he returned, Xhan listened to the man's description of what he'd seen, then beckoned Gunder to approach.

"There are three ways into the building. Through the front, a back door, and a third entrance that can only be opened from the inside. With only two Fists I cannot guarantee no one will escape."

"We don't have time to bring in more," explained Gunder. "This must happen tonight. By tomorrow this place will be protected. Some of its patrons are quite influential." Xhan's mouth twisted again as if he'd tasted something bitter. "I will fight."

So far the Drassi had done their best to keep him away from the fighting. Although he'd pretended not to notice, there were always two men within arm's reach at all times. It didn't make very good business sense if the person holding your contract died.

"Do you see this?" said Gunder, gesturing at the rank sewn on his uniform. "That means I'm a Captain. I have no powerful friends or relatives, no family name on which to barter. I earned this. I can guard the door."

Xhan took a moment to weigh up his choices. He could refuse to attack the brothel, but not following orders would go against the contract and sully the Drassi name. Internationally they were known for being the best swords money could buy, and they always followed orders. There was also the unpleasant truth that after tonight the brothel would continue trading children's flesh unless destroyed. On the other hand, if they did attack there was a risk Gunder might be injured or even killed.

"Lei will stay with you," said Xhan, gesturing at the Drassi who had scouted the building.

The rest of them checked their weapons, then split into two groups, moving silently to encircle the brothel. Gunder followed Lei towards an iron door which had no keyhole or handles on the outside. There was a small slot at eye level, but it was sealed tight.

A few seconds later he heard a crash, then another as the Drassi broke down both doors and entered the building. A series of screams followed and some back and forth of steel ringing against steel. Even from where he was standing Gunder could hear the fight was gradually moving through the building towards him. When he heard a scraping sound of bolts being drawn back, Gunder and Lei prepared themselves. A bald fat man, wearing only a belt and a pair of shoes, stumbled out clutching a pile of clothes. Coins rattled down from a loose purse, but he paid them no attention. When his frantic eyes settled on Gunder's sword they widened in terror. Even as the man tried to turn around and go back, others inside were shoving their way forward. He stumbled and fell onto his face, before being trampled by several other men whom Gunder recognised as influential figures.

Lei looked towards him for a signal.

Gunder's sword swept down, slicing through the fat man's neck, severing his head from his body. "No one leaves."

With death coming for them from behind and in front, the worms did the only thing they could. They begged, pleaded and made promises to fulfil every wish Gunder could imagine, if only he'd spare their lives. As he chopped down the deviants, Gunder imagined scything corn on the farm from his youth, instead of slicing people into chunks of meat. Working together, he and Lei cut down eight men in the doorway before they could flee.

Xhan and the others found Gunder wiping the last spots of blood from his sword. Although he didn't say anything Xhan was obviously pleased to see Gunder without injury. Most of the

Drassi were covered with splatters of blood and patches of gore, but all of them moved as if the brothel had been the first target of the night.

"What is our next target?" asked Xhan.

"There's just one more," said Gunder and this time he allowed himself a smile. It took a while to reach the building, but before long they stood in front of its elaborate doors; Xhan and the others knew where they were headed.

The newly completed Temple of the Chosen was a hideous monstrosity that loomed over the city. Its golden walls, vast white dome and four blue minarets were inoffensive, but the enormous statue of Taikon sickened everyone. The sculptor had taken a number of artistic liberties, and the handsome and benevolent figure had very little in common with the real Mad King of Zecorria.

Despite the chaos elsewhere in the city, two dozen Chosen were guarding the temple. As Gunder stepped into the street he wasn't surprised to see several officers of the Watch emerge from side streets. At first the Chosen didn't look worried, until the number of Drassi warriors swelled to outnumber them four to one. Every man was bruised and bloody, yet he could see each was utterly determined to destroy the eyesore that blighted the city.

"Tear it down," whispered Gunder. A moment later the signal was given and he charged forward with his sword held high.

CHAPTER 43

The sun beat down on Vargus's head as he walked through a field of ripe wheat. Unbroken blue sky stretched as far as he could see in every direction. Sweat trickled down his back making his skin itch, but he didn't mind. Today he was coming home. His last visit had been so long ago he could barely remember it. Despite his discomfort and aching muscles, a smile would not stay away from his face.

Small birds wove in and out of the hedges, twittering as they went. The only other noise in the world was the wind rattling through the grain. The quiet peace of the land was broken by a distant cry. At first Vargus thought it was a child, but the sound was constant. It stretched on and on, and then suddenly stopped as soon as it had begun.

Vargus put it from his mind and the frown slowly eased away until his features were smooth once more. He reached the edge of the field, jumped the dry stone wall and rejoined the narrow track that sloped down to the village nestled in the heart of the valley. Smoke rose from a few chimneys and as more of the village came into view, he saw sheep and cows milling about in nearby fields. Looking towards the wooded hills beyond the village, he fancied he could see trees swaying and hear the rasp of the woodcutters' saws. A couple of groups would be up there, chopping down trees for fuel and planting seedlings to replace them. The surrounding fields, forests and the river running through the heart of the village gave them everything they needed.

For those used to living in cities, with ready access to certain luxuries, it took a while to adjust, but they'd all come here for the same reason. After long years of wandering the world every single one of them sought peace. For a time they were content and truly happy. They embraced the silence and the simple life, shedding decades of customs, bad habits and accents from distant lands, until all that remained was the essence of self. Eventually something new would be born or created, the wind would change and a new age would begin. One day they would be walking in the hills, or working in the fields, and the next they would be gone, back into the wider world. No one threw around blame or passed judgement, because eventually it would happen to them all. Inevitably a time would come when they grew weary of the world and would come home again to the village.

The awful noise rose again, louder and sharper. Looking across the hills Vargus saw no birds taking flight in alarm and the animals in the fields paid no attention. Even as he looked down at the worn trail beneath his feet it began to fade.

Home. Soon then, but not just yet.

Vargus opened his eyes and Orran jumped back, covering his alarm with a grin. "Thought you were going to sleep all day. Past your bed time, old man?"

"This better be good, I was having a really nice dream."

"About sheep, was it?" said Orran with a leer.

After wiping the last remnants of sleep from his face Vargus stretched and stood up. He was still on the battlements then, and the western army was still out there, waiting for the order to attack the city again, perhaps for the last time.

"Actually it *was* about sheep. They were running away from a naked man who kept chasing them. He looked a lot like you, Orran."

Black Tom guffawed and a ghost of a smile briefly touched Hargo's lips. The big man's mood was consistently melancholy these days. The war had changed all of them, and if they survived it, each man would deal with it in his own way. Vargus couldn't say what the long-term effects would be on Hargo, but he spoke little these days, which wasn't a good sign.

"You're twisted in the head," said Orran, shaking his head.

"Didn't you used to work on a farm?" asked Vargus. "Tend your own flock, eh?" he said, and a couple of lads laughed.

Before Orran could make a witty retort a crisp note from a bovine horn blasted the air. It was so loud it made Vargus's ears hum. Several other horns followed in quick succession, echoing along the walls and across the city. It was the sound from his dream.

"Fuck," muttered Hargo, as he tightened the leather straps on his shield and drew out the cleaver from his belt.

"Why are they still fighting?" asked Orran. He didn't address the question at anyone in particular and wasn't really expecting an answer. They were all thinking it, though. They'd all heard the stories, civil war in the north, rebellion in the south and the Yerskani liberating Perizzi in one night. With the capital free it wouldn't be long before the Queen dealt with the rest of the Chosen in her country. The whole western alliance was falling apart, but no one seemed to have told the army marching towards them.

What little colour remained in Orran's battered face quickly drained away when he saw who made up the bulk of the approaching army. Normally, before individual faces emerged they saw a sea of brown, grey and silver. After a time they would be able to make out armoured men spattered in mud. But on what was probably one of the last days of the war, Vargus saw a horde of green, brown and blue. After the first thousand he stopped trying to count the number of Vorga marching towards the city.

"Right lads, we've faced these slimy bastards before. You know the drill," yelled Vargus before spitting over the wall. "They're big, slow, and twice as ugly as your wife's mother. Don't try to outmuscle them, and don't bother with dismembering. Slicing works best. Go for their elbows and knees with anything blunt, get them down, and don't stop hitting them until you're sure they're dead. Let's show these fish-heads what it means to be a Seve."

"Show them the colour of our guts, you mean," muttered Orran, but Vargus heard him anyway.

"Something to say, Orran?"

"No, just talking to myself."

Vargus lowered his voice so only those nearby could hear. "You know today is probably the last day of the war. You've just got to hold on for a few more hours. Can you do that?"

The little man looked up at the sky and Vargus could see his eyes were wet with unshed tears. "I'm so tired my bones ache. How can that be? How is it I can feel every single one?"

"We'll get through this."

"I'd like to think so," said Hargo, staring out at the Vorga horde, "but I don't recognise many of the lads around me any more."

There were a lot of drawn and anxious faces bordering on terrified. Facing a few units of Vorga, mixed in with men, was one thing. Facing an army full of them was a nightmare. The men around him were drained and physically exhausted beyond anything they'd ever experienced. No matter how much they ate or slept, they were still hungry and tired. The chasm inside would only begin to heal when the war ended.

Vargus grabbed Hargo and Orran by the shoulders, digging his fingers into their flesh until their eyes met his. Black Tom and a few other lads huddled around and a hush fell over the men at the sound of Vargus's voice. "I don't care about kings, politics or religion. It's all games. Strategies for those with crowns and power. What's important to me is making sure you survive, so you can go home and forget about the war. Remember the Brotherhood. Remember how far you've come because of it. We fight as one. Save the life of the man beside you, because without him you're already dead. Don't give up now when we're so close."

Some of the tension eased from the faces and shoulders of those nearest. Orran shook himself like a wet dog and rolled his shoulders in readiness, while Hargo just nodded. Black Tom said nothing but spat over the wall and offered Vargus a grisly smile. It would have to do. They were out of time. He could see individual faces and already the Vorga were starting to run at the walls with ladders. With hooks and pikes, brute force and a lot of shouting, many ladders were toppled, and whole squads of Vorga plunged to their deaths. But after a while their numbers began to tell and some of the ladders were not repelled by the defenders.

Some of the men waited in stony silence, while others began to curse and scream at the enemy, working themselves into a frenzy. If the Vorga expected their reputation to cower the Seves they were sorely disappointed. By the time the first made it onto the battlements they faced men who had become veterans after only one war. The fat and gristle had already been cut away, and all that remained was muscle and unrelenting bone.

A green-skinned Vorga barged its way onto the battlements to his left. To his right a squad of green- and brown-skinned Vorga started hacking into the defenders and pushing them back.

"Send them back to the sea!" shouted Vargus, charging towards the larger group. Before he was within range Vargus saw one of the Vorga stab a warrior in the throat with its spiked dagger, take a bite out of another man's face and rip open a third with its claws, spilling entrails over the stones. Pushing off the battlements to add extra weight he leapt at the closest Vorga, aiming his blade at its head. The force of the impact sent a shockwave up both of his arms, but thankfully the blade didn't break. The steel bit into the Vorga's face, snapping off several bony protrusions around its jaw and cleaving its face in two. The tip of his sword burst one of its eyes like an overripe melon. With a high-pitched keening sound it stumbled back and was quickly finished off by others.

"They bleed like anyone else!" roared Vargus. "Kill the fish-fuckers!"

Without turning to see if anyone stood with him, Vargus pressed forward into the melee. A whirling on his right told him Orran was whipping his daggers about and he heard frequent plopping sounds as bits of innards splashed down. A more rhythmic series of screams and high-pitched whines came from his left, as Hargo butchered anyone that tried to flank him on that side. When a burly brown Vorga pressed Hargo against the battlements, Black Tom rushed in, slicing open the creature's stomach and then driving his pike into its body up to the haft. Instead of dying it hissed at Tom and swiped at his face, catching him across a cheek with its claws. With his right arm still pinned Hargo took a dagger from his belt and drove it into the Vorga's eye, twisting it from side to side. Jelly and bits of brain dribbled down his hand. Finally the Vorga released its grip and died. Two more Vorga quickly took its place, but just as Vargus was about to assist, someone shoved him backwards.

Before he could see who had attacked him something flashed by his cheek, leaving a white hot trail. Stumbling back with one hand pressed to his face, he swung his sword in tight arcs to keep the enemy at bay. When his vision cleared a blue-skinned Vorga was bearing down on him with a bloody axe. He parried two attacks that threatened to split him in two, and riposted with an underarm slash that forced the Vorga back. Although it looked as vicious as the others, Vargus sensed the reluctance of its attacks. When their eyes met he saw a fierce intelligence and regret. It had no desire to be fighting in this war.

Offering his enemy a smile Vargus gave it a little salute then charged. Brushing aside the axe he put a hand under its jaw, shoving its face up. At the same time he lashed out with a boot which connected with its right knee. There was a dull cracking sound and the Vorga lurched to one side, but grabbed his arm on the way down, pulling him off balance. Someone stepped on Vargus's hand and another heavy foot stomped on his right arm, turning it numb. Something pierced his leg and another blade found its mark on his back, cutting a narrow trail across his ribs. The crippled Vorga wasn't faring any better and was kicked, stabbed and stomped several times before it sloped away.

Crawling on elbows and knees, Vargus tried to move away from the heart of the melee, but someone grabbed him by the back of the neck. He was hauled into the air and held aloft by the biggest and ugliest Vorga he'd ever seen in his life. The seven-foot monster was covered with a network of old scars which cross-crossed its face, arms and body. Bony spurs were missing all over its head and the only weapon it carried was a huge stone mallet.

"Crawling little worm," it whispered, giving him a bloody smile littered with bits of skin and hair. Before it could take a bite out of him a Seve warrior tried to drive a spear into its side. The blade glanced off its rubbery hide and didn't even leave a mark. The Vorga looked annoyed at the interruption, but only as long as it took to cave the man's head in with its mallet.

While it was distracted, Vargus drove both feet into its face. All of the air was knocked out of his body as he slammed to the ground. While he scrambled around for a weapon the stone mallet came down on his chest, breaking several ribs. In desperation Vargus kicked out with both legs. One of his feet hit something, giving him a moment of respite. His clawing fingers closed around something sharp, cutting the flesh on his palm, but he pulled the weapon towards him until he found the hilt.

As he wheezed and tried to stay conscious, Vargus saw the huge scarred Vorga battling three Seve warriors and managing to hold its own against them. Crawling forward again he waited until it was distracted before driving the sword into its groin. Bright green blood spurted but he kept pushing upwards, using the strength in his arms and legs until he'd buried all four foot of steel inside the monster's body.

The Vorga coughed and took a step backwards as Vargus regained his feet, leaning against the wall for support.

"You are not a child of Nethun," said Vargus in its native tongue. The Vorga's eyes widened, perhaps in shock at the curse more than pain from its wound. Hargo pressed a sword into his hand and Vargus opened the Vorga's throat before kicking it over the wall. The men around him cheered, but the victory was brief as more Vorga charged towards them.

The press of bodies swept Vargus along the wall until he found himself separated from the others. Someone slammed into him and a white hot lance of pain shot up his side. An axe came out of nowhere biting into his right leg, gouging a chunk out of his thigh. He stumbled backwards and only stayed upright because he was squashed against the battlements in a press of bodies. When the melee moved on he looked around for his attacker and saw a pair of brown Vorga looking at him. All of the Seve warriors nearby were engaged, leaving him to deal with them both by himself.

Working as a team they charged, forcing Vargus to choose an opponent. He feinted to the right with his sword, then struck the other Vorga in the throat with his fist. It gagged and fell to one knee but the other came forward, slicing its axe into his shoulder. His right arm went numb and his sword dropped to the ground. Blood was pouring down his side, and as the Vorga wrenched its axe free he howled and almost blacked out from the pain. As he reached for a dagger a spear pierced his side, driving out what little breath remained in his body. Blood trickled down his leg and there was something stuck in his throat.

As the pair of Vorga charged again, Vargus spat a wadge of blood into the face of the first and made a desperate grab for its axe, keeping its body between him and the other. His opponent's grip was impossibly strong and instead of trying to wrestle for the weapon he swung its whole arm. The axe sliced across the chest of the second Vorga and a flurry of green and yellow innards spilled out. Forgetting the axe the Vorga wrapped its arm about Vargus's throat and started to choke him, then bit down into his shoulder. With a roar he pulled the Vorga close, then with the last of his strength, threw it over his shoulder. It hit the battlements and started to slide over, but made a desperate grab for purchase. Its unbreakable grip wrapped around his injured right wrist, and before he could scream Vargus was pulled over the wall. Even as they fell the Vorga tried to kill him, but as the ground rushed up towards them it was the last thing Vargus cared about. He was going home.

There were only a few candles in the hospital room, but they provided enough light for Balfruss to make his way to the narrow cot without bumping into the furniture. He sat down beside Eloise and tried not to grimace at the stench that clogged the air. For a time he just listened to the frail rattling breath that hissed in and out of her burned lungs. It was such a small noise, one that barely seemed capable of sustaining life, and yet she persisted. Hours and now a day beyond what the surgeons expected.

Yesterday, when her breathing stopped for a short time the hospital had sent for him, thinking it signalled the beginning of the end. Now they were at a loss to explain it. Every twenty or thirty breaths there would be a strange hiccup, her breathing would pause for three heartbeats and then resume.

The thick stone walls kept out the noise from other parts of the hospital, leaving him wrapped in an oppressive silence broken only by the sound of her breathing. For a brief moment he thought it sounded louder than yesterday. But he knew hope was a spiteful mistress that played tricks on desperate minds. More than anything he wanted to heal her. To find a way to mend the ruined flesh and see her returned to full health. But Eloise was dead. The charred thing in front of him was not her. Soon, even the faint spark that lingered in the ruined flesh would fade.

The worst part, through a cruel trick of fate, was that half of her face remained unblemished by the burns that covered the rest of her body. Bandages dipped in a mix of oils and lotions meant to calm and soothe the flesh covered her from head to toe. If he focused all of his attention on that unmarked half, he could almost convince himself that she was sleeping.

Eloise hiccupped again and this time his heart beat five times before her breathing resumed with a faint catch. They were getting further apart. It wouldn't be much longer now. No matter how many times they soaked the bandages, or dribbled tonics into her mouth to numb the pain, the agony she was experiencing was beyond imagination.

"It's only now, at the very end, that I realise how rich I was," said Balfruss.

He reached out and touched the Source, channelling a trickle of power until a tiny blue flame appeared on the tip of his right thumb. The flame remained unnaturally steady and it made no sound as it washed the room in a pale glow, a weak imitation of daylight. With an impotent shake of his head Balfruss extinguished the flame and stood up to leave. As he turned away from the bed he noticed her features looked more relaxed. Perhaps Eloise was drifting away and was now in a place beyond pain. He certainly hoped so.

"I've never believed in the Gods, or a golden place after," Balfruss admitted, "but if I'm wrong, I hope Darius is waiting there for you."

Pressing two fingers to his lips Balfruss gently touched them to Eloise's unblemished cheek. The air in the corridor outside felt cool and fresh, but it was busy with groups of teary-eyed relatives. All of the patients on this corridor didn't have long and their families were just waiting for the inevitable.

To his left a Lantern priest, dressed in a pristine white hooded robe, sat praying with a group of women. Beyond them a group of local warriors, rangy men from the south, were discreetly passing around a flask and talking in quiet voices. Next to them was a burly priest of the Maker trying to console a grey-haired woman. Two young boys ran past her screaming in delight, oblivious to her pain and the general mood. A shame-faced mother chased after the boys, trying to grab hold of them, but they eluded her grasp and ran on. For a moment Balfruss considered offering to help, but then he saw the expression on every face as they recognised him. It wasn't just fear any more; they were terrified.

Ignoring them Balfruss strode away, trying to put as much distance between him and the mourners as possible. After passing through a heavy door he emerged in a busy area bustling with surgeons, nurses and Sisters of Mercy. Bodies lay at the edge of the room, row after row covered with white shrouds. Priests of every denomination said prayers over the dead, while others tried to extricate the recently deceased from sobbing relatives. There was too much activity for people to notice him, but even so Balfruss kept his head down.

"*They all know who you are. You can't hide from them,*" said a voice in his head.

Balfruss stopped and frantically looked at the faces of the people around him. The thought was not his own.

"Thule?"

"*I am here.*"

"Where?"

A nurse gave him a peculiar look, but hurried away when she recognised him. Balfruss stormed along the hospital corridors and out into the street. It was past midday and the sky was a hazy blue clogged with grey clouds. The streets immediately surrounding the hospital were busy with a constant flow of people, making it difficult for him to find somewhere quiet. Choosing streets and alleys at random he kept moving east, deeper into the heart of the Old City.

Eventually Balfruss found himself in a quiet square surrounded on three sides by shops that sold fruit, pulses and vegetables. The fourth side of the square held an ancient shrine devoted to the turning of the seasons. Balanced on its edge stood a seven-foot stone disc. Its surface was worn and pitted by the weather, but he could still see the old markings. Offerings of food, flowers and even wine sat at the base of the stone disc, but no thief would ever steal them.

Mercifully the square seemed deserted. Balfruss sat down on one of the benches in front of the shrine, scanning nearby windows for faces before speaking.

"Thule?"

"*I am here.*"

"Where? Where is here? Are you alive?"

"*No,*" said the now familiar voice in Balfruss's mind.

"I don't understand."

"When we first met, I shared a piece of myself with you. It was the only way for the others to hear about the plight of my people. Now that I am dead, this small echo is all that remains. But it too will fade in time."

The desperate spark of hope that Thule lived was extinguished.

"I'm glad to hear your voice. At least I won't be completely alone for what's about to happen."

"What's that?" asked Thule.

"I'm going to kill the Warlock, but it will cost me my own life."

"It may not come to that."

"Perhaps," said Balfruss. Images of Thule and Eloise falling from the wall wreathed in flame rose in his mind. He pictured the city gates being blown open and the western army marching in, slaughtering everyone in their path. Crouched among the dead, Balfruss saw Vannok cradling the bodies of his wife and children. A thousand pairs of unblinking eyes stared at him as his city started to burn. Deep inside, buried beneath layers of self-control, a river of rage started to bubble up.

Balfruss looked up at the sky, where clouds were starting to gather. It wouldn't be long now.

"Why are you so certain that you will die?" asked Thule.

"I've never pushed myself to the absolute limit. I'm afraid of what might happen."

"You will still be in control."

"Maybe, but I'm more worried because I know the Warlock and I share the same hunger. When I controlled the Link I felt unstoppable, that there wasn't anything I couldn't achieve. What if I become addicted to the power? What if I want more?"

"The Warlock might be a reflection of you, but he is not you. You will come back from the edge."

The sound of running feet made Balfruss look up, but a part of him already knew it was time.

A boy with long legs and flapping feet sprinted into the square, skidding to a halt. He was out of breath and it took a while before he could speak.

"General Vannok," gasped the boy. "The Warlock—"

"It's all right," said Balfruss, getting to his feet. "I know. Lead the way."

The boy took another deep breath then started off at a slow jog. Balfruss followed at a more sedate pace.

"There's no need to run."

The boy stopped and looked over his shoulder. "But the Warlock is waiting."

Balfruss maintained his pace. "Let him wait."

CHAPTER 44

A light rain started to fall as Balfruss marched through the capital. On every street, people were lining up to see him pass: merchants, labourers, children and groups of warriors. Their expressions were a mix of admiration, excitement, worry and fear. Most were afraid. An eerie hush fell on every group as he passed, but occasionally someone would cheer or shout a few words of encouragement. Mostly it was the children who seemed unafraid and he smiled or waved back at them.

Instead of heading to the battlements, he carried on along the main street towards the gates. The messenger kept talking, but Balfruss couldn't hear him. There was a rushing sound in his ears, like the tide rolling back and forth. All other sounds in the world faded away until he was alone with the Source. It was always there, just out of reach, an ocean of power waiting for him.

As he approached the gates Balfruss expected an argument. Instead he found Vannok, his face set in an expression of grim determination. Several times his friend tried to say something, but couldn't find the words. In the end he settled for gripping Balfruss by the shoulder. Then Vannok turned away and gestured at someone in the gatehouse.

A dull throb ran through his bones and with a high-pitched

squeal the city gates slowly opened. As Balfruss walked out of the city he barely registered the carnage. Piles of rotting corpses, chunks of men, and bits of pink and purple meat were stacked up against the outer wall. The scavengers had been busy, as many bodies were missing limbs and coils of intestines were stretched out across the ground. At his passing a huge blanket of flies lifted from the bloody mounds, then settled again to recommence their feast.

Faint voices cried out, broken men on the border between life and death, desperate for succour or release from their torment. Their pleas went unanswered and soon they were behind him as he strode across the stained grassland. Here and there the grass was smeared with blood, but mostly it had been ground up into a huge muddy bog from thousands of feet. A massive black crater stood out ahead. It was the only thing that remained of Finn, a stark reminder of what Balfruss now faced.

He continued walking away from the city, and as the land sloped upwards his sides started to burn and sweat rolled down his face. When he reached the top of the hill he paused and turned his face towards the sky. The drizzle cooled his head and eased some of the flush from his cheeks. With eyes closed he felt the tiny droplets tapping against his eyelids and deeply inhaled the cool misty air of his homeland. He savoured the feeling as it crept into his lungs.

Opening his eyes to the madness once more, Balfruss raised his voice and bellowed a challenge that rang out across the plains. The call was heard and then answered as the Warlock, dressed in his crimson robes, made his way towards Balfruss. The western army drew back, slowly at first, and then with increasing speed as many realised they were still too close. A full rout began with men throwing away weapons and armour, anything that slowed them down, in their panic to escape. Soon the two men were alone, facing each other across a shallow valley.

Striding forward Balfruss climbed onto a large grey rock on the western rim. A gentle wind tugged at his clothes and cloak, making it flap about him like a black sail. As he thought about the last few weeks, and what the Warlock had cost him, Balfruss's face twisted into a mask of fury. The only thing that stopped him from lashing out in anger was his training. It took considerable effort, but slowly he forced the rigid muscles of his face, shoulders and neck to relax. The grimace eased until he faced the Warlock with absolute calm and without any expression.

The Warlock was saying something. His words were amplified so that they carried to Balfruss's ears, but the only voices he heard were the ones inside. The dead spoke to him. He recited their names as a prayer to stay in control. He thought of all the people inside the city. He thought of Vannok and his family, the Queen and her brothers, even his father. He thought of all the lives that would be destroyed if the madman before him was allowed to live.

As he drew more and more power from the Source, his eyesight sharpened until he could see the Warlock's irritated expression across the valley. His mouth was still flapping, no doubt with words meant to provoke Balfruss into acting rashly, or to erode any remaining hope. Today, all words were just meaningless noise. The only things that mattered were strength and will.

When the Warlock finally realised he was wasting his time with talk, a faint smile touched Balfruss's face. Opening himself to the Source he drank even more deeply, until power emanated from every pore in his body. The sky darkened as he gathered his will and energy built up in the air. Tiny bolts of lightning flashed down around him, splitting stones and tearing up chunks of earth, but he didn't care. Black clouds rolled in from the east and the wind started to blow stronger, flattening the grass and driving rain into the face of his enemy.

Across the valley the air started to crackle as both men brought their will to bear. Overhead the heavens echoed in response and thunder rumbled over and over again like a giant drum.

As he approached his limit, Balfruss took a moment to marvel at how his view of the world had changed. Even though he'd not moved, it felt as if he were looking down on the plains and everyone on it from on high. Everything looked so small. The people in his city were like insects, hiding in an anthill and just as easily crushed underfoot. The western army was nothing but a pack of wild dogs, easily scattered by a loud noise. For the length of a heartbeat he teetered on the brink, but quickly stepped away, coming back to earth. Even at this distance he could feel the Warlock's disappointment.

Stretching out with both arms, as if trying to reach for the Warlock, he directed all of his power towards his hated enemy. At the same time the Warlock unleashed his power and the two forces collided with a clap of thunder that shook the earth. A twenty-foot crevice opened in the middle of the valley between them. Balfruss stumbled but managed to stay on his feet.

The recoil made them both pause for a moment. Then as Balfruss began to frantically weave a shield with one hand, the Warlock launched a green ball of something at him. The emerald comet screamed as it blazed towards him, leaving a brown streak across the sky in its wake. Redoubling his efforts Balfruss focused on his shield, sketching another on the ground, a trick he'd learned from Ecko.

The comet slammed into his shield, but instead of breaking apart on impact it started to congeal and swell in size. The slimy substance stretched and grew, coating his shield like a layer of skin. He could hear a faint whispering at the edge of his mind and quickly realised the pulsating slime was alive. It seemed to be feeding on the energy from his shield and continued increasing in size and mass. A few seconds later it had him completely surrounded and his entire view of the world had been blotted out. When the air inside his shield started to get warm Balfruss began to worry. Fire seemed like the obvious response, but if the creature fed on energy he doubted it would work. As the air became difficult to breathe Balfruss dropped to his knees.

Drawing heat from the air made breathing worse still, but as he only had a few breaths left it didn't matter. A layer of ice coated the rock beneath his feet and his hands started to stick to the surface. As a layer of ice crystals crept up the inside of his shield, Balfruss felt the creature squirm in discomfort.

He took one last long deep breath, held it and drew more heavily on the Source, pulling all heat from the air. A thick crust of ice raced up the shield on all sides until he was encased in a solid block that began to thicken. Ice formed on the end of his nose, snowflakes clung to his eyelashes and his hands and legs started to shake uncontrollably as any exposed skin started to turn blue. What little air remained in his lungs began to burn and black spots danced across his vision. The creature's screams grew louder and more high pitched until he felt it shatter, with a final wail, into a thousand tiny pieces.

In honour of Finn he summoned a hammer, shattered the ice dome and stood up, drawing in deep breaths of fresh air. The Warlock didn't wait for Balfruss to recover as a fireball streaked towards him, followed closely by a second and then a third. Even as he regained his breath Balfruss shook his head in dismay. Rather than attempt to block the fireballs he deflected them, turning them around and using their momentum until they were hurtling towards the Warlock.

While he had a moment to gather his thoughts Balfruss wove something together and immediately released it. By the time the Warlock had turned the fireballs aside, a small blue ball the size of a grape was flying towards him from Balfruss's outstretched hand. It struck him on the side of the face, bounced off his ear and rolled away before dissolving on the ground.

The Warlock's smile turned into a chuckle and then a full-belly laugh as he started to pull something together. His good humour slipped and then disappeared as he stumbled and fell to one knee. The tainted water trickled further into his ear canal and he dropped to the ground, vomiting all over himself. With a twist of one hand Balfruss squeezed the Warlock's weak shield, popping it like a soap bubble. A flick of his wrist looped a hook of energy around one of the Warlock's ankles, lifting him upside down into the air. Twirling one finger he made the Warlock spin vertically, over and over again, just slow enough to increase the vertigo and nausea. A vicious smile stretched across Balfruss's face as he watched the Warlock wail and retch, splashing bile onto his face, skin and clothes.

As the Warlock continued to spin, Balfruss stretched out one hand towards a large boulder the size of a horse. At first nothing happened, forcing him to draw yet more power from the Source until his skin felt stretched to its breaking point and all of his joints started to ache. Slowly the boulder lifted out of the squelching mud and then it too began to rotate, bits of mud and grass flying off in all directions.

Splitting his focus proved more difficult than Balfruss had anticipated and a fresh wave of sweat burst from his pores, soaking his already damp clothing. Putting all of his energy behind its momentum Balfruss hurled the boulder towards the Warlock with a scream of rage.

Despite being covered in his own filth, somehow the Warlock saw it coming. He slashed the cord of power holding him upside down and frantically started weaving a shield to protect himself. He hit the ground in a heap but quickly rolled to one side and came upright, swaying from side to side. A second later the boulder struck his shield full on, shattering it like an eggshell.

The granite cracked and started to break apart, but not before it slammed into the right side of the Warlock's body. With his enhanced vision Balfruss saw it shatter the bones in the Warlock's right arm, snap his shoulder, and smash half of his pelvis and upper leg into bone fragments. This time when the Warlock collapsed onto the ground Balfruss knew he would not be getting up again.

It was time to end it. Looking towards the sky Balfruss began to summon the lingering storm, knitting the clouds together, and somewhere thunder began to rumble in the distance. A whistling sound was his only warning before something punched him in the side. Looking down Balfruss saw the hilt of a dagger protruding from his body above his belt. Before he could react he felt it shift and fall to the ground. The weapon had been badly thrown, and the wound wasn't deep or life threatening.

Across the valley the Warlock had managed to get himself into a sitting position. Balfruss had thought him done but despite having no colour in his face the Warlock had managed to blot out his pain and summon power from the Source. He made several flipping motions with his one good arm and more discarded weapons on the battlefield were lifting off the ground. Working as fast as he could Balfruss wove a shield, adding layer upon layer. A second later a spear collided with the invisible barrier, crumpling on impact with a screech of metal. Several axes and maces thumped into it next, and although none broke through, Balfruss felt each blow bruise him and make his concentration wobble. Sensing weakness the Warlock increased the barrage, pulling every discarded weapon out of the mud as far as the eye could see. More weapons bounced off Balfruss's shield until the ground in all directions was littered with hundreds of weapons.

In what he thought could be the final minutes of his life Balfruss took a moment to think back over everything that had brought him to this moment. All of his struggles, the countless hours of studying, the arguments, the friendships, the tragic losses and brief moments of peace in a lifetime of struggling for acceptance and a sense of belonging. He thought about his father and the rage that had been his only companion. It had cost Graegor much and left him bitter and alone.

Taking a deep breath Balfruss pushed away all of his anger, unwilling to become his father, driven by emotions instead of intellect. As another cloud of swirling weapons flew towards him Balfruss shook his head and idly flicked them aside. Childish tricks from an immature mind.

Using a broken spear as a crutch the Warlock pushed himself upright. An ugly leer pulled his features tight as he started to create something Balfruss had never seen before. Huge amounts of power were being poured into a tiny black vortex that hung in the air beside the Warlock. A sharp stabbing pain just under his navel made Balfruss look down, but he wasn't injured. His body and mind had reacted on a primordial level to the horrifically unnatural tear in the fabric of the world.

The Warlock's abilities had always seemed superior to those of any Battlemage, beyond even the Grey Council, but this was the manifestation of the darkest rumours any pupil of the Red Tower had ever dared utter. Opening a doorway to somewhere else beyond the Veil.

There were stories of ancient things that existed beyond the Veil, monstrous immortal beings who granted immense power in return for favours, usually the person's immortal soul. As with all fables the risk outweighed the reward to any sane person, but the Warlock seemed beyond caring. He would risk all and expose the entire world to something beyond anyone's control or comprehension in order to win. What if while they fought one another something tried to come through from the other side?

The Warlock had to be stopped at any cost before it was too late.

Balfruss threw a lance of power at the Warlock to distract him with one hand while he pulled at some trailing threads of the vortex with the other. He didn't know how it had been constructed, but that didn't matter. All he needed to do was keep the Warlock occupied as he ripped the binding apart. Balfruss felt that he was walking along the razor's edge, threatening to push himself too far and be consumed by the Source, but he didn't hesitate in mounting a ferocious assault on the Warlock. Lance after lance of raw energy hammered into the Warlock's shield while Balfruss kept severing the tear with a narrow filament of power.

As the last thread snapped, the portal vanished with a loud crack that echoed across the sky. A wave of energy flowed outwards from the source like ripples on a pond. When the swell passed through Balfruss it made him shiver involuntarily as a spasm ran through his muscles.

Screaming in hatred the Warlock brought his full power to bear, throwing it against Balfruss, who struggled to keep it at bay. Balfruss pushed back with his power, drawing more and more energy from the Source. Gone were the tricks, the lost Talents and the word games intended to weaken his resolve. In his mind's eye he saw the Warlock's power as a giant wave trying to drown him. The pressure made his ears pop, and now he was truly deaf to the outside world. At the same time he knew that the Warlock was also under stress as the full weight of his strength sought to crush him to dust.

Silently they battled back and forth, first one gaining an advantage and then the other. Time had no meaning. The world was swept away and nothing remained except the Warlock. Balfruss could feel his opponent's will pushing against him, pressing and squeezing as it sought to tear him apart and squash him to naught all at once. Huge mounds of earth erupted as if they were volcanoes, and stones the size of horses flew through the air. Lightning forked down towards one and then the other, suddenly moving aside at the last second, splitting earth and stone. The rain began to beat down harder, and the wind began to swirl into a small typhoon in the middle of the battlefield. Bodies and weapons were thrown into the air and just as suddenly the wind died and everything fell to the earth. Apart from small gestures neither man moved during the battle as the world fell apart around them.

Despite the wind and rain, sweat poured down his face from the pressure, and Balfruss knew the Warlock would be feeling the same. It could not go on for much longer. Channelling this much power was starting to take a physical toll. Balfruss could feel his skin hardening and becoming brittle like glass. Soon his flesh would begin to peel, or perhaps whole limbs would shatter and break off. His mind was slowing and his insides felt as if they were simultaneously being squeezed and stretched at the same time.

As his mind started to become fuddled, the truth finally became apparent. They were evenly matched in strength. He was struggling but still managing to hold the Warlock at bay. With that realisation he let go of any remaining fear and doubt. He embraced the power that was a part of him and rejoiced in his connection to the living heart of creation. The Source coursed through his veins. It echoed in his mind with a pulse louder than his own. He marvelled in its majesty and surrendered himself to it completely.

Reaching down into the Source, into the deepest corners of his being, Balfruss summoned even more power until he went beyond his breaking point. The air burned as it moved in and out of his failing lungs. His eyes seemed too big for his skull, and it felt as if his head would explode from the pressure building up inside. His heart pounded in his chest, louder and louder, until it was ready to burst. A scream ripped its way out of his body, and with every fibre of his being he directed every drop of power towards the Warlock.

The energy surged from Balfruss's body, flowing out of his eyes, mouth and nose, and with it came an agonised, unholy scream that echoed across the valley and beyond. The force of his attack shattered the Warlock's shield as raw energy from the Source ripped through his body, consuming what little was left of his soul and destroying his fragile mind. The Warlock's body flew back a hundred feet and landed with a sodden thump on the bloody grass. He was dead long before he hit the ground.

The Warlock's glazed eyes stared at nothing. The storm broke and the rain tapered off, but a pool began to gather in the dead man's gaping mouth.

Besides the rain all else was silent and still.

Walking slowly and with purpose, Balfruss stepped down from the rock and turned to face the western army. Some fell to their knees in supplication, others screamed in terror and many dropped their weapons and ran. Balfruss watched them for a moment and then with slow and deliberate steps, made his way across the shattered battlefield towards the city.

The gates stood open, and like a conquering army of one, he walked into Charas unopposed. Everywhere faces watched him, from the walls and along the streets, but they were all a blur. Something kept him moving forward, but he didn't know where he was going. His mind was moving in circles that were becoming slower and slower. It was only when he felt the cold stones against his cheek that Balfruss realised he'd fallen down.

Vannok was saying something. Maybe it was to do with his mother. She didn't like it when they played out after dark. They should have set off for home a long time ago. He didn't like to worry her. But he was so tired, and his whole body felt so heavy. It wouldn't hurt to have a little nap. He closed his eyes and the darkness swallowed him.

CHAPTER 45

The bell above the door chimed and Gunder, once more dressed in his merchant disguise, looked up from his seat behind the counter. Schooling his expression had become second nature, but a smile briefly quirked across his face at the sight of his visitor.

"Good morning, my Lady," he said with a small bow. "How may I serve the Palace on this glorious day?"

"You honour me, but I am not a Lady," said Roza, dressed once more as a palace servant. "I'm here with thanks from her Majesty."

"I'm delighted, but very surprised her Majesty would notice a humble spice merchant, such as I."

Roza glanced around the shop, her expression never changing. "Is someone else here?"

"No, we're alone," he said, escorting her to the padded seats by the window. "But I'm sure it won't be long before someone is watching. Better to maintain appearances."

"Very well."

Roza waited patiently while he brewed a pot of tea and then served it with a plate of pastries. After serving, Gunder remained silent for a while, enjoying the quiet in his shop. The streets outside were also extremely quiet in the wake of the revolt. It wouldn't be long before the city recovered and the normal hustle of city life returned.

"Any news from the palace?" he said finally.

Roza put down her glass, folding her hands in her lap. "The Watch is still on high alert. Most of the bodies have been cleared away and people are starting to return to a normal routine. The Guardians of the Peace have been busy investigating as well. It seems there were a number of murders during the revolt. Some of the bodies were not discovered until this morning."

"Fascinating."

One of Roza's eyebrows quirked up. "Several of those killed were high-profile people in the city, including three foreign ambassadors."

"That's shocking," said Gunder, taking a slurp of his tea, "but I suspect replacements will be dispatched very soon. Or perhaps not, since relations between nations in the west are so difficult at the moment."

"That will change."

"Of course, but it buys Shani some time to get more of our people in place."

"There's also a rumour that six of those killed were operatives from other nations."

Gunder eyed the pastries and finally gave in to temptation. He gobbled one in two bites and resisted the urge to lick his fingers. After wiping his mouth he noticed Roza was still waiting for an answer. "What?"

"Was that authorised?" she asked, and Gunder made a vague dismissive gesture. "You're playing a dangerous game."

"Dangerous?" he said, and all hints of the fat merchant drained from his expression and body language. Roza leaned back in shock at the sudden change until he relaxed and forced a friendly smile. A tense silence stretched between them.

"I hear most of the Drassi are on their way home," Roza offered.

"It made sense to release them. The Queen cannot be seen to be relying too heavily on foreign support to retake the rest of the country. What remains of her army is on its way back, but their numbers are severely depleted. I suspect the recruiting offices for the Watch and the Queen's army will be busy in the next few months."

"There's also talk of subtly improving the city's defences, but nothing overt. Now, more than ever, trade is going to be vital, so they can't put up walls."

"How soon before the Queen reopens trade with Seveldrom and the far east?"

Roza shrugged. "Officially I'd guess another week, ten days at most. Missives are being drafted as we speak. Celebrations are planned for the next four days with a tour of the cities. Once that's done, and everyone has settled down, I would expect them to reopen."

"Good. I've asked Shani to send a few new faces. We need to shake things up a bit."

"Was that why you wanted to see me?"

"I'm retiring from the spice business and you will take over the shop."

"Am I being punished?" snarled Roza. "Do you have any reason to complain about my work?"

Gunder held up his hands in an attempt to placate her. "No, I've received no complaints."

"Then what is it?"

At first he didn't answer, but eventually he found the words. "During the revolt, I was dressed as a member of the Watch."

"I know. I helped with the boots for the uniform."

"For the first time in two years, I felt free." Roza's frown was not unexpected but she didn't comment. "This disguise has become something else."

"That happens to everyone," she said with a relieved sigh. "Maybe you need to take a little time. Close the shop for a few weeks. Blame it on the war and just go and be yourself."

"You don't understand. You're being promoted."

Roza stared into his eyes for a moment then looked away. "You're not joking."

"No. You will run the network in Yerskania. I've sent word to Shani about the change. Congratulations," he said, but Roza wouldn't be distracted.

"What are you going to do instead?"

"The same. I'll still be around and will offer advice, if you need it."

Roza looked appalled. "You're going freelance?"

"No, no. My loyalties haven't changed, I'm just taking some time, but afterwards I won't be returning to the spice business," he said with a gesture at the racks.

"What happened?" pressed Roza, sitting forward on her chair until she was slightly too close for comfort. "Something changed. You've been different for a while now."

"It's not important."

"Regori, tell me," she said, laying a hand on top of his.

He considered brushing her off, but then changed his mind. They'd known each other for many years before he'd come to Yerskania, and they had been close friends at one point in the distant past.

"It was during the revolt, or just afterwards." He scratched at his head through the felt cap. He couldn't wait to be rid of it and the garish clothes. "The Chosen had been defeated and I'd dismissed the Drassi. As I was walking home through the chaos, I saw a lot of damaged buildings, burned-out shops, and piles of bodies. And then I had a terrible thought."

"You were disturbed by the destruction."

"Hmm, oh, no. I've not developed a weak stomach.

Something far worse than that," he said with a laugh that held no mirth. "I realised that all of the shops and buildings would need to be repaired. Then there's also the priests and grave diggers that would be kept busy for weeks. No, in the midst of all the chaos, I smelt profit."

"Profit."

"Money. That was my first thought. Not how we could exploit the situation to benefit our cause." He disgusted himself. Regori straightened his back, standing at his full height for the first time in years. "I've been Gunder the fat merchant for too long. I'm starting to think like him. No, he has to die. We'll blame it on his weight and heart. You, his niece, will inherit the business."

"But, what about my contacts? And my other identities? I've made some good connections."

"Pass on those you can to others, burn the rest."

"When are you leaving?"

"In a few days. I'll give you time to wrap things up, but leave no trace." It was clear she didn't like it, but eventually Roza nodded. "Come by in a couple of days and we'll sort out the details of my death. As my niece you'll inherit the house as well, but you can decide if you want to live there or somewhere else."

He walked her to the front door before holding it open. Roza stared at him for a while with an unreadable expression before going through. She probably thought he'd lost his mind. That, in itself, was part of the problem. He didn't know his own mind any more.

Despite the padded suit, Regori felt much lighter as he walked back to the home of Gunder the merchant for the last time.

CHAPTER 46

Talandra picked up the latest report from the top of the pile and sat back in her chair to read it. She was tempted to put her feet on the desk, but apparently it wasn't something a Queen should do, according to the head steward who'd caught her yesterday.

Putting the report to one side for a moment, her eyes were drawn back to the letter she'd received this morning. She didn't need to read it again as she'd memorised the words. Even so she couldn't stop staring at it. She knew it was only the first of many. It would change everything, just when she was beginning to build a new life for herself.

She left the report on the desk, opened a window and stared out at her city. It was two days since the war had officially ended. Two days since a delegation from the western army had approached the city under a flag of peace and offered their formal surrender. Two days without the ring of steel and the cry of the dying men echoing in her ears. Their pleas still found her, in the darkest hour of the night, but she no longer had to watch men die on the walls.

At least the city was starting to return to a semblance of normality. Most of those evacuated before the siege had returned, although there was still a stream at the city gates each day.

Businesses were reopening, and already a slow but steady trickle of caravans were readying to leave for the west. Despite the official declaration none of the merchants were taking any chances, as each train was protected by a Fist of Drassi, mercenaries or private guards.

Several delegations had already left for the west, Morrin and Zecorran citizens, as well as ambassadors who'd been trapped here during the conflict. Somewhere on her desk were several letters from enraged citizens complaining about the intolerable living conditions they'd been forced to endure, including one from Ambassador Kortairlen of Morrinow. He'd been happy to receive her protection once the fighting had begun, but now claimed he had been held in squalor. According to Shani, the Morrin ambassador was fond of indulging, and Kortairlen had spent the whole war getting drunk and receiving visits from expensive escorts.

In two days General Vannok would lead several thousand men into the west, where they would join up with soldiers from Yerskania. Her father had made a promise to Sandan Thule that she intended to keep. Shael was still a nation in chaos. Several cities had been liberated by Shael's rebel forces, but the Vorga were not like other people. They would not simply walk away if they lost one battle. The end of the war meant nothing to them. Given what she knew about the Vorga, she doubted they'd ever agreed to be ruled by Taikon. The Mad King had simply included them in his plans. Always happy to test their strength and skill in battle, the Vorga had agreed to march into Seveldrom.

Although so far she'd only exchanged a few short messages with the Queen of Yerskania, Talandra felt she could learn a great deal from her as she had successfully ruled for many years. From the tone of her messages, Talandra also sensed a sharp mind and a dark sense of humour. She believed they were going to get on very well in the future.

Standing at the window, her eyes drifted over the rooftops, and the great spire of the Maker, before coming to rest on the city walls. They were still washing off the blood and many of the stones by the gates were indelibly stained from the siege. A few apothecaries were offering their skills to remove the marks, mixing potions that made the stone sizzle and crack as it ate into the surface. City engineers were on hand as well, talking about tearing down a whole section and rebuilding it bigger and stronger than before, with a few nasty surprises. For now, she left them alone to test their theories. Eventually they would stop squabbling and come to her with all of the options, and then she would make a decision.

Yesterday she'd walked along the wall where countless warriors had died, the hem of her gown dragging across the bloody stones. The dress was still hanging outside the wardrobe in her bedroom, and she'd forbidden her maid from taking it away. It served as a reminder, but she knew it was only temporary. Something more permanent was required, not just for her, but for everyone who lived in the city, as well as those who came to visit.

A sharp double rap on the door disrupted her chain of thoughts. She moved to her desk and quickly rearranged the papers, hiding one amid the pile. "Come in."

Shani marched into the room, dressed in a pair of tight sky blue breeches and matching jacket. Her black hair was held back with a narrow comb, which accentuated her long face. It really didn't suit her. On the other hand, the colour and cut of Shani's clothes were very becoming, and the trousers showed off her gorgeous legs. Talandra was about to make a comment to that effect when she remembered herself. Shani offered a formal bow, which saddened Talandra more than a little.

"Your Highness. Are you well?" she asked formally.

"Well enough. Please, take a seat," said Talandra, sitting down in one of the chairs in front of her desk.

"Thank you," said Shani, sitting down opposite. Her amber eyes briefly passed over the stack of papers. Talandra noticed faint purple lines running across Shani's cheeks and up the sides of her neck, an indication that she wasn't getting enough sleep.

"Busy, your Highness?"

Talandra pushed one letter deeper into the stack. "Always, but I have time to meet with you. What do you have for me?"

Shani took several small pieces of paper from her jacket. Talandra noticed several had been folded many times, no doubt from being attached to the leg of a bird or bat. It was hard to believe that only days ago she had been the one visiting the belfry and aviary to collect coded messages from her spies.

"This morning I received a report from Zecorria. Civil war has officially broken out."

Talandra heaved a long sigh and took a moment to consider the consequences. Shani waited until she gestured for her to continue. "Yesterday High Priest Filbin publicly spoke out in front of a huge crowd against King Taikon. He called on the people to cast out the false prophet. He also admitted to being fooled and begged for their forgiveness."

Talandra grimaced. "Let me guess: he received it?"

Shani gritted her teeth and nodded. "He offered to stand down as head of the Church of Holy Light. He said he was not worthy to lead them."

"Which only made the people able to relate to him, and now they love him even more."

"He's a public hero. There were marches and peaceful protests until a soldier killed one of the protesters. The governors of various districts convened an emergency Council and unfortunately split into two factions. Taikon's group of supporters is smaller, but there are many people who still believe he's their saviour and prophet. Since then Filbin has beseeched the people to learn from his mistake and join him and the others in opposition."

Talandra was fuming. "Did you read my reports about High Priest Filbin?"

"I saw them."

"Then you know what kind of a man he is. It turns my stomach to think of people worshipping that deviant as a hero and saviour."

"He could have an accident," suggested Shani. "He's overweight, and not exactly a young man any more."

Talandra waved the idea away. "Even if it were made to look natural, someone would claim it was done by one of Taikon's supporters. It would only make things worse, and I don't want him made into a martyr. It's bad enough I have to hear about him, I don't want my grandchildren hearing his name."

An awkward silence settled on the room at her words. This high up in the city the only sound she could hear from the streets below was an occasional faint cry of a street vendor.

"Temples devoted to Taikon are being defended by the Chosen in Zecorria," said Shani, breaking the uncomfortable silence. "Elsewhere the Chosen don't really exist any more. They never had a foothold in the southern kingdoms, and I can only guess what's happened to them in Morrinow."

"Thanks to the rebellion the temple in Perizzi is nothing but ash, and they're planning to build something else on the site. I've also heard directly from the Queen of Yerskania about this. She's pledged to find any dedicated Chosen who went underground, and she strikes me as a very determined woman."

"Your Highness—"

"Please Shani. Don't call me that when we're alone."

"Your Highness," Shani said again, and Talandra sighed. "I would advise reserving judgement on the Queen. While she is to be admired for her recent efforts, she did allow Taikon to manipulate her. I appreciate the circumstances were extreme, and I've no doubt she will be more alert going forward, but we cannot solely rely on her to avoid similar situations from developing in the future."

Talandra moved to the window and stared out, unable to look at her former lover and, apparently, former friend. "What do you advise?"

"Gunder has asked for a number of new agents to be sent as soon as possible to establish a larger presence in Perizzi. Yerskanja is still the trade heart of the west, and everything will pass through the capital as before."

"I agree. When can they be ready to leave?"

Shani coughed politely. "I anticipated your response, Highness. They left this morning with the first group of merchants."

"Very good. Keep me informed."

"Yes, your Highness."

"Before you go, I have a gift for you," said Talandra, moving to her desk.

She took out a small set of three black iron keys and passed them across to Shani. "Those are the keys to the Black Library," said Talandra. "Every secret I've accumulated over the last twenty years. As head of my network, it's now yours."

Shani was speechless.

"Was there anything else?" asked Talandra.

"No, your Highness."

Shani got up to leave, but paused beside the desk, pulling one of the sheets of paper from the middle of the stack.

"May I ask what this is?"

Talandra saw she was holding the sketch she'd made a few hours earlier. "The idea came to me in a dream."

"What is it?"

"A monument," said Talandra, taking the sketch of the monolith from Shani. "For those who died, and for the future, so that no one will forget what happened. I considered having the names of the dead carved into it."

"It would be taller than the city walls if you did that," said Shani, and the thought sobered them both.

"Tempting, but it would be depressing to have its shadow hanging over everyone. Even so, it needs to be big, so that everyone coming to Charas can see it from far away."

The pain from everything must have been constricting her throat worse than she had realised, as Shani laid a hand on top of hers. Talandra looked into her amber eyes and Shani offered a friendly smile.

"I think it's a good idea. Something needs to be built. No one should ever forget." Shani withdrew her hand and stepped back. Perhaps friends, then.

"I can't decide if it should be made from local yellow stone, or something else," mused Talandra.

"It will come to you," said Shani. "I have to go."

"Of course."

"Highness," said Shani, with another little bow, and this time the title didn't sting as badly as before.

Once Shani's footsteps had receded Talandra pulled out the other letter she'd hidden at the bottom of the pile. The wax crest wasn't familiar, a fox and three swords, but she'd heard of Lord Bragnon and knew him to be a powerful man from the south of Seveldrom. He was a rich noble who owned thousands of cattle used to make the famous Seveldrom leather armour. What she hadn't known, until she read it in his letter, was that Lord Bragnon had a son who had fought in the war as an unranked warrior.

The marriage proposal was worth a moment of her time to consider, but it would be the first of many.

Talandra slipped the letter into a drawer to look at another day, and picked up the next report.

CHAPTER 47

Hargo felt uncomfortable. And itchy. The itchiness came from the bandaged cut on his right arm and the gash in his scalp. He knew it meant the wounds were healing and likely weren't infected, so he'd live and have more scars. Not that it mattered. Zera used to be a Sister of Mercy. She'd seen far worse. He shuffled from foot to foot as if on hot stones. The others looked at him again, as if they expected him to do something. His sense of unease grew.

"What?"

Black Tom sidled closer, his breath stinking of liquorice as usual. Hargo used to like the stuff every once in a while. Now the smell of tarr made him think of the war. He never wanted to smell it again. "Are you gonna say something?"

Not for the first time Hargo wished Orran was here. The little rat-faced bastard had an easy way with words. And women. Not that he often talked his way into a woman's bed, but it didn't stop him trying. He took the knocks and just tried again with another. Eventually he got it right. If only he'd done the same with his wounds and kept trying, not gone and died. Just like Tan and Rudd and all the other lads. Just like Vargus.

They'd all seen him fall. It was right after the Vorga champion had cut up a dozen of them and Vargus had taken it down. Stuck a sword right up inside it, like it was fucking the blade. Even then the big bastard was too stupid to know it was already dead. They'd cheered, but only for a short time. Soon enough more of the green- and brown-skinned bastards came at them, whooping and clicking their teeth. He'd been stuck fighting two with Orran, but he'd seen the ones that went for Vargus. Maybe they were angry about their champion, or maybe they just didn't like his face. Hargo hadn't been worried, until one of them cut Vargus and then everyone saw him fly over the wall with the other.

After, when the Warlock was dead and they opened the gates, he and some of the others searched outside for Vargus. The stench was worse than anything he'd imagined. Rotting bits of men and piles of pink and blue innards. Giant swarms of flies and crows had already eaten their favourite bits, eyeballs and the like. The rest was just a giant pile of purple, green and black meat, some of it bloated and ready to burst. Some of it didn't look like it had ever come from a living creature.

There must have been two thousand men who started the search for Vargus. After two days with nothing to show for sticking their hands into innards, there was just him and a handful of others. Some reckoned he was still alive and was out there somewhere. Some thought he would come back, like the old pagan God that rose from the dead. After the third day, even Hargo knew the truth. Vargus was gone. He might have been the start of the Brotherhood but the huge crowd of men gathered today showed that he wasn't the end of it. And suddenly he knew exactly what to say to them. Hargo cleared his throat and turned to face the others.

"Vargus wasn't a great man, and he wasn't no saint," he said looking out at a sea of faces. Most he didn't know, but all of them had that look in their eyes. They'd all lost friends and family. They'd all lost brothers, and they were all the same. That was why they were here, stood in front of an empty grave. "He was a tough old bastard. And he was my friend. The first day we met he knocked me on my arse. I'm strong, always have been, but I was cocky. Thought I knew how to fight, but he taught me otherwise. And he taught me about family."

There were lots of grunts and noises of agreement. Men turned to look at those around them, and even though there weren't two that looked the same, they all saw the truth.

"I had a brother when I was a boy, but he fell and broke his neck. Can't much remember him, so I grew up without brothers, until a few weeks ago." Hargo hadn't spoken about his brother in more than thirty years. It felt strange to share it with so many. Like he was telling them all a secret no one was supposed to know about him. "Most of you won't know this, but someone in the west heard about the Brotherhood. They knew we were fighting better than before, so they sent someone to kill Vargus, thinking that without him it would end. But it won't." Hargo clenched his fists and stared out at the hundreds of men, daring just one of them to argue with him. But all he saw was smiling faces, nodding heads and then came cheers of agreement.

"Vargus always told me the Brotherhood wasn't his. It was just something he'd been taught and passed it on to us. Might be true, might be bullshit, but he said it so we wouldn't think he was some sort of priest, like those Lord of Light fellas. Always telling you what to do and how bad you've been."

"Lantern fuckers," muttered Black Tom. His words were echoed by many in the crowd and there were other curses and grumbles. Hargo waited for it to go quiet again. He wasn't going to shout. He still didn't know why he was the one saying these words and not someone else. But they all seemed to be listening, so he would say what was in his head. Slowly the crowd went quiet again and they all stared at him, making his skin itch worse than before. He didn't like having so many people watch him all at once.

"Make up your own mind. I'm not here to tell you what to do. It's what Vargus would've said if he were still alive. The war might be done, but I'm not going to forget the Brotherhood. I don't think I could, even if I wanted to. It's part of what kept me alive. I don't know what will happen next year, or the one after that, but I've seen crops get blighted and animals die in the fields, and no one knows why. I expect times will get hard again, but when they do, I'm not facing them on my own any more." Hargo slapped Black Tom on the shoulder and the little man grinned. "And if he gets in trouble, and needs help, I'll do what I can. Because he's family."

There was nothing else to say. Hargo took a moment to think on Vargus as he stared down at the grave. It didn't seem as if they'd met only a few weeks ago. It felt like Vargus had always been there, always been a part of him. His body was gone, probably stripped down to bones by now, but Hargo knew he wouldn't forget him, or stop talking about him.

Black Tom offered him a skin of something and Hargo took a long pull. Something fiery hit his stomach and its warmth quickly started to spread. Black Tom took a drink and then tipped the rest onto the grave.

Hargo started the long walk back to the city with Black Tom at his side. It took him a while to notice, as others usually stepped aside when they saw him coming, but all of the other men were staring at him. It was the same look they'd given Vargus. One that meant he was someone special, someone to listen to. For once Hargo wished he wasn't such a big man and could disappear into the crowd. Once they were back in the city he wouldn't be noticed in such a large place. After that he'd gather his things and set off for home.

"Where you headed, Tom?"

Black Tom spat out a greasy wadge of tarr. "Not sure. Could go home, but don't much fancy it."

"Why's that?"

"My old man. He expects me to take over the family business. Never wanted to before, can't see it happening now. Expect my younger sister will do it instead. She'll do a better job anyway."

Now that they were past the last of the crowd Hargo breathed a little easier. Looking over his shoulder was a mistake. Lots of them were still watching him. He turned away and ignored them.

"What's he do?"

"Owns a bunch of Sorenson bulls in the south."

Hargo considered it. "Quiet life as a cattle farmer sounds good after all the noise."

"He's not a farmer. He owns ten thousand head of cattle. Others do the farming. He just runs the abattoirs and tanneries for making armour."

Hargo stopped and turned to face Tom. "Ten thousand?"

"Yeah."

A cold prickle ran across the back of Hargo's skull. "Who's your father, Tom?"

Tom spat again and resumed walking. "Doesn't matter."

"Are you noble born?" asked Hargo, and Black Tom cackled, but then his face tightened into something sad and bitter.

"There's nothing noble about me."

"That's the truth," agreed Hargo.

Tom laughed and his pained expression eased. "Did you mean what you said?"

"About what?"

"That I could call on you if I was in trouble."

"I wouldn't have said it otherwise," said Hargo.

Black Tom said nothing and Hargo was happy to walk in silence. All around them the land was scarred and battered.

Everywhere the earth was torn up and much of the plains had been churned into mud. It took them a while longer, but they skirted around the valley where Balfruss had killed the Warlock. No one liked to go there. Some of the others had stood on the walls and watched the whole thing, right up until the end. Hargo had been in the hospital with Orran choking out his last few breaths. Even so he'd heard the thunder and the crack of lightning. At the end, Orran had gone quiet in the arms of a Sister, a big busty one with a kind face. He'd died snuggled up to her tits with a big smile on his face. After seeing how some had died, Hargo thought Orran had it lucky.

When they'd closed his eyes and covered him with a sheet, Hargo had gone outside and started walking. Somehow he ended up at the wall, and by then it was over. All the faces around him were happy, with people cheering and laughing. Some were even drinking but then Balfruss came back, walking through the gates by himself. He walked right past Hargo and the others as if he couldn't see them.

In the last few weeks Hargo had seen hundreds, maybe thousands of men die. He'd come close a few times himself, and had even ended up in the hospital twice. None of those who lived were without scars. Even the freshest spotty-faced lad who'd not held a sword until two weeks ago was now a veteran.

Every single one of them had stared into the face of death. They'd come to know it, to hate it, to loathe it for taking people away they cared about. But they'd all courted the black-hearted bitch, and now they knew her better than their own wives.

The look on Balfruss's face that day was something Hargo would never forget. On that day, death wasn't a woman, it was a Battlemage.

After he'd walked past, some men and women fell to their knees, one or two cried and more whispered to their God. They prayed they never saw him again and gave thanks he was on their side.

"My father is Lord Bragnon," said Tom, breaking the silence. He took out his tarr pouch and for the first time Hargo noticed a crest on the side. A fox and three swords.

"Never heard of him."

"No reason you should. So, where you headed?" asked Tom.

"Tyrnon. It's a town about a hundred miles east. Up in the hills."

Black Tom grunted. "I know it. Been there a couple of times. Lots of miners and woodcutters."

"Next time you're there, find me and we'll have a drink."

"Sounds good."

"You're buying," said Hargo. "Rich boy."

Black Tom laughed and stuffed another wadge of tarr into the side of his mouth. "Fair enough."

"Good."

"It goes the other way as well," said Tom, and Hargo looked at him. "If you ever need anything, ask and I'll do what I can. I won't forget the Brotherhood."

"Glad to hear it."

They walked the rest of the way back to the city without talking, but it was comfortable and familiar. All Hargo wanted to do now was go home and see his wife. It had been so long since he'd seen her, part of him wasn't sure he'd recognise her any more. And maybe she wouldn't know him either. He'd worry about that, and what came after, another day. In the morning he'd start the long walk home, but tonight he was still a warrior in the Queen's army and he intended to get drunk.

CHAPTER 48

"Get me a camel. Now!" roared Emperor Taikon.

The mad Emperor was sat on a throne, surrounded by piles of his belongings that had been brought to him from throughout the palace. In the last few days the throne room had become the only place he felt safe. Whenever he left the room he heard the voices. They always seemed to be far away and he couldn't understand the language, but sometimes he thought he could see figures moving in the shadows. Creatures with tentacles, beaks and razor-sharp claws. That was why he kept lanterns burning in the room at all hours of the day and night, to keep the shadows at bay.

He slept and held court amid piles of bedding, rumpled clothes, broken glass, plates of rotting food, maps, books and an assortment of exotic animals. A white goat, painted with black stripes, was happily munching its way through the pages of an ancient text on the importance of wheat. Across the room a box full of mewling kittens writhed and cried out for milk from their absent mother. They weren't interested in the five-foot lizard Taikon had placed in the box with them. In the rafters a brightly coloured songbird slept perched on one foot. It briefly opened its eyes at Taikon's outburst, took a shit on the clothes below then went back to sleep.

"And a mirror. I need my special mirror!" shouted Taikon. From another part of the palace came the flapping sound of feet, and eventually a sandalled servant arrived carrying a standing mirror.

Nirrok, the last in a long line of royal servants, was sweating profusely and tried his best not to stare at the Emperor, the piles of rubbish, or the rotting corpse of the previous herald propped up in one corner. He tried extremely hard to ignore the cloud of flies, the stench, and the apple that had been inserted into the dead man's mouth.

"What's this?" asked Taikon as Nirrok slowly crept towards the throne, trying his best to avoid standing on anything.

"Your special mirror, Most Holy."

Taikon looked confused and put a hand to his ridged forehead. "Yes, yes, I did say I wanted that, but it doesn't look like my special one. Are you sure it's my special mirror?"

Nirrok took a moment to consider before replying. "That mirror was . . . broken."

"Kill them!" screeched Taikon. "Have whoever broke the mirror stabbed, hung and quartered. Then bring me their eyeballs in a bowl of pea soup. But it must be cold, not warm."

"Yes, Most Holy," said Nirrok, although there was no way he could fulfil Taikon's request since it was the Emperor who had broken the mirror in a fit of rage.

"Hmm, well I suppose this mirror will have to do. Stand it up over there." Taikon gestured vaguely towards a pile of books to his left and Nirrok edged towards it. Finding no room to set it down he slowly pushed everything to one side until there was enough space. Thankfully none of the piles tipped over and he heaved a sigh of relief.

"Is my camel on its way?" asked Taikon as he stared at his reflection. Nirrok kept his face towards the floor, as was proper when stood in the presence of a living God.

"Yes, Most Holy."

"Is it a green one? It has to be green."

Again Nirrok paused before answering. He took a moment to consider if the truth was more or less likely to get him killed. "We can't find a green one, Most Holy."

"Did you say you can't find one?"

"Yes, Most Holy." Nirrok waited patiently, staring at the ground, trying to breathe as quietly as possible.

"Look at me. I command it."

Nirrok took a deep breath then slowly raised his eyes towards the Emperor. The sight of Taikon proved to be even more disturbing than the first time he'd laid eyes on him. Even in that short space of time there were a number of visible changes. The black horns that had appeared out of his forehead had grown larger, and were now starting to curl backwards and loop behind the Emperor's ears like a ram's. Hung over one of the horns, as it would no longer fit onto his lumpy head, was a crown inlaid with diamonds and precious stones. The Emperor's skin had become a sickly shade of pale blue and it was shot through with a broken network of black lines that pulsed like veins. But those things carried no blood, and they seemed to writhe under the skin as if they were independently alive. Even though he knew nothing about the latest tailoring fashions, Nirrok was aware that the Emperor's purple jacket and green breeches clashed terribly with his skin tone. He resembled a giant bruise.

"Did you say you can't find a green camel?"

Nirrok gulped, certain that his final moments were approaching. "Yes, Most Holy. I have searched everywhere."

"I see." A long silence stretched out, broken only by the chewing of the goat starting on another chapter.

"Perhaps I could look again?" suggested Nirrok, edging backwards in a desperate attempt to get out of the room before his luck ran out. "I could definitely find a different-coloured camel, if that would be suitable."

"Don't be ridiculous," scoffed Taikon. "If you can't get me a green one it's just not worth it."

"No, Most Holy."

Taikon sighed dramatically. "Very well. Send in my Generals. We need to discuss ending this tedious war."

Nirrok dithered again and this time decided to err on the side of caution. All of the Generals were dead, as were four sets of replacements, and then three more groups of junior officers who had been rapidly promoted. Any remaining senior officers had stayed on the front line after the first group had been butchered by the Emperor. Not that it had mattered; it just took the Chosen a little longer to find them and send back their heads for the Emperor's collection. "Yes, Most Holy. I will bring them immediately."

Nirrok scuttled out of the room as fast as his bandy legs would carry him. The guards outside were gone. He made it all the way to the front door of the palace without seeing a single person. He started running down the street and was still running an hour later.

Vargus had watched Taikon's antics for the last hour, concealed behind a tapestry that led to a secret passage. The Mad King was so wrapped up in his own world, he'd never once looked in Vargus's direction.

"Silly, silly," muttered Taikon before preening in the mirror and trying to balance the crown on top of his misshapen head. Vargus had heard more than enough. After pulling on a pair of thick gloves he pushed the tapestry to one side and strode into the room, knocking aside whatever stood in his way. Plates cracked beneath his boots and broken glass was ground into powder. The goat wisely decided to move elsewhere and chew on something in another part of the room. Taikon didn't even notice Vargus until he was climbing up the steps to the throne.

"Ah, there you are, General," said Taikon, shaking his head as if he were admonishing a child. "I'm bored. Bored, bored, bored. This war is dull. We need to make it more interesting, don't you agree?"

Vargus ignored his ramblings and looked deeper into Taikon's body, seeing beneath the skin and muscle to what lay beneath. Buried in the middle of his intestines lay the artefact, which was consuming the Mad King bit by bit. As he watched, another black tendril started to crawl its way up the side of Taikon's left cheek beneath the skin. It writhed for a few seconds, stretched and then settled.

"Which one are you? Are you the smelly one?" asked the Emperor.

Seizing Taikon by one shoulder Vargus made a spear with the fingers of his other hand and rammed it into the Emperor's torso, passing through clothing and skin without difficulty. As green blood began to gush from the wound, he started to feel around for the artefact. Taikon tried to shove him off and started screaming, more in alarm than pain, but no one came to investigate. No doubt they were probably used to hearing far worse.

Slightly more worrying for Vargus was that he could feel Taikon's skin starting to heal around his forearm. Before he became a permanent part of the Mad King's body, he yanked out his hand. The skin began to stretch across the wound and once it met in the middle it started to knit itself back together. Within a few seconds there was no sign of the wound. The blood quickly dried, turned brown and started to flake off.

Taikon slumped back on the throne, gasping for breath as his eyes rolled up in his skull. The artefact started pulsing again, creating even more tendrils, which made Taikon convulse. Drawing his sword Vargus approached the throne and swung at

Taikon's neck using all of his strength. The Mad King had some remaining instincts of self-preservation, as he held up one hand in a vain attempt to ward off the blow. The sword cut through Taikon's arm just above the wrist before biting deep into his neck. Blood gushed out, spraying across Vargus's face and he quickly spat out the sweet green liquid.

The sword had only partly severed Taikon's head from his body, but even as Vargus tried to saw the blade back and forth to finish the job, the wound started to close again. Taikon's severed hand turned black, the flesh putrefying at an accelerated rate, but something white pushed its way out of the stump of his wrist. New bones were starting to grow at the end of his arm, and muscles started to weave around them like a spider spinning a web. Taking a dagger from his belt Vargus stabbed Taikon a dozen times in the torso, then six more to make sure. The artefact was not without limits and the number of wounds caused the rate of healing to slow. This gave Vargus enough time to press Taikon's head against the back of the throne and force the blade through the remainder of his neck. The mangled head of the Mad King toppled to the littered floor below where it continued to scream and babble. His body remained upright, independently alive from the head. Taking a deep breath Vargus tried again, this time cutting open a wide gash across Taikon's stomach before reaching inside his chest. It took longer than he would have liked, buried up to his elbow in another man's guts, but eventually he managed to get a solid grip on the slippery stone. Using one foot to brace himself against Taikon's body, Vargus yanked his arm back and the artefact came free with a loud pop.

Almost immediately Taikon's skin started to blacken and decay. The head on the floor stopped screaming and the Mad King's final expression was one of stunned bemusement, as if he couldn't quite believe what had just happened to him. By the time Vargus had finished wiping his weapons clean on a discarded jacket, all that remained of Taikon was a pile of clothes and a few scraps of black hair.

Gripping the artefact tightly between his palms, Vargus slowly began to apply pressure, squeezing it tighter and tighter. Although he could feel it pulsing with energy, he was careful not to let it touch his bare skin. Even through his leather gloves he could feel it writhing and squirming, as the parasite inside the stone tried to find a way to bond with him. With relentless determination he squeezed harder, the muscles bunching in his hands and arms until he heard a loud crack. Bright purple light leaked out from between his fingers, bathing the throne room in strobing waves of colour.

Something tried to penetrate his mind and latch on to his thoughts, but he brushed away the weak attack and pressed harder with both hands. There was another crack and a shrill scream in his mind that quickly trailed off. The light faded until he held nothing more than bits of coloured glass, which he dropped to the floor. He cast one final glance around at the mess in the throne room before walking out.

Herakion, the capital city of Zecorria, had the blessing of being host to The First Church of the Holy Light, an enormous cathedral that sought to copy the oldest house of the Maker. The gaudy cathedral dwarfed every other structure in the city, forcing all inhabitants to live in its shadow. And much like the few buildings not touched by the church's shadow, those who did not follow the Way were treated as outsiders. It was far easier to pay lip service to the Lord of Light than be treated as if you were a carrier of the red pox by the community.

With a sad shake of his head, Vargus pulled his hood forward again, just in case. Although foreigners were not uncommon in the city, it would be better if few people saw him, given what he might have to do.

The huge doors to the First Church were closed, but they opened easily at his touch. The doors had no keyholes, locks or bars of any kind. The church never closed its doors to its followers and a priest was always on hand, day or night, to offer guidance. The church was huge inside with a high vaulted ceiling, stained-glass windows and long rows of hard wooden pews. The gold-coloured stone floor sparkled, reflecting the light from a thousand candles. Not content with having a monstrous edifice devoted to his worship, the Lord of Light had gone one step further in his First Church. Nine paintings covered the entire ceiling, which depicted the Lord of Light creating the world, showing the First Men how to plant crops, how to make fire, how to till the land and seven more lies for which he'd claimed credit. Vargus paid them no mind, although he did stop to stare at one small painting tucked away in a dusty corner.

Here was the truth, or at least an approximation. Even though the colours had faded, the paint was peeling and, at a glance, it looked like one giant black blob surrounded by white, Vargus could still make out the figures sat feasting at the long table. Twenty-eight men and women. A gathering that no mortal, other than the artist, had ever seen since time began. It had been a whim, a passing fancy of ego that some had embraced and others indulged. A meeting that would and could never be repeated, as some of those depicted no longer existed. The painting showed a glorious feast with a massive table heavily laden with food from all over the world. Light in the room came from candles on the table and a small boy holding a lantern. A small girl, her face smudged with grime, sat beside the hearth and attended to the fire. The flames bathed the room in golden light, driving the shadows to the far corners where a few more faces lurked.

Turning away from the painting with a heavy heart, Vargus focused again on the present. Ignoring the golden ornaments, marble statues and other gaudy displays of opulence, Vargus stared at the hunched figure sat in the front pew. The man hadn't moved since his arrival, but Vargus doubted his presence had gone unnoticed.

Despite the late hour there were one or two other worshippers with their heads bent in prayer. He ignored them and sat down immediately behind the man. An overzealous priest started to rush over, but he stopped in his tracks when Vargus frowned in his direction. The young man gulped and hurried away, suddenly finding something pressing to do elsewhere.

"Do you remember that night?" asked Vargus. "The meal seemed to last for days. The plates of food were heaped so high the table groaned under the weight."

The hunched figure sat back and threw off his white hood. "I don't like to think about it," said the Lord of Light.

"So much has changed since then. Some of it happened almost overnight," mused Vargus.

"Is that a threat?"

"An observation."

The Lord of Light kept his face turned away as he stared up at the benevolent idol of himself. "Why are you here?"

"To tell you that the war is over. The fighting has stopped, and though the west is still in turmoil, it will heal in time."

"I am pleased. Taikon's perversion of my faith, and that of the Blessed Mother, was most disturbing." The Lord of Light shivered. "Thank you for bringing me this good news."

Vargus remained silent for a long time before he spoke again. "I know it was you."

That made the Lord of Light turn around in his seat. "What was me?"

"You taught the Warlock. You showed him Talents that were lost for centuries, like spirit walking. You gave him the parasitic artefact from beyond the Veil."

"That's absurd. Why would I do that?"

Vargus shrugged. "Because you're young, arrogant and greedy. Because despite all your power, you want more."

"I grow more powerful every day. Why would I take such a risk by teaching such things to a mortal?"

"That is the only thing I don't know."

"Do you have any proof?" asked the Lord of Light with a knowing smile.

"The artefact was destroyed. The Mad King and the Warlock are dead, but even if they were alive, I doubt you were stupid enough to teach them directly."

"I respect you, Vargus, but I'm deeply offended and hurt by your accusations. What you're suggesting is that I interfered with the mortals. Something which is forbidden, as was recently pointed out to us all."

Vargus snarled and leaned forward, but the Lord of Light didn't move away. "It is forbidden, boy, and the punishment is not one you would enjoy."

"You seem very fond of threats, and yet I doubt you have the power to back them up," said the Lord of Light with a mocking smile. Here, at the heart of his power base, in a country dominated by his followers, he felt utterly secure.

The smile that slowly crept across Vargus's face unnerved the Lord of Light and his bravado faltered. "You're right," said Vargus, completely confusing the Lord of Light. "I don't have any proof, but this is not a court of justice. There is no judge or jury, only the execution of will."

"You wouldn't."

"Really?" said Vargus, sitting back on his pew, completely at ease. "What do you think happens to one of our kind when they've been living, in the same body, for thousands of years? Do you have any idea what that does to the mind?"

"I don't understand," said the boy.

"Of course you don't. You're a child. You haven't even seen a millennia yet. But the Maker, he's been here almost since the beginning. All that time he's been amassing more power than all of us put together, and yet he became trapped in a body that was broken. His mind was rotting. Sometimes he appeared sane, but the moments of lucidity faded every year."

All of the candles in the church flickered in unison. An expression of horrific realisation dawned on the boy's face.

"It was you," whispered the Lord of Light.

"He begged me," said Vargus, his voice hoarse. "He couldn't bear it any more. He was suffering and even put the weapon in my hand."

All colour drained from the Lord of Light's face until he was as pale as his robe. "But, with so much power, he must have come back."

"He was reborn almost immediately, born to a barren woman, but the time between was too short. His mind was still broken. He cried out to me from across the world and I answered his call. I strangled him in his crib. Over and over we've done this. Eventually he will be reborn whole, because he is eternal, but you are not."

"Mercy," he pleaded, but Vargus chose to interpret the word differently.

"It was a mercy when I killed him the first time. The body died and I cast his essence onto the wind where Summer carried him to every land."

"Have mercy, Weaver."

Vargus sat forward again and this time the Lord of Light flinched. "If you ever interfere with the mortals again, I will destroy you. Then I will hunt you down and bash your skull in as a babe in arms. And I will keep doing it until your star wanes and your power fades. You will stay in the Void, deaf, dumb and blind, until you are nothing. Do you understand?"

The Lord of Light frantically bobbed his head up and down. "I'll be watching you, boy."

Before the Lord of Light could offer excuses or plead for mercy, Vargus turned and walked slowly out of the church.

CHAPTER 49

Somewhere in the darkness a voice beckoned, and with it came the promise of warmth. As Balfruss rose up through the layers of fog, he could feel sunlight warming the skin on his face. Waking up was so difficult. It felt as if he were wading through mud for a long time before he managed to claw himself into the real world.

Sitting upright in bed Balfruss stared around at an unfamiliar room. It was plainly furnished, with only a bed, a basin and a chair occupied by a sleeping man. It looked more like a cell than a bedroom, and the thick wooden door only added to his first impression. Golden sunlight shone down from a high window, and judging by the angle of the sun, he guessed it was approaching midday.

The man in the chair looked familiar, but it took Balfruss a while to recognise him without his armour. He looked smaller, although the eye patch, scars and axe did nothing to lessen his villainous appearance. Balfruss let him sleep. He looked exhausted, his eyes ringed with dark smudges. The skin on his face was heavy with wrinkles, and even asleep the lines of tension were deeply etched in his forehead.

Looking down at himself Balfruss saw he was dressed only in a long brown shirt that reached his knees. As he adjusted to his surroundings, a familiar and unpleasant smell assaulted his nose. That of unwashed bodies, blood and death. Part of it came from him, but something far worse crept into the room from beyond the door. That meant a hospital, and he must be in Charas.

Standing up proved to be far more challenging than he'd anticipated. He supported himself against the wall until he regained his balance. All of the muscles and bones in his legs cracked as he stretched, his back twinging in pain. As the memories came flooding back Balfruss was surprised a few sore muscles were the least of his injuries.

Leaving Graegor to sleep he tiptoed out of the room in search of a bath and fresh clothes. A doctor hurrying elsewhere stopped and stared in shock. His mouth hung open and he started to babble. When Balfruss asked where he could take a bath the doctor just pointed down the corridor. A little further along an equally startled nurse directed him until he found the bath-house. He ignored the steam room and went straight to one of the copper baths. The place was deserted except for an attendant, but Balfruss sent him away and filled the bath, pumping the water into a bucket himself. It felt good to exercise the muscles in his arms and shoulders after lying in bed. He guessed he'd been there for some time, but he wasn't quite ready to deal with that just yet. Some of the cramp in his body faded, but the exercise seemed to awaken a host of small agonies in his legs and lower back.

Once the bath was full of cold water Balfruss realised he couldn't put off what he'd been dreading since waking up. He focused his will and reached out for the Source. The power flooded into him with ease and he continued to draw on it until it filled his being. Part of him felt enormous relief, but another part disappointment that nothing had changed. As ever, the unlimited well of power called to him, but it did not tempt him in the way he'd feared.

Balfruss released a small trickle of power into the water, heating it until steam rose from the surface. He added some herbal salts and placed a wash cloth and coarse bar of soap beside the bath. The hot water eased away the aches that were lingering in his muscles, and for a while he forgot about everything. When the water began to cool he scrubbed his skin with soap until it was red. His beard was long and scraggly so he tidied it as best as he could manage with a borrowed pair of scissors.

The attendant had anticipated his next request, as a pile of clean clothes waited just outside the door. The breeches were well made and comfortable, but the shirt too long in the sleeves. Balfruss rolled them up to his elbows and donned the pair of boots, which proved to be his own. They fitted so perfectly he sighed in pleasure, then went in search of something to eat.

No one tried to stop him on his way out of the hospital, but every person paused in what they were doing to stare as he walked past. On the streets Balfruss thought things might be better, but it was only more of the same with more people. When he stopped at a street vendor to buy some fruit, the merchant refused his money and wouldn't change his mind. The same happened when he stopped at a bakery for some bread and cheese.

After a short walk Balfruss found a quiet square where he was able to sit and eat alone. And for a little while he could pretend that nothing was wrong. Both merchants had given him too much in their eagerness to get rid of him, but Balfruss found he was ravenous and managed to eat everything. The bread was warm and delicious and the red berries so sweet and tangy they left his fingers in a delightfully sticky mess.

Closing his eyes he turned his face towards the sky and enjoyed the heat of the midday sun. Warm, and with a full stomach, he wanted nothing more than to live in the moment forever. An hour passed unnoticed in silence, but slowly, as the familiar smells and sounds of the city wrapped around him, a host of recent memories returned and with them the anguish of what had been lost. The full weight of recent events once again settled on his weary shoulders. The time for pretending was over.

On the long walk to the palace he ignored the terrified glances and the mothers who pulled their children behind them at his passing. He paid no attention to the way conversations stopped and laughter was cut short.

During his first week at the Red Tower, Balfruss and the other children had been told that people would be afraid of them. They knew nothing of the Source, its joy and majesty, and how it connected all living things. His teachers had told him to ignore their fear and prejudice, because it came from ignorance.

In spite of everything he'd done to protect them and the city, his own people still treated him as something monstrous. Seeing fear in the eyes of strangers was one thing, but seeing it on the faces of those he'd nearly died to protect was something else entirely.

"*Can you really blame them?*" came the echo of Thule's voice.

"I wondered if you were still there," said Balfruss to the ghost in his mind. "I don't blame them, I'm just disappointed."

"*You destroyed the Warlock. He was the most powerful Sorcerer alive. He manipulated the entire world into a war and thousands died. If he was capable of that, they wonder what you will do.*"

"I would never do that."

"*I know that, but they don't.*"

Word must have been sent ahead, because the palace gates stood open and the guards offered him a salute as he approached. Balfruss ignored them as well and kept walking, paying no attention to the palace servants and warriors who stepped aside or hurried away when they saw him coming.

The doors to the throne room were closed, but the warriors threw them open and let him pass. The Queen waited on the throne, flanked on one side by her brothers and Vannok on the other.

Vannok offered an apologetic smile and a shrug of his shoulders, as if to say he didn't know why everyone was suddenly so scared of him. Not a hint of fear showed in Vannok's eyes, for which he was grateful. He knew Balfruss would never harm any of those he'd fought so hard to protect. The others were more difficult to read, but Balfruss could sense a lot of uncertainty and the air hummed with tension.

"Are you well?" asked the Queen and Balfruss allowed himself a brief smile. The throne had rightfully been hers all along. He'd seen how the others deferred to her. As well as that, for which he felt glad, she was also still a young woman with a kind heart. For now, at least.

"I am recovering, Majesty. Thank you for your concern."

"You've been asleep," she said, then shook her head. "You've been unconscious for five days. They didn't think you would ever wake up."

"I'm happy to prove them wrong," said Balfruss, but he knew there were many who were less pleased. It would have been a lot simpler if he'd died. There were a few other Battlemages out there, and many people with small Talents, but they had not answered the King's call to arms. They would not be a threat to anyone, and because of what he and the Warlock had done, they might live the rest of their days without revealing their abilities.

"As am I," said the Queen, but Balfruss wasn't sure if her words were genuine.

"Thank you, Majesty."

Queen Talandra spread her hands wide. "Ask any boon, and if I have the power, I will grant it."

The tension in the room stretched further and Balfruss sensed more eyes watching him than those he could see. Before answering he slowly looked around the room, noting the large tapestries that were new additions. Poised behind them were several men armed with crossbows, no doubt dipped in something toxic. Without looking behind him Balfruss knew the guards who'd let him into the throne room so quickly were now stood inside the door with hands resting on their weapons. Visibly nothing had changed, and yet staring at the Queen he saw many layers beneath the naïve exterior she presented. In a way he was glad. She would need to be ruthless, driven and just as determined as her father to rule and maintain peace in the west.

"All I ask, your Majesty, is that you honour the promise your father made to Sandan Thule. Shael must be free."

The Queen gestured towards Vannok. "General Lore is leading men into Yerskania and then south. The Queen of Yerskania is also sending warriors. An army will march into Shael to liberate its people. I swear it."

"*Thank you, brother*," said Thule.

"What else? What about something for you?" asked the Queen.

Balfruss shook his head. "I don't want anything."

"Surely there must be something?" pressed the Queen. He understood why she kept asking, because to sacrifice so much and receive nothing in return did not sit comfortably. But he wasn't there to ease their collective conscience.

"What I would like returned to me is beyond your power, or mine," he said, and saw understanding in the Queen's sad and knowing smile. She made a little fluttering gesture with one hand and the tense atmosphere quickly eased. "I am leaving Charas, your Majesty."

"Where will you go?"

"North, to visit the First People. An old friend told me that one day I would stay with them."

"Then the least I can do is offer generous provisions and a

steed for your journey," said the Queen. She stood as if preparing to leave, but instead came down the steps towards him. Balfruss saw a few guards start to move towards him, but the Queen frowned and waved them back. Much to his surprise she embraced him and after a moment he wrapped his arms around her slender frame.

"I'm so sorry for your loss," she whispered in his ear. "And I'm sorry that it's come to this. Thank you for everything. You don't deserve this."

Before he could reply she kissed him on both cheeks, which left him lost for words. The Queen stepped back and retook the throne, once more an official ruler in state.

"On behalf of the people of Seveldrom, and the free kingdoms of the west, I thank you for your service. We owe you our lives."

Balfruss bowed deeply to the throne and then backed out of the room. By the time he'd packed up his meagre belongings and walked to the palace gates, Jonkravish, the Queen's quartermaster, stood waiting for him beside a black stallion. Its saddlebags were bulging with food and provisions, and a heavy roll was tucked behind the saddle. Despite the extra weight the horse looked eager to run and he wasn't about to disappoint his new steed.

Balfruss climbed into the saddle, took the reins from the Morrin and looked around at his city. There were too many painful memories and so much had been lost. He had no reason to come back. There were still many places he had yet to explore, many mysteries to uncover.

With his eyes on the horizon, Balfruss rode out of the city. A short way down the road he found Graegor waiting for him astride a black horse. He looked dressed and armed for war and carried provisions for a long journey. For a long time the two men just stared at each other in silence.

"I will never forgive you for what you've done," said Balfruss.

"I know. I'm not here to say I'm sorry. It would be meaningless. I can't change what I've done."

"Do you even regret it?" asked Balfruss. Graegor didn't answer, but the emotion in his eyes spoke volumes. "Then why are you here?"

"Your past is lost to me. I wasn't part of it, but I want to be part of what comes next."

"Do you even know where I'm going?"

Graegor shook his shaggy head. "It doesn't matter."

Balfruss didn't know the man beside him. They weren't family. He didn't think anything could bridge the gap between them. Only time would tell.

"Try to keep up," said Balfruss, spurring his horse down the road.

From a tower on top of the palace Talandra watched the two figures ride away from the city. She heard footsteps on the stairs and a minute later Shani moved to her side. They stood in silence for a while, each lost in their own thoughts. Talandra's mind turned to the future and the challenges that lay ahead.

"We should never have let him go," said Talandra, more to herself than Shani.

"You had no choice."

"This is his home. His family and friends are here," said Talandra. Shani sighed. "The people are scared of him, and to be honest, so am I. It had to be this way." A shiver ran down Talandra's back and Shani put a comforting hand on her shoulder. "What is it?"

"The only reason we're safe today is because of Balfruss. He sacrificed everything for us and we rewarded him with exile. What if one day that turns to bitterness? What happens tomorrow if he, or another Warlock, walks up to our gates? Who can we call on to stop them?" asked Talandra, but Shani didn't have an answer. They were on their own.

ACKNOWLEDGEMENTS

Writing may be a solitary endeavour, but getting published is not. I'd like to thank my remarkable agent, Juliet Mushens, for her unwavering enthusiasm, her belief in my writing and her ongoing hard work. Sarah Manning, for all of her brilliant work behind the scenes. The team at Orbit, in particular Jenni, Susan and Joanna, for making me take a hard look at the story. I'd also like to thank the rest of Team Mushens, a disparate bunch of rogues, who have been incredibly supportive and now feel like they're family.

Look out for

BLOOD
MAGE

by

STEPHEN
ARYAN

Coming soon!

www.orbitbooks.net

extras

www.orbitbooks.net

about the author

Stephen Aryan was born in 1977 and was raised and educated in Whitley Bay, Tyne and Wear. After graduating from Loughborough University he started working in marketing, and for some reason he hasn't stopped. A keen podcaster, lapsed gamer and budding archer, when not extolling the virtues of *Babylon 5*, he can be found drinking real ale and reading comics.

He lives in a village in Yorkshire with his partner and two cats. You can find him on Twitter at @SteveAryan or visit his website at www.stephen-aryan.com.

Find out more about Stephen Aryan and other Orbit authors by registering for the free monthly newsletter at www.orbitbooks.net.

interview

What prompted you to start writing _Battlemage_?
Before writing _Battlemage_ I'd written several novels, mostly in the science fiction and fantasy genres. This was the latest novel in a fifteen-year journey to get published. Inspired by _Legend_ by David Gemmell, the initial seed for _Battlemage_ actually came from a short story I'd written a few years ago. It was about a mature wizard and his oldest friend going on one last mission together. They were in the twilight years of their lives and I began to wonder what had led the wizard, Balfruss, to that moment. Where had he come from? What about his adventures as a young man? I started building his story and it went from there.

Who are your favourite wizards in the fantasy genre?
While I like Gandalf, you always know that deep down he's a good man trying to do the right thing. Raistlin Majere, created by Margaret Weis and Tracy Hickman, from the Dragonlance novels is fascinating because he's so grey and multi-layered. You never really know where his true loyalties lie or what he's up to, which stops him being predictable. Ged, from the Earthsea novels by Ursula Le Guin, is another favourite. His story is really unusual and unexpected, and its dark tone left a mark on

me at an early age. Harry Dresden, created by Jim Butcher from the Dresden Files, is a fantastic character who I absolutely love after spending so much time with him over the last fifteen years.

Tell us about your writing routine.
My writing routine is very traditional. I'm a planner, so I always have the start, end and milestones of the novel worked out before I actually begin writing chapter one properly. There's always some creative wiggle room in there, so I'm making some discoveries as I write, which keeps it interesting, but the story never deviates dramatically from the plan. I don't use any index cards or special writing software, just a basic word processor. I write during the evenings and at weekends, and I try to write as often as possible but that's not always every day. My best hours are first thing in the morning and late at night when everyone is asleep and everything is very quiet.

It's very easy to write magic and wizards badly – characters who can make all their problems go away with the wave of a hand and the words of a spell. How do you write them well?
Exerting any kind of force, physical or mental, takes a toll on the body and the mind. Whether it's chopping down a tree or concentrating for hours trying to solve a mental puzzle. It taxes you and is draining. Using magic, when it's done right, should reflect this as well. Magic must have a cost and I've stuck to this, so if you push yourself too hard it will kill you. Also I've tried to make it realistic like any other acquired skill in the world. Therefore no single wizard can know everything, or do everything with magic, and there's always going to be someone out there who is stronger, more skilled or cunning. There also has to be a learning curve,

otherwise someone could do anything just by waving their hands. The more I can ground the magic system in a logical structure, the more realistic, and hopefully satisfying, it will feel.

What do you do when you're not writing?
I like to read a lot, and mostly it's SFF novels and comics. I'm always trying to stay up to date with a growing number of TV shows, but am constantly falling behind. I've been podcasting for the last eight years and love talking about all things in geekdom. I've recently taken up archery and am finding it quite challenging but a lot of fun. I also love walking in the countryside, particularly if there's a nice pub at the end of it where I can get a pint of real ale and some good food.

Who are your influences in the fantasy genre and without?
From within the fantasy genre David Gemmell is undoubtedly the biggest influence on my writing. Other fantasy influences include David Eddings, Terry Brooks, Ursula Le Guin, James Barclay, Margaret Weis and Tracy Hickman, Tad Williams, Jim Butcher. Outside of fantasy, Stephen King, Dean Koontz, J. Michael Straczynski and Joss Whedon, particularly for their work on television.

The old epic mythology films like *Clash of the Titans*, *Jason and the Argonauts* and the Sinbad films with visual effects by Ray Harryhausen, influenced me from an early age. After seeing those films I read every book of Greek and then worldwide mythology in the library.

Balfruss loses a lot of friends in this book. How difficult is it to write scenes with character death, and which were the hardest to write?

I've lived with all of these characters in my head for many years, so it was incredibly tough writing the final scenes for all of them. The most challenging to write were Finn's death and Ecko's funeral scene. While writing Ecko's death scene itself was difficult, it was even more of a wrench to have each of the characters talk about how he'd affected them. For a moment it lays each of them bare and reveals something about their characters. It was a way to sum up each of them in a few sentences.

What's coming next in the world after *Battlemage*?

I didn't want to write a series where everything resets at the end of book one. So at the start of book two the story begins a year after the war and the world has been irreparably changed. The West was previously stable, but now there's civil war in Morrinow, power struggles in Zecorria for the throne, general unrest and greater distrust of neighbouring countries. Magic was already on the downward spiral, but now people are more afraid of it than ever before because of the Warlock. Some of what Balfruss foretold has come to pass and the world is entering a new Dark Age for magic, hence the Age of Darkness title. Now, if some new terror was to rise up, there are no more Battlemages to call on for help as most of them are dead. There's a lot of anger and blame flying around because of the many warriors who died in the war, and now someone has to pay.

if you enjoyed

BATTLEMAGE

look out for

AGE OF IRON

by

Angus Watson

Chapter 1

"Mind your spears, coming through!"

Dug Sealskinner shouldered his way back through the ranks. Front rank was for young people who hadn't learned to fear battle and old men who thought they could compete with the young.

Dug put himself halfway in that last category. He'd been alive for about forty years, so he was old. And he wanted to compete with the young, but grim experience had unequivocally, and sometimes humiliatingly, demonstrated that the young won every time. Even when they didn't win they won because they were young and he wasn't.

And here he was again, in another Bel-cursed battle line. Had things gone to plan, he'd have been living the respectable older man's life, lord of his broch, running his own seaside farm on Britain's north coast, shearing sheep, spearing seals and playing peekaboo with grandchildren. He'd been close to achieving that when fate had run up and kicked him in the bollocks. Since then, somehow, the years had fallen past, each one dying with him no nearer the goals that had seemed so achievable at its birth.

If only we could shape our own lives, he often thought, rather than other bastards coming along and shaping them for us.

Satisfyingly, the ragtag ranks parted at his request. He might not feel it, but he still looked fearsome, and he was a Warrior. His jutting jaw was bearded with thick bristle. His big head was cased in a rusty but robust, undecorated iron helmet. His oiled ringmail shone expensively in the morning sun, its heaviness flattening his ever-rounder stomach. The weighty warhammer which swung on a leather lanyard from his right hand could have felled any mythical beastie.

He'd been paid Warrior's wages to stay in the front rank to marshal the troops, so arguably he should have stayed in the front rank and marshalled the troops. But he didn't feel the need to fulfil every tiny detail of the agreement. Or even the only two details of it. First, because nobody would know; second, because there wasn't going to be a battle. He'd collect his full fee for a day standing in a field, one of thousands of soldiers. One of thousands of *people*, anyway. There were some other Warriors – Dug knew a few of them and had nodded hello – but the rest were men and women in leathers at best, hardly soldiers, armed with spears but more used to farm equipment. Quite a few of them were, in fact, armed with farm equipment.

What, by Camulos, is that doing here? he thought, looking at a small, bald but bearded man holding a long pole topped with a giant cleaver – a whale blubber cutter, if he wasn't mistaken. He hadn't seen one of those for a while and wanted to ask its owner what it was doing so far inland. But an interest in fishing equipment wouldn't help his battle-hardened Warrior image.

He pushed out into the open field. Behind Barton's makeshift army, children in rough wool smock-frocks ran across the bright field, laughing, fighting and crying. The elderly sat in groups complaining about the army's formation and other things that had been better in their day. To the left, sitting in a heap of rags and shunned by all, was the inevitable drunken old druid, shouting semi-coherently about the imminence of Roman invasion, like all the other dozens of drunken druids that Dug had seen recently.

Over by the bridge were those others who escaped military service – Barton's more important families. A couple of them were looking at Dug, perhaps wondering why their expensive mercenary was taking a break.

He put his hands on his hips in an overseer pose and tried to look like he was assessing the line for weaknesses. *Very important, the rear rank of a defensive line*, he'd tell them if they asked afterwards.

Dug hadn't expected to be in the Barton army that sunny morning. He'd been stopping in Barton hillfort the day before when word came that the cavalry and chariot sections of King Zadar of Maidun Castle's army would be passing on their way home from sacking the town and hillfort of Boddingham.

Boddingham was a smaller settlement than Barton, forty miles or so north-east along the Ridge Road. It had stopped paying tribute to Maidun. Perhaps Boddingham had felt safe, a hundred miles from the seat and capital of King Zadar's empire, but along good metalled roads and the hard chalk Ridge Road, that was only three days' journey for Zadar's chariots and cavalry – less if they pushed it. It would have taken much longer to move a full army, as Dug well understood, having both driven and hindered armies' movements in his time, but everyone Dug had spoken to said that Zadar's relatively small flying squad of horse soldiers was more than capable of obliterating a medium-sized settlement like Boddingham. If that was true, thought Dug, they must be the elite guard of Makka the war god himself.

The Maidun force had passed Barton two days before, too set on punishing Boddingham to linger for longer than it took to demand and collect food, water and beer. Now though, on the way back, swords bloodied, slaves in tow, the viciously skilful little company might have the time and inclination to take a pop at weak, underprepared Barton.

"You!" A man had shouted at Dug the night before. So courteous, these southerners.

"Aye?" he'd replied.

"Know anything about fighting?"

You'd think his dented iron helmet, ringmail shirt and warhammer might have answered that question, but southerners, in Dug's experience, were about as bright as they were polite.

"Aye, I'm a Warrior."

And that was how he'd ended up at the previous night's war council. He'd actually been on his way to sign up with Zadar's army – finally fed up with the strenuous life of a wandering mercenary – but he saw no need to mention that to the Barton defenders.

Fifty or so of Barton's more important men and women, the same ones who weren't in the battle line, had been packed into the Barton Longhouse for the war council. Calling it a longhouse was pretentiousness, another southern trait that Dug had noticed. First, it was circular. Second, it was only about twenty paces across. At most it was a mediumhouse. It was just a big hut really, made of mud, dung and grass packed into a lattice of twigs between upright poles. Four wide trunks in the middle supported the conical reed roof. Dug could have shown them how to build a hut the same size without the central supports, thereby freeing up space. Perhaps the hall predated that particular architectural innovation, but there was a wood at the foot of the hill and plenty of people, so rebuilding would have been a doddle.

This tribe, however, was clearly neither architecturally diligent nor building-proud. One of the support posts leaned alarmingly and there was a large, unplanned hole in the roof near the door. At the end of a long hot day, despite the hole, the air inside was thick and sweaty. It could have done with double ceiling vents. Dug could have shown them how to put those in too.

King Mylor of Barton sat on a big wooden chair on a platform in the centre, rubbing the back of his hand against his two remaining rotten teeth, staring about happily with milky eyes at his visitors and hooting out "Oooo-ooooh!" noises that reminded Dug of an elderly seal. He looked like a seal, now Dug came to think of it. Smooth rings of blubber made his neck wider than his hairless, liver-spotted skull, which was wetly lucent in the torchlight. Whiskers sprayed out under his broad, flat nose. Dug had heard that Barton's king had lost his mind. It looked like the gossipy bards were right for once.

Next to Mylor sat the druid Elliax Goldan, ruler in all but name. You didn't cross Barton's chief druid, Dug had heard. He was a little younger than Dug perhaps, slim, with tiny black eyes in a pink face that gathered into a long nose. Rat-like. If you could judge a man by his face – and Dug had found that you could – here was an angry little gobshite. Dug had seen more and more druids as he'd migrated south. There were three basic types: the wise healer sort who dispensed advice and cures, the mad, drunk type who raved about dooms – almost all Rome-related these days – and the commanding sort whose communes with the gods tended to back up their plans and bolster their status. Elliax was firmly in this latter camp.

On Mylor's left was the druid's wife, Vasin Goldan. Her skin was shiny and mottled. Big eyes sat wide apart, far up her forehead, very nearly troubling her hairline. Frog-face, Dug had heard her called earlier. *Spot on*, he mused. Seal-head, Rat-nose and Frog-face. Right old menagerie.

Behind Elliax and Mylor were four Warriors in ringmail. It was never a great sign, Dug thought, when rulers needed protection from their own people.

Elliax silenced the hubbub with a couple of claps, interrupting Dug's explanation to a young woman of how he'd improve the hut's roof. "The meeting is convened!" he said in a surprisingly deep voice. Dug had expected him to squeak.

"Could we not do this outside?" asked Dug, pulling his mail

shirt away from his neck to get some cooler air down there. Spicily pungent body odour clouded out. The woman he'd been talking to shuffled away. Blooming embarrassment made Dug even hotter.

"Barton war meetings take place in the Barton Longhouse!" Elliax boomed, also reddening.

"Even when it's hot and there's plenty of room outside? Isn't that a bit stupid?" Several people around Dug nodded.

"Hot-t-t-t-t!" shouted King Mylor.

Mylor, it was said, had lost his mind along with Barton's wealth and position ten years before, when he'd bet his five best against King Zadar's champion. The champion, a massive young man called Carden Nancarrow, had slaughtered Barton's four best men and one woman in a few horrifying moments. Barton had paid painful taxes to Maidun ever since.

By persuading Mylor to accept the five-to-one combat rather than defend the highly defendable fort, Elliax claimed he'd saved Barton from annihilation. Over the following decade he'd continued to serve his town as Zadar's representative and tax collector. Zadar's taxes would have starved Barton in a couple of years, said Elliax, but he was happy to mislead Maidun about Barton's assets and collect a little less. All he asked in exchange were a few easy gifts like land, food, ironwork or the easiest gift of all – an hour or so with a daughter. While others became steadily malnourished, Elliax thrived, his wife fattened, and unmarried girls bore children with suspiciously rodent faces. Anyone who complained found themselves chosen by Elliax's druidic divinations to march south as part of Zadar's quarterly slave quota.

"We have nothing to fear," Elliax continued, ignoring Dug and King Mylor. "I have seen it. We pay our dues and it's in

Zadar's interest that we keep paying them. He will not attack."

"But Zadar can't be trusted to act rationally!" shouted a young woman at the back. "Look what he did to Cowton last year."

Dug had heard about Cowton. Everybody had. Zadar had wiped out the entire town. Men, women, the elderly, children, livestock ... two thousand people and Danu knew how many animals had been slaughtered or sold to Rome as slaves. Nobody knew why.

Elliax looked sideways at King Mylor. The king was picking at the crotch of his woollen trousers.

"Who is your chief druid?" Elliax asked. Nobody had an answer. Elliax smiled like a toad who'd caught a large fly. He held out his arms. "This morning, on the wood shrine, I sacrificed a seabird from the Island of Angels to see its tales of the future. As the bird quivered in death, I was distracted by a sound. I looked up and saw a squirrel hissing at a cat. The cat passed by, leaving the squirrel unharmed." Elliax looked around smugly, eyes finishing up on Dug's.

Most people looked at each other and nodded. More often than not the gods' messages were too cryptic for Dug to grasp immediately, but he got this one.

"Can't argue with that!" said a stout man.

"Yeah, if it was true. Ever heard a squirrel hiss?" muttered a woman behind Dug.

"No one would dare lie about something like that!" whispered a man who, by the frustration in his voice, Dug took to be the woman's husband.

Elliax continued. "I looked into the bird's viscera and found Danu. She told me we had nothing to fear from Zadar. Next I found Makka. He outlined our strategy. The weather has been dry, so Zadar will leave the Ridge Road and take the quicker lowland road, as he did on the way to Boddingham. Makka told me that we should gather everyone on the valley floor and form a spear and shield line between the two curves of the river on the other side of the bridge. Cavalry and chariots cannot charge a spear line."

"Unless the spear line breaks," said Dug. He wouldn't have usually challenged any god's proclamations, especially Makka's, but these people didn't know battle and needed to be told. A few older voices murmured agreement, which encouraged him to continue: "In which case you might as well have a row of children holding wet reeds. Why not bring everyone up into the fort? Do a bit of work on the walls overnight – sharpen the angles, tighten the palisade, few spikes in the ditch – and they'll never get in."

"And leave all our farms, homes and crops to the whims of Zadar's army!" Elliax spat, his voice becoming steadily higher. "You're as stupid as you look, northman! You shouldn't be in here anyway. You're not from Barton. There's no reason for a spear line to break. I think two gods know a little more than some shabby has-been Warrior. And actually I have the advice of three gods, because further into the guts of the bird, I found Dwyn."

"Pretty crowded in that bird," said the woman behind Dug. Her husband shushed her again.

Elliax ignored the interruption. "That cunning god perfected the plan. He told me to send a rider to Zadar to tell him that we'll be lining the route to celebrate his passing with a ceremonial battle line. We'll defend our land with something that looks like a show of respect. That's the sort of strategic thinking you won't have seen much of where you're from."

"Are you sure that's what Dwyn told you?" Dug had never

questioned a druid before, but Elliax's plan was madness. "Forewarned, as most kids where I'm from know, is forearmed."

Elliax sneered. "We have slings, many more than Zadar can possibly have. His troops will be on horseback and in chariots, we'll be behind shields. If Zadar tries to attack, our shields will protect us and we'll send back a hailstorm of death. Zadar is not stupid. He will not attack! He knows how futile it would be. Besides, the gods have spoken to me. Perhaps if you'd listened to them more, you wouldn't be walking the land begging for work. At your age too. It's shameful."

Dug's ears were suddenly hot. Elliax turned away from him and outlined his plan in detail. Irritatingly, thought Dug, the jumped-up prick's idea made some sense. Charging a line of spears on horseback or in a chariot was indeed suicide. Horses knew this too, so it was also near impossible. He was right about projectile weapons as well. Barton's more numerous slingers and shields should neutralise any projectile threat.

Geography also favoured Barton. To get from Zadar's likely route to most of Barton's land, you had to cross a river. The only bridge for miles was in the centre of a long bend. The best way for cavalry to beat a line of spearmen was to gallop around and take them on the flank or from behind. With the army bracketed by two loops of the river's meandering course, that would be impossible. But there was still one big, obvious flaw.

"Why don't we stay this side of the bridge?" Dug asked. "We can hold the bridge with a handful of soldiers, protect most of the land and you can still have your wee procession. If Zadar attacks and your long line of bakers and potters doesn't hold, which it probably wouldn't, then we're trapped between him and the river and in all sorts of bother."

Elliax grimaced as if someone had just urinated on a relative's funeral bed. "Still you challenge the gods? They know, as you don't, that there's valuable property just the other side of the river."

"This property wouldn't happen to be yours, would it?"

"Why don't you shut up and stop embarrassing yourself? We share property. It's *everyone's* land, you northern fool."

Elliax stared at him furiously, but then, as if recalling a pleasant memory, smiled. "Or maybe you'd like a stronger reading? Why don't you come up here and we'll see what your spilled entrails say about Zadar's intentions? We'll see the next ten winters in your fat gut! Bob, Hampcar, why don't you find out just how much this know-it-all knows about fighting?"

Two of the four guards stood forward and slid swords a couple of fingers' breadth from scabbards. They were both big men. One had a long face with a pronounced muzzle and drawn-back lips showing uncommonly white teeth. The other was beardless, with a scar soaring redly from each corner of his mouth into his shaggy hairline. That injury was caused by making a small cut at each corner of a person's mouth, then hurting them; an iron auger screwed between wrist bones was one method Dug had seen. The victim would scream, ripping his or her flesh from mouth to ears. If the wounds healed and they didn't die of infection, they were left with a smile-shaped scar. Way up north this was called a Scrabbie's kiss, after a tribe keen on handing them out. Men generally grew beards to cover the scars, but this guy had shaved to show them off. It was, admittedly, quite effective, if you were going for the scary bastard look. His mate looked even tougher.

Dug decided not to take them on.

"Are you coming? Or are you a coward?" Elliax sneered.

Dug stared back in what he hoped was a cool, Bel-may-care manner. He didn't need to take on four Warriors to prove a point. Or even two. Besides, if Dwyn, god of tricks, Makka, god of war and Danu, mother of all the gods, had all been involved in the planning, who was Dug to argue? He might as well negotiate a decent fee for standing in the line, then leave the following evening a richer man with his guts still in his belly.

"Are you coming, I said?"

"I'll stay here."

"Stupid, fat and cowardly too. Some Warrior!" Elliax looked around triumphantly and seemed to grow a little. "Ignore this oaf's ignorant comments. I have been shown the way. The plan is made and King Mylor agrees." Mylor looked up and smiled at hearing his name, then returned to plucking at his genitals. Elliax continued: "Have no fear. Zadar hasn't got where he is today by attacking against impossible odds. We are completely safe."

So the following dawn everyone who wasn't too young, infirm or important to hold a weapon, around four thousand men and women in all, wandered at first light across the bridge to the big field and gathered between the two river bends. The mixed bunch of farmers, crafters and woodspeople from Barton village and its outlying hamlets and farms shuffled about confusedly but good-naturedly as Dug and others formed them into an as effective a line as possible, putting those with relatively decent shields and spears at the front. Dug herded a few people with longer spears to the rear, going by the theory that if those in front were engaged in a hand-to-hand mêlée, the back rank could still

thrust their long weapons at the enemy. He knew it was futile –
if this front line engaged with even half-trained troops then they
were all fucked – but it kept him busy and showed that he knew
his game.

The children and the elderly crossed the river and gathered
behind them, standing on carts, boxes and barrels to watch
Zadar's army pass. The chief families arrived last, dressed in
well-worn finery. Mylor, Elliax and his wife Vasin arrived last,
with their chairs from the longhouse mounted on the biggest
cart.

As the day warmed, a carnival atmosphere developed behind
the spear line. The crazy druid stopped shouting, children played
less frantically and the elderly forgot their gripes as they drank
and talked of battles past. Puppies scurried between feet.
Older dogs padded around looking for pats and scraps. The
line grew ever more ragged as its members left to grab a drink,
find somewhere to squat or just wander about.

Dug was pushing back through the line to say hello to some
old boys with a gigantic barrel of cider that he'd spotted earlier
when Zadar's army rode into sight from behind a stand of trees
some four hundred paces away. A few shouts got everyone's
attention and silence spread through the crowd like blood soaking into sand.

"Lift me up, please?" It was a small, skinny boy with huge
brown eyes and a tuft of hair the red-brown of freshly ploughed
earth. He stared up at Dug. "Please?" The boy's eyes widened
ever further.

Dug sighed and hoiked the boy onto his shoulders. He hardly
weighed a thing.

"Is that Zadar?!"chirped the child.

"Probably. Yes." A lone rider headed the procession. He wore a huge, golden, horned helmet, a shining black ringmail jacket and black leather trousers. His black horse – by far the largest Dug had ever seen – was similarly attired in a golden-horned pony cap and a draped sheet of black ringmail protecting its rump.

"What's he wearing on his head?"

"Can't you see?"

Dug felt the boy slump a little. Dug could see well over long and short distances, but he knew that a lot of people had trouble with either or both. As a young man, he'd made no allowances, convinced that everybody could see just as well as him but pretended not to be able to for perverse reasons. Age had made him more tolerant.

"His helmet has horns on it."

The boy perked up. "Why?"

"Maybe to make him look scary, or maybe he's trying to persuade people that he's Kornonos, the horned god of animals. Probably he's not very tall and he thinks people will think he's taller if he wears a big hat. But of course people will think he's just a wee man in a big hat."

The boy giggled. Zadar in fact looked like quite a big man, but Dug was never one to let truth get in the way of belittling people he suspected to be puffed up.

"That coat he's wearing – and that rug covering the arse of his horse – is ringmail. That's hundreds or thousands – probably thousands in this case – of rings of iron all linked together. It'll protect you from slingstones, a sword slash, that sort of thing. But it's not much use against this." Dug raised his warhammer. The boy jiggled with glee. The hammer was an effective but simple weapon, no more sophisticated than the rock-tied-to-a-stick design that had been popular for aeons. An iron lump the size and shape of a large clog was moulded around a shaft of fire-hardened oak a pace long and held in place by a tight criss-cross of leather strips. Both ends of the handle were sharpened into points.

"Only kings and Warriors are allowed to wear ringmail."

"But you're wearing ringmail!"

"Aye. That's right. I'm a Warrior . . . Mine is more the hundreds of rings type, though not as supple or as light as his'll be."

"And is his horse a Worrier? Or a king?"

"Uh . . . neither. Thing about rules is that if you become powerful enough, you get to break them. And make them."

"Your voice is funny."

"I'm from the north."

"What are you worried about?"

"What?"

"You're a Worrier?"

"A Warrior. It's a title, like king. But this one you earn. You have to kill ten people in a battle. If five people who are already Warriors agree that you've done that, then they say you're a Warrior, and you get one of these." Dug tapped the crudely made iron boar that hung on a leather thong around his neck. "And you're allowed to wear ringmail, which is a neat way of making sure fewer people become Warriors and making life safer once you do. Being a Warrior also means you can claim a certain price as a mercenary. And people treat you better, like you might be given food at an inn on the understanding you'll protect the place."

"Can I have a boar necklace?"

"No. You've got to earn it."

"But our smith could make one for me?"

"Aye, he could, but the punishment for pretending to be a Warrior is death by torture."

The kid mused for a few moments on Dug's shoulders.

"Probably not worth it."

"No."

"And the man dressed in black behind Zadar?"

"That must be his head druid, Felix." Dug spat for good luck. They said that Felix, Zadar's Roman druid, could command the gods' magic like nobody in Britain had for generations. Dug had heard tales of Felix thwarting enemies' plans by reading their minds from afar, and other stories of him ripping souls from people's bodies or tearing them apart just by looking at them. You couldn't believe all, or even most, of what the bards said and sang, but Dug had heard so much about Felix's powers that some of it must have been true. He shivered despite the warmth of the day.

"And who's that next lot? Oh gosh!" squeaked the boy.

"Aye." Following King Zadar and Felix were fifty mounted men and women. Their helmets were hornless, their mail less polished and their horses' spiked pony caps were dull iron. "Those are Warriors."

Two hundred paces away they rode by, eyes front, not deigning even to glance at Barton's suddenly pathetic-looking spear line. They'd obviously been ordered not to look to the side for effect, thought Dug. That told him two things. One, that Zadar was a showman, and two, that discipline was strong in the Maidun army. Worryingly strong.

The chariots came next.

"The chariots are built with wooden struts under tension so they can bounce over bumps, narrow burns, corpses … Two people in each, a driver and a fighter. See that first lot, with the armoured soldiers?"

"Yes!"

"Those are the heavy chariots – less bouncy, more solid. They'll drive up to a battle line. The fighter will lob a javelin at the enemy. That probably won't kill anyone, but it might stick in a shield, making it useless or at least difficult to use. Or it might go through two overlapping shields, pinning them together when the iron spearhead bends. Then two soldiers have the choice of fighting joined together or chucking—"

"What would you do?" the boy interrupted.

"The only time it happened to me I chucked the shield away. There's something to be said for using a sword without a shield. It can free your senses, changing the whole direction of your—"

"What do the fighters do after they've thrown their javelins?" said the boy.

Dug nearly dumped the boy off his shoulders, but he remembered that his daughters had always interrupted his advice and stories, so, in their memory, he decided to give some leeway to the impertinent wee turd.

"Javelins away, the soldier usually leaps off the chariot and wades in with sword, hammer, spear – whatever. Most people down here use swords, great iron double-edged swords, for swinging. The Romans use shorter pointy swords, for stab—"

"Have you got a sword?"

"Me? No. I had one. I've had a few, but I'm a hammer man now. So, the soldier starts killing people and trying not to get killed, while his charioteer mills about in the background keeping an eye on things. When the guy on foot gets tired or hurt, he retreats or waves to the chariot, which picks him up and they shoot off to safety. They'll have a snack and a piss, maybe take a shit, grab a drink, and then head back to the battle. Brilliant way to fight if you have the means."

"Why do they have those big swords sticking out of the chariots?"

Dug had been trying to ignore the curved blades that protruded a pace from the boss of each of the heavy chariots' wheels. He shuddered at a memory. "If your enemy runs, you chase them. Those blades are sharp. One moment someone's running, the next they've got no legs from the knee down."

"What are these other ones? They're smaller."

"Light chariots. Unarmoured or lightly armoured driver, plus a slinger or sometimes an archer. No blades, thank Danu, but they're still nasty. They're all about speed. They fight from a distan—"

"My mum said that the bravest fighters go naked into battle to show how brave they are not needing armour."

"That does happen. But it's not bravery. Battles are dangerous enough. You don't have to be naked to appreciate that. It's mostly because they've drunk way too much, or it's men showing off; usually a mix of the two. And it is always men. Women are cleverer than that. Nobody likes the naked ones, they always get killed the quickest. Often by their own side."

"Have you ever gone into battle naked?"

"I have not. But there was one time a whole gang of naked men charged a group of us. It was a cold day, and their wee blue cocks were pointed straight at us, like mice looking out of hairy holes, somebody said. They were still a way away and a girl on our side hit one of them in the bollocks with a slingstone. The noise he made!" Dug chuckled. "We were laughing almost too much to fight. It was up on the banks of the Linny Foith, a great channel miles north of here but way south of where I'm from. I'd just sworn a year's service to a—"

"What about going into battle painted blue?"

"I've done that, but I don't like it. When I was with the Murkans I was in a battle and each side had blued up, trying to intimidate the other. We all felt like arseholes, and it was hard to tell who was on which side. I'm pretty sure I killed a friend that day. Sometimes your blood gets up. I was lashing out at anybody blue, forgetting ..."

"Will you kill me if Zadar attacks?"

"I will not."

"Will Zadar's army kill us both?"

"No, no. They can't do a thing. They may all be Warriors but it's just a small part of his army, and we outnumber them ten to one. They can't outflank us because of the river, and they can't attack us head-on because we've got spears and they've only got horse troops. If we stay in this line we're fine. Although if they get off their horses we might have problems, and if we break we're in all sorts of bother, whereas if we'd stayed on the other side of the river or, even better, in the hill-fort ..."

"What?"

"Don't fuss. We'll be fine."

The procession continued. After the chariots came the cavalry, again in heavy and light order. Those fifty horsemen who had followed directly after him were plainly Zadar's famous elite, but the couple of hundred heavy cavalry didn't look much less useful. Dug wouldn't have been surprised if they were all Warriors too.

Most interesting to Dug were the light cavalry – one section in particular. On the near side of the procession were six mounted female archers with long hair and bare legs. The blonde one at the front was staring at the Barton line. She was the only soldier in Zadar's army who'd turned her head.

"Are they goddesses?"

"Aye, son, I think they might be."

"And what are these?"

"Musicians."

As if to prove his point, the men riding at the rear of Zadar's army raised brass instruments to their lips and blared out a cacophony. The wooden clackers fixed on hinges in the instruments' mouths added a buzz like a swarm of giant bees.

"I say musicians, but that's no music!" chuckled Dug.

The men and women in Barton's battle line looked at each other then back to the horn blowers. Other than thunder, this was the loudest noise that most of them had ever heard. The boy's legs tightened around Dug's neck.

"Don't be scared, it's just noise!" Dug yelled over the increasing din, for the benefit of those nearby as well as the boy. "We'll be fine! Can you loosen your legs?"

Zadar's army was all in view now, stretched out to match precisely the length of the Barton line. *That probably isn't an accident*, thought Dug. The cavalry and chariots wheeled as one to face them. The trumpets screamed louder. Mylor's ramshackle pseudo-army took a step back. The horns ceased. A gap opened in the centre of the Maidun line, and a lone chariot wobbled slowly towards Barton. Instead of horses, it was drawn by two stumbling, naked, blood-soaked men. They were harnessed to the chariot by leather thongs attached to thick iron bolts that had been hammered through their shoulders. Standing in the chariot, whipping the men forward, was a young woman with large, wobbling bare breasts.

Chatter spread through the Barton line like wind through a wheat field. Someone said one of the men drawing the horrific chariot was Kris Sheeplord, king of Boddingham. The other was the messenger sent by Elliax to Zadar to tell him about the parade plan.

The king of Boddingham toppled forward, pulling the messenger down with him.

"Big badgers' balls," said Dug. "I don't like the look of this."